I NEVER KNEW I NEEDED YOU

A ROOM 223 STORY

ANDY LAPLANTE

For my girls
Casey and Lauren

I Never Knew I Needed You

Andy LaPlante

1

CASSANDRA

On a Friday evening, in the era of tube tops, low-rise jeans, and boybands, Cassandra Williams was in a battle against time. Hunched over her word processor, she furiously tapped away at the keys. Around her, a collection of organized, detailed notes and highlighted references sat on her desk. They were a clear sign of her commitment to her craft as a writer. She was drafting an Op-Ed about the recent tuition hikes for The Mount Holyoke News, and the piece wasn't just another assignment; it was her chance to leave a mark as an accomplished college journalist.

As she tried to concentrate, she felt her focus slipping away. The culprit? The unmistakable sounds of NSYNC blasting from a room just a few doors down. The catchy beats and infectious harmonies invaded her thoughts, making it impossible for her to keep her mind on track. She was being pulled away from her work and towards the appeal of a carefree Friday night in college.

With a frustrated sigh, Cassandra cupped her hands over her ears, attempting to block out the noise. Her inner voice reassured her, "They'll all be out soon, and then it'll be quiet. Then, I'll be able to finally concentrate."

As she fought to regain her focus, her patience was tested further as the door to her dorm room flew open. Cassandra's roommate, Leah Simmons, entered with a blast of energy and sparkle.

Leah's entrance was as striking as her fashion sense. Her outfit was a blaze of color that seemed to light up the room, making her appear as if she had stepped out of the very music videos echoing down the hall. She was decked out in a sequined top that sparkled brilliantly and a pair of form-hugging bell bottoms. Her energy clearly stated that she was ready to take over the night by storm.

Leah's electrifying presence, full of life and vibrance, completely contrasted Cassandra's 'plain Jane' style. Leah embraced the bold and the bright, a living embodiment of the era's fashion-forward attitude. Cassandra, however, preferred the simplicity and comfort of a pair of jeans and a well-worn hoodie. Their differences in style were not only reflected in their fashion choices but also their personalities; while Cassandra always had her nose buried in a book, Leah regularly had her head in the clouds.

Leah's voice cut through the tension in the room, "No more work! You're coming out tonight."

Looking up from her screen, Cassandra revealed eyes that danced between exhaustion and determination. "You know I can't go out, Leah. This piece I'm writing about the tuition hikes—it's a big deal, and my deadline is Monday. I can't afford to lose tonight."

Leah's sigh was heavy, echoing her growing frustration. "Cass, you're always working," She groaned. "When was the last time you did something fun?" Without waiting for a response, she reached over and shut down Cassandra's word processor, forcing the screen to go dark. "Taking one night off isn't going to kill you. You've got the whole weekend to write about all the world's problems."

"Cassandra's reaction was immediate and sharp. "What the hell, Leah!" she screamed, "I was working on that!"

Leah softened, her tone turning persuasive. "Listen, Cass, you need a break. You've been grinding non-stop this semester. College is flying by, and soon we'll be drowning in 'real life' problems."

Cassandra remained unmoved, her dedication to her work unwavering as she scrambled to turn the machine back on.

Seeing this, Leah played her final card. "It's college night at The Nook; you know what that means," she sang before selling hard a night out that no girl in their right mind would ever willingly sign up for. "Flat dollar draft beers, guaranteed crappy music from the jukebox, pickup lines from townies." She nodded, her eyes wide, trying to paint a positive picture before offering her closing hook. "Plus, you know that new guy I'm seeing from UMass? He's got a cute friend in town." She offered, wiggling her eyebrows."

After a barrage of whines and pleas, Cassandra gave in, trading her casual, "staying in for the night outfit" for a modest dress and a pair of sensible heels. She felt cute but not flashy. Her plan was that if she was going to go out, she'd do everything she could to blend in. She would allow herself one glass of wine before getting back to her room and her more comfortable universe of writing and academics.

At The Nook, Cassandra sat in a dimly lit booth, holding onto a glass of merlot and wondering why she'd let Leah drag her out. She watched from a distance as her roommate and boyfriend mingled with his friends. Their table was alive with laughter; everyone was having a blast—everyone except her.

As she sipped her wine, trying to make herself as small as possible, Cassandra surveyed the crowd. Her mind was locked on getting back to her dorm room and finishing her Op-Ed.

She needed an escape plan—one that didn't include getting an earful from Leah for bailing on her. Sneaking out without being noticed would be extra tricky, considering that Leah and the group she was with had settled in at the table closest to the front door. If she went out that way, she would definitely be seen.

The side door was an option that would allow her to sneak out unnoticed. Still, that exit led to an alley where there was usually a gang of townies smoking cigarettes, always looking to pounce on unsuspecting college students. She wasn't interested in facing whatever that path could have in store.

Out of options, she decided to finish her glass of wine, silently hoping that Leah would pick up on her misery and offer to go home with her without making a fuss.

In the meantime, she'd have to entertain herself. So she studied the room, making up imaginary backstories about the people around her, writing their tales in her head. While she hated going to dive bars like The Nook, they always made for quality people-watching.

As her eyes wandered back over to Leah's group. Hoping to get her attention, she spotted him.

His laugh was deep and infectious, echoing over the roar of the bar's atmosphere. The group was recounting tales of their recent misadventures, talking trash about their favorite sports teams, and insulting each other at every given opportunity. In the center of it all, there he was, holding court.

Even from a distance, his energy was magnetic; all eyes were on him as he spoke. He exuded this fearless charm as if he had mastered the art of embracing life's unpredictable journey.

She took in his outfit, a snapshot of late 90s fashion that did him no favors in her book. The jeans were comically oversized, hanging off his hips in a way that defied gravity. His sweater, a cream color, was more appropriate for someone who shopped in the big and tall section of Filene's. And then there was his stupid hat. A black baseball cap perched at an awkward angle on his head as if it had fallen from the sky and landed there by accident, and he'd simply never bothered to adjust it.

She couldn't help but think he looked like a clown, someone desperately clinging to a trend already on its way out. He was the opposite of the more understated, intellectual types she was usually drawn to.

When their eyes met across the crowded room, he felt an irresistible attraction— She felt repulsed.

"Who the hell does he think he is?" she thought, her gaze narrowing. His overly cheerful demeanor struck her as trying too hard, too eager to impress.

Inevitably, as if guided by fate or perhaps the laws of bar logistics, he approached her. The distinct scent of his Polo Sport cologne filled the air, blending with the room's smell of hops and sweaty college students.

"Hi, I'm Jeremy, D.C.'s friend. You're Leah's roommate, Cassie, right??" he asked.

"Cassandra," she corrected with an icy tone. "My name is Cassandra. Nobody calls me Cassie."

"Sorry, Cassandra, got it," he said dropping his head, his cheeks coloring slightly. "I didn't mean to—"

"It's fine," she interrupted, her voice edging toward impatience. "Listen, I was just about to leave, so—"

"Wait, don't go yet," he pleaded, trying to stop her. "We just got here; the night's still young. Let me buy you a drink."

She had heard that line before and knew what would follow it. After a meaningless conversation and a string of empty compliments, he'd eventually ask for her number. She'd give it to him, and he wouldn't call. Or worse, he would, but only after a night at the bar or a house party looking for a quick hookup.

"I already have a drink, thanks," she replied curtly, lifting her glass as evidence.

Unfazed by her resistance, Jeremy asked, "I see; how about a joke then?"

His eyes had a playful spark, all mischief but totally harmless. "Fine, just make it quick," she replied, setting down her glass.

Dramatically clearing his throat, he started, "Alright, here goes. Why did the Buddhist refuse Novocain during a root canal?"

Cassandra offered a slight shrug, "I don't know, tell me."

Unable to hold back any longer, Jeremy burst out, "Because he wanted to transcend dental medication!" His eyes were wide, with his mouth open, making a goofy expression. "Get it? Transcend Dental—"

She stopped him, waving her hands in front of her face, letting out a soft chuckle. "Yeah, yeah, I get it."

It wasn't the punchline that caught her off guard; it was how he delivered it. As much as she tried to hold it in, she found herself laughing—not a deep belly laugh, but just enough to crack the door open for him to continue the conversation.

"Wait, what's that?" he said, turning his head to the side while cupping his ear. "Is that a laugh I hear?"

She gave a slight but sincere curve of her lips. "Maybe a little."

"I knew I'd get you with that one; it's one of my favorites," he chuckled. "So, how about it? Let me buy your next drink."

"Look, you're cute and all," she said, gathering her purse and putting on her coat, "but you're just not my type."

He responded with a respectful smile, "Fair enough, you can't blame a guy for trying."

Just as she stood up, a burst of commotion broke out from the far end of the bar. Two drunk townies shouting slurred insults quickly escalated into a fistfight, capturing everyone's attention.

Jeremy, acting on instinct, didn't hesitate, didn't speak; he just moved, positioning himself between Cassandra and the action, shielding her.

In a flash, a beer bottle, launched by one of the brawlers in a moment of reckless anger, sailed through the air towards them. With swift precision, Jeremy deflected the bottle, causing it to smash on the floor harmlessly.

With the immediate danger passed, his eyes darted to the two men grappling fiercely, slamming violently into the tables and chairs surrounding the bar, causing havoc.

Moving with purpose, Jeremy approached them, not with fists, but with authority. Inserting himself between the two men and pulling them apart, he demanded, "Hey! Chill out, take it outside!" his voice firm and confident.

As the bar staff stepped in and the townies were thrown out, the party atmosphere quickly returned to its usual buzz of lively chats and laughter as if nothing had ever happened.

With the drama over, Jeremy quickly returned to Cassandra to check on her; his concern was genuine. "Are you okay?" His voice conveyed warmth that dissolved any awkwardness between them, leaving Cassandra at ease.

"I think so," she replied. Looking down to inspect herself, she noticed her wine had been knocked onto the floor during the commotion. "Maybe I will take that drink after all," she said softly.

"You got it!" Jeremy responded, his adrenaline shifting. I'll be right back; don't move!" he shouted, dashing off like a golden retriever chasing his favorite toy.

When he returned with their drinks, she felt a surge of courage that was entirely out of character for her." If I am going to have this drink with you, you need to let me do something first," She demanded.

Jeremy looked at her, spellbound. "Anything."

Reaching across the table, she grabbed the brim of his hat, straightening it. Their eyes met as she held her face close to his. "There," she whispered, "much better." She let her eyes linger before slowly lowering herself back in her seat.

They spent the night having those first-date-type talks, with the bar's hustle and bustle fading into the background. It felt like they were in a bubble, away from the world.

At the end of the night, when the bartender yelled, "Last Call," Jeremy insisted on walking Cassandra back to her dorm. Stopping at her door, he gathered his courage before asking, "Can I call you?"

Her smile was instant as she felt the start of something special. "I'd like that," she said, her heart buzzing from the thrill of new romance.

The unlikely courtship of Cassandra Williams and Jeremy Anderson continued from that fateful evening. Despite their personalities' oil-and-water nature—her practical and him a dreamer—they found remarkable compatibility. They fell into a pattern of Saturday night dates, with him making weekly trips to South Hadley from his college in Vermont.

Over time, he won her heart with his sincere affection and unique sense of humor. After graduating college, they moved in together. Their apartment was small and not in the best part of town, but it was theirs.

A few years later, they got married. Their wedding didn't have a massive guest list, but some say it felt like the biggest party they'd ever been to. Cassandra planned every detail and even handcrafted many of the favors and decor herself. Jeremy supported every choice and participated eagerly in the planning. The result was pure elegance, reflecting their balance, her meticulous planning, and his spontaneous spirit.

Not long after, their family grew as they welcomed a daughter, Jenny, into their lives.

Jenny was a perfect blend of her parents' qualities. She had Jeremy's bravery and Cassandra's smarts. She mirrored her father's sense of humor and her mother's depth of thought. As they watched her grow, Cassandra and Jeremy knew Jenny was special. She was everything to them, the heartbeat of their family.

To Jeremy, Cassandra was not just his wife; she was a force of nature. She wrote poetry, taught high school English, and volunteered as a tutor at the local community center. She believed in words and the power they held. But more than that, she believed in love—her love for Jeremy and their shared love for Jenny.

Their days were filled with laughter, epic family adventures to uncharted places, lazy picnics under the sun, and snug weekends where they would drown themselves in popcorn and endless movie marathons.

Life unfolded like a beautifully crafted novel until the plot took a devastating turn. Shortly after Cassandra's 47th birthday, her world was turned upside down.

During an ordinary checkup, the fragile fabric of life was unraveled. Like a sudden thunderclap on a clear day, the doctor's words pierced the room: "Cancer."

It was a revelation that shook Cassandra's core. Words like "tumor markers," "chemotherapy," and "staging" invaded their lives, transforming each day into a relentless fight for survival.

Jeremy stood by Cassandra like a rock. They tried every available treatment, fought through every round of chemo, and consulted with every specialist they could find. Money, time, and comfort took a backseat to her health.

During this time, Jenny was entering her sophomore year in college, and the struggle took its toll on her relationship with her parents, particularly her father. The once close-knit family was crumbling under the pressure, but Jeremy and Cassandra fought to maintain a semblance of normalcy for Jenny's sake.

In time, despite their best efforts, Cassandra's body began to lose strength and wither away. There were good days when she could sit up in bed and smile, ask about Jenny's studies, and even joke about their hospital "vacations." But the good days were often followed by horrific days of unbearable pain, unimaginable fatigue, and the kind of despair that can break even the strongest spirit.

In her lucid moments, Cassandra would look into Jeremy's eyes, those deep wells of sorrow, and her heart would break for him.

———

In the soft glow of their bedroom, where memories danced in the shadows, Jeremy felt a surge of emotions as he and Cassandra pored over old photo albums. Every picture showed moments from their brighter days, filled with endless laughter and warm sunshine. Each image was a tiny glimpse into the depth of their love, tugging at their hearts with a fierce and emotional pull.

Their soft laughter was a bittersweet symphony, echoing off the walls with a resonance that spoke to their deep connection. As each memory flickered by, so too did the moments of silence.

In one of these silences, Cassandra's strength waning, yet her spirit undimmed, looked deeply into Jeremy's eyes—a look that could shatter his entire world and then put it back together in a heartbeat.

"Do you remember that first night we met?" she asked, her voice a whisper against the storm brewing in his heart.

"Of course I do," he replied, the corners of his mouth lifting in a melancholy smile. You hated me," he chuckled, the sound more of a sob than anything as he recalled his less-than-stellar first impression.

"No, I did not hate you," she corrected with a gentle sigh, "I just thought that you looked silly at first, with those ridiculous pants and that God-awful crooked hat," she said with a faint smile.

Her voice softened as she continued, her words painting a picture of a past filled with unexpected turns. "That night, when the fight broke out," she paused, closing her eyes and returning to the events of their first meeting. "You protected me, just like you always have."

"I wish I could protect you now," he sobbed, "but I can't. You're my purpose, and I can't do anything to save you," he cried, his words barely a whisper against the weight of his grief.

Yet her resolve never wavered in the face of such raw emotion. "Jeremy, you need to listen to me," her voice, soft yet steady. "When my time comes, promise me you'll embrace the life that awaits you and take care of yourself the same way you've always taken care of me."

Her words shattered him, and his chest tightened as tears streamed down his face. "I can't," he gasped between sobs, struggling to catch his breath. "I don't know how to live without you." He swallowed hard, fighting through the depth of his despair. "You're my reason for living; you're my purpose," he whispered, his voice breaking with emotion.

"You can, my love. You can, and you will," she whispered, her voice guiding him through his emotional darkness. Just keep me in your heart. There, I'll live on until the day we meet again."

———

On that tear-soaked evening, with Jeremy by her side, holding her hand, Cassandra passed peacefully, leaving him devastated and forever changed.

In the aftermath, Jeremy allowed himself to be consumed by grief, living in the emptiness of a home that once thrived on Cassandra's vibrance. He became a broken man.

As the years passed, he failed to live up to the promise to embrace life and take care of himself.

Day after day, he struggled to find motivation, just going through the motions without truly living.

His health was no longer a priority. His career turned into a sequence of keystrokes and mouse clicks, meaningless tasks in a world that had lost its color. His diet was a blur of convenience. Fast food picked up on the way home from work was usually his first and only meal of the day. While he was always tired, he rarely slept. Heavy doses of caffeine kept him awake. Exercise or physical activity of any kind was a thing of the past.

After years of failing to take care of himself, he wasn't surprised when one night, while sitting in his recliner, scarfing down a Double Whopper and onion rings, he felt a sharp pain in his chest. As his heart attacked him, he gasped for air, and the walls closed in around him.

He could have reached for the phone to call 911, but he didn't. He wanted to go. As he took his last breath, his only thought was of Cassandra and how all he wanted was to be reunited with her in the afterlife.

He wouldn't be.

2

GOIN BACK TO CALI

Jeremy's face was lined like an old map. Each wrinkle told a story, and every line was a choice—many, the same choice, made repeatedly across multiple lifetimes.

Most drift through life unaware of the full impact of every decision they make. Jeremy was different. His fate—or curse, depending on the day—was to experience his life in repetition. So far, he'd lived twenty-five lifetimes, and now, he was staring in the face of life twenty-six.

To say he was an old soul would be an understatement. At 57 years old, an age he'd never lived past, he had an air of cosmic exhaustion that suggested the weight of ages.

Yet, the indigo sky of his eyes still held a flicker of excitement, a spark that had yet to be snuffed out. Maybe it was the prospect of potentially finding a loophole in his karmic cycle and being set free from the relentless grasp on his soul, or perhaps it was the exhilaration of seeing life through a lens most people couldn't dream of.

Today was the day he'd be returned to his youth. May 5th, 2036. Cinco de Mayo. He often wondered if there was any significance to that date, whether the universe had been trying to send him some sort of riddle he had been unable to solve.

Weary of living multiple lives and certainty of his fate, he had made a deal with himself. If destiny dictated when he would greet death, time and again, he would do it on his terms, in a place where his life once shimmered most brilliantly: The Roosevelt Hotel in Hollywood, California.

The hotel represented a moment he'd carried in his heart across all his lifetimes—a moment spent with Cassandra in his first life, a life untouched by endless cycles.

Their honeymoon had been there, in an era of innocence, marked by the clinking of champagne glasses and warm sunshine streaming through palm trees. It was a safe space that held a once-pure emotion in him that his cyclical existence had worn down long ago.

Walking through the hotel doors, each step he took was heavy. He knew that within a few short hours, his body would betray him, and this life would end, no matter how many healthy lifestyle choices he'd made this time around.

The hotel had changed over the years. Once overflowing with glitz and glamour, it now felt empty and soulless as it buzzed with automated kiosks and futuristic tech. Seeing the place he once cherished lose its magic saddened him deeply. But one thing still mattered: the particular room he'd requested, Room 223, a cabana suite overlooking the iconic Tropicana Bar.

That sacred room had once been a haven of bright futures, brimming with hope and dreams. It was a place where possibilities seemed endless and unknown. But its role had shifted dramatically— tonight it would mark an end.

As he stood at the door to Room 223, his hand trembled as he pressed the key card to the electronic lock. Deja vu enveloped him as the lock's tumblers clicked open with a familiar, comforting sound.

Entering the room, he was bathed in the soft glow of the setting sun pouring in from the balcony. Unlike the rest of the hotel, the cabana suites were kept to their historic glory, just as he remembered. For a brief moment, he was transported back to that first honeymoon with Cassandra. Reliving that innocence felt like it was lifetimes ago— because it was.

He stared out the window, where the fading light played hide and seek with the letters of the Hollywood Sign. The dying day cast a soft glow over the hills that cradled so many broken dreams.

He remembered the first time he'd seen that sign, bright and bold against a clear blue sky, a symbol of ambition for a young man with stars in his eyes, his bride by his side, and not much else.

With a sigh, he reached into the minibar, searching for a temporary escape or, at the very least, a momentary distraction. He decided on an old favorite—a scotch that reminded him of both good and bad times.

Pouring himself a glass, he watched it swirl, a miniature whirlpool of memories and reflections.

Raising the glass, he offered a toast to the room, the city, and the relentless march of time. "To endings and beginnings," he whispered, his words barely more than a breath.

Sitting down on the edge of the bed, he cradled the glass in his hand. The 18-year-old single malt scotch was the same he'd bravely ordered decades earlier and lifetimes ago at the hotel's bar. Back then, he desperately desired to blend in with the high society that had seemed so out of reach.

He remembered how cool he had tried to sound ordering it that night. "I'll have a single malt 18, neat," he'd said, trying to mimic the confidence of the glamorous crowd around him. But that first sip had been a shock to his system, a fiery trial by alcohol that had almost made him puke.

Back then, Jeremy was more of a beer guy, unaccustomed to the punch of a good scotch. But time had changed him. His taste had evolved as it was refined by centuries of success and failure. Now, the scotch was a familiar warmth, a reminder of how far he had come and of all the roads he had traveled.

He drank again, chasing away the existential chill of the evening and the shadows of the past. Closing his eyes, he toasted again silently to the man he'd once been and to the uncertain future that awaited him.

As life twenty-five was ending, he wondered whether the number twenty-five could signify some sort of completion, like the final piece of a cosmic puzzle. Was there anything behind the number twenty-five, an importance in the number itself that he hadn't uncovered? He thought about all the philosophical theories and ancient wisdom he'd studied throughout his many lives, searching for some answers, but none came.

Taking his last sip of scotch, he looked out upon the terrace surrounding the pool. He fixated on the flickering flames in the fire pits lining the patio. They were in their own cycle of life and death, never the same fire twice. It made him think that maybe he wasn't the only one caught in this rhythm of existence.

Closing his eyes, he clung to a sliver of hope, desperately wishing for a way out of the cycle he was trapped in. He'd lived through it all, exploiting his past lives' knowledge for all they were worth. Each new existence brought a series of achievements, from the buzz of celebrity to the quiet accumulation of fortunes.

He had nothing left to achieve, and now, he was drowning in boredom. Deep down, he knew that his next life had to hold more meaning, something real. Maybe that was the only way to break free from this endless series of cycles.

For now, Room 223 would be his sanctuary, where he could reflect on his past, cherish his memories, and bid farewell to life twenty-five before setting off on another journey into the unknown.

3

ROOSEVELT RESET

AT 8:45 PM SHARP, it started.

Jeremy looked at his watch as his chest tightened. "Right on schedule," he grunted as the intensity of the experience increased. His face flushed as if blood were racing away from it in anticipation of what was to come. His chest tightened, his nerves tangled into knotted webs of pain, each thread pulling tighter with every breath. This was a dance of agony he had become accustomed to.

But it wasn't the physical discomfort that haunted him the most. It was the raw experience of his soul—his very essence—being separated from its mortal shell and thrust into an alternate existence.

The air around him shimmered as if heat waves were distorting it. His vision blurred; objects in the room stretched and warped like they were made of liquid crystal.

Then, a sensation best described as 'ripping' enveloped him. It was as though invisible cosmic hands had reached into his being, gripped his soul with a vise, and pulled with a relentless force that defied all laws of physics and metaphysics alike. This wasn't just an out-of-body experience, where one might float peacefully above, looking down on their physical self with detached curiosity. This was an existential dislocation, a displacement so severe that it felt as if the very fabric of his being was tearing at its seams.

. . .

Then came peace.

Whispers of an idea, spoken in a language beyond words, wrapped him in a blanket of calmness. This journey into the profound wilderness of being wasn't new to him. He had drifted into this state of pure existence in his previous resets. He found himself floating in his consciousness. He seemed to be drifting in an eternal ocean—calm and boundless, in a realm of unbroken stillness.

For a moment, he wondered if this was the end he had longed for—one where he would not be forced to relive his life and would be set free of his cyclical curse.

The thought dissolved as quickly as it formed as he realized he was merely hovering between being and nothingness. He recognized this moment well. It was the brief pause between lifetimes. Here, his essence remained; he was aware, existing as pure thought alone, unbound by physical form.

Then, like a sudden flash of lightning, the realization jolted through his formless self. He was going back— not to an undefined future, but to a time when he would have another opportunity to reweave the intricate fabric of his life.

Cassandra's name flickered in his mind like the flame of a candle dancing in the wind. Every one of his lives had been a quest to find her, be with her, and save her—a pursuit to reconstruct a family, to piece together the jigsaw puzzle of a lost love and an incomplete future.

Every attempt had failed, leaving time and space fractured, sometimes having cataclysmic consequences, splintering the timeline and rupturing the fabric of humanity's destiny. Yet, he was ready to take that cosmic gamble again. His soul had matured. He was no longer a rookie player in the dark; he was a seasoned veteran, a pro at the game of life.

In the most intricate recesses of his mind, he cataloged all the pivotal moments and crossroads of destiny he needed to navigate with surgical precision. He knew all the events that would bring good fortune and every obstacle he needed to avoid, like landmines scattered on the field of fate. He disassembled the mosaic of minor details and grand events that needed to be matched perfectly, and in his mind, he reconstructed each tile so that his desired future could be achieved.

In that fading yet infinite moment, he felt a newfound strength. He felt ready, in ways he never had before, to hoist the sails of existence and embark on yet another journey into the unknown. This time, he held the compass of experience, the map of knowledge, and the wisdom of past failures. This time would be different—different in a way that was carved into the essence of his being.

He took one final metaphysical breath as the realm he was suspended in began to disintegrate, giving way to the shadow of rebirth. A breath not drawn from lungs but from the depths of his eternal self, swallowing the silent tranquility around him.

Then came the chaos.

Imagine a square peg being forced into a round hole. But the square peg isn't made of wood or metal—it's made of memories, dreams, love, sadness, the laughter you've shared, the tears you've cried, your first kiss, even your deepest fears.

Now imagine that hole isn't a gentle emptiness but a swirling vortex of chaos, a medley of alternate realities, each pulling at the fragments of that peg, reshaping and contorting it into something entirely new.

This part of the transition between realities always had a psychedelic fever-dream quality to it. Ethereal landscapes merged into intricate cityscapes; shadows of people he had once known—or thought he knew— crossed his vision like wraiths. Time warped, stretched, and collapsed in on itself. He felt like an intricate origami being unfolded and refolded into the same design, yet each time, never quite the same as before.

Everything ended with his soul slamming into a new reality like a comet crashing into a barren planet. The initial sensation was often one of exhilaration, a mix of adrenaline and serotonin flooding his system. A bizarre byproduct of what he called 'reset sickness.'

As the wild journey he had just been on faded, he felt misplaced. It was as if his life story was being rewritten in an unfamiliar language—the plot was the same, but the words no longer matched him."

When he opened his eyes, the familiar scent of stale socks and Polo Sport filled his nose. "Shit," he muttered as he looked over at his alarm clock. The red LED display flickered the date: Oct 24, 1996.

The irony of his existence lay in the date of his rebirth: his 18th birthday. The anniversary of his entrance into adulthood became the day every reset returned him to, marking both a beginning and an unending cycle.

He always approached this familiar starting line with a more refined strategy in each new life. During his time in the existential abyss, he developed a comprehensive manual of actions to take and which pitfalls to avoid. Each step on his path was defined by the wisdom he had compiled from his previous lifetimes.

His plan for this 26th life was a carefully woven blend of proven theories and practical tactics, all geared towards one primary objective: to reunite with Cassandra.

Although his plan was rigid, he would allow for minor deviations and small ripples that wouldn't disturb the flow toward his ultimate goal. This approach gave him a small amount of control in an otherwise unpredictable existence.

Throughout his repeated journeys, he learned how to separate the meaningless events from the critical ones. The daily dramas of high school had revealed themselves as largely unimportant.

However, there were pivotal moments and unchangeable events that he needed to navigate with precision. Each step was carefully planned out. Sticking to this plan was critical in reaching his ultimate goal of a reunion with Cassandra.

Among these goals, the most important was attending a particular college in Vermont and being at a precise location at a specific time to recreate the night they would first meet. This first encounter was a fixed point in time, an unchangeable event that needed to happen exactly as it did in his first life.

He was intimately familiar with these critical events. He understood that while some aspects of his journey could be shaped or reshaped for his benefit, others were set in stone. This knowledge was both a burden and the light that guided him through many lives. Each step he took was a deliberate move in an intricate dance with fate.

As Jeremy swung his legs over the side of his bed, he took a deep breath. Yes, it was "Reset Day," but for the first time in a long time, he felt a spark of something that had long been snuffed out inside him—hope. And in a life that was an endless cycle, hope was something he rarely had.

Getting out of bed, he looked at himself in the mirror and smirked. "Life 26, prepare to have your ass kicked."

The first rays of the sun streamed through the cracks of his blinds, casting a golden glow on his room eerily similar to one of the setting sun he had observed in his room at The Roosevelt moments earlier and years ahead.

The similarity felt like a good omen, or at least, he chose to see it as one. In this life, he would have structure, a plan, and, most importantly, a little wiggle room for harmless errors that he believed would make this version of life unique. He was armed with the wisdom of a man who had lived 25 lifetimes and the heart of a young adult eager to break free. Whatever this life held, he was ready.

Thus began Jeremy's 26th life; this time, he had a feeling it would be different.

Very different.

4

THE LABRADOR

GREGG ANDERSON WAS a human hamster wheel of disappointment. He'd wake up, reluctantly put on a shirt and tie, drag himself to work, and come home nine hours later to down a six-pack like water while watching the nightly news. The entire time, he would shout comments lashed with prejudice as if the people on TV could hear him. Often, the neighbors did. Eventually, he would pass out on his recliner until the morning.

Rinse and repeat.

It was as if he were engaged in a never-ending dance with mediocrity, a grotesque ballet performed solo because no one wanted to join him on stage.

Jeremy often wondered how his father managed to weave his web of misery so effectively. Gregg had a unique way of pissing everyone off, co-workers, grocery store clerks, even the mailman who'd occasionally and "'accidentally" drop the mail in puddles before delivering it.

Jeremy's mother—the resilient woman who raised him until he was 13—left the state to escape the gravitational pull of Gregg's bullshit., and Jeremy never blamed her, not one bit. He figured, after putting up with Gregg for as long as she did, she deserved her freedom, even if it came with the companionship of a mysterious Floridian man named Otis, who smelled like sea salt and Old Spice. At least, that's how Jeremy imagined him. He'd never met the man. Not once in 25 lifetimes.

Then, there was Jeremy's grandfather, Henry, a saint of a man whose laughter used to fill the house during holidays. Once upon a time, Henry had been the town's mayor. Not just a figurehead mayor but a full-throttle, all-guns-blazing leader who had wrangled this place like a cowboy tames a wild stallion. After years of shaking hands and kissing babies, Henry longed for a life beyond the confines of public office.

Seeking a new challenge where he could make a difference, he dove into real estate development. He wasn't interested in ordinary projects; Henry had a vision for something bold and unprecedented, a project that would redefine the town's landscape.

Henry set his sights on a 47.5-acre piece of land hidden within the wooded hills surrounding their town. Beyond the cookie-cutter suburban single-story ranch homes and the lower-class housing known as "The Mills," this land was destined for Henry's most significant achievement: The Labrador.

The Labrador was more than just a construction project. It was to be a colossus of tourism, a venture that would transform the failing town into a bustling destination. Henry imagined it as a palace in the woods, a symbol of luxury and relaxation that would attract visitors from every corner of New England. He imagined parties, where the air buzzed with the lively sounds of jazz music, champagne flowed freely, and laughter filled every corner.

The journey to bring The Labrador to life was no walk in the park. There were construction delays, financial challenges to overcome, and bureaucratic red tape to cut. On top of it all was the ever-present chorus of naysayers who believed the project was doomed to fail from the start.

Construction was completed in the spring of 1947, and The Labrador stood tall amongst the trees as a towering testament to Henry's vision and perseverance. It was everything he ever dreamed of and more.

The grand opening was a spectacle, a festival of fireworks and fanfare. The town, once skeptical, basked in the newfound prosperity that The Labrador brought. Tourists flocked in droves with their wallets open and ready to inject life into the local economy.

In the summer months, the place was always fully booked. People didn't just stay at The Labrador; they experienced it. The beds were so plush it felt like you were sleeping in the clouds. The on-site 5-star restaurant offered a menu that was an adventure in every bite. The centerpiece of it all was a grand ballroom that was so exquisite that it looked like it had been designed by Jay Gatsby himself. The cocktails were legendary and artfully crafted, making each drink a life-changing experience. They say even the staff seemed like they'd waltzed out of a Hollywood film, polished, professional, and too good-looking to be real.

The Labrador reigned supreme for nearly two decades, bringing in piles of tourism revenue, revitalizing the area, and breathing new life into the community. Shops flourished, restaurants thrived, and the streets, once empty, buzzed with excitement.

But the twist is always the cruelest part of a story. For Henry, it was a fire—an overnight transformation of his empire into ashes. A blaze erupted in the kitchen while the Labrador slept peacefully in the night. For hours, teams fought to extinguish the fire. Nothing they did could stop the destruction. It was as if Hell opened the earth beneath The Labrador, and the devil himself reached up to claim it as his own. By sunrise, nothing remained but the blackened bones of a once majestic structure.

Lives were lost, futures vanished, and a vibrant history filled with lively nights and hushed secrets faded into ash and distant memories.

The tragedy left the town in ruins, and Henry was no exception. His once vibrant swagger faded, resembling a flower deprived of water. The man who used to stride with the confidence of someone who had mastered life had become a shell of himself.

Henry passed away in the winter of 1988 on the anniversary of the fire that wiped The Labrador from existence. Lung cancer was the official cause, yet Jeremy couldn't shake the feeling that the disease was a cover for the old man's escape from the agony of his shattered dreams.

After his grandfather's passing, Jeremy uncovered a hidden secret: Henry had set up a trust fund with enough money to propel Jeremy into adulthood. This gift, which would become available on his 18th birthday, was Henry's way of providing a foundation for his grandson's future.

Henry had always envisioned The Labrador as a source of generational success for the Anderson family. After it went up in flames, he was determined to realign the family legacy. This financial endowment was designed to give Jeremy the freedom to pursue his dreams and chase after his own great white whale, with nothing to hold him back.

5

EIGHTEEN AND LIFE

JEREMY SURVEYED HIS ROOM, looking for any clues of change in the life he'd just started. He knew at this stage that everything would be exactly as it always had been, and this life was no exception.

He felt tired. Not physically tired but spiritually exhausted. He needed to get his blood pumping.

Shuffling over to the set of free weights at the corner of his room, he felt excited to use his young body again. At this age, he was an athlete, a three-year letterman on the football team, and a wrestler. He didn't hate the part of a reset where he got to wake up young and fit. Sixty push-ups, forty curls, and a set of burpees later, his body was awake, but his mind was still somewhere between "screw this" and "what's the point."

He stood in front of his mirror, tracing the contours of his chiseled abs, his frame a testament to physical fitness. His eyes darted to the clock; its numbers seemed to sneer at him, ticking away at a reality he could no longer escape. A young and strong body with a mind in turmoil, his physical shape seemed like a cruel joke when contrasted with his inner state.

"Fuck it," he groaned to himself before getting ready for school.

He turned on the shower, allowing it to warm up before stepping in. As the spray washed over him, he felt a little cleaner, a little more human, a little more ready to put on an "everything is awesome" act. With a sigh, he shut the water off and toweled dry.

His next stop was his closet. His choices were limited to athletic gear, graphic tees, flannels, and worn-out jeans. He was not a snappy dresser.

Thankfully, the birth of Grunge helped him hide the fact that his father hadn't taken him back-to-school shopping since the 8th grade. He chose a vintage Beatles tee he bought at a garage sale, paired it with some baggy jeans, and called it a day.

He could hear the grumbling and muttering downstairs. That would be his father, up early for a breakfast of coffee, cigarettes, and disappointment.

Taking a deep breath, he grabbed his backpack and headed downstairs. His grip tightened around the strap of his bag as he rounded the bottom of the staircase and was greeted by the chaos that was the home of his youth.

The small Cape Cod-style house was a testament to neglect. Peppering the living room were overflowing ashtrays, beer cans, and piles of empty TV dinners, fossils of meals eaten without pleasure or company.

The place was like a realm of desolation, a snapshot of time forgotten. It was as though the outside world had marched forward, leaving this space and its lead occupant trapped in a bubble of despair.

In a corner of the living room, Jeremy's father, Gregg, sat reading his newspaper while sipping his coffee spiked with bourbon, lost in a self-crafted fortress of failure.

"What's the matter? Are you too cool to say good morning to your old man?" his father growled, his words slurring from behind his newspaper.

Jeremy gritted his teeth. "Morning, sir," he managed, his voice carrying forced cheerfulness.

Gregg grunted, setting the paper down before taking another swig of his boozed coffee. "Eighteen today, you think you're a man now?"

"Age is just a number," Jeremy replied, attempting to sidestep the confrontation.

Faced with a day brimming with plans, he had no intention of starting it fighting with his half-drunk loser of a father who was oblivious to the world beyond his own narrow view.

Jeremy's understanding of life's complexities far surpassed that of Gregg, and he knew engaging in a pointless argument would only waste precious time. His immediate challenge was to get out of the house with minimal disruption to his timeline.

Any unnecessary confrontations with his father could derail his day. The task required tact and a careful balancing act, skills Jeremy had mastered living under such unique circumstances.

As he quietly planned his exit, Gregg's words, muddled by the early morning bourbon in his coffee, belted, "I'll bet you're having dinner at your little cheerleader's house tonight, huh? Just don't go getting her in trouble if you know what I mean; I can't handle another pain in the ass like you running around here."

The words pulled Jeremy back into a painful past he had long since left behind. Sure, engaging in a battle with his father would likely throw off his plans, but quietly slipping out the door and ignoring Gregg's taunts as he always had left a hollow feeling in his gut.

A newfound confidence surged within Jeremy, a desire to push back against the weight of his father's oppression. For once, he felt an urge to break free from the abusive chains he'd had wrapped around him.

Jeremy knew it was now or never. If he didn't make a move, he'd be stuck dealing with his father for years to come. He eyed Gregg, feeling the heavy air around them. The room was charged with nerves and unease. He could feel his heart racing. His hands balled into fists, his knuckles turning ghostly white. Everything blurred into the background, leaving him and his father in a long-overdue face-off.

He thought about the unfolding scenario, a crossroads that could redefine his future. What if he confronted Gregg now, in this moment? He let his imagination roam, lining up each potential outcome. Each hypothetical path fell like dominos, reshaping his world with every imagined confrontation.

In one scenario, he envisioned the words erupting from his mouth like molten lava, irreversibly scorching everything in its path. Gregg's face would contort in anger, and he'd scream some nonsense about disrespect. Maybe they'd even have a full-blown shouting match, shattering the false harmony they'd maintained for years. This was the most likely scenario.

Then, Jeremy's mind flickered to an alternate reality where Gregg stopped and thought about his actions. In this unlikely scenario, his father might recognize his mistakes and consider changing his ways. He knew that the odds of this happening were slim to none, somewhere between 'not a chance in hell' and 'never in a million lifetimes.'

However, there was a third path that he couldn't ignore—the one where he kept his mouth shut, and everything continued just as it had always been—a status quo experienced in every iteration of his existence.

Gregg would torment him emotionally in that timeline, like a perpetual storm with no end in sight. He would keep weathering it, bearing it like a martyr, until Gregg would die, most likely when Jeremy was in his late twenties, taking with him only the bitterness that had soured their relationship for years.

Standing there, Jeremy couldn't help but picture the torment he'd endure for years if he chose to back down. The risk of causing a ripple this early in life was foolish, but something deep within him, a mystic energy, urged him to stand up for himself.

With determination burning in his eyes, he decided. He was going to face his father right there, right then, consequences be damned.

His heart pounded in his chest. It was go-time, the moment of reckoning. He'd been through lifetimes of his father's crap, again and again, each existence teaching him something else about the human condition. But this lifetime, this was the one he was going to take control of, the one where he didn't let an abusive, alcoholic dick influence his choices or define his path.

It was as if the universe itself had grown tired of his hesitation, its cosmic hand reaching down to shove him off the cliff of indecision. This wasn't just a minor deviation from his plan; it was a complete overhaul, a leap into the unknown with nothing but raw, unfiltered courage as his parachute.

He weighed every possible scenario, every potential fallout of confronting his father, but in this electrifying moment, all that calculation didn't seem necessary.

"Fuck it," he thought, a rebellious whisper in his mind that grew into a deafening roar.

Ready to step into the storm that awaited him. Jeremy squared his shoulders and drew a deep breath.

"Dad," he began, his voice steady but laced with an unmistakable edge, "we need to talk, and this time, you're going to listen."

"Talk? Since when do we 'talk,' huh?" Gregg's voice dripped with venom.

He took a deep breath and let it out, steadying his resolve. "I want my trust fund Dad, I know you've been skimming from it."

Gregg's face flushed an angry red. "You ungrateful little shit! How dare you accuse me!" He screamed.

"Stop," Jeremy interjected, his voice icy calm. "I know all about what you've been up to, and I just want what's mine."

For a moment, the room descended into chaos. Gregg roared, his temper flaring like wildfire, hurling insults and curses. But Jeremy remained calm, each word from his father rolling off him. The power dynamics had shifted, and they both knew it.

"You think you can stand there and demand things from me?" Gregg spat out; his eyes narrowed into slits. "I raised you; you owe me—"

Jeremy interrupted, his eyes locking onto Gregg's as though ready to disarm a ticking time bomb.

Twelve lifetimes ago, Jeremy was one of the most successful sports agents in the NFL, a real-life Jerry Maguire. He had worked tirelessly wheeling, dealing, and negotiating the contracts of prima donna athletes. The rush he got from closing high-valued extensions pulsed in his veins. He was no stranger to the art of persuasion; he had stared down NFL linebackers and convinced them to take hometown discounts for the 'greater good.' Facing off against the man who claimed to "raise him" wouldn't be as tricky as Jeremy initially feared. "You didn't raise me, Gregg; you fucking used me as a cash cow, helping yourself to my college fund to feed your poor life choices. That all ends now!"

Gregg glared at Jeremy.

"I want my freedom, and I want my money. The money Henry left for me, not you, not your failing 'investment opportunities' or whatever you call your scams these days."

Shifting his posture, embodying a confidence as sharp as a blade, Jeremy leaned forward, his voice slicing through the air with a hushed, iron-edged whisper. "Listen closely—it's straightforward. That fund is mine. I'm eighteen today, and I can access it without your consent, and I know exactly how much money is in that account."

This was no bluff. Jeremy's claim was rooted in truth, born from his unique insight into past lives. He knew, with the certainty of someone who had seen for himself, that despite his father's habitual embezzlements, the account's balance on this particular day would be no less than $26,054.68.

This money would be enough to get him through the rest of his senior year, the summer, and up to Vermont for his first semester at college. He could turn what was left into a steady income stream from there. With his knowledge of market trends and lottery numbers, taken from the wisdom of his 25 previous lives, generating wealth was not just a possibility but a guarantee.

He locked eyes with his father, "Look, Gregg, it's simple: let me take what's rightfully mine, and you'll never hear from me again. Unless you sober up, which, let's be honest, isn't going to happen any time soon." The words hung in the air, a gauntlet thrown, a challenge issued.

The balance of power had shifted, and with it, the course of their lives. For Jeremy, this was more than just a confrontation; it was a declaration of independence, a first step into a world where he was the architect of his destiny.

The room fell into an uneasy silence. Gregg looked at him, his eyes no longer filled with the fury that Jeremy had grown accustomed to seeing. Instead, there was a glint of something else—recognition. Acknowledgment that the tables had turned. Jeremy couldn't be sure, but he felt a shift, a realignment in the universe that spelled the beginning of his freedom.

"Do we have a deal?" Jeremy pressed on, locking eyes with his father.

Gregg sighed with defeat heavy in his voice. "Fine."

Opening the closet, he shuffled out an envelope and handed it to his son.

"Everything you'll need to access the account is in here; just take it and go," he said, holding the envelope in front of Jeremy's face. I had a feeling you'd try to pull something like this," he said with an evil grin.

Jeremy yanked the tattered envelope free and turned to walk away. He paused, turned back, and looked at his father. "Gregg, get your shit together; life's too short," he hoped the words would strike a chord, urging his father to take them seriously and consider making a change. A change that Jeremy had never seen in every iteration of his life. And with that, he walked out the door.

So much for not making waves, he thought to himself. The unbearable uncertainty of how the severing of his relationship with his father at this stage in life twenty-six weighed heavily on him.

6

HUXLEY HIGH AND THE CONCRETE RULE

JEREMY SHOVED the stubborn stick shift of his 1987 Wrangler into gear, revving the engine of the beat-up Jeep as if trying to awaken some dormant beast. The vehicle growled back, its frame vibrating like it was pissed off at the world or maybe just pissed off at him.

"Come on, don't crap out on me now," Jeremy muttered, patting the dashboard affectionately. The Jeep—orange as an Arizona sunset—was a labor of love, or perhaps more fittingly, a labor of stubborn independence. Gregg had promised to pay half for a "nice" Jeep, perfect for the beach on The Cape. After months of radio silence, Jeremy bagged groceries and rounded up enough shopping carts to buy the rusting relic he was driving.

The 4x4 was a shitshow on wheels—tire pressure inconsistent, a crappy transmission, and a rickety axle —but it was his shitshow. It was the best vehicle he'd ever owned, and given his unique existence, he'd owned a lot.

As pulled out of the driveway, still feeling the rush of adrenaline from the confrontation with his father, he couldn't help but wonder if the ugly family showdown would ripple through time and space and screw up his quest to reunite with Cassandra.

He thought about her wavy hair and brown eyes that could look directly into his soul. For the past 25 lifetimes, he had been chasing that gaze and the connection he'd once had with her.

The butterfly effect—that's what this was. He had studied enough physics to understand the concept. A butterfly flaps its wings in Brazil and sets off a tornado in Texas. Or, you stand up to your dad on your eighteenth birthday and end up alone for the rest of your 26th life.

The concept came down to simple cause and effect. Each choice, each confrontation, each whispered, "I love you" or "I can't," had the potential to throw his destiny off course.

Jeremy's thoughts were a collection of Deja Vus. Fragments from 25 previous lifetimes danced at the edges of his consciousness. First kisses, final goodbyes, victories, and screw-ups all haunted him like ghosts.

He remembered life seven, where he'd been too consumed with school even to notice Cassandra when he had the chance.

Life thirteen was a bitch; they were together but torn apart by war.

Life twenty was almost a fairytale, but he hesitated and lost her to someone else.

One thing was clear in all these narratives of his existence: the tiniest miscalculations had cost him dearly.

He tightened his grip on the steering wheel. The Jeep seemed to growl approvingly as if urging him to push through his doubts. "Alright, focus," he told himself. If he'd just messed up, the question was, how bad?

He'd twisted some events in past lives with zero effect, significant events, and nothing major happened.

In Jeremy's twelfth lifetime, he failed at trying to reunite with Cassandra and wanted to "force an early reset." So, he decided to mess with the Y2K bug, the infamous glitch that everyone thought would bring about the end of the world as the year 1999 ticked over to 2000. The whole planet was in a panic, imagining planes falling from the sky and bank accounts vanishing into the digital abyss. With an uncanny knowledge of code gained after years of reincarnation, Jeremy hacked into the mainframe of central global servers. He reversed the fix, reinstalling the original bug, cackling as he imagined the mass chaos that would ensue. But when the clock struck midnight, nothing happened. The world kept spinning, computers kept humming, and people cheered. It was as if the universe shrugged and said, "Nice try, kid."

On the other hand, in his 14th life, Jeremy failed to woo Cassandra and ended up alone in his 40s. He decided to get a puppy to soothe his loneliness. The dog ended up being a real asshole. One summer day, she got free from her leash while out for a walk. Even though he knew that she could run like the wind and that he'd never catch her, he chased after her into the street. They were both flattened by an F-250 flying a Don't Tread on Me flag off the back—instant reset.

Maybe this event with his father wouldn't affect anything. He had to believe in the power of positive ripples too.

Roaring down the road, the Jeep's tires hummed on the pavement, echoing Jeremy's newfound resolve. Every stop sign and every red light along the way felt like the universe's way of asking, "Are you sure?" And each time, Jeremy hit the gas, surging forward as if he was saying, "Hell yeah, I'm sure."

As he pulled into the parking lot of Huxley High School, Jeremy's heart was a strange mix of anxiety and hope. The odds were stacked against him; the variables were infinite. But as he killed the Jeep's engine, he felt gratitude wash over him. He was armed with something invaluable: the wisdom of 25 lifetimes and a rusting orange 4x4 that, against all odds, just wouldn't quit.

And so, as he stepped out of the Jeep, slamming the creaky door behind him, Jeremy couldn't help but feel that maybe, just maybe, the butterfly had flapped its wings in the right direction this time. Perhaps this was the lifetime he'd get it right—imperfections, screw-ups, and all.

Jeremy had a brief moment of clarity. His heartbeat had settled into a rhythmic lull, eyes half-closed as he leaned against the school's infamous Wildcat—the dilapidated school mascot that stood like a rusty, sad sentinel on the edge of the parking lot. A sense of calm washed over him as if someone had turned down the volume on the universe.

Suddenly, out of nowhere, screeching tires shredding against asphalt shattered the peace. He whipped his head around to witness the horror: a brown 1984 Plymouth Turismo—ugly as sin—barreling through the parking lot like a bat out of hell.

The car's rusty exterior reflected the sun's rays in jagged, unholy ways, making it look like a death machine out of a Mad Max film. Students scattered out of the car's warpath like a school of panicked fish evading an apex predator.

Backpacks went flying; a skateboard shot off into the distance, and some poor nerd's lunch became a smear of defeat on the pavement.

Jeremy's eyes went wide, and his body froze. Part of him was scared, sure—who wouldn't be when faced with a two-ton speeding hunk of metal? But the other part of him, the dominant part, was absolutely fucking livid.

"Are you shitting me?!" Jeremy internally screamed, his heart pounding not in fear but in full-throttle anger. If the ripples were going to force an early reset, it certainly wasn't going to come by the hands of Dutch "Fucking" Wyatt and his piece of shit Plymouth.

Jeremy could almost feel the car's grill laughing at him; its headlights the menacing eyes of a mechanical beast about to devour its prey.

Time slowed like it often does in those gut-check moments when every millisecond counts. Jeremy glanced at the school's Wildcat statue beside him, its tarnished metal layers screaming years of neglect. He considered taking cover behind it for a second but then thought, "No Way. Fuck this."

He felt a fire ignite within him, propelling his limbs into action. His eyes narrowed, his jaw clenched, and his muscles tightened with adrenaline and rage. With a determined pivot, Jeremy lunged away, giving the Turismo's death path a wide berth.

His heart pounded, and his eyes filled with fury as he turned to watch the car roll to behind the school. He was neither a victim nor a passive observer; he was a raging storm, ready to unleash. But before he could get to his feet and storm after his vehicular assailant, Jeremy heard a chuckle from above him, "Fucking Dutchie. Man, that dude's bad for your health."

Jeremy immediately recognized the voice, setting him at ease. Looking up, he saw Del, his best friend since the 7th grade, smiling down at him with his hand extended. "You good, dude?" Del inquired with a half-smirk and half-genuinely concerned look. Yeah, I'm cool," Jeremy responded as he popped up to his feet.

"Good, it's game day tomorrow, Friday night lights; we need you strong." he said, flexing his arms and puffing out his chest, "Finally gonna get that first win," Del boasted confidently, relaxing his form.

Jeremy dusted himself off and nodded. "Yeah, big game, for sure," he muttered, grabbing his book bag from the back of his jeep before heading toward the school entrance with his best friend by his side.

In the chaos of high school in the late 90s, Antoine Del Coronado emerged like an unblemished diamond in a pile of half-hearted rhinestones. He wasn't your average teen cliché; he was an anthology of all things aspirational, a blend of the archetypes you'd find flipping through an old-school teen magazine, only far more captivating.

For starters, there was his style. Del didn't just wear clothes; he wore statements. Imagine a kaleidoscope of vivid colors flirting with subdued khakis, and vintage band tees paired with designer jeans. And shoes? Oh, man—he had more kicks than The Foot Locker at The Ingleside Mall.

When he stepped into a room, his fashion sense screamed, "Here's someone who knows his shit," and you couldn't help but agree. Even his school bag was a carefully curated item. It wasn't a bland sack of canvas like Jeremy's. It was a sleek leather messenger bag that didn't look worn-out and chaotic but mysterious and organized, like the inside of his brain.

Then there was his athletic prowess. Del wasn't just physically gifted; he was the epitome of athleticism. Basketball, football, track—you name it, he'd not only participated, he dominated. He had Division-1 schools coming out to see him play football as a freshman— in Western Massachusetts— on a winless team. Now a senior, he had his pick of scholarships. His future was bright.

His movements on the court or field were like poetry in motion: swift, calculated, elegant. He dribbled the basketball as if it were an extension of his body, evading his opponents with a charisma that left the crowd in awe. And when he sprinted, it wasn't just a mad dash towards the finish line; it was an art form, a spectacle, like watching a jaguar chasing the wind.

You'd think someone like Del would be a cocky asshole, but that's where you'd be dead wrong. The guy had the humility of a monk and the charm of a lead in a blockbuster Rom-Com combined. His laughter was infectious, a wholesome melody that made even the most cynical folks believe in the inherent goodness of the world. His eyes, hazel with flecks of gold, didn't just look at you; they looked into you, making you feel seen, heard, and undeniably important.

The guy had it all. It's as if the Universe had looked down one day and said, "You, Sir Antoine, are my golden boy, my embodiment of absolute fucking awesomeness, and you shall remain untouched."

Grades? A breeze. He nailed every paper and aced every exam as if he had some psychic hotline to the academic gods.

Love life? Steady and passionate, as though Cupid had aimed his bow with extra precision.

Antoine Del Coronado was a walking, talking charm offensive without the superficial pretenses that plagued many of his peers. Life didn't just happen to him; he happened to life, leaving an indelible mark wherever he went. You couldn't hate him because to do so would be to hate the very concept of hope and potential. Del was a reminder that sometimes, just sometimes, the universe gets it right.

As the two friends made their way up the path through the school's courtyard, Del's words were a stream of consciousness that flowed over the gravelly crunch of footsteps on the pavement, their strides perfectly synced, like they'd been walking this route together for years. Because, well, they had.

"Man, you don't even get it, Jer. 'Just a Girl'? That shit is an anthem!" Del said full of enthusiasm, his arms waving wildly, barely missing Jeremy's nose. "Gwen Stefani is so cool. I do love those alternative babes."

Jeremy chuckled. "I bet you've got your feminist mixtape all sorted, too, huh?"

Del shot him a look that was equal parts resentment and pride. "Hell yeah! You know I do. Alanis, Fiona, Cranberries, Garbage—they're all on there. All good shit, dude."

His musical preferences were an extreme departure from what one would think he'd have in his CD player.

"I mean, sure, I love Hip-Hop and all, but nothing gets me more fired up than hearing some hottie laying it down." I just love chicks, man,"

It was almost comical how these contrasting musical worlds coexisted in Del—a six foot two black jock who was as passionate about women's empowerment anthems as he was about scoring touchdowns. But that's what made Del, well, Del.

He'd always been a beautiful paradox, the kind of guy who'd paint his nails black but wouldn't hesitate to throw a punch if you disrespected his friends—or his musical queens.

Just last week, or more appropriately, the last week of Jeremy's 25th life, the two were having a conversation about Taylor Swift. Del was out of his mind with the recent news of her upcoming tour to support her latest release, her 22nd Album "Neon."

During one of their regular video chats, Del went on and on about her. "She is amazing, man. I met her at this swanky party back in 25'. I nearly passed out. She smelled like cinnamon and dreams."

When he said this, Jeremy nearly died from laughter. Del could always kill him with these hilarious little bits that almost made perfect sense as if they were true. He couldn't help but laugh at Del's theatrical description. "Cinnamon and dreams, huh? Sounds like a new Yankee Candle scent."

It was strange for Jeremy to think of a conversation that, for him, happened in the past but never happened for Del. In fact, in this current time, Taylor Swift is only six years old.

As the two walked in lockstep towards the school, Del droned on with excitement about The Spice Girls' upcoming US release of their first single. Just after the school year started, Del bought an imported CD of "Wannabe." It immediately became a cornerstone of his musical rotation. He often credited himself with introducing The Spice Girls to Western Massachusetts.

Jeremy got caught in the flow and almost mentioned their recent chat about Taylor Swift, but he stopped himself and went deep into his head, reminding himself of his one concrete rule.

THE CONCRETE RULE:
NO ONE CAN EVER KNOW

Jeremy had a secret he couldn't share even if he wanted to. Sure, you could say that everyone had their own cross to bear, their own closet of skeletons. But Jeremy's secret was a doozy—it defied the very fabric of time and reality. He was living his life for the 26th time, not like a metaphorical do-over after a bad breakup or a failed college course. No, this is the real deal, Groundhog Day-type shit, only without Bill Murray and the comedic relief.

By now, he had lived enough lifetimes to know the crucial laws that governed his existence, and the most unbreakable one was Rule Number One, The Concrete Rule: Never, ever, under any circumstance, let anyone know he's reliving his life. It wasn't just a matter of preserving the mind-bending nature of his reality. It was a matter of survival. The stakes were sky-high.

In Life Number Three, Jeremy, overwhelmed by the isolation that came with his secret, had cracked. He had spilled the beans to Del, thinking a bond of a lifetime—or, rather, lifetimes—would be strong enough to handle it. Wrong move. It took less than a week for Del to let it out. Del had tried to be supportive; he really had, but the weight of Jeremy's revelation became too much for him. He'd had started to question his own reality, his own sanity, and finally, in an act of self-preservation, he had done the unimaginable—he turned Jeremy in.

Doctors, psychologists, therapists—the whole nine yards. They all thought Jeremy was insane, a danger to himself and others. Pills, therapy sessions, and eventually institutionalization followed. Jeremy found himself strapped to a bed, drugged until his thoughts became as murky as a swamp and monitored like a lab rat. Life Three ended in a premature, voluntary, and incredibly painful reset brought on by the acts of an over-medicated young man not working with a sound mind.

He had good reasons to keep his mouth shut tighter than a maximum-security prison.

The significance of The Concrete Rule wasn't just about avoiding the torture of life in a psych ward or the emotional agony of losing the trust of everyone he cared about. It was about the irrevocable ripple effects on the people he confided in. It was like a mental contagion, a virus that, once unleashed, couldn't be contained.

Knowing that Jeremy was living life on a perpetual rerun caused Del to question his own choices and free will until he was swallowed up by existential dread. It had a way of unhinging the doors to one's sanity until all that remained were shattered relationships and splintered minds.

And, God forbid, if the word spread wider—if more people began to find out—the ripple effects could turn into tidal waves. Social constructs would crumble. Religion, ethics, and the entire belief system of what's possible would be torn apart. The world would lose its shit, and anarchy wasn't as fun as it sounded in punk rock songs. Jeremy figured that there was no need to drag anyone else into his shitstorm.

So there he was, on day one of Life 26, already tiptoeing through existence, knowing full well the incendiary power of his secret. He had to wear his poker face well, making mundane choices while grappling with wisdom and weariness most teenagers couldn't even understand. It was like being a war veteran in the body of an 18-year-old, and every day was a high-stakes game of Russian roulette. One slip of the tongue, one moment of vulnerability, and everything could go to complete shit. Jeremy wasn't 100% sure if anyone else shared his experience, but that was one bit of information gathering that wasn't worth the risk.

The air crackled with teenage chatter as Jeremy and Del reached the gates of Huxley High. Conversations swirled around—Who broke up with who? Did you see what she wore? Can you believe he got a C on that paper?

Jeremy felt like he was drowning in a sea of teen angst. His eyes darted around as if scanning for a lifeboat or at least a tolerable floatation device in the hellhole of high school melodrama.

As Jeremy got swept up into the crowd, he watched as Del greeted his classmates. High-fives and hugs for everyone was Del's approach to every morning. Del's locker stood out amongst the chaos in the school's maze of hallways, Its exterior was boldly painted in Huxley High's blue and gold. Smack in the center; a giant Miami Dolphins sticker claimed its territory, a pop of color against the school spirit backdrop. The locker was an island of personality in a sea of uniformity; its inside was as meticulously organized, as its outside was proudly decorated. Inside, textbooks, mixtapes, and snacks were arranged carefully, a statement of identity hidden from the outside world.

As Del swung his locker door shut, a sudden brash voice cut through the bustling crowd, drawing the attention of everyone nearby. The voice oozed with a dramatic, theatrical tone that could only belong to one person.

"Well, well, well," the voice boomed, dripping with sarcasm and a hint of playful admiration, "if it isn't the two dreamiest boys in all of Huxley High." The words were laced with a charm that was as irresistible as it was sarcastic.

As she pushed her way through the crowd, Stacy McMillan, the whirlwind of their high school trio, approached them.

Del and Jeremy exchanged glances and braced themselves for whatever mischief Stacy had in store. Her wild hair framed her face like a rebellious halo, and her cropped top exuded just the right amount of confidence.

There she stood, in all her 90s alternative glory: black combat boots, a plaid flannel shirt tied around her waist, and a choker necklace that looked like it could double as a weapon. She was, in all terms, gorgeous. She had a petite frame and was in fantastic shape, although she'd never played a sport in her life.

Del and Jeremy both encouraged her to try out for something, anything. The three had gym together the previous year, and she consistently dominated every assignment. She even made Dennis Winston cry during a volleyball game once. It wasn't her fault. Dennis is a nice kid, but he's a total wimp.

"Stacy!" Jeremy gasped with excitement upon seeing his friend. He had known her for years, and once upon a time, in the 9th grade, they had even dated. She had been his world for a brief and intense month, a blazing comet shooting across his monochrome sky. But to be perfectly honest, she scared the ever-loving shit out of him.

Stacy was as passionate as she was aggressive, an emotional force of nature that Jeremy had no clue how to navigate. And so, their romantic relationship had crashed and burned, leaving them to emerge as platonic allies in the war against high school.

"Looking grim, boys; did someone die?" she asked, arching an eyebrow as she looked them over. Her gaze fell on Del, and then it lingered on Jeremy as if challenging him to say something interesting.

"Same old, same old," Jeremy managed to say, scratching his head, "You know, the impending doom of pop quizzes and lunchroom drama."

Stacy rolled her eyes. "God, I can't wait to get out of this shithole." She paused, looking deeply at Jeremy, "Seriously, you okay? You look sad or tired or some such shit," she hesitated, "I dunno, you just look— off."

He smiled sweetly back at her, "Yeah, Stace, I'm good."

As much as Jeremy feared Stacy at this stage in life, the two were to be lifelong friends. In life one, when Cassandra was ill, Stacy was there. So was Del, but Stacy made it her mission to check in on Jeremy.

While not all lifetimes ended with the three being tight until Jeremy's end, there was always a strong tie between them.

"Alright, men, let's saddle up and Carpe' the fuck outta this diem,"— she called out, her voice trailing back to the two boys as she walked ahead, the young men eagerly following her lead.

And with that, they pushed through the crowd of students, a trio bound by their own complicated, exhilarating, and sometimes terrifying friendship.

Jeremy felt a rare sense of relief wash over him. Sure, high school was still a swirling vortex of existential dread, but at least he had a few good friends to help him re-acclimate to life as a teenager.

With a determined look, he quickened his pace as he walked alongside Del and Stacy through the bustling crowd of students.

He leaned in toward them, his voice earnest but filled with urgency. "Hey, I need to shoot over to the library really quick," he explained. "I've got some books to return. I'll catch up with you at lunch, okay?"

Del nodded understandingly, his eyes filled with curiosity. "Sure thing, Jer— Don't take too long, though. We might stumble upon some juicy high school drama without you."

Stacy chimed in with a teasing grin. "Yeah, you don't want to miss out on my amazing storytelling skills."

Jeremy chuckled, appreciating their lighthearted banter. "I'll be there. See you guys later!"

The truth was, there was no errand to the library; he just needed a minute to breathe and collect himself before tackling the day. Thoughts needed collection; emotions needed inventory. He needed clarity.

7

DUTCH WYATT

As HE MADE his way through the arts and science wing, Jeremy kept his head down, peeking up occasionally to scan the halls for differences from previous lives. "Nope, all the same," he thought to himself.

The ghosts of forgotten locker combinations and teenage drama haunted every inch of these walls. His eyes narrowed as he surveyed the scenery, taking a mental inventory of the passing notes, gossip-fueled conversations, and glances that were either lust-filled or dripping with contempt. It was as if the whole building were a stage, and the students were actors playing their parts to an almost comical degree.

Jeremy's eyes landed on Dennis Winston. The kid was a portrait of insecurity – pale skin almost translucent under the harsh fluorescent lights. His eyes were perpetually wide with a mix of caution and alarm. Dennis's build was slim but not exactly weak. He was still waiting to hit the growth spurt that would eventually redefine his physique. To anyone who noticed him, Dennis seemed like the tallest short guy they'd ever seen, an oxymoron in human form. He moved with a careful, measured gait, as though each step was a calculated move to avoid drawing attention.

There he was, clutching his Trapper Keeper like a shield, a barrier between him and the unpredictable tides of high school life.

Jeremy held in a laugh. "A fucking Trapper Keeper," he mused darkly. The sight of it was almost absurd to him.

Dennis, with his dated school accessory, looked like he had stepped out of a time capsule from the '90s. Yet, there was an innocence and simplicity about him that made Jeremy nostalgic.

Jeremy was about to make another mental joke when the atmosphere shifted, heavier than a thousand-pound anvil plummeting from the sky.

Enter Dutch Wyatt, cruising onto the scene like a human wrecking ball.

"Fucking Dutchie," Jeremy thought to himself. The name brought back memories of a soul torn and tattered by life's cruel sense of humor.

Once upon a time, they'd been friends. They would hang out every day after middle school, often riding their bikes to the abandoned former home of The Labrador. They'd explore the ruins and claim the old maintenance cottage as their own. They'd stay there long past when the streetlights came on, regularly camping out there on the weekends.

Before everything went to shit, Dutch had been something to behold—his potential was blinding. Strong as an ox and smart as a whip. His mind gravitated toward all things technical. He was the first kid Jeremy had ever seen solve a Rubik's cube after he got one for Christmas in the fifth grade. After failing to solve it over the holiday break, Jeremy got frustrated and abandoned the puzzle. Dutch took one look at it, spun it around a few times, and, poof, solved.

In middle school, Dutch and Jeremy, along with Del, played pop-warner football together. Dutch was a behemoth of a kid, even back then, standing taller than the other boys in his class. They used to say he was born with a football in one hand and a ten-pound weight in the other. With every carry, he would bulldoze his way through the defensive line, his legs churning like two cylinders of a supercharged engine. And he could throw too; every pass he threw was delivered with the precision of a surgeon.

When Del moved to town in the 7th grade, the trio made for an unstoppable force. It was magic. That year, the three boys brought their team to the championship and won. They often talked about how High School would be theirs to run—kings of the school.

In the spring semester of 8th grade, life came crashing down on Dutch like a tsunami of raw sewage. The world had taken his mom, his last anchor, as suddenly as a candle blown out in the wind. Hopelessness settled on Dutch like a heavy fog, and he descended, spiraling into a pit of brooding, and assholery. The tragedy had cooked him into a different person—a dirtbag meathead stew.

Dutch did not become a king; he became a tyrant.

And now, here he was, swooping in on Dennis like a hawk on a helpless field mouse, all for the cheap thrills of petty high school bullying.

"Dennis, you're still carrying that bullshit around?" Dutch sneered, knocking the Trapper Keeper to the floor. "You're such a fucking dork."

Dennis's face flushed a deep red, a mixture of embarrassment and quiet defiance flickering in his eyes. He looked like he wanted to disappear into the ground, yet there was a trace of something new in his stance, perhaps a sense of self that wasn't there before.

Feeling a surge of protectiveness, Jeremy stepped in, positioning himself between Dennis and Dutch. "Hey Dennis, class is about to start; you should head out," he said, his tone calm but firm.

Grateful for an opportunity to escape, Dennis gave a relieved nod before hurrying away, casting a quick, thankful glance in Jeremy's direction.

Jeremy met Dutch's gaze squarely, his voice steady. "Take it easy, Dutchie. No need for drama today, alright?"

"What's your deal, Anderson?" Dutch said, peering back at Jeremy, "You want some?" He continued.

Jeremy locked eyes with Dutch, like a wolf sizing up its next meal. The tension between them was electric. It was the kind of showdown you'd expect to see in a gritty Western film, except this was high school, and the stakes were much higher.

Dutch, unsettled by Jeremy's attitude leaned in, his eyes narrowing, his voice a low, menacing growl. "What's your fucking problem, man? You know I've got zero beef with you."

A smirk toyed at the corner of Jeremy's mouth.

"See you around, Dutchie," Jeremy said after holding for a beat, his voice perfectly mimicking Dutch's aggressive tone. Without waiting for a response, he pivoted, his Chuck Taylors making a soft squeak on the linoleum floor as he walked away, leaving a river of students to flow around him.

"Fuck you, Anderson! you're not as cool as you think you are!" Dutch's voice ricocheted through the air, an arrow missing its mark.

Jeremy's grin widened. "Great burn, Dutchie," he thought, not even needing to look back to know that Dutch was left standing there, clenched fists and boiling ego, a spectator to his humiliation.

8

THE ESCAPE

Mrs. Pritchett taught first-period English. Her voice sounded like gravel being dragged across more gravel when she spoke. Each syllable was an expression of her disdain for the youth sitting before her. If eyes could roll themselves, hers would have done double backflips every time she had to explain the significance of the green light in "The Great Gatsby" for the umpteenth time.

She had a perpetual expression that made you think she was simultaneously smelling a fart while sucking on a lemon. It was a look that could only be described as "sourpuss meets roadkill." That expression could silence a room.

She only wore long skirts that seemed to have been stitched together from the drab curtains of an abandoned theater, the kind where they used to play Shakespeare but now just hosted mice and old memories. On her upper half, she usually sported an oversized cardigan; its faded colors and worn textures did nothing to brighten her ensemble. Picture a color wheel comprised of the most vibrant hues of the rainbow, then imagine the exact opposite. That's what she wore. It was as if her clothes were trying to say, "Yeah, we've given up too."

Her classroom was another beast altogether. The air felt thick, as though it had been sitting there since the 1970s, absorbing every sigh and every dream that had ever died within those four walls. The walls were covered in off-white cracked paint that looked like the skin of an ancient mummy. Overhead fluorescent lights flickered intermittently, just enough to make you question your sanity but not enough to justify a complaint to the maintenance department. The room was adorned with old-school literary posters: Dickinson, Hemingway, Poe—faces that looked equally disenchanted to be there as Mrs. Pritchett herself.

Jeremy sat hunched over his desk, staring blankly at his teacher as she droned on about literary devices and the importance of metaphors in understanding the human condition. Her incredibly consistent monotone was the stuff of legends. The woman could hypnotize a rattlesnake.

He scanned the room for any differences from previous lifetimes. Donna Reynolds sat up front, gnashing her juicy fruit, as she furiously scribbled away in her yellow-lined notepad like a court reporter.

"Nope, all the same," he confirmed quietly.

As he turned his attention to the windows lining the classroom, a flicker of sunlight poured in through a cracked window, illuminating Tomoyuki Matsuo's spiky hair.

"Ah, Tomo," Jeremy smiled. Tomo was a gift from the cosmos in an otherwise monotonous world and there he was, with his head on his desk, snoring like a baby rhino with one arm dangling as if he'd given up on life in the middle of a sentence.

Mrs. Pritchett had grown tired of jabbing the sword of education into Tomo's impenetrable armor of sleepiness. But Jeremy knew a soul blazing with life lurked beneath Tomo's lazy exterior.

"Classic Tomo; I can't wait to give him shit for this later," he laughed to himself as the snoring got louder.

Even Donna, the quintessential grade grubber, shot an annoyed glance over her shoulder. He could almost see her thoughts like subtitles in a foreign film: "Unbelievable. How does he get away with it?"

Without the energy to wake the sleeping giant, Mrs. Pritchett continued her lecture, her voice piercing through the classroom.

"The tragedy of Macbeth lies in the character's own hubris," Mrs. Pritchett droned. "In Shakespeare's world, arrogance and ambition always lead to a catastrophic end."

Jeremy could practically recite it backward at this point. Once upon a time, he thought that the rise and fall of the Scottish king was a badass tale. But that was lifetimes ago. Now, each word felt like a strike against his soul. Lady Macbeth's cries of "Out, damned spot!" might as well have been him yelling, "Out, damned class!"

He'd read them all. All the classics, all the bestsellers, and all the hidden indie gems. Life one's library was a graveyard now, filled with the decaying skeletons of tales that had once sparked his imagination.

Now, all that remained was an endless loop of recycled thoughts, a literary echo chamber where he was the lone survivor, desperately trying to claw his way out.

If only he could write his own ending. If only he could pen a tale so captivating, so totally original, that it'd break the monotony of his never-ending series of lives. But that was the crux of it, wasn't it? The true torture of immortality wasn't just the repetition; it was the stifling of creation. He was a captive audience in a theater that never changed its program, forever stuck in the nosebleed seats while his soul screamed for something—anything—new.

As Mrs. Pritchett waxed poetic about the nuances of iambic pentameter and his classmates scribbled down notes as if they were gospel, he stared blankly at the worn-out pages before him. Shakespeare once wrote, "All the world's a stage, and all the men and women merely players." Well, Jeremy thought, if that's the case, then where the hell is my goddamn exit?

Just as the thought of forcing a premature reset entered his mind, he felt something, eyes, on him, from across the room.

As he looked, she was there just as he'd remembered, Missy Winston, Dennis' older sister. He could have sworn she was burning a hole in the back of his head with her gaze, but she wasn't. She was staring out at the grassy fields surrounding the school, lost in some of the deepest thoughts one could ever imagine. The early morning sun pouring in through the tattered blinds washed across her, casting an angelic glow on her lightly freckled face and adding an extra sparkle to her pale blue eyes.

As she looked up from her daydream, her eyes locked onto his, and for a second—just a tiny, inconsequential fragment of time—it was as if she recognized him, as if she knew him, knew what his curse was.

The thing was, in Jeremy's first life, his original life—before resets and ripples became a part of his vocabulary—she was just Dennis' older sister. Nothing more, nothing less. To Jeremy, looking at Missy was like looking at a vintage photograph that never aged. To him, she was forever young. He often had opportunities to see what happened to his classmates in multiple versions of life, but not Missy. Never Missy.

Her eyes unfocused, and she returned to her contemplative state, her gaze shifting back to the endless fields that stretched beyond the window. A scenery she'd never grow old enough to tire of. His gut twisted with a grief that was etched in the pathways of her destiny. She was a character in his life's story that would be tragically short-lived.

Even after she turned away, he couldn't help but keep his eyes on her. She was an unchangeable constant. While others painted themselves in vivid colors and screamed their identities from the mountaintops, Missy was content to exist in softer hues, melting into the scenery, a whisper lost in a crowded room.

She was the kind of girl whose name teachers always remembered but never had to call on because she was always there, quietly jotting down notes with her meticulously kept gel pens. Unlike the others, her backpack was a practical, no-nonsense companion containing only what she needed —no flair, no distractions, maybe a novel hidden away, dog-eared at a chapter that would forever remain unfinished.

He wondered what kind of world was hidden behind those calm, wise eyes. What passions did she hide? What dreams did she tuck away in her closet along with her uniformly casual outfits?

And the question that nagged him the most was: Could one decision, one moment of breaking character and becoming someone noticeable, change her path? After all, sometimes, even a whisper can change the course of a hurricane. But much like Dutch, Missy's essence seemed to defy alteration.

She was a constant in a sea of variables, a fixed point in his lives. Seeing her again, just as she'd always been, felt like a haunting. She was a ghost from a life he once knew, symbolizing the puzzling rules that controlled his cyclical existence.

The bell, that god-awful electronic tone over the PA system that somehow managed to be both shrill and lifeless, blared through the classroom.

Like a cluster of Pavlov's dogs trained to salivate at the sound, the room erupted into a sudden frenzy of slamming notebooks and shuffling feet. High schoolers, each encased in their cocoon of teenage stress, spilled into the hallway, funneling towards their next battleground of academia.

For Jeremy, that meant a double math period. Trigonometry. Not just any day of trig, but an exam day.

A sharp exhale escaped his lips, a reluctant release of the tension he'd been holding. For a moment, the universe seemed to mock him: "Here you are, big guy, gifted with the ability to relive your life in infinite loops and still bound by the dread of a fucking math test."

"You ready for the exam?" said a voice behind him. Gary Reynolds, the de facto 'mathlete' and wunderkind, treated trigonometry like his personal playground. In another life, Jeremy had envied him; in yet another, they'd been rivals; and in one particularly bizarre life, they were friends. Now, Gary was just another variable in his complex equation of life.

"Ready as I'll ever be," he responded, his voice carrying a subtle undertone of resignation that only he could understand. The word 'ready' was a term whose definition had been obliterated by years of resets and cosmic do-overs.

As he settled into his seat, Jeremy felt the familiar surroundings close in on him—a blackboard scribbled with equations, the sterile scent of disinfectant, and the apprehensive murmur of his classmates.

The teacher, Mr. Stevens, who was as enthusiastic about math as a drill sergeant was about discipline, walked in carrying a stack of papers. "Take one and pass it down," he commanded, his voice devoid of emotion as if he were automating a task he'd performed in countless semesters past.

The room grew quiet, punctuated only by the sound of papers shuffling and pencils scratching. Jeremy stared down at the test in front of him. Sine, cosine, tangent—they all danced on the paper like a secret language, a language he'd learned and relearned across lifetimes.

As he worked through the problems, his mind couldn't help but wander back to Missy. Solving trigonometric equations felt almost like mocking his inability to solve the more profound equations of human life and fate. Each number he scribbled down, each solution he found, underscored the cruel reality that some problems had no solution, some stories no alternative endings.

With a sigh, he finished the exam in record time and put down his pencil, letting a sense of emptiness overtake him. He had completed the test in less than twenty minutes but couldn't turn it in yet. If he did, Mr. Steven would question him and the validity of his efforts. The last thing he needed was to be caught up in some disciplinary drama for suspected cheating on a test. This was a valuable lesson he learned in life five. He would have to sit quietly with his head down and pretend that he was working hard to solve the mathematical dilemmas in the exam.

As he sat there, he thought about Cassandra. He needed to get back on track. He'd only been in this lifetime for a few hours and already felt like he was losing his grasp. He reached down into his backpack and pulled out his journal, the leather cover was cold against his fingers, an untouched canvas that beckoned him to spill ink and thoughts across its barren landscape. It was an early birthday gift from Stacy—her generosity, another constant in the fluctuating rhythm of his lives.

He lifted the journal to his face, inhaling deeply. The fresh leather scent mingled with the memories it triggered, a bittersweet aroma laced with nostalgia. As his exhale broke the silence, he felt a sense of grounding.

For a moment, the classroom, the exam, and even Missy's tragic fate faded into the background, allowing him to focus on the task at hand. Cassandra.

His heart stirred at the mere thought of her name, a kaleidoscope of emotions flashing before his eyes: love, regret, yearning, hope. The paths that led to her and away from her in each of his lifetimes had been full of pitfalls and detours, a cosmic game of chess that required moves planned years before they would happen. But he had a plan, and this journal would be his strategy book.

With a resolve that sent a shiver down his spine, he uncapped his pen. It hovered above the page as if waiting for the universe's permission. With the first stroke of ink, he felt he was making a contract, not just with himself but with the laws that governed his reality—written in a code of words and choices that could free him or chain him in perpetual misery.

And so, he began to build an inventory of his actions.

He contemplated the effects of the careless deviation from his plan by getting into an argument with his father and leaving home earlier that morning. He accepted the outcome, as the risk far exceeded the reward.

In Life One, during his junior year of college, he and Gregg had gone to blows over Thanksgiving dinner. This event severed ties between them for years. They wouldn't reconnect until just after Jeremy and Cassandra were engaged. Jeremy mapped this out in his journal.

He recounted the relationship with his father for each of his previous 25 lifetimes and scribbled notes furiously, taking care to cover his writings from any nosey classmates.

In no timeline were they close or accepting of one another. In all events, Gregg's behavior remained consistent. So did Jeremy's. They'd eventually fall out in every case, and Gregg wouldn't survive his 60s. His end was always a result of hard living. There were lives where Jeremy tried to get his father clean. Sometimes, he did, but it always ended the same way. Gregg was never destined to see an AARP card.

After recounting all significant possibilities, Jeremy felt at ease. Nothing between him and his father mattered; it didn't shape any future. This, however, gave him cause to shift his thoughts to what other events he knew to be fixed in existence. Under the last line in his journal about Gregg, he wrote the word "Clear" and put a checkmark next to it.

He then turned to a fresh page and wrote the word: CEMENTED.

Under the word, he made bullet points.

The first simply read Del.

Jeremy sat hunched over his journal, staring at the name, almost daring it to challenge his preconceptions.

Del was flawless, for lack of a better term—the perfect example of all the achievements a young adult could wish for.

"Could someone like that even be derailed?" he asked himself.

In life 8, Del had become an Olympic gold medalist, breaking records in the 1000-meter sprint like it was a morning jog. Jeremy remembered sitting in the stands, gripping the edges of his seat as Del's muscles coiled like springs and then exploded, carrying him across the finish line in a blur of human potential.

Life 17 had cast Del as a humanitarian, and Jeremy had stood beside him in war-torn countries and disaster-stricken areas. Whether it was airlifting supplies, negotiating peace between warring factions, or spear-heading public health initiatives, Del had a knack for being in the thick of it. But what made it jaw-dropping was how he navigated the complex socio-political landscapes with an ease that opposed his age. The man had been nominated for a Nobel Peace Prize—twice!

Then, during Life 22, Del was an activist, a voice that refused to be silenced. He fought against injustice, inspiring movements, and provoking change. And God, his speeches—each word felt like a bullet, each sentence a war cry.

But here's the kicker: no matter the lifetime, no matter the achievement, Del remained Del. Humble as ever, he'd take his accolades with a pinch of salt, his focus was always on the next big challenge. And he was always, without fail, there to lend a helping hand or offer a shoulder to lean on. His generosity knew no bounds, often establishing charitable organiza-tions or funding scholarships with the millions he'd earned, making heroes out of ordinary people.

"How many lives have I lived where Del's not just excellent but tran-scendent?" Jeremy wondered, scribbling furiously.

In each of these lives, despite his different paths, Del remained that same incredible person: kind-hearted, humble, and brimming with a sincerity that made you want to be better. It wasn't just what he achieved that left Jeremy in awe; it was how he wore these achievements. Never a crown to lord over others, he was more like a torch, lighting the path for those around him.

Jeremy stopped writing as he reached the end of the page. He felt like he'd been trying to capture a galaxy on a postage stamp, each star of accomplishment merely a pixel in the vast constellation of Del's existence.

"Fucking untouchable," he finally whispered, placing a decisive check-mark next to Del's name. It was like trying to imagine a crack in a diamond. Some beings were just meant to be unbreakable, resilient, and unwavering in their path.

Jeremy sighed, letting a mixture of relief and envy wash over him.

"Alright, Del, you magnificent bastard, you're safe," he thought, picking up the pen again, ready to delve into the maze of other lives he had yet to examine.

With each name that followed, Jeremy hoped he'd find another unbreakable thread, another constant in a chaotic universe.

Jeremy glanced up at the clock on the classroom wall. Its second hand was ticking away, counting down to the inevitable interruption of the bell. But there was still time to dive into other characters in the epic narrative of his multiple lifetimes.

He blew out a deep breath, his lips fluttering as if he were blowing out invisible candles. His pen hovered over the paper, hesitating for a heart-beat before diving in. Under the long ode to Del, Jeremy scribbled two new names: Missy and Dutch.

When the bell sounded, releasing them from the mathematical purgatory, Jeremy felt neither relief nor dread, only a profound sense of calm. He was bound by rules he never understood, haunted by constants he was trying to manipulate. Exiting the classroom with the trig exam completed, he felt relieved that his potential timeline remained unchanged.

The world seemed bound by equations he never got the hang of. Pythagoras and his damn triangles. Imaginary numbers—what even was the point of numbers that didn't exist? They taunted him, a "middle finger" from the universe that told him he was never going to crack the code.

He grabbed his backpack, slinging it over one shoulder as if it were filled with bricks—which, metaphorically speaking, it was. Bricks that were made up of unfulfilled expectations, questions he didn't have the answers to, and uncertainty about his place in an increasingly complex universe. The pack hung low, dragging his posture like the weight of his thoughts dragged his spirit.

Before leaving the classroom, Jeremy's eyes lingered on the chalkboard at the front, taking in Mr. Stevens' chaotic mix of symbols and numbers. He hoped to find some hidden message, a cosmic clue that would break the spell of his endlessly repeating life. Maybe, just maybe, those scribbles held the key to freeing him from this cycle that felt more like a curse than a life.

But as he scanned the board, no revelations came, all those numbers and symbols just hammered home the truth: he was stuck. He was like the reluctant star of some B-movie playing on repeat, the kind that played on Cinemax late at night. Only, in his case, he never signed up for the role.

The hallway was a chaos of hormones and high school hysteria, a combination of locker slams and laughter. But Jeremy waded through it, oblivious to the manic energy around him, unresponsive to the occasional slap on the back or half-hearted greeting from classmates who knew him but didn't really know him.

Deep down inside, buried under layers of self-doubt and lifetimes of angst, there existed a glimmer of hope. He had emerged from the trig exam with a lingering calm. He hadn't catastrophically screwed up; he hadn't set his potential future with Cassandra aflame with a deviation from the status quo by standing up to his father this early in the game. And for a second, he allowed himself to entertain the thought that maybe, he could learn to manipulate those haunting constants and master the rules that bound him.

His attention was drawn to a locker, its surface a canvas of graffiti—names, sketches, and teenage declarations. Among them, a line from Rage Against the Machine's "Killing in the Name" stood out, echoing in his mind: "Fuck you, I won't do what you tell me." The defiance in those words struck a chord with him, stirring thoughts of rebellion against the usual expectations. For a moment, he thought about letting go of his pursuit of Cassandra, questioning if it was just another setup for disappointment. But a resolve hardened within his heart.

"No," he assured himself, "I got this. Game on." Taking a moment to regroup, he shifted his backpack, its weight somehow feeling lighter. With a renewed sense of determination, he made a pivotal decision. He might not understand all the mysteries of the universe, but he was determined to master the complexities of his own being.

Gym was next on the agenda, a class taught by Coach McHale, the eternally optimistic football coach who had been with the school since Jeremy's freshman year. If optimism could win games, McHale would have been Vince Lombardi. Unfortunately, his record was more of a laundry list of creative ways to snatch defeat from the jaws of victory. The Wildcats hadn't won a game in years, but nobody dared fire the coach. It was as if the school had collectively embraced its role as the perennial loser.

Gym would be a breeze to skip. McHale operated on the honor system, a policy as flawed as his defensive strategies. All Jeremy had to do was say something about needing to rest before practice or an existential crisis and McHale would wave him off with a thumbs-up and a clichéd motivational quote like, "Go get 'em, tiger!" as if Jeremy were about to run off and conquer the world instead of dodge a senseless high school experience.

After gym would come study hall—a holding pen for future under-achievers—after that, lunch, the social minefield of the day. Now was the perfect time to ditch school and figure out the next play.

As he entered the gym, his eyes narrowed as he watched Coach McHale stride out of the locker room, biceps flexing under the strained fabric of his Huxley Wildcats polo. Once upon a time, McHale's gym-teacher-by-day, inspirational-coach-by-afternoon persona might have stirred some grudging respect in Jeremy's teen heart. But today, it ignited a wildfire of disgust.

McHale lifted his whistle to his lips and blew, piercing the air like a vulture's screech. Jeremy cringed as memories flooded back—memories of the pathetic pep talks that once echoed through this very gym. Each word from McHale had felt like an insult, a thinly veiled implication that they, the players, were the sole reason for the Wildcats' unbroken losing streak rather than his poor coaching decisions.

"What an absolute loser," Jeremy muttered, the words slipping out through a nasty exhale.

In the storybook of life, some characters are heroes, others are villains, and then there are those who are neither. To Jeremy, McHale had long since cemented his place in that last category. He was a legend in his own mind, a walking contradiction in the world of high school football.

Sure, he had the physique of a man who'd easily be mistaken for an NFL veteran instead of a gym teacher. Broad-shouldered, square-jawed, with just the right amount of gray peppering his hair to make him look distinguished rather than washed-up.

His past was like an epic Greek tragedy staged in locker rooms and football fields across America, as if Achilles had donned pads and cleats. McHale was no slouch in his heyday. He had graced Arizona State with his God-given talent as an All-American wide receiver. Then, he'd hustled his way into the NFL, playing for the San Francisco 49ers. During the first preseason game, he caught passes like a hawk snatching fish out of water —five catches, sixty-eight yards, and a touchdown. People had started to talk. "This McHale guy—he's one to watch."

But Fate is a wicked bitch with a dark sense of humor.

During his next game, with his eyes on the prize, McHale sprinted off the line for a 15-yard slant route when bam! A safety crossing over the middle absolutely destroyed him with a collision you could hear from the nosebleeds. That play ended it all. His ACL and MCL were both obliterated, and his career was over. Just like that, he went from being a rising star to a tale that would never be told.

Then came a coaching gig at The University of Massachusetts, a "favor" job as an assistant coach shrouded in mystery and punctuated with rumors. No one talked about what went down there, but whatever it was had gotten him fired. Everybody chose to believe the worst rumors rather than seek the truth, as McHale was no one's favorite teacher.

So, there stood McHale, a complex combination of triumph and failure, coaching The Wildcats like a man who'd once touched the sky. Given the circumstances, his optimism was impressive. It was like watching a rock 'n' roll star do covers at a rundown bar; everyone knew he was out of place, but no one could deny the energy he brought into the room.

***

Jeremy approached McHale, and while he was still 20 yards away, their eyes met, and when they did, the coach made a B-line to one of his Senior Captains.

"Jeremy, my man! Are you ready to unleash the sweat-drenched beast that's howling inside you, itching to be an MVP?"

McHale's voice detonated like a firework in a tin can, bouncing off the sterile linoleum floors and high-school stink of hormones and disinfectant. Jeremy rolled his eyes so hard he thought they'd get stuck staring at his brain.

"Coach, I'm not feeling it today. I might have pulled a muscle at practice yesterday."

"Are you hurt or injured?" McHale aggressively interrupted.

Jeremy didn't answer immediately; instead, he looked away, trying to contain his ability to verbally shred the man in front of him.

The coach squared his jaw, eyebrows crashing down like two hairy anvils. "Hurt or injured, Anderson. Choose your words like you'd choose your last meal."

Jeremy, letting out a reluctant sigh, his voice barely graduating from a mumble, responded. "Neither Coach. I'm just not jonesing for the great sport of kickball today. I'm saving my chi or whatever for tomorrow night's game."

McHale's eyes narrowed, laser-focused. "Don't fuck around, son. We can't afford to go into battle missing one of our generals—Copy?" Jeremy gulped, keeping his eyes on the championship banners from the 80s that hung from the rafters, representing a more prestigious time for the school's athletics program.

Trying to avoid eye contact, he responded, "Got it, Coach. I'll show up at practice. I'll unleash my inner beast or whatever."

McHale sniffed the air as if he could smell the bullshit Jeremy was trying to feed him. "Are you on something, Anderson? 'Cause you look like you've seen a ghost, and if you've been ripping doobies, I swear to all the gridiron gods, I'll boot your ass off this team so fast you'll enter another dimension."

Both knew that McHale's threat was emptier than a politician's promise. The man struggled to field enough players to avoid forfeiting the season.

Jeremy's patience snapped. "Coach, I'm not stoned. I've just got some personal shit to sort out, okay? Life's not all orange slices and halftime pep talks."

"Fine." McHale huffed, "But I want you at a hundred and ten percent at practice this afternoon. Otherwise, prepare to have my foot up your ass. Am I clear?"

"Crystal," Jeremy sighed, finally making eye contact as if sealing a demonic pact. "You will have your gladiator."

"Good, just haul your ass back here in time for practice, and we won't have a problem, understand?" McHale barked, though Jeremy had already started heading toward the school exit. The coach's voice, now in the distance, was just static fuzz in the airwaves of his mind.

9

NEAR MISS

Jeremy shoved open the door leading out of the building with his shoulder. The worn-out wildcat emblem was barely visible on the frosted glass. The sunlight pounding on the concrete made him squint against the blaze of early day's light; even his knockoff Ray-Bans couldn't fend off the glare.

"No time for reflection big guy," he said as he tossed his book bag onto the passenger seat, nearly knocking over a half-full Mountain Dew. He eyed the bottle of neon liquid. To him, it looked ancient, like a relic from a forgotten era, yet it had probably only been there for just a couple of days. Shrugging, he grabbed the soda and twisted off the cap before taking a swig. The flat, warm drink hit his lips with a disappointing lack of fizz. He winced slightly at the taste, more out of habit than anything. As it trickled down his throat, the sensation was oddly comforting—a reminder of his need for a caffeine kick in a life where days blended into centuries. Downing it, he felt the familiar jolt, a momentary buzz in his otherwise numbing routine.

Jamming the key into the ignition and giving it a turn, the Jeep's engine roared to life, filling him with a sense of raw vehicular power. He wrestled with the stick shift and grunted as he forced it in reverse.

"Gym, Study Hall, 45 min each, another 45 for lunch," he muttered, almost like a chant. His fingers drummed on the steering wheel as he calculated the time. "That gives me a little over two hours to get back in time for Mr. Deegan's snooze-fest of a history class." The clock on the dashboard read 11:17 AM. It felt like a dare.

Easing off the clutch, his eyes were locked onto the rearview mirror. His mind was a sea of problems—getting back to school before anyone missed him, avoiding ripples, getting through the next three years, getting back to Cassandra.

His thoughts were everywhere, on everything, everything except what was directly behind him.

"Hey, creep! Watch out!" A voice shouted from out of nowhere.

The scream tore through the air like lightning, shocking Jeremy's senses; it yanked him back to reality, pulling him out of his mental maze. He slammed on the brakes, jerking the Jeep to a halt, his seatbelt tightening like a noose around his chest. His heart pounded as if it wanted to escape his ribcage.

Missy stood just inches from the bumper, her face held a look of fear and fury. Her eyes were wide and glaring, her fists clenched like she was ready to go twelve rounds. Her fine blonde hair, usually cascading like a waterfall, was pulled back into a ponytail, and a few loose strands clung to her flushed cheeks. "Jesus Christ, Jeremy! She yelled.

Those words penetrated his soul. "It could never be my fault, never." He thought to himself.

Throwing the Jeep into park, he rolled down his window, leaning his arm casually against the door as if he hadn't just nearly backed into her. But his facade of indifference crumbled under the weight of her glare.

"What the hell! Are you trying to kill me before lunch?" She screamed.

"Shit, Missy. I didn't see you. I'm sorry, I swear." he stuttered, his eyes flicking back to his mental schedule—gym, study hall, lunch, back before history. Missing history would suck, but running someone over would be much worse.

"You didn't see me! She scolded, "You could have killed me!"

His heart sank.

Her arms flailed wildly as she screamed at him."You're so weird; you were staring right at me during first period. It was creepy as hell. What's your deal anyway?"

His eyes narrowed. He felt cornered, caught between his embarrassing near-accident and the unspoken tension between them in English class. Was he staring? Absolutely, but not for the reasons she thought.

"Look, I spaced out. It wasn't about you. But back to nearly turning you into roadkill—seriously, I'm sorry."

Her eyes softened slightly, but the storm of anger hadn't passed. He half-expected her to whip out a key and give his Jeep a lasting memory of their encounter. Rumors of Missy's wrath in the debate team circulated the halls like wildfire. He braced himself for a verbal slaughter.

"Fine, just watch where you're going, okay? And maybe pay attention in class; it wouldn't kill you," She reprimanded.

He nodded, the weight of the moment lifting off his shoulders.

As she walked away, he found himself watching her again. He thought about the narrow escape from the vehicular mishap and a complicated mess that could have caused irreparable ripples through this life.

His mind returned to the ticking clock, to the schedules and plans that framed his life like the borders of a jigsaw puzzle.

"Gym, study hall, lunch, and back before anyone notices." The list now seemed like a foolish attempt to control time. This life was already getting messy, and it had just reminded him who was in charge, and it wasn't him.

10

CHERRY BOMB

Mr. Donnelly was the gatekeeper of third-period study hall, a collection of hormone-ridden teenagers and the echoes of grunge music and teen angst.

Once upon a time, he'd been a passionate educator, a crusader with chalk and textbooks. He had seen himself as John Keating in "Dead Poets Society," inspiring young minds to seize the day. But now he counted the days, hours, and minutes until his pension kicked in and he could escape this dungeon of pre-adulthood.

He was the epitome of burnout. He once believed he could set the world on fire or at least spark a flame in the minds of his students. Now, all he wanted was to read his paper in peace.

In the third row, Kristen Ray found herself exiled to the kingdom of boredom, a barren landscape where the clock seemed to move at a snail's pace. Each tick was a drop of water, each tock an echo, reverberating in the cavern of her impatience.

Kristen was the sun around which Huxley High orbited. A blend of charisma, beauty, and unattainable perfection. She was the girl whose name you'd hear echoing through the hallways, ricocheting off lockers like a hit single everyone knew the lyrics to but never fully understood. Junior class president, varsity cheerleader, dance team captain; The titles cascaded down her résumé.

With a family rooted in affluence, she was bred to shine, programmed from childhood to be a combination of all things magnificent. Her parents, pillars of community and prosperity, had honed her into a Swiss Army knife of social brilliance: poised, graceful, smart, and above all—better.

The mission was clear: outshine, outclass, outperform.

She wielded her popularity like a scepter, ruling over the school with a firm and often bitchy fist, an act she had perfected over time, a necessity to maintain her place at the top of high school society.

This high school royalty status put Kristen on a pedestal, a lonely spot despite the constant buzz around her. Admirers and imitators surrounded her, yet she often felt isolated.

Her inner circle saw her as the invincible queen, yet she felt like she was playing a part. She appeared confident and in control to the outside world, but inside, she was a bundle of insecurities, constantly second-guessing her every move. Her so-called 'bitchy' attitude was a way to keep others at bay and maintain her spot in the teenage hierarchy without revealing her vulnerability.

She longed for deeper connections beyond the superficial bonds of high school cliques. She wanted to be seen for who she truly was, not just as the prom queen or the cheer captain, but as Kristen – complex, real, and craving authenticity.

Yet, in the tricky game of high school politics, revealing her true self was a risk too significant to take. So, she continued to wear her crown like a queen ruling a kingdom where she often felt like an outsider, playing a role scripted by expectations and guarded by her carefully constructed facade.

Then there were the boys, who looked at her like she was an item on a menu, ready to be ordered, consumed, and rated for taste. For the most part, she tolerated it. She played the game, flirting just enough to keep her popularity intact but never crossing lines she considered sacred. However, if anyone dared to look at her as nothing more than an object, that's when her quick wit and fierce words would spring into action, cutting down anyone who underestimated her.

For this reason, it was widely understood that you don't cross Kristen Ray.

Thankfully, this wasn't something that happened often, as she had someone to shield her from the advances of teenage hormones. Her boyfriend of over two years, Jeremy Anderson.

Kristen found her sanctuary in Jeremy. They'd been together since she was a freshman and he a sophomore. From the moment they first locked eyes, something clicked—like two puzzle pieces that didn't know how incomplete they were until they found each other.

Before Jeremy's life became a series of repeating cycles, Kristen colored his late teens with a love that left a lasting mark. In their early days at Huxley, she set her sights on him with her fiery spirit and undeniable beauty. She was the light in the darkness of his troubled home. She was not just his first love; she was the first person who made him feel like he mattered.

He took her "off the market." With Jeremy by her side, Kristen felt untouchable, bulletproof, wrapped in an emotional Kevlar that shielded her from the often unwanted attention of the male population of Huxley High. He didn't objectify her; he saw her complexities. He was the one person who made her feel comfortable enough to remove her porcelain mask without fearing it would crack. With him, she was more than just a string of titles or a set of expectations to live up to. She was simply Kristen.

The fact that Jeremy came from a lower-class background didn't matter to her. If anything, she found his humility and grit endearing. He wasn't born with a silver spoon like she was. He had to fight for every inch of respect and opportunity to come his way. She admired that about him. She always viewed his home as a patchwork of disappointment, where the shabby walls wore the scars of unfinished DIY projects—a living metaphor for his father's big ideas and failed plans. The house echoed the hollow promises of a better life that never came.

Kristen's feelings towards Jeremy's father were a delicate balance of empathy and disgust. She maintained her sweet demeanor around him, but deep down, she couldn't shake the creeping sense of discomfort he inspired. She pitied him for his struggles but harbored a deep-seated disgust for how he treated her boyfriend.

Her parents, on the other hand, were awesome. They'd let Jeremy crash on their couch whenever Gregg went off the rails, and there wasn't a meal where Jeremy wasn't invited to join them.

After a memorable summer together, at the beginning of the new school year, Kristen's heart was filled with worry about her future with Jeremy. His upcoming graduation hung over her like a shadow. It was a ticking time bomb, counting down to the moment he'd walk across the stage, diploma in hand, preparing to set off for college without her as she was still a year behind him. The thought of him moving away to college, even if it was only a few hours away, filled her with a sense of loss. They rarely fought, if ever, but when they did, it was about this.

In Kristen's perfect world, he would choose a school closer to home, UMass, or maybe Westfield State, closer to Amherst College, where she planned on applying and was more than confident she'd get accepted. She had the grades, and tuition wouldn't be a problem for her parents.

She thought they could continue to be each other's safe haven if they were both in the five-college system. She envisioned the two of them huddled in the campus library, textbooks and notes scattered across the table as they tackled their coursework. In this imagined world, late-night ice cream runs would be spontaneous escapes from academic life. Their laughter would echo through the empty streets as they savored their frozen treats.

Then there would be the quiet moments, nestled in Jeremy's dorm room when his roommate would conveniently be out for the night. They'd sit close, legs intertwined, on his worn-out couch that had seen better days. There would be a bulky TV set resting on a rickety wooden stand with a VCR perched on top, ready to play some movie they'd already watched a million times.

This was a future she dreamed of, a way to preserve the sanctuary they had built over the years. She couldn't imagine a life without him by her side. She was concerned about the potential temptations of college life and the new experiences that could pull him away from her.

In her most private moments, when the lights were off and the world outside her window was silent, Kristen allowed herself to hope. She would pray that Jeremy would choose a school close to home; maybe he could walk onto the football team and eventually be offered a scholarship. She could see herself in the stands, cheering him on like always. It was a future where they could navigate college life together, where she could be his anchor as he ventured into uncharted territory.

"Ugh. Twenty-five more minutes," she groaned as she chewed the remnants of the cherry-flavored gum she'd had since morning. Breakfast was an event Kristen usually skipped; her morning fuel was typically more carbonated and less nutritious—a Diet Coke, a stick of gum, maybe a Strawberry Pop-Tart—she never needed more. This particular morning's breakfast, Bubble-Yum, wasn't her favorite. The burst of artificial sweetness it once had now felt like a tasteless wad occupying her mouth.

"I gotta get rid of this gum," she resolved.

With that thought, Kristen pushed her chair back and stood up. As she did, she stretched her arms above her head, elongating her toned body like a cat waking from a luxurious nap. Her muscles were firm but fluid; each limb was a testament to years of disciplined cheer routines and dance competitions. She was a living, breathing work of art—a Venus sculpted not from marble but from sweat, grace, and the will to excel.

As she readied herself to make the trip to the trashcan near Mr. Donnelly's desk, her eyes instinctively flicked to the window, where a familiar figure caught her attention.

Jeremy, her gridiron hero boyfriend, was striding purposefully toward his bright orange Jeep. "Where's he going?" she wondered, her brows a combination of confusion and annoyance.

"That jerk is bailing out, and I am stuck in this prison?"

With her curiosity piqued but her mission clear, Kristen strolled toward the front of the classroom.

Dennis Winston had a perfect view from the back of the classroom, a spot that offered both seclusion to protect his safety and, more importantly to him, a clear view of Kristen. He had been watching her long before she got up from her seat, but when she did, it was as if someone had turned up the volume of his favorite movie.

He couldn't help but stare as she glided toward the front of the classroom; he watched how her red curls seemed to dance, each tight ringlet performing its private choreography. It was like watching the embers of a fire rise and fall, unpredictable and mesmerizing.

In Dennis' daydreams, Kristen was always cast in the lead role. He imagined moments of closeness with her, creating events that would bring them together.

He'd imagine them sharing an umbrella during a sudden rainstorm, their bodies close as they struggled to stay dry.

He fantasized about his hands accidentally brushing against hers as they both reached for the same book in the library. The thought would send a bolt of excitement coursing through him, lighting up his neurons like a string of holiday lights.

His imagination would picture their faces inches apart, close enough to share secrets, confiding youthful hopes and dreams.

The thought of experiencing her laughter up close, of being the one to make her smile, would fill him with a warmth that seemed to radiate from his core.

Yet, he always knew where to draw the line. His fantasies never strayed too far from reality, nor did they cross into territories that would compromise his respect for her.

He was always aware of this invisible boundary, a line in the sand that he was careful not to cross, even in his most vivid daydreams.

He locked his eyes on her as she reached the teacher's desk, where Mr. Donnelly was engrossed in his newspaper.

As she approached the front of the class, she delicately spat her now useless gum into a scrap of paper.

Dropping the wad into the trash, she felt the weightlessness of discarding something insignificant, a meaningless connection to the morning now left behind. It was a small action, yet it carried the gravity of a statement: Kristen Ray didn't hold onto things that had lost their flavor.

As Kristen looked back toward the window, she was lured by an image that punctured her well-curated tranquility like a graffiti tag on a freshly painted wall.

On the other side of the glass, Jeremy was sitting in the driver's side of his Jeep in what looked like an intense debate with Missy Winston—a girl so inconsequential that she might as well have been wallpaper.

Kristen's eyes locked onto the window like she was zeroing in on a target. For a second, the world around her—Third Period Study Hall, Mr. Donnelly's shuffling newspaper, the tick-tock of the classroom clock—all blurred into nothingness.

Just outside the glass, her boyfriend and Miss Goody-Two-Shoes Winston were engaged in a full-on, arm-waving confrontation.

"What in the actual fuck?" Kristen's mind screamed, her internal voice practically spitting the words like shards of hot glass. Her eyes narrowed to icy slits, each blink capturing snapshots of the scene as if her mind was cataloging evidence for a future trial.

Missy, ordinarily soft-spoken, was on the offensive, her arms flailing and slicing the air with forceful gestures as if she were in the middle of one of her debates and going for the throat. Jeremy, sunken in the front seat of his Jeep, looked mortified. His usually confident posture had melted into something far more vulnerable, far less composed. He was cornered, and by the look on his face, he knew it.

As Kristen watched the drama unfold, a storm of emotions swept over her. Was she being paranoid, or was there something going on between Jeremy and Missy?

Meanwhile, from the depths of the rows of desks and lifeless study mates doodling and passing notes, Dennis felt like he was peeking through a keyhole into Kristen's soul. When her eyes darted toward the window, her face momentarily darkened, he noticed. It was like watching a summer storm roll in, clouds casting a brief shadow over an otherwise sunlit day. He didn't know what was clouding her sky at that moment, but he felt an arresting break in the beat, a hiccup in her otherwise seamless façade.

Just as she was spiraling in her internal storm of thoughts, Kristen felt eyes on her, undressing her emotional armor. Her gaze shifted to the back of the classroom, catching him, his wire-framed glasses gleaming back at her. Her eyes constricted further. "What's your damage, nerd!" she spat out. "Why don't you take a picture? Frame it above your Star Wars sheets, God!" She roared, breaking the otherwise peaceful study hall.

As heads turned to see who the target of Kristen's offensive was, Dennis shrunk in his seat. It was as if he'd been slapped; his cheeks flushed a shade that almost matched the color of Kristen's vibrant curls. It was a hit below the belt, a reminder of the unspoken boundaries that separated them. His pen fell from his hand, landing with a soft thud on his notebook, marking the end of whatever fantasy he'd had in his head.

"The Winstons are double-teaming my sanity today," she thought. First, Missy and the drama in the parking lot with Jeremy, and now Dennis, her dorky younger brother was staring holes into her like she was a priceless piece of art he could never afford.

Mr. Donnelly, noticing Kristen lingering near his desk from the corner of his eye, was startled by her sudden outburst. He sighed inwardly, his patience wearing thin. Peering over his newspaper, he addressed her with a voice heavy with the weight of many disappointments. "Miss Ray," he said, his tone firm yet weary, "unless you're here to clean my desk, please return to your seat." The subtext was clear: 'Why can't you just stay in your damn place so I can stay in mine?'

"Sure thing, Mr. Donnelly," Kristen chirped as she snapped back into a polished form, more befitting a lady. Her words were laced with a sugary sweetness that could give you cavities.

She was good—a master at hiding her emotions behind a veil of politeness and cheer. Only someone paying close attention could spot the slight squint of her eyes or the tight press of her lips, hidden signs of the anger brewing under her cool facade. But Mr. Donnelly wasn't looking that hard.

As she returned to her desk, The moment of tension with Dennis hung in the air. Sitting down, her eyes darted back to where she last saw Jeremy and Missy, and her heart sank at the sight that greeted her.

Jeremy's Jeep was pulling out of the parking lot, his silhouette visible through the windshield. His grip on the steering wheel seemed intent, focused as if he were grappling with thoughts as knotty as the laces of a well-worn football. And then, just like that, he disappeared out of sight, leaving behind a cloud of unsettled dust and an even more unsettled girlfriend.

Kristen's eyes redirected to Missy, who was now walking up the hill toward the school. Missy was the prototype of softness; each step she took seemed as gentle as the fluttering of a butterfly's wing. She was the sort of girl who would apologize for stepping on a crack in the sidewalk; totally sweet and completely harmless.

Kristen's thoughts began to reel themselves back in, focusing on what she knew—or at least what she thought she knew—about Missy. "Come on, this is Missy Winston here," she reasoned internally, trying to soothe the emotions churning inside her. "She's not exactly the aggressive type; she's more like the human version of a lullaby. Jeremy wouldn't give her a second thought."

In Kristen's mind, Missy was, in every sense of the word, a sweetheart. Her goodness was as predictable as the sun rising each morning, a prime example of decency in a high school that was often anything but.

If life were simpler, if the rules of social hierarchy didn't exist, Kristen knew they would probably be friends. In fact, they had been once, best friends.

In Kristen and Missy's early years, elementary school was a blissful blur of childhood innocence. Their days were filled with sleepovers where the night air was thick with whispered secrets and giggles. They were inseparable, united against the struggles of adolescence, from harboring unrequited crushes on T.V. stars to the anxiety of math tests.

However, the transition to high school brought a significant change. Missy, academically gifted and ahead of her peers, was offered a rare opportunity: to skip the eighth grade and go directly to high school. She did not take the decision lightly, as it meant leaving behind friends and the comfort of her established social circle. As challenging as it was, the opportunity was too good to pass up.

When Missy left for high school a year early, Kristen felt a deep sense of loss. The sleepovers stopped, and their friendship fell apart as Missy immersed herself in her studies, trying to keep pace in an environment that pushed her academically.

As she prepared to enter eighth grade, Kristen's parents, sensing her loneliness, indulged her in an extravagant back-to-school shopping spree. She was given free rein to choose her wardrobe, selecting designer jeans and top brands that seemed to leap straight out of the glossy pages of Seventeen Magazine.

On the first day of school, her new wardrobe, combined with a summer growth spurt, caught the attention of the popular clique. She was quickly absorbed into their ranks, and the acceptance was intoxicating. Kristen had found a new world, one where popularity reigned supreme.

When the next year rolled around and both girls were enrolled at Huxley, their paths diverged further.

Missy remained committed to her studies, her world revolving around academics.

Kristen, on the other hand, continued her radical transformation. Popularity was her driving force, evolving into an all-consuming ambition. She joined the cheerleading squad, her demeanor shifting from playground innocence to a carefully crafted poise.

Missy, in contrast, became a living reminder of a simpler past, a remnant of an uncomplicated friendship that now seemed like a distant memory.

Kristen harbored a growing resentment towards Missy. When she'd arrived at Huxley, she hoped for a gesture from her former best friend, a sign that their past still had some meaning. But no such effort came from Missy, who seemed completely absorbed in her academic world. This perceived indifference only fueled Kristen's feelings of abandonment, intensifying her resentment.

Kristen soon realized friendships were tactical moves based on mutual benefits and survival rather than genuine connection. She knew that being friends with Missy did nothing to help her carefully crafted image. It was a harsh reality, but she accepted it as an unspoken rule of the high school hierarchy.

Kristen watched as Missy disappeared at the school's entrance. With her departure, the ghost of Kristen's past retreated into the shadows, awaiting the next moment of vulnerability to haunt her again.

She released a salty. "Whatever," under her breath, shaking her head as if she could physically dislodge the swirling thoughts from her mind. It was her go-to mantra when the world became too much, a single word to encapsulate surrender and dismissal.

As she settled back into her chair, she twisted her hips to crack her back. Rolling her shoulders, her eyes returned to Dennis. He was visibly straining to keep his eyes anchored to his notebook, but like a compass that couldn't help but find North, his eyes uncontrollably went back toward her.

With a malicious glint in her eye, she mouthed the word— "dork," before curling her mouth into a smirk that sent chills down his spine.

Dennis was busted—again. He hung his head, staring at his closed notebook, hoping there would be no further scolding from his secret crush.

Watching him, Kristen couldn't help but shake her head, a hint of a smile playing on her lips. The mess of her feelings—caught between Jeremy and Missy—seemed a bit less heavy as she allowed herself to get lost in this brief high school drama.

With a resigned sigh of equal parts frustration and surrender, Kristen reached into her bag and fished out a fresh piece of gum. Peeling off the wrapper, she popped it into her mouth, her teeth sinking into its sugary flesh. The burst of artificial cherry flavor served as a palate cleanser, not just for her mouth but for her spirit. It was a minor act, insignificant in the grand scheme of things, but right now, it felt like taking back a sliver of control, a tiny win in a game she wasn't even sure she was playing correctly.

11

THE COTTAGE

JEREMY'S EYES lingered on the tattered sign, its rusty nails clinging to the splintered wood. "Brador," he read, the half-word hanging in the air, a ghostly remnant of grandeur long gone. It was poetic in its sad way; the fallen castle of his grandfather's dreams was now reduced to a barely legible sign and stories that gathered dust in the attic of his memory.

As his Jeep bumped along the uneven gravel, every jolt seemed to represent the turbulence churning inside him. This place, these woods, brought a positive sense of being. They were connected to his family's past, rich with tradition and history. And right now, that was exactly what he needed.

A "No Trespassing" sign, with graffiti scribbled across its warning, was nailed to a tree hanging over the dirt road. The sign's presence seemed almost comical in this forgotten stretch of woods.

Jeremy smirked at the rebellious graffiti sprawled across the warning. "Eat it, ya pig." "The poetic expression of teenage anarchy made him smile. "That has to have been Dutchie's handiwork; no two ways about it," Jeremy thought to himself. He could almost hear Dutch screaming the words out the window of his car as he ripped past the cops on a Friday night on the town's main drag.

"Fucking Dutchie," he thought to himself as the smile faded from his face, feeling a pit of sadness in his gut.

Pulling up in front of the cottage, Jeremy took in the state of the building, "This could work," he thought, mentally running through a list of essentials he'd need to convert the dilapidated structure into a livable space. "Some elbow grease, a little ingenuity, and it could be a bona fide home base."

The cottage was the former home to the staff of the Labrador and the only one left standing after the fire. After years of neglect, it was shrouded by overgrown weeds and weighed down by history's heavy hand.

Jeremy felt a strange surge of emotion as he walked up to the front steps. "This is it, I guess," he thought to himself. "A place to lay low, to think, to strategize."

The Cottage stood in contrast to the world it was born into. The wood siding had seen better decades; some planks were warped, and others had holes the size of fists where rot had eaten its way through. But despite its run-down state, the structure was more or less intact. It still had all four walls, and the roof, although missing a shingle or two, seemed sturdy enough to hold its own against the weight of seasons passed and those to come.

The door hung slightly off its hinges as if it had given up trying to keep the world from entering. A rusty padlock dangled from a latch, but Jeremy knew the trick of it. A slight jiggle, a push-up, and a twist to the right—click—open sesame.

Walking through the door was like stepping into a time capsule, a pocket of the past preserved in dust and cobwebs. There were signs of boyhood adventures strewn about— an old deflated football lying in a corner, a stack of yellowed comic books on a makeshift wooden shelf, and a graffiti-covered workbench that had once served as a "command center" for countless imaginary battles and schemes.

Gregg still owned this piece of land, a forgotten extension of what had once been The Labrador. The wars over the property had been long and messy, but this unassuming cabin had somehow stayed under the radar, too insignificant to fight over. It was the last existing piece of property that still belonged to the Andersons, and only he, Del, and Dutch knew about it.

Technically, he had every right to be here. No one would look for him there, and no one could kick him out. It was as close to a home base as he could get on such short notice.

He stepped back outside and surveyed his would-be home. It wasn't much, but it was private, and more importantly, it was a place where the world couldn't touch him.

In a life of eternal repetition, it was a corner of the universe where he could set the rules. And right now, that felt like everything.

In his mind, Jeremy could already see the sequence of events playing out like a well-rehearsed play. Kristen, twisting her curls as she waited by the gym doors, would start scanning the hallways looking for him, her forehead creasing in irritation when she realized he would be a no-show. She'd shoot off a couple of eye rolls, maybe vent to her girlfriends, before shrugging it off and heading to lunch alone. He could practically hear her voice already, her cadence that shifted between excited chatter and sultry undertones, usually reserved for their more private moments.

Typically, they'd meet at the gym, where she'd talk his ear off for a solid ten minutes. Those gabfests were once the highlight of his day. Kristen would talk about everything and nothing—gossip, her plans for the weekend, and some piece of high school wisdom she'd conjured up. Jeremy usually just nodded, threw in a few uh-huhs, and basked in her presence. Then they'd sneak into an empty classroom or stairwell for a quick make-out session that sent tingles down his spine, a secret recipe of lip gloss and hormones, a ritual of teenage passion that was never skipped.

Afterward, they'd stroll into the lunchroom hand-in-hand. They'd meet up with the popular clique—a collage of jocks, pretty girls, and preppy kids. Kristen would watch in amusement as Jeremy shoveled down whatever slop the cafeteria offered that day as if he were trying to win an eating contest. It wasn't like the food was any good; he was just always starving.

Finally, the lunch period would end, and he'd walk Kristen to her next class, which was in some far-off corner of the building, a million miles from his history class. He'd barely have time to catch his breath as he'd sprint through the halls, dodging clueless freshmen, and skidding into the classroom just as the final bell rang with sweat pooling at his temples.

Like many other events in high school, he knew this ritual didn't matter. The daily routine with Kristen, the lunchroom spectacle, and the breathless dash to History class were all footnotes in a story already written. Jeremy had done it enough times to know that missing out on today's episode wouldn't rewrite his entire future or shatter the world as he knew it.

His footsteps echoed through the cottage as he walked back outside. He couldn't help but feel anxious as he locked the door behind him. The old wood gave a final creak, sealing him from the rustic shelter that was now his home. With one last glance over his shoulder, he turned and walked towards his jeep.

The sun was relentless in its midday blaze, casting harsh shadows over the uneven dirt road ahead of him.

———

Jeremy's thoughts raced as he drove down the rugged path, kicking up dust in his wake. The clock was ticking louder in his mind, a constant reminder of the time slipping through his fingers. He couldn't afford to waste any more of it. He had to get back to school before anyone missed him. But first, he had to get to the credit union and secure his trust fund before Gregg had second thoughts.

He knew his father all too well. The man had a knack for trouble, and alcohol only made things worse. Sure, Gregg had conceded the cash holdings in the shabby envelope now living in the glovebox of Jeremy's jeep. Still, the bulk of what Henry had left him was locked away in the local credit union, shielding it from Gregg's impulsive spending and squandering.

Jeremy's heart broke as he thought back to his original youth, and he vowed this time to make sure Gregg would no longer have an opportunity to fuel his reckless lifestyle with the funds he needed for his future. Fortunately, on his 18th birthday, he could access the account without his father's presence.

He tightened his grip on the steering wheel as he thought about the consequences of failure. If Gregg got to the credit union first, he could withdraw the total balance, leaving Jeremy with nothing to do but go crawling back home. Jeremy had no intention of allowing that to happen.

As he pulled into the parking lot, Jeremy could practically hear the clock ticking. He dashed inside, his eyes scanning the room for any sign of his father. The place was relatively quiet, with only a handful of customers. He approached the counter and was greeted by the teller, a young woman with a bright smile.

"I need to close my account and transfer the funds to a new one," he said, his voice unwavering despite the anxiety that gnawed at him. The teller nodded and she pulled up the account. His eyes watched the clock on the wall, the seconds slipping away. He couldn't afford any delays. Just as he signed the final document, he heard the credit union door swing open behind him. His heart skipped a beat as he turned to see his father stumbling in, reeking of alcohol and anger. Their eyes met, and a chill ran down Jeremy's spine.

"Jeremy!" Gregg slurred, a malicious grin on his face. What are you doing here?" Clearly, his alcoholic haze was so strong that he'd forgotten about the argument that had taken place earlier that morning.

Jeremy knew he had to act fast. He grabbed the paperwork and quickly signed off on it before handing it back to the teller. "Transfer the funds now, please," he instructed.

Sensing the urgency, the teller worked quickly, transferring the money to a new, undisclosed account. Jeremy's hands were clammy as he watched the process.

Gregg stumbled closer, his eyes narrowing as he realized what was happening. "You little punk! You think you can take what's rightfully mine?"

Jeremy clenched his jaw, refusing to engage with his father. The transfer was almost complete, and the clock in his mind was ticking louder than ever.

Finally, the teller handed Jeremy a receipt. "All set," she said with a reassuring smile.

After grabbing the receipt from the teller's hand, Jeremy bolted out the door, leaving his father's angry shouts fading behind him.

He felt a mix of triumph and dread—sure, he had just managed to protect his funds, but he knew this was just one win in an ongoing battle with his father.

Every time he'd relived his life, those initial years were marred by the constant shadow of Gregg's cruelty. But this was more than just about money or escaping his father's wrath; it was about setting his path. In every life, those first 5-10 years, set the tone, and this time, Jeremy was determined to take control. The satisfaction of knowing he had secured a piece of his future was undeniable. Still, he knew he had to stay vigilant and, more importantly, remain a step ahead of his father.

12

MISSY'S LAMENT

Missy sat alone at her desk long after class ended. Her pale eyes were focused on her notebook. Her golden hair, kissed by the soft glow of the classroom's overhead lights, was parted down the middle in a style that suggested simplicity rather than high fashion. She was a unique blend of beauty and brilliance, but the strength of her character often overshadowed her looks.

Her determined approach to life was admirable. She wasn't just smart; she had a ferocious ambition that set her apart from her classmates. Her dedication to academics and extracurriculars was unparalleled, making her a force to be reckoned with in classrooms and competitions.

Boys found her intimidating. Many were not used to a girl who held her ground so firmly. Her unwavering confidence and often reserved demeanor unintentionally placed her outside Huxley High's typical dating scene. And it wasn't because she wasn't attractive. Any young man would consider himself lucky to have her on their arm.

Her reputation as a fierce competitor on the debate team was highly celebrated. She was an unbeatable force with her razor-sharp wit, articulate speech, and ability to dissect an argument with precision. One thing was certain: you never wanted to argue with Missy Winston. Not just because she'd win but because she'd do so with a grace and eloquence that would leave you questioning your point of view.

She spoke with authority and passion. But outside the debate team, in the hallways of Huxley High, she was very different. There, she navigated the buzzing crowds quietly, her voice rarely rising above a whisper.

To many, she appeared as the classic shrew: someone too caught up in her own world, too high above typical high school drama.

Yet, this interpretation of her couldn't have been more wrong. She wasn't a diamond that dazzled at every angle, catching every eye. She was a sapphire, mesmerizing and brilliant in its own right—a gem that didn't seek attention but, when truly seen, was appreciated for its true depth. Only those with an eye for rare and genuine beauty could understand the complexity of Missy Winston.

So, She sat alone, pen in hand, refining her notes into a personal study bible. Her handwriting was the stuff of calligraphic dreams, each letter a work of art, curving and flowing with the grace of a ballet dancer. She chose her pens with the care most people reserved for life-changing decisions. For this session of re-copying her notes, she opted for a fine tip that wouldn't blot or cause a smudge. Something like that would ruin an entire page, and aesthetics mattered.

She lived in the details, leaving no concept unexamined, no theory unexplored. She penned side notes in the margins, scribbled asterisks next to essential points, and used different colored highlighters to flag various categories of information. Her notebooks were like a Da Vinci journal if he'd been an honors student in the 1990s with an affinity for gel pens.

Her innate kindness and burning desire to make the world a better place were what truly set her apart. While she had the brains and talent to succeed, her soul—generous, empathetic, golden—made her extraordinary. She wasn't just aspiring to greatness; she was aspiring to goodness, to be the kind of person who didn't just climb ladders but extended a hand to help others.

Already making waves as a high school senior, she was tackling courses part-time at Western New England College, a testament to her academic strength. In the complex game of life, she was strategizing moves far ahead, playing chess with her future while her peers were still grappling with the basics of checkers.

Her plans were not just ambitious; they were crafted with precision. Boston College was her top choice to attend after graduation. She wasn't just hoping for admission— she was a strong candidate for early acceptance.

Her strategy was clear: move to Boston right after graduation and immediately start working on her bachelor's degree. Her goal was to complete her undergrad studies in three years, which would require intense dedication and discipline.

Despite her quiet brilliance, she was locked in an unending tug-of-war between her aspirations and the world's expectations. The struggle wasn't loud or explosive; it was a simmering tension, a perpetual unease that lodged in her soul's depths.

With all its drama, high school was only part of a larger struggle for Missy. She knew her purpose—to make people's lives better.

This was something none of her classmates cared about. They were tangled in a web of insignificance, obsessed with who dated who, who made varsity, and which Baywatch babe was the hottest. That wasn't Missy's scene, but she often felt the draw of 'fitting in,' the temptation to let her guard down and join the ranks of the typical teenager.

She had watched Kristen, her former best friend, become the reigning queen of the social ladder, surrounded by people who seemed to hang on her every word. She had seen the way heads turned when Kristen entered a room. The air charged with an electric buzz as if everyone had just woken up. Missy was happy for Kristen, or at least she told herself she was.

But some days, especially when she was alone in her room, surrounded by textbooks and journals filled with lofty ambitions and perfectly laid out plans, she wondered what it would be like to be the kind of person people couldn't help but notice. What would it be like to walk into a room, feel the air shift, and see heads turn? It was a silent struggle, one she waged each day. It was a battle between the woman she was becoming—a woman of depth, kindness, and integrity—and the popular girl she wished she could be.

As she glided her pen across the paper, she knew that she was doing more than just jotting down notes; she was laying down the cobblestones of her future, each one placed with precision and care, leading to a destination only she could envision. One that would make the world a better place for us all.

Between each flourish of ink and each sentence she committed to paper, her eyes would drift, if only for a second. They'd drift to the court-yard where groups of friends gathered, laughing without a care. They'd drift toward the door every time someone walked by, hoping they would walk in, searching for her. Her heart would flutter, entertaining the fantasy that things could be different for her, dreaming that she'd be the irresistible force pulling people into her orbit. But no one was coming in to look for her.

As the last few lines of her notes materialized on the page, each character etched with the same meticulous precision she applied to every aspect of her life, and she allowed herself a momentary detour. Her mind couldn't help but wander, and it wandered straight to Jeremy.

She remembered the depth in his eyes as he looked at her in English class. Those weren't the eyes of the confident jock everyone knew him to be; those were the eyes of someone searching for something, maybe even aching.

Jeremy had always been a sturdy rock in the landscape of her high school life. The kind of guy who could send ripples through a crowd just by walking into a room. But what she saw earlier was different; it threw her for a loop. His eyes weren't just darting around the room like they usually did; they were intense. And then, when they locked with hers, it felt like a window opened briefly, revealing an unfamiliar vulnerability.

For the first time, she really saw him, and something was different— not off, just different. She felt the age of his soul. Was he really that complicated, or was it her imagination running wild? She couldn't quite tell, but it had her curious.

And then there was the incident in the parking lot when she saw her life flash before her as Jeremy's Jeep lurched towards her, narrowly missing her by inches, leaving her heart pounding in her chest. For a moment, she was someone else entirely—someone bold, fierce, empowered. She'd stood her ground.

It unsettled her, this newly perceived depth in Jeremy. The Jeremy she thought she knew was a total jock, the king of avoiding any genuine emotional depth. When she called him out for his reckless behavior, he didn't snap back with a sarcastic remark; he didn't offer an arrogant smirk like she'd expected. Instead, he seemed to—shrink. It was as if her words had punctured some inflated version of him, letting the air out slowly. It was a vulnerability that she'd never seen.

Shaking her head, she tried to snap herself out of the daydream. She was almost finished copying her notes. But instead of the letters and words in her artistically perfect handwriting, all she could see were those moments with Jeremy—his old-soul eyes in English class and his unexpected vulnerability in the parking lot.

As she wrestled with her thoughts, losing her concentration, her pen slipped, creating an inkblot that marred the otherwise perfect page.

"Dammit!" She muttered.

A sigh escaped her lips. Here she was, an A-student, already part-time in college, building her path to her future brick by careful brick, and yet, she was letting herself get distracted by her high school's crowned king.

She picked up her pen and looked at her notes, which were nearly immaculate aside from the inkblot in the middle of the page. Every line, every bullet point, was part of her carefully planned future, a future that would help her make a real difference and bring about change.

"That damn mark!" Missy scoffed again.

As much as she was laying down the cobblestones for a brighter future, she couldn't help but wonder what would happen if she went off her path, if only for a moment. It was an exciting and terrifying thought.

As she looked down at the ruined page, the inkblot taunted her—screaming imperfection in a world she so painstakingly curated for precision.

"That damn mark," she muttered again, letting a soft cloud of exasperation escape her lips. The urge to tear the page out and make it vanish from her life was almost unbearable. But that's not what Missy did. She didn't throw things away; she fixed them.

"I'll do it again later," she promised herself quietly as she carefully packed her pens and notebook in her bag, each item finding its designated spot.

She took a deep breath as though inhaling the resolve she'd need to recreate her notes with the same meticulousness, only this time without the cursed inkblot.

There was no place for inkblots in Missy Winston's life. Everything needed to be perfect; her path and how she followed it was set in stone.

13

DENNIS THE DORK

THE LINGERING echo of embarrassment rang in Dennis's ears as he fumbled with his locker combination. As he thought about Kristen's devilish glare in the study hall, he could feel the heat rising in his cheeks, a constant reminder of the crimson hue that had painted his face when she had caught him staring at her.

As he swapped his textbook for his lunch bag, his hands betrayed him, causing it to slip and fall to the floor, letting an apple escape before rolling across the hallway. A chorus of giggles erupted from nearby students, making him shrink further into his shell. He cursed himself silently, wishing he could erase that awkward encounter from his memory.

"Smooth move, Dennis," he muttered to himself.

As he bent down to retrieve his lunch from the floor, he felt the peering eyes of his classmates, or so he thought. In reality, nobody had paid any attention to his clumsiness.

The truth was, his lunch had fallen with such a soft thud that it had gone unnoticed. But in his mind, it was a different story. He could hear the imagined giggles and chuckles and feel the invisible weight of judgmental gazes burning through him. His heart raced, and his palms grew sweaty as he imagined the entire school erupting into laughter at his expense.

He quickly reached down, scooped up the brown bag, and reached for the apple just as a passing classmate kicked it further down the hall. His head sank again, and with a sigh, he stood up, clutching his lunch as if it were a shield against ridicule. His cheeks burned with embarrassment, and he couldn't shake the feeling that everyone was watching him, waiting for his next clumsy move.

The truth was, Dennis blended in seamlessly with the background of Huxley High. He was, in essence, a nobody who went about his day-to-day existence without drawing the slightest hint of attention. In the grand scheme of things, he was just another face in the crowded halls. His fear of the spotlight was a personal struggle that gnawed at him from within. He had crafted an image of himself as the clumsy, awkward guy who always stumbled through life, but in reality, most people didn't give him a second thought.

-And then there was Kristen.

When he locked eyes with her in study hall, it was as if he'd walked straight into a tornado and come out the other side questioning the laws of physics. Their staring contest only lasted seconds, but it felt like an eternity.

In his mind, Kristen was not just a pretty face with lip gloss and dazzling basket tosses. She was not just the centerpiece of high school fantasies. She was a complex soul waiting to be discovered, a kindred spirit who shared his passion for art and science and the profound depths of love. He believed that behind her bubble-gum exterior was a fire of passion waiting to be fanned into a blazing inferno, and in secret, he wanted to be the one to ignite it.

As he often watched her from a distance, he couldn't help but feel a deep sense of connection, as if their souls were destined to be together. In his heart, he knew that she was more than just a crush; she was his soul-mate. And with that conviction burning brightly within him, he wanted to take the risk, step into the light, and find a way to show her that he saw beyond her mask. His daydreams of a romantic connection with Kristen were plagued by a harsh reality he couldn't ignore. She had a boyfriend, and not just any boyfriend.

Jeremy embodied the kind of high school dream guy you'd expect to be dating someone like Kristen. He was good-looking, with a strong jawline and an athlete's physique that turned heads wherever he went. But it wasn't just Jeremy's looks that made him stand out. He had a sense of humor that was just as sharp as his reflexes on the field were. At social gatherings, he was the life of the party, cracking jokes and making everyone laugh. His easygoing nature made him popular not just among the jocks but with students from all walks of life.

It was no surprise that he had been crowned Homecoming King in his junior year, a title that seemed tailor-made for someone like him. His charm and charisma had won over the entire student body, and his peers adored him. But what set Jeremy apart was that he was a genuinely good guy. He wasn't just a popular athlete, he was a friend to everyone, including Dennis. Jeremy had a heart of gold and had bailed Dennis out countless times when he faced the wrath of Dutch Wyatt and everything that came with being a target for the bully's torment.

The uncanny timing of Jeremy's interventions in Dennis's life had become the stuff of legends. It seemed as if Jeremy had a sixth sense for when Dennis was about to be on the receiving end of a brutal beatdown, always appearing in the nick of time to intervene. It was as if Jeremy was his guardian angel, swooping in to protect him from harm's way. And what made it even more remarkable was that Dutch would always back down whenever Jeremy stepped in.

People had often whispered about the power dynamic between Jeremy and Dutch. How was it possible that Jeremy could make Dutch, the brute force of the school, fold with a mere word or gesture? It defied all logic, especially given how Dutch put on a public beat-down on a senior twice his size during the Spring assembly in his sophomore year.

Whatever the truth was, one thing was clear: Jeremy's presence was a shield that protected Dennis from the relentless storm that was Dutch Wyatt. He couldn't help but feel a deep sense of gratitude and admiration for Jeremy, the hero who had come to his rescue time and time again.

So, every time Dennis's mind wandered into romantic fantasies about Kristen, the doors of his imagination would slam shut, reminding him that she was in a committed relationship with someone who deserved her.

And so, he remained a silent observer who, deep down, couldn't help but hope that fate had something else in store for him, a chance to find his happiness, even if it meant taking a risk and stepping into the spotlight.

14

FUCKING DUTCHIE

AT HUXLEY HIGH SCHOOL, Dutch Wyatt was impossible to ignore. The hallways, alive with the energy of youth, would fall into a sudden silence whenever he made an entrance. Conversations halted in mid-sentence; glances were exchanged. An unspoken agreement was clear: don't get caught in Dutch Wyatt's path.

From the outside, Dutch was the poster child for teenage rebellion, a walking middle finger to rules and order. His careless swagger and belligerent demeanor gave off an unmistakable 'devil may care' energy. But his exterior was just the tip of an emotional iceberg, below lay a disturbing sea of angst, frustration, and pain.

Many of Dutch's signature moves amounted to little more than nuisances—a stolen lunch here, a shredded notebook there, disruptions in class, small actions that hinted at the more profound struggles beneath his surface.

The acts weren't random. They were the manifestation of a young man, trying in his own tortured way, to gain control in a world that perpetually kept him down. He lived by an unspoken philosophy: If the world was determined to screw him over, he'd make damn sure he wasn't suffering alone.

Whenever he'd see someone at ease, smiling, or simply in a good mood, it was as if a spotlight was pointed at his misery. That's when he'd strike, pulling them down into the shit with him, making them taste the bitter flavor of his existence.

Most students hid in the background, hoping to avoid his wrath. Others had tried and failed to confront the bully, standing up for the underdog. But Dutch's mission was clear: Huxley High would feel first-hand the storm that raged within him.

Before sophomore year, Dutch's reputation had never stretched beyond that of an annoying wiseass. He was the kind of guy who seemed stuck in the role of the class clown, always ready to shoot off a tasteless comment or a wisecrack, but that was about it. His favorite targets were his female classmates. He'd chirp at them incessantly, trying to be charming but ultimately coming off as disgusting.

Dutch's antics had become predictable, his presence an all-too-familiar annoyance that had worn thin on his classmates and the faculty. He was never regarded as a real troublemaker or a rebel. He was simply a nuisance that everyone hoped would eventually grow out of his immature phase. He was little more than an annoying fly buzzing around the halls, a perpetual wise guy whose bark far outweighed any bite.

But on one fateful spring day, in the school's gym, Dutch's reputation as one to never mess with would be sealed forever.

Dutch's patience wore thin during the school's annual spring assembly and midway through Principal Mitchell's excruciatingly dull speech about school values and upcoming events. Sitting through assemblies was never Dutch's things thing, and that snoozefest pushed him to his limit. Unable to fight the urge, he decided to do something to liven up the event. To him, it was his duty.

Taking a deep breath, he stood up in the bleachers and shouted, "Suck a fat turd Mitchell!"

The unexpected outburst echoed through the gym, shattering the dry atmosphere and unleashing a wave of laughter. The crowd's reaction was exactly what he hoped for— Mission accomplished.

However, big-shot senior Brad Prescott wasn't having it. He saw the move as an attack on school spirit, which made him furious.

Towering over most with muscles that screamed 'wrestling god,' he spun around to face Dutch, his voice thundering, "Hey Wyatt! Why don't you shut the fuck up and act like you've got a single brain cell for once!"

Dutch, ablaze with fiery defiance, stood his ground. "Or what, golden boy? You gonna attempt one of your pathetic wrestling holds on me?" He shot back, scanning the crowd for any signs of approval for his response, but was met with silence.

Brad's face flushed, veins in his forehead standing out as his anger boiled over. "You're treading on thin ice, punk," he growled, eyes locked on

Dutch, leaning in, "Keep pushing it, and I'll personally make sure you get a beatdown that you'll never forget."

Dutch's grin widened, that infamous shit-eating smirk that spelled nothing but trouble. "A beatdown? That'll be the day," he quipped, his voice dripping with mockery as he glanced over at Brad's girlfriend, who watched the confrontation with concern and annoyance.

"Oh, and by the way," Dutch continued, not one to let an opportunity slip by, "tell your girl to stop calling me late at night. I need my beauty sleep, you know?" He punctuated his insult with a wink in her direction, fueling their already fiery tension.

Losing all composure, Brad lunged at Dutch.

What followed was pure, unfiltered chaos. Everyone expected Brad, with his sheer size and years on the wrestling team, to wipe the floor with Dutch. But Dutch fought like he was possessed. He ducked, swerved, and landed punch after punch, turning Brad's face into a messed-up canvas of red and blue.

The gym roared with shouts and cheers as Brad, the wrestling prodigy, was being absolutely wrecked by the sophomore menace. Dutch moved with an agility and ferocity that defied his usual careless demeanor. He ducked, weaved, and struck with a precision that left Brad stunned.

Then came the moment that shocked everyone. Bloodied and winded, Brad found himself on the floor, his pride shattered along with his nose. Tears welled up in his eyes, embarrassment washing over him, begged Dutch to stop.

But Dutch didn't stop; he kept going, landing blow after blow, each one accompanied by a cutting word of advice that no one would ever welcome.

The gym, once filled with the roar of hundreds of students, now held a heavy silence, punctuated only by the sounds of the struggle. It took a handful of teachers and administrators, rushing from all directions, to pry Dutch away. With wild, triumphant eyes and adrenaline coursing through his veins, Dutch seethed.

As he was dragged to the exit, he wrestled himself free. Just before storming out, he turned to face the crowd, defiantly raised two middle fingers, and shouted, "Eat it, pigs!"—A total Dutch move.

Gossip spread like wildfire that he would be expelled. But, in a twisted turn, the Prescott family, maybe out of embarrassment or sympathy for The Wyatt family's tragic past, asked the school to be lenient in punishing Dutch.

The verdict? A one-week in-school suspension—a slap on the wrist.

The student body was in an uproar, but one thing was for sure: Dutch was no longer just a nuisance; he was the guy you didn't mess with if you knew what was good for you.

After the fight with Brad, Dutch did some soul-searching. Not in the cheesy after-school special kind of way, but in the raw, honest contemplation of someone who's seen the edge and knows how close he came to tumbling over.

As Dutch replayed the scene repeatedly in his mind, he couldn't deny the satisfaction he felt about the message he had sent to the popular crowd by correcting Brad with his fists. It was a declaration that he wouldn't be pushed around. But deep within himself, there was a profound recognition of what the school meant to him.

Huxley High was his sanctuary. It wasn't about pride, reputation, or even the thrill of a good brawl. It was something far more primal than that. For Dutch, home was a wasteland—lacking love, warmth, and the most basic necessities.

Huxley provided what his so-called 'home' couldn't. At school, he had access to at least one daily meal that wasn't stolen or scrounged up from somewhere. It was a simple luxury that he never took for granted. It meant that, at least for a few hours each day, he didn't have to fight off the gnawing hunger that plagued him outside of school.

Then, there was the auto shop. It was his fortress of solitude, a place where he could drown out the world with the roar of engines and the scent of motor oil. In the auto shop, teachers weren't trying to mold him into something he wasn't. They were just trying to keep the students from burning the place down.

Facing the threat of losing a decent meal and a space where he could be himself, Dutch decided it was time to draw a line and establish limits around his role as the school's troublemaker. Mind games, the mental torture that he loved to inflict, and maybe the occasional shove in the hallway were fair game. But anything that put him at risk of getting kicked out of school was off the table.

Even though he wasn't walloping someone daily, his presence in the hallway was enough to send a cold draft through the bravest of souls. But beneath the armor of indifference and rage, Dutch clung to two anchors that kept him from drowning in his tempestuous sea: community-subsidized lunch and the school shop where no one cared who he was.

He hustled enough money the summer before his senior year to buy his 1984 Plymouth Turismo for $100 from his neighbor. The car had been sitting lifeless for the last five years, and although it hadn't been road-worthy in years, Dutch was confident he could bring it back from the dead.

The Turismo wasn't the sleek beast you'd imagine hearing its name. No, it was a cranky, rusty hunk of shit that seemed hell-bent on defying every ounce of Dutch's mechanical skills. No matter how much blood, sweat, and swears he poured into it, the car refused to purr like it was supposed to. Instead, it coughed, sputtered, and groaned like a senior cat with a bad attitude. But to Dutch, it was more than just a car. It was a metaphor for his life. A challenge wrapped in rust and peeling paint. Every failed attempt to get it roaring was a mirror to his setbacks, yet he kept going back, with a wrench in hand and hope in his heart.

The Turismo was Dutch's white whale, his never-ending project. It stood as a testament to his stubbornness, his refusal to accept defeat, and his relentless spirit.

Every greasy hour he spent under its hood, and every night he stayed late in the auto shop, was a middle finger to the universe, a declaration that Dutch Wyatt would not be beaten easily, not by fate, and sure as hell not by a stubborn piece of shit car.

Away from the judging eyes of his peers, in the auto shop, Dutch's demeanor transformed. The brooding mask he wore so well would slip, replaced by a look of intense concentration. It was here, among the smell of motor oil and the clanking of tools, that he was in his happy place. And at the center of it all was his obsession, the Plymouth Turismo.

Dutch was defiant to any supposed curse that hung over his family. He had convinced himself that it was just a ghost story that spread through the town for decades. As far as he was concerned, he just had terrible luck, and that was it. He despised the hand he had been dealt. He'd lost anyone he'd ever cared about, and his current home life was less than a storybook environment, but he just chalked that up to life not being fair.

Working on his car was the only thing that allowed Dutch to escape the harsh realities of his world. It would help him forget about his lost family, the weight of his current life, and the dreams that had been shattered along the way.

As he tinkered with the car, every wrench turned, and every dent repaired was a spiritual release. It was as if the world faded away for those precious moments, and Dutch was in complete control. The car was not just a machine; it was a lifeline that helped him cope with the scars of his past and the uncertainty of his future.

While he might have been resigned to the belief that his life was destined for hardship and misfortune, Dutch's devotion to his car was an act of defiance. It was a declaration that, at least in this one small corner of his existence, he could hold onto something that brought him joy and purpose. With all its quirks and challenges, the car became his refuge, relief for his wounded spirit, and a reminder that even in the darkest times, there could be some hope.

The frustrating part about the Turismo was that no matter how much Dutch poured into it, no matter how flawlessly he executed his repairs, the car never ran smoothly. There was always something, some elusive problem, that stubbornly resisted his every effort. It felt like an endless game of cat and mouse, a relentless chase to make it run like it should.

With wrenches and tools scattered around him, Dutch's greasy hands were deep in the guts of his car's engine. His focus was laser-sharp, the world around him fading into the background as he worked to tune up the stubborn machine. But just as he was beginning to make progress, a sudden crackle over the school's PA system jolted him back to reality.

Kristen Ray's voice dripping with pep and enthusiasm announced the upcoming football game, scheduled for Friday at 7 p.m. against Regional High.

His mind split in two, shattering his concentration. On the one hand, there was Kristen's image, her attractive body, her social status in Huxley High's hierarchy of popularity, and on the other, his hatred for the football team, more specifically, their coach.

In Dutch's eyes, Coach McHale was nothing more than a loser in a coach's uniform, desperately clinging to dreams of glory that seemed forever out of reach.

McHale's relentless pursuit of Dutch to join the football team only served to fuel his hatred. The coach had heard stories about Dutch's athletic abilities in middle school and knew that wasn't something that just went away. He saw Dutch as the key to turning the team's fortunes around.

The ferocity of the beating Dutch had unleashed on Brad Prescott had only deepened the coach's admiration for the young man's raw power. But Dutch wasn't the kind of person who believed in empty promises. He wasn't interested in entertaining the coach's desperate attempts to get him to join a losing team. He already had his fair share of losses in life, and he wasn't looking to add more to the list.

What nobody realized was that Dutch had a well-kept secret. Despite his hatred for the coach, openly talking trash about him to anyone who would listen, he still went to every home game. Hidden under the bleachers, he would watch with the scrutiny of a seasoned scout, keeping an eye on McHale's bad decisions, shitty coaching techniques, and consistently failing results.

His interest lay in the performance of his former friends, Jeremy and Del, who had once been as close as brothers. In middle school, the three ruled the Pop Warner field together, forming a formidable trio that struck fear into their opponents. Their shared triumphs were etched into the archives of their formative years.

Dutch knew that Jeremy and Del deserved better. They were talented athletes, their skills shining through even in the face of repeated losses. Rumors had circulated that college scouts were recruiting them despite the history of defeat surrounding their team. It was a glimmer of hope that, brought Dutch comfort.

Week after week, he would watch as Jeremy and Del took beating after beating on the field, their faces full of determination despite the mounting losses. He hated to watch them lose, and as much as he wanted to be by their side, he knew it was impossible. He had resigned himself to watching them play from the shadows, silently cheering for his friends while carrying the weight of his demons.

As the announcement over the PA ended, Kristen, having forgotten to switch off the microphone, rambled on about the football team's slim chances of winning. As her nonsensical chatter filled the airwaves, a faint scuffle could be heard before falling silent.

Dutch couldn't help but smirk at the chaos. He shook his head, reveling in the small victory of hearing her fumble over her words. But as he turned his attention back to the Turismo's engine, his smirk faded into a look of intense concentration.

Something caught his eye—something that shouldn't have been there. A spark plug wire was loose, barely making a proper connection.

He had meticulously inspected and tuned up the engine countless times before, and he took pride in his attention to detail. Yet, here was something so simple, so glaringly out of place.

"What the fuck," he muttered to himself in frustration, his hands deftly working to inspect the wire. He couldn't comprehend how something like this had happened. The engine had been perfect in his eyes, a testament to his meticulous care and attention. He reached in and disconnected the wire, his fingers running over it as he inspected every inch.

"Somebody fucking with this?" he asked himself, his suspicion rising. But after a closer examination, he couldn't find any signs of tampering or damage to the wire. It was, as it should be, perfectly fine.

He continued his inspection, checking every detail before firmly securing the part back in place, ensuring the connection was tight. There was an unease in the air, a sense that even in the world of machines and mechanics, there were mysteries that couldn't be explained.

He wiped his grimy hands on a nearby rag before sliding into the driver's seat of the car. His expectations were well-defined by a history of disappointment. He knew that the car would likely struggle to start, run poorly, sputter, and die.

Frustrated, he turned the key with a resigned sigh. The Turismo responded with its usual groans as the engine struggled to turn over. It sounded like shit, just as he knew it would. The motor began its familiar sputtering, but then, something unexpected happened.

As he sat in disbelief, the idle became steady, and the engine's sound shifted from a pitiful wheeze to a robust growl.

His eyes widened as he listened to the engine's miraculous transformation. It was as if it had defied its nature, casting aside its history of failure to run with newfound strength and purpose. Dutch couldn't contain his excitement. He let out a triumphant howl, matching the roaring tones of the car's engine.

At that moment, he forgot that he was surrounded by classmates working on their own projects. His outburst was a raw expression of joy and disbelief as he celebrated the unexpected triumph against his long-standing battle with his car. He couldn't help but cackle, his laughter filling the shop. His earlier frustration faded into the background as he basked in the moment's thrill.

Dutch couldn't wrap his head around how such a minor issue had plagued his car for so long. It was as if some unexplainable force had stepped in to transform the Turismo's performance. Whatever it was, he didn't care. The important thing was that his car sounded like a badass machine for the first time in years, and he would savor this feeling for as long as it lasted.

When the welcome sound of the bell rang, signaling the start of the lunch period, Dutch's stomach growled, reminding him of his constant hunger. "

Shit! Chicken Burger Day!" he thought to himself with a smirk.

With his car's engine finally purring smoothly and the prospect of a decent lunch ahead, he felt that today might actually be a good day after all.

With that in mind, he put away his tools, wiped his greasy hands on a rag, and headed for the cafeteria, his mind still buzzing with the unexpected success of his beloved Turismo.

15

COLLISION COURSE

FINDING HIMSELF AHEAD OF SCHEDULE, Jeremy raced his Jeep into the Huxley High parking lot. With time on his side, he had a moment to quickly catch lunch with Kristen before the mad dash to History class. Things were looking up, and the promise of a good meal was the boost he needed to keep going.

After parking the Jeep, he snagged the worn envelope from the glove box that reeked of Gregg's schemes and shoved it deep into his backpack. As he headed up the hill, he broke into a sprint, racing toward the school's entrance.

Making his way into the building, he headed towards the stairs leading to the cafeteria. As he rushed to catch the end of the lunch period, he felt gratitude for one of the quirks of his peculiar existence. Every time he 'reset,' he was at the peak of his teenage athleticism. His feet barely touched the ground as he bounded up the stairs, making the climb effortlessly.

But as the proverb goes, pride comes before a fall.

Lost in his thoughts, he didn't notice another student descending the staircase he was sprinting up. Their collision was both sudden and violent. His momentum and physical strength resulted in an impact that sent the unsuspecting student flying, landing with a loud crash on the level above them. Papers, textbooks, and a collection of essentials spiraled in a chaotic tornado around them.

When the dust settled he took in the scene. There, sprawled on the landing and trying to recover, was Missy— winded from the impact and with a bloody nose, she struggled to get to her feet.

"Missy, of all the people he could've barreled into, it had to be her," he thought as he scrambled to his feet. His heart raced as he watched her cough and gasp for air. Seeing the crimson streaks of blood dribbling from her nose made his heart sink. Gone was the triumph of the earlier victory at the credit union and in its place was raw panic.

"No, no, no!" he muttered, his voice filled with genuine horror as he knelt beside her, extending a shaky hand. "Missy, I am so sorry. I didn't see you."

She looked up, her blue eyes glassy and filled with tears, either from the pain or the shock—he couldn't tell.

"I wasn't looking. I was rushing, and— God, this is terrible," he stammered, unsure if any apology would be enough.

She tried to speak in a daze, her voice barely a whisper. "It's okay," she winced— just help me up."

He cringed, his guilt evident, as he gently wrapped an arm around her, carefully helping her sit upright against the cold wall. He quickly began collecting the contents of her backpack tossed everywhere in the collision —loose papers, textbooks, a few pens, and her glasses.

Handing her the glasses, he was thankful that they were unharmed. As she put them on, her vision sharpened. Now able to recognize her accidental adversary, the shock in her eyes was replaced by a blazing fury.

"YOU!" she spat, her voice dripping with disbelief and annoyance. "Of course it's you!" Her sudden transition from dazed victim to fiery accuser would've impressed him had he not been on the receiving end. In a rapid motion that seemed almost magical, she snatched her belongings back from him, her anger pouring out like a dam that had burst. "First, you nearly flattened me in the parking lot this morning, and now you try to pile-drive me into the wall in the stairwell?"

Already feeling small, he tried to correct her, "Missy, that's not how pile drivers work."

Shooting him a glare, "That's not the point!" She snapped as she tried getting to her feet. But as she shifted her weight onto her left leg, her face contorted in pain, and gave a sharp cry, nearly collapsing. She steadied herself and continued her verbal assault. All he could do was stand there, drop his head, and take it. All of it

His eyes darted around the hallway for a moment, as if searching for an escape route. Finding none, he met her fiery gaze. He took a deep breath, and, with sincerity in his eyes, he picked his head up and looked at her. "Look, Missy, everything today has been chaotic, to say the least; the parking lot, this," he gestured to the disarray surrounding them.

"I don't really know how to put it into words," he hesitated, his voice faltering, the weight of the day pressing down on him.

"Today has been surreal. Nothing has played out like it usually does. It's like some cosmic joke, and for some reason, you're getting caught up in the middle of it."

She raised an eyebrow, her confusion evident. "What do you mean 'like it usually does?'— that doesn't make any sense; no one knows how any day is supposed to go. What are you, some sort of psychic? She snorted as a light smirk hit her lips.

He panicked, and in his emotional exhaustion from day one, he'd slipped. If experience taught him anything, he needed to make sense of what he'd just said, and he needed to do it quickly. "I mean, I needed to leave school for an emergency and wasn't prepared for it. I've been scrambling all day. It's exhausting. I don't know why you've been dragged into my drama today. You aren't supposed to be. I can't explain it."

Her stance shifted from defensive to genuinely intrigued. "So, what? I'm just an unlucky bystander in your rollercoaster of a day?" Her tone was half mocking, half serious.

Feeling cornered, he grimaced. "Yeah, I guess that's one way to put it." Taking a deep breath, his mind racing, he tried to regain control of the situation. "I really am sorry, Missy; let me help you to the nurse; you need to get that ankle checked out. I will do whatever I can to make this right."

Recognizing the sincerity in his eyes, she backed down before grabbing a tissue from her bag and placing it on her nose.

"Please, let me help," he pleaded.

She agreed with a nod as he gathered her scattered belongings from the floor and neatly placed them into her backpack. He collected the remaining textbooks, and with one swift motion, he securely tucked them under his arm. With his free hand, he extended it toward her, an unspoken invitation for support.

They moved in tandem as he guided her down the halls towards the administration wing, a simple gesture rooted in compassion.

To anyone watching, it would appear as a harmless act of kindness. Though, knowing Huxley High's rumor mill, whispers would certainly float around about the unexpected pairing of the school's homecoming king and their future valedictorian.

Wanting to fill the silence, he asked, "So, how's the school year treating you?" It might seem like a mundane question to most, but it had an underlying weight for Jeremy. He had engaged in this conversation with Missy in past lifetimes, always around the same time. The answer was predictable.

"Pretty Good," she responded with a wince as she stepped down on her weak leg, her voice a soft murmur. It was the same brief reply he had expected, a scripted moment in the ever-repeating play of his existence. The words were always the same. As was the tone, the subtle nuances of her voice, and even the look in her eyes, those things rarely varied. Today, however, there was a hint of weariness in her voice, a touch of reflection in her eyes that he didn't remember from before.

She glanced at him, a strand of hair falling in front of her face. "Thanks for helping. Even if you were the one to knock me down in the first place."

He chuckled softly, a smile tugging at his lips. "Yeah, it was the right thing to do, I guess.

They continued in a comfortable silence, punctuated by the distant chatter of other students and the hum of fluorescent lights overhead. When they reached the nurse's office, He gently placed her textbooks on a nearby bench.

Taking a deep breath and leaning into him slightly for support, she said, "You know, despite today's bizarre turn, it wasn't all bad. I mean, when was the last time we talked?"

He searched his memory; it had been ages since he'd thought about pre-cycle life. As the memory came to him, he blurted out, "That middle school play? When I was the tree, and you were a squirrel?"

She laughed," Yup, The Sound of The Woods Musical."

"Yeah, Good times," he responded, feeling the innocence of a time long forgotten.

As they stood at the door of the nurse's office, there was a shared moment of nostalgia as memories of simpler days passed through their minds. He cherished moments like these in each cycle, the unexpected connections that made every life feel unique and worth living.

Clearing his throat, he said, "I should probably let you get checked out. Let me know if I need to replace any of your things. She looked thoughtful for a moment before smiling sweetly at him, "Don't worry about it; I know it was an accident."

As he turned to walk away, he couldn't help but wonder what other unexpected moments this cycle would bring. The thought brought on a wave of anxiety.

Just as he thought this event was behind him, her voice rang out, causing him to stop in his tracks.

"Hey, Homecoming!" she shouted with uncharacteristic confidence and a hint of mischief in her tone. "Next time you feel like undressing me with your eyes in English class, maybe just try to say hi instead."

His face turned a deep shade of red as he looked at her. "Fair enough," he responded sheepishly before turning to walk away.

Seated in the nurse's waiting area, Missy's ankle throbbed with a dull pain as she replayed her parting jab at Jeremy.

"Hey, Homecoming," she immediately cringed. "Why did I say that?" she thought, scolding herself for her newfound boldness. While he was the reason she was in this mess, he'd also gone out of his way to help her. The snarky comment seemed inappropriate, and she couldn't pinpoint the sudden burst of confidence that compelled her to say it.

Over the years, from elementary school antics to high school dynamics, as far as she was concerned, Jeremy had always been the poster child of positivity. Always the golden boy, everyone's friend. She remembered whispers about his family — tales of a mother who disappeared and public sightings of his father. Was there something more to the story? Something that might explain his behavior today?

Missy had always been wary of his constant good nature. She thought no one could be that perfect without a hidden agenda. She thought about how he'd often gone out of his way for others, even helping her brother out of tight spots, time and time again. But today, something was off. The infectious charm that drew people to him felt overshadowed by a heaviness she couldn't quite put her finger on. It was as though an internal battle raged within him, a struggle she was beginning to see.

Once more, her mind circled back to her bold remark. Was it crazy to hope he'd brush it off and not make a big deal out of it?

She replayed the scene, agonizing over each word. To think that he might see her as anything more than the school's overachiever felt like a stretch. And yet, there was no mistaking how he'd looked at her in first-period English. His eyes held a depth she couldn't figure out. What was going on in his mind? What was he grappling with?—she wondered.

Her eyes fell upon a clock with a second hand that seemed to move painstakingly slow. She tapped her fingers on her knee, the rhythm aligning with the muffled sounds of school life outside the door.

Her mind wandered back to Jeremy, but she told herself to stop. Thoughts like that were a distraction. She'd always been a focused individual. Academic excellence, leadership roles, college applications—these were the things she should be thinking about. Jeremy Anderson and his mysterious depths had no place in her head.

Fortunately, her racing thoughts were interrupted by the entrance of the school nurse, Ms. McKinstry. Glancing at Missy's swollen ankle with concern evident in her eyes, she asked in a gentle yet firm voice, "What happened?"

A little taken aback by the nurse's directness, Missy quickly responded. "Oh, I twisted it during Gym class."

Nurse McKinstry gave a tsk of disapproval. "Coach McHale again? I swear, his over-the-top drills will be the end of me. That man's machismo antics are more trouble than they're worth. Don't get me started on that infernal game he has you kids play; what's it called, Bombardment?"

"Yeah, Missy replied, I hate that game. I call it Dodgeball on steroids. I usually take myself out early and just let the meatheads play."

Nurse McKinstry chuckled, "That McHale is the king of the meatheads."

Missy couldn't help but smirk, grateful for the nurse's light-hearted jab. The nurse's practiced hands moved over Missy's ankle, pressing lightly here and there, gauging her reactions. After a few moments of careful examination, she concluded, "It's a mild sprain. I suggest you ice it and keep it elevated for a while."

A glint of mischief appeared in the nurse's eyes as she added, "I'll write you a note. Tell Mr. McHale to take it easy on you for the next few days."

A surge of relief washed over Missy. Being excused from Gym was like winning the lottery for her. It granted her extra invaluable time — time she could utilize to pore over her notes and solidify her understanding for the impending Honors Chemistry exam. She could already imagine herself tucked away in her favorite quiet corner of the library with her textbooks sprawled out and her mind laser-focused.

A faint smirk crossed her lips as she momentarily entertained a silent word of gratitude. 'Thank you, Jeremy Anderson,' her thoughts echoed in her head. But she quickly caught herself. Now wasn't the time for distraction, no matter how intriguing. She had plans. Her future was shaped by discipline and dedication, and she wasn't about to let a chance collision alter her course.

16

SMOKING IN THE BOYS ROOM

As Jeremy slipped into the bathroom where the vocational wing intersected with Arts and Science, a quick look around told him he was alone. The stalls in this particular bathroom had long been stripped of their doors, a testament to Huxley High's finest vandals. What it lacked in privacy, it made up for in character.

The walls were decorated with layers of graffiti, each mark telling its own story, each doodle a memory of past students. And among these countless inscriptions, the word "pig" was prominently featured. Everyone at Huxley knew that if "pig" was scrawled anywhere, it was Dutch. There was something about how he used the word like it was the vilest word he had ever spoken or written.

The stall furthest from the entrance offered the most privacy possible in a doorless environment. It was as good a place as any to collect his thoughts away from the day's chaos.

Settling into the stall, he reached into his backpack, pulling out the envelope his father had given him and the documents from the account transfer at the credit union. He gingerly placed the envelope on the tiled floor, ensuring it was out of harm's way, and slowly unfolded the bank record. His eyes darted immediately to the bottom line as he inspected the receipt. The balance read $2,000. The number crushed his soul.

In every single life, that college fund had been a reliable constant. Regardless of all the differences, twists, and turns each new life brought, it always held $26,054.68. It was meant to cushion his college journey, acting as a buffer alongside the partial athletic scholarship he was set to receive. But now, staring at the glaringly small balance, his mind raced.

How? Why was this different? What variable had shifted in this lifetime to reduce the fund to almost nothing? He re-read the statement several times, hoping that he'd missed a zero or misread the number.

Desperation took over his thoughts. Had there been some mistake? Or worse, had Gregg tampered with the fund before he could move it into another account? The questions raced in his mind, each more distressing than the last.

There had to be more. He reached into the envelope to find another sealed envelope, a handwritten note, and a crisp hundred-dollar bill.

"What the actual fuck," he whispered as he examined the now empty envelope before opening the note and reading it to himself:

Jeremy,

Well, look who's finally grown a pair. I always figured the day would come when your balls would finally drop, and you'd stand up to your old man. It took you long enough. And let me tell you, son, you've got me to thank for that boldness. All those years of tough love? You're welcome.

If you have this note, I've already been to the bank and made some adjustments to the account. Don't worry, you won't need that cash; your education is a useless endeavor that'll never provide any return on your investment. That money, I have plans for it, big ones.

The remaining $2k? That wasn't oversight or generosity. It's my parting gift, a reminder of my presence in your life. I could have taken it all and left you nothing. But where's the fun in that?

You're probably wondering about the envelope. Let's just say it's got something I never really wanted. Something I *knew would come back to haunt me someday. Frankly, the weight of what's inside? It's better suited for a thankless punk like you. Enjoy the curse.*

Oh, and the C-note? Consider it a parting gift. Grab yourself a decent steak, wash it down with the coldest beer you can find, or maybe get in a little trouble.

Good luck,

Gregg

"What an incredible asshole," Jeremy thought, folding the note and putting it away. Reaching for the sealed envelope.

The slight crinkling of the paper seemed deafeningly loud to Jeremy as he began to peel it open. Just as he was about to glimpse its contents, a sudden burst of noise echoed throughout the room—the bathroom door violently flinging open, followed by boisterous laughter. Jeremy's heart leaped into his throat.

"Fucking Dutchie," Jeremy whispered to himself; he was in no mood for another confrontation.

The conversation was animated and loud, filled with disdain as they vented about a recent run-in with a particularly annoying school administrator. The detailed retelling, laced with teenage hyperbole and snark, was unmistakably Dutch's style. It was a story of rebellion, of sticking it to the man, and Jeremy could practically see Dutch's signature smirk as he spoke.

Every instinct in Jeremy screamed to stay hidden. Quietly, he tucked the letter and the sealed envelope back into his backpack before quickly slipping the $100 bill into his pocket. He pressed himself against the cool, graffiti-laden walls of the stall, pulling his feet up, hoping the deep shadows would keep him hidden.

Encounters with Dutch were unpredictable on a good day. With everything that had already happened today, Jeremy was not interested in any ripples, no matter how large or small any off-script interaction with Dutch Wyatt could cause.

For what felt like hours but was only minutes, Dutch and his friend continued their conversation, punctuated with the occasional outburst of laughter. All the while, Jeremy remained silent, hardly daring to breathe. He mentally willed them to leave, desperately wanting to avoid confrontation and get back to the envelope in his backpack.

Jeremy's chest tightened with dread and irritation as the door creaked open again. What happened next seemed to happen in slow motion.

The echo of a third set of footsteps entered the bathroom, accompanied by the suppressed laughter of Dutch and his sidekick, who decided to linger for some added amusement.

"Hey, dork!" Dutch's voice cut through the room.

Jeremy could visualize the sly grin on Dutchie's face as he called out to this new and unknown person. "Your golden savior ain't here to bail you out now, is he?"

"Dutch, please, just leave me alone," the voice begged.

Jeremy's heart plummeted. "Dennis!" he inwardly gasped, grappling with the timing and the person involved. "Why Dennis?—Why now?"

"No way, Jose," Dutch retorted with a cruel chuckle. "I've been hunting you down. You owe me."

Jeremy's senses heightened. He could hear the shuffle of shoes on the tile floor and the faint rustle of clothing. The atmosphere grew thick with tension. Jeremy wished with all his might that Dutch would settle for some harmless teasing and move on. But deep down, he knew the bully wasn't the kind to let things slide.

"Listen, you little puss," Dutch sneered, his voice dripping with evil delight, "You made the bet. You lost, and now you gotta pay. Simple as that."

"Dutch listen, I never agreed to any bet with you; you told me you'd kick my ass if I didn't do it," Dennis pleaded.

"That's not how I remember it," Dutch scoffed. You bet me the Wildcats would win last week, and they lost, like always. You owe me ten bucks; time to pay up."

Inside the stall, Jeremy's heartbeat echoed loudly in his ears. He silently willed Dutch to let it go with a minor humiliation. Just a wedgie, maybe a swirly, but don't cause him any real harm, he hoped.

But fate had other plans. With the quickness of a striking cobra, Dutch lunged at Dennis. Before Dennis could react, Dutch's beefy sidekick clamped a vice-like grip on the skinny teen, rendering him immobile. The air grew thick with tension, sweat, and adolescent bravado.

Jeremy heard the gut-wrenching sound of a fist thudding against flesh.

Dennis's breath whooshed out in a painful grunt, and his body crumpled like discarded paper under the force of the blow.

Basking in his dominance, Dutch looked down at Dennis and sneered as he barked at his lackey. "Pick him up!"

On command, the goon hoisted Dennis up like a rag doll, his limbs flailing as he tried to break free.

However, the sheer physical advantage of Dutch and his henchman quickly countered Dennis' desperate attempts to escape. The duo exchanged a wicked look. Their synchronized chuckles were hauntingly harmonious as they sang, "Swirly time!"

Jeremy's heart raced faster as they dragged the helpless Dennis towards the stalls. The predatory pair were blissfully unaware of the one stall that wasn't vacant. The one occupied by Dennis' ever-present guardian angel.

As their footsteps grew louder, echoing in the narrow confines of the bathroom, Jeremy braced himself. He was about to be thrust into a confrontation he didn't want to be a part of, one that he couldn't avoid, not with Dennis's safety on the line.

As Dutch and his sidekick approached the stall, the shadows cast by the dim overhead lighting shifted, momentarily revealing Jeremy's sneakers beneath the stall's partition.

"Let him go!" Jeremy demanded in a firm tone as he exited the doorless stall. Time seemed to stop as realization dawned on Dutch's face.

"Anderson!" Dutch exclaimed, his eyes widening in surprise, replacing his previously overconfident demeanor. The odds had changed.

Dennis's limp body seemed to gain some life.

"Jeremy!" he gasped, his voice filled with relief. The mere presence of Jeremy had shifted the dynamic in the room, making the walls close in on Dutch and his goon.

Jeremy didn't hesitate. Stepping out from the shadows, standing eye to eye with Dutch, he commanded again, "I said let him go, Dutchie," this time with more force than before, his voice steady, resonating with authority.

Dennis's captors hesitated before eventually releasing their grip on him.

Jeremy stepped forward, piercing Dutch with a glare that seemed to see right through him. "We're going to settle this, Dutchie, right here, right now."

The atmosphere was intense. For a moment, the only sound was the muted hum of the fluorescent lights overhead.

"Beat it, wimp," Dutch sneered as Dennis made his way to the exit. His eyes then shifted to his sidekick, giving a subtle jerk of his head, indicating for him to leave. The goon lingered, his loyalty to Dutch making him reluctant to abandon him.

With a steely gaze, Jeremy looked at him and warned, "If you lay so much as a finger on him again, it'll be the last thing you ever do, understand?"

Seeking guidance, the thug's eyes darted to Dutch. With a subtle nod from his would-be leader, he took it as his cue to retreat. Disappearing with a swagger and a final wary glance at Jeremy, he left the two alone in the bathroom.

———————

The electric atmosphere grew even more charged as Dutch and Jeremy stood facing each other. While they had once been as close as brothers, time and circumstances had driven a wedge between them. The intensity of their shared gaze softened as Jeremy broke the silence, his tone infused with frustration and brotherly concern.

"Seriously, Dutchie, why do you always have to be such a dick to Dennis?"

Casually leaning against the bathroom sink, Dutch shot Jeremy a sideways glance. "He's soft, Jer. If he's ever going to survive in the real world, he's gotta toughen up. Think of it as me giving him a crash course in some tough love," He smirked as he dropped his shoulders and gave a nonchalant shrug, clearly not expecting a physical confrontation with Jeremy. "He's gotta toughen up. I'm doing him a favor, teaching him to stand up for himself."

With his arms crossed, Jeremy shot back, "Dutchie, we both know Dennis is never going to stand up to you, not in the way you're pushing for. He's not built for the kind of 'lessons' you're trying to teach him. He just wants to keep his head down, do his own thing, and be left in peace. Can't you just leave him alone? He doesn't need your 'tough love.'"

Jeremy's mind flashed back to Gregg's words, the familiar justification echoing in his ears—"tough love." He refocused, the sting of that memory sharp and fresh.

"Dennis is trying Dutchie. He's doing his best, finding his own path. He doesn't need to be knocked down by you every step of the way. One day, he'll surprise you with what he becomes." He hesitated as he said the last words.

He knew exactly who Dennis was now and who he would be. He couldn't help but admire Dennis's journey, especially witnessing his trans-formation in college. It was there that Dennis would end up meeting his own kind of people; he'd find himself and gain confidence in who he was. He was destined to grow into a great man, a committed husband, and a caring father. Dennis got what he always wanted in each of Jeremy's lives: a quiet and happy life.

Dutch seemed momentarily taken aback by Jeremy, but before he could respond, Jeremy continued.

"You're better than this, man. The Dutchie I used to know, the guy I grew up with, was different. Where's that guy?"

Jeremy could no longer see the spark that once shined bright in Dutch's eyes. The dreams and aspirations of a young boy full of hope were long gone.

Across countless lifetimes, Jeremy had witnessed the repeated and inevitable tragedy of Dutch's early and violent end. Each attempt to inter-vene, to change the trajectory of Dutch's fate, had ended with an agonizing and soul-crushing failure. The echo of these defeats haunted Jeremy's soul.

Yet, in his heart, hope flickered, refusing to be extinguished. He hoped for Dutch to find peace, not just for the sake of everyone at Huxley High who dealt with the brunt of Dutch's anger, but for Dutch himself.

Lost in this fantasy, he met Dutch's eyes, and memories of happier times surfaced. Perhaps the true salvation wasn't in changing Dutch's inevitable end but in altering the quality of the days he had left. He wondered if maybe he could help Dutch find a sense of purpose that might, in some cosmic way, offer peace to his restless soul.

He took a deep breath, trying to reconnect with the person he once knew.

"Dutchie, I know the guy you are under all that tough exterior. I've seen it." He paused, "How about we make a deal? You lay off Dennis, stop the bullying, and in exchange, I'll promise to have your back whenever you need it."

Dutchie's eyes narrowed, his defenses going up. "Oh, how generous of you," he replied sarcastically. "I don't need a savior, especially not you. I'm doing just fine. I don't need your charity, bud."

"That's not what I meant, Dutchie," Jeremy said with a hint of a smile, knowing exactly where to go next, his eyes sparkling with mischief. "Remember the game against Beecher Middle in 8th grade?"

Dutchie's eyes lit up at the memory. "Hell yeah, I do! I was on fire that day. I threw for 325 yards. Not bad for a 13-year-old, huh?" He chuckled, a hint of boyish pride peeking through his tough facade.

"And after our big win?" Jeremy prompted with a knowing smirk on his face.

Dutch grinned. "Oh yeah! Del somehow scored us invites to that high school party. Man, walking in there, we were so cool."

"We weren't just cool, Dutch," Jeremy said, his tone wistful. "We were legends in the making. For one night, it felt like we were on the verge of greatness, about to rule the world."

Dutch hesitated for a moment, then sighed, "Julie Nichols, man. Such a babe."

"Exactly!" Jeremy said, smirking. "She thought you were older, all thanks to me. I told her you were my sophomore cousin visiting from Canada. Do you remember what happened between you two?"

Dutch's face instantly flushed, a hint of the boyish charm peeking through. "Yeah, man. It was awesome."

"That was your first real kiss, wasn't it?" Jeremy prodded.

Dutch scratched the back of his neck, sheepishly admitting, "Yeah, It was."

Jeremy leaned in, eyes locked onto Dutch's. "So, you could say that without me, that magic moment wouldn't have happened. You owe me, Dutchie. You owe me big time."

Jeremy watched as a brief moment of vulnerability flickered in Dutch's eyes before his tough demeanor snapped back into place.

"Alright, alright, I'll lay off the kid," Dutch grumbled, folding his arms defensively.

"Look, Dutchie," Jeremy began, choosing his words carefully. "I'm not here to babysit or control you. But I do remember the bond we once had." Reaching into his pocket, he pulled out the $100 bill and held it out. "This isn't charity. It's just so you don't have to hassle kids for their lunch money. Maybe you can get yourself something decent to eat."

Dutch stared at the bill, clearly battling with his pride. After a moment, he took it, nodding slightly. "Thanks, man," he mumbled, not quite meeting Jeremy's eyes.

"Anytime"— Jeremy responded, dipping his head trying to connect his eyes to Dutch's, "and hey, this stays between us, okay?"

Dutch lifted his eyes, a hint of the old fire returning. "It better, or there'll be hell to pay."

But even as he said it, Jeremy sensed his voice's absence of genuine menace. The moment was a truce between past friends.

Jeremy held Dutch's gaze for a moment, sensing the layers of pain and frustration underneath.

The anger and defiance was all an act, a defense mechanism built over the years to protect him from the world's harsh judgments. Jeremy realized that beneath the rugged exterior, Dutch was still the kid he'd grown up with, still carrying the weight of dreams lost and potentials unfulfilled. He could see the internal conflict in Dutch's eyes, a clash between the person he once was and the person he thought he needed to be.

Both stood in a silent acknowledgment of their shared history. Jeremy hoped that in this moment of vulnerability, Dutch would remember the potential he once held and, perhaps, find a way back to it. Jeremy felt a renewed sense of purpose, but when he thought he had Dutch figured out, an unexpected comment surprised him.

"Oh hey," Regional tomorrow, "you've got to cover Tony Jefferson, right? Dutch asked, not looking away from his reflection.

"Yeah— why? Jeremy replied, confused.

"He's really good, but he always leans left before a post, back off a little, give him some cushion," Dutch offered.

"Uh, Okay, thanks," Jeremy's eyes furrowed, "I thought you didn't care about football anymore, Dutchie."

"I don't care about football," he said as he turned to look at Jeremy. "I'm just saying, you guys are going to get totally smoked tomorrow night. I just thought you could use the tip." He shrugged, checking his reflection in the mirror, smoothing back his long hair, "You guys are way better than what McHale lets you be. It's total bullshit."

"You know, Dutch, there's still time for you to—" Jeremy started.

"Alright, Anderson," Dutch murmured, cutting Jeremy off, pushing away from the sink's edge, "It's been nice chatting with you, but I've got more important shit to do."

With a brief nod, he walked out, letting the bathroom door swing closed behind him.

Alone among the faded graffiti and years of Dutch's rebellious declarations scrawled on the walls, Jeremy sighed.

"Could've been worse," he thought, attempting to find some humor in the aftermath, hoping he hadn't caused tremendous ripples that might throw his quest off course.

Glancing in the mirror, he washed his hands and collected his thoughts.

Dutch, Missy, and the mysterious envelope in his backpack all battled for his attention. He needed a moment to himself, a break from the chaos. He needed to sort out his mind.

He was still transitioning back to his youth, and he was drained. The first day of a reset was always the hardest. It was a day where he was sucked from an existence he'd grown into, and accepted, and forced back to the starting gate. The process was exhausting.

He splashed some water on his face and dried off with the inside of his t-shirt. Taking a deeper look at himself in the mirror, he inspected his youthful face and became weary of his placement in now his 26th life.

"Great start," he said to his reflection before grabbing his book bag and its mysterious contents, throwing it over one shoulder, and heading for the door.

After exiting the bathroom, Jeremy found a secluded corner in the nearly empty hallway. Slumping down against the cool brick wall, he reached into his backpack and pulled out the envelope again. The secrets within taunted him as his fingers traced its edges.

What could be such a big deal that his father never wanted it? What curse was Gregg talking about in his horrible note? Jeremy had never known, not in any lifetime, any burden so significant that would cause his father such difficulty.

Suddenly, the piercing sound of the bell echoed through the hallway, and a crowd of students spilled out. Caught up in his thoughts, he'd completely lost track of time. He shoved the envelope into his backpack. The bell's shrill tone yanked him back into the present. "History!" He gasped.

For him, this particular class was a waste of time—hours lost in multiple, repeated lives spent listening to Mr. Deegan's lectures. Studying history when he had explicit knowledge of multiple futures seemed senseless. Most believe that history is doomed to repeat itself. Often, for Jeremy, so was the future.

As he was swept up in the flow of students hurrying to their next class, Jeremy heard a commotion behind him, marked by the distinct sound of pushing and shoving that could only be Stacy making her way through the crowd.

"Hey you!" she shouted over the dull roar of high school class transition, "the blonde jerk with the baby blues—wait up!"

He looked back to see her slicing through the sea of his classmates like a knife through warm butter.

With her wild brown hair and equally fierce eyes circled in a healthy amount of dark eyeshadow, Stacy was impossible to ignore. Her voice, always a mix of theatrics and mischief, seemed to bounce off the walls, reaching Jeremy's ears above the crowd's murmur.

Turning to face her, he watched her navigate the crowd with grace, pushing past students with a finesse that was uniquely her own. Her expression sparkled as her eyes locked onto him. She moved with tremendous agility, weaving against the flow of students with no resistance.

"Jeremy Anderson!" she huffed, finally catching up and slightly out of breath, her cheeks flushed. "Do you ever stop, or is 'fast and elusive' your permanent setting?" she teased, poking him in the ribs as the two rejoined the flow of students. "We missed you at lunch; where were you? Off sucking face with Big Red?"

Stacy hated Kristen with the heat of a thousand suns. While most saw Kristen as the queen of the universe, to Stacy, she wasn't good enough to be anywhere near Jeremy's orbit.

He chuckled, "What can I say, Stace? I had something to do." His tone was light, not letting her in.

She rolled her eyes dramatically, "Well if you'd hold on for just a second, I've got something for you." Reaching into her bag, she pulled out his journal.

"I think you left this in English," she said, handing it over. "I saw it sitting on one of the back shelves when I had Pritchett in third period, and I was going to give it to you at lunch, but you were a ghost," she sang in a spooky tone.

"Don't worry, I didn't read any of it. I couldn't bear to; I'll bet it's loaded with sugar-sweet love poems to Miss Cherry Bomb," she punctuated with a gag.

He accepted the journal with a grateful nod while dismissing the verbal assault on Kristen. "Thanks, Stace."

Her eyes held a hint of concern. "Something's up with you today, I know it." Her expression momentarily turned from devil to guardian angel. I saw it all over your face this morning. What is it? Bad day, bad month, bad year?"

He gave a half-smile, "Yeah, you could say that."

Suddenly, her face transformed; her mouth dropped open in shock, and she gasped, "Oh -my -God, it's your birthday! How did I not remember?" Her voice wavered between guilt and disbelief but quickly rallied with her distinctive playfulness. "Seriously," she groaned, "I am the absolute worst friend ever. I'm really sorry, dude. You must think I am a real shit for forgetting."

"No, it's not that," he replied, gently dismissing her concern. It's just been a crazy day so far."

"Tell me all about it later," she offered, her standard mischievous expression returning. We'll hang out; I totally owe you."

"I might have a few things to do after practice," he added.

"I'll be home after 7—just come by whenever. You'll talk, and I'll listen. We'll unpack whatever is rattling around in that skull of yours," she chuckled, tapping him on the forehead.

"Okay, Stace. I'll try to stop over," he agreed, a small smile breaking through his melancholy expression.

"Well, see you around handsome," she winked before dashing off, her wild mane waving as she bopped through the crowd, shouting for everyone to clear a path for her.

A sense of irony hit him as he reached the door to his history class. Here he was, about to study historical events of significance when he had lived through countless versions of the future. The door handle felt cold under his grip, and for a brief moment, he wished he could escape, leave it all behind. But he couldn't. He had to stick to the script and maintain the order.

So, with a resigned sigh, Jeremy walked into the classroom. Sliding into his usual seat in the back of the class, he pulled out his textbook and pretended to be just another student.

17

SUPER PISSED

Mr. Deegan droned on with his lesson, a monologue so familiar to Jeremy that he could recite it backward. "He really is the worst," Jeremy thought as he looked over the middle-aged teacher in the same plaid suit he'd worn every day, every class, in every lifetime.

Jeremy's eyes drifted to the window, yearning for the freedom of the outside world. He'd promised himself a flawless run for this cycle. Yet, the early confrontations with his father, Missy, and now Dutch, had thrown him off balance.

There was a peculiar sameness in the air, but with an undercurrent of something different, something shifting.

From his multiple lifetimes, he had become skilled at recognizing which moments in time could be reshaped and which ones were stubbornly set in stone. No matter the approach, no matter the strategy, some outcomes just wouldn't budge.

This thought, the unchangeability of some events, gnawed at him the most.

Even in a world of endless do-overs, there was a rhythm to life, a series of events that, for most people, shifted and changed with every decision. But for Jeremy, the road was all too familiar. Even when he veered off the beaten path, there were landmarks, events, and choices that seemed immovable, like boulders in a flowing stream.

His eyes settled on Missy, who sat a few rows ahead. She looked no worse for wear after their earlier collision, but he couldn't help but feel guilty. As much as he knew some moments were fixed, there was always the temptation, the belief that perhaps he could change the outcomes this time. Every reset came with a fresh set of hope and pain.

As his mind wandered, droning out Mr. Deegan's monotone dissertation on The Cold War, Jeremy's head became filled with a whirlwind of thoughts. He drifted to the two looming tragedies that shadowed Huxley High's graduating class of '96. The events would cast an unseen shadow over the school's bright and hopeful atmosphere. There was a twisted pattern in play, one that he had witnessed over countless lifetimes. One that he could not change.

With his rebellious streak and untamed spirit, Dutch was always a ticking time bomb. In every replay of Jeremy's life, Dutch's tragic end was an inevitable chapter. The Wyatt family curse was local folklore, but its pull was undeniable. What pained Jeremy the most was that Dutch's impending doom often played a part in another's tragic fate.

With her untapped potential and future brimming with possibilities, Missy stood in opposition to Dutch's chaotic existence. Yet, their destinies seemed intertwined, like two stars caught in a tragic dance of cosmic fate.

Dutch's fall would be discussed in hushed tones and viewed as the unfortunate end to the Wyatt legacy—a reflection of a family history filled with heartbreak and tragedy.

Missy's end, however, would send ripples of grief through Huxley High. A bright future was extinguished too soon, leaving a trail of unfulfilled dreams and the haunting question of what might have been.

The school's memory of them would take on distinctly different tones: Dutch would be remembered with a sense of sad inevitability and hope that the Wyatt family's tragic tale had ended.

On the other hand, Missy would be remembered with profound sorrow and a lingering feeling of the potential that was never realized.

Yet, as time passed and new batches of students filled Huxley High's halls, their stories faded, eventually finding a quiet resting place on a forgotten yearbook page tucked away on a dusty shelf, rarely to be revisited.

This tragic tale had a consistent element at its center: Dutch's notorious Turismo.

The car's presence was impossible to miss in the Huxley High parking lot. Each time its engine roared, it overpowered even the piercing bell that signaled the end of class. Just like Dutch himself, the car was bold, brash, and teetering on the brink of disaster. Its overworked engine and battered exterior made it far from a sight for sore eyes. Yet, in a way, it was the perfect extension of Dutch. The car's unruly nature mirrored his rebellious spirit. More than just a way to get from point A to point B, the Turismo was a loud, glaring symbol of Dutch's defiance. With all its flaws and raw power, it wasn't just a car but an unapologetic declaration of Dutch's wild essence on four wheels.

It would be no surprise that when Dutch met his end, it was behind the wheel of that awful machine.

However, what was genuinely heart-wrenching was how Missy always seemed to get caught in the crosshairs of Dutch's automotive recklessness.

Time and time again, Missy's fate was cruelly intertwined with Dutch and the Turismo's path of destruction. Whether she found herself as an unintended victim in a neighboring car or simply an innocent pedestrian, Missy seemed inescapably drawn into the car's tragic trajectory.

On one agonizing occasion, she was casually walking by a known intersection when the Turismo, pushed beyond reason, hurtled directly into a telephone pole. As the car crumpled and smoke began to rise, Missy, driven by courage, raced to pull Dutch from the mangled wreckage. But just as she was about to reach him, the vehicle exploded into a fireball, the sudden blast snuffing out their young lives in an instant.

Certain elements never wavered in every replay of events: Dutch's notorious Turismo, his careless actions, and the unexplained way Missy always got caught in the crossfire.

For Jeremy, the pain he felt wasn't just from seeing their tragedies unfold but from the soul-crushing predictability of it all. No matter how hard he tried or how many lifetimes he'd lived, their destinies were set in stone. The force binding Jeremy to this ceaseless loop of life seemed to have a cruel grip on Dutch and Missy, too.

But what if he could rewrite that story?

Jeremy knew that while he couldn't change the dark cloud hanging over Dutch and Missy's futures, he could, however, try to bring some light to their present.

Lost in thought, Jeremy made a silent promise to himself, and whatever mysterious force ruled his existence. If he couldn't save their lives, maybe he could influence how they would be remembered.

Dutch had more layers than most gave him credit for. Sure, he had his wild side, especially when behind the wheel of that notorious car. But Jeremy had seen glimpses of a different Dutch, one who laughed genuinely, showed raw pain, and occasionally let his guard down to do something unexpectedly sweet. If Jeremy could somehow highlight those moments, maybe the students at Huxley High would see past the bully and remember Dutch for the complex person he was.

Missy's fate was undeniably tragic, but Jeremy could help craft a legacy that celebrated her life rather than mourn her death. Instead of becoming a faded cautionary tale, her memory could inspire change, pushing her peers to live their lives with more purpose and passion.

Jeremy found himself with unwavering determination. With the wisdom gained from lifetimes lived over and over, he planned to create new legacies for Dutch and Missy. His goal was simple yet profound: to ensure they were remembered for the positive impacts they made, not just the way their stories ended.

This plan fit with his bigger picture—his future reunion with Cassandra. As long as he managed to be in the right place at the right time, specifically visiting Del at UMass in the spring of '99, everything would fall into place.

The bell's shrill ring yanked Jeremy back to the reality of the classroom. A distinct clatter grabbed his attention as students hustled about, preparing to head to their next class. At the front of the room, Missy grappled with crutches, books, and a rebellious backpack.

"Jesus Christ! Crutches?" he internally gasped, taken aback by the scene. He was so consumed in his thoughts that he hadn't noticed them tucked under her desk. He got up to help her, making sure not to rush and seeming too eager. After their awkward moments earlier, he realized that moving too fast wasn't helping his case. He waited for the right moment, but the next thing he knew, he was staring. And again, she caught him.

When their eyes locked, Missy, showing off her surprising, playful streak again, teased, "Back at it with the staring, huh? — I thought we'd covered this earlier." Her lips curled into a playful smirk, "Aren't you the resident hero here? Feel like lending a hand?"

He chuckled, still caught off-guard by this bolder version of her. "Who even is this girl?" he thought to himself. The Missy he remembered was always composed, never this feisty.

Her teasing smile mellowed a bit, giving way to a more genuine warmth. "So, are you just going to stand there, or are you going to give a girl a hand?"

"Of course," he said, moving quickly as the room emptied. Hurrying over, he gathered her belongings. "Let me walk you to your next class," he offered.

Raising an eyebrow and in a playful tone, she accepted, "Considering you're the reason I'm like this, it's the least you could do."

A blush tinted his cheeks, but he rallied with a soft smile, extending his arm for support. The understanding in their eyes spoke volumes, hinting at gratitude and shared secrets from earlier encounters. This day had taken their dynamic to a different level; one neither had seen coming.

"Let's wait a bit; let the halls clear out," he suggested, hoping to make their journey less chaotic. "Which class are you heading to next?"

"Home Economics," she replied.

His eyebrows shot up in surprise. "Home-ec? Isn't that considered a breeze class? I thought only jocks took it for an easy period and a guaranteed good grade."

A shade of pink spread across her face. "I like cooking, okay? For your information, I'm also taking courses at WNEC, and I plan on transferring the credits to Boston College in the fall. I want to get a jump on my bachelor's right after graduation. I plan on having my Master's in 4 years.

Taken aback, he remarked, "I had no idea, that's impressive. It sounds like you have a solid plan." His eyes sparkled with admiration, even though he already knew she always excelled at everything she did.

"Hold on a sec," Jeremy said, pausing at the classroom door. Let me grab some late passes from Deegan. We don't need to rush and risk another injury."

She smirked, "We're really batting a hundred today, aren't we?"

"Actually, Missy, 'batting a hundred' isn't really—" he began to correct her before catching himself and waving it off. "Never mind. Just give me a moment."

Jeremy initiated some sports talk using his usual charm and tapping into Mr. Deegan's known weakness.

"You think the Pats will clinch the AFC East this year?" Jeremy asked. Knowing the teacher's passion for sports always served Jeremy well. "I don't know," Deegan replied, "4-3 is a pretty good start. We've got the Bills this weekend; they'll be tough to beat. Thank God we have Bledsoe, what a cannon!"

Jeremy nodded in agreement as Missy watched on, puzzled. To her, it was like they were speaking a foreign language.

After a brief chat and a few predictions, Jeremy secured the late passes.

With their buffer against tardiness in hand and the second bell ringing in the distance, the two made their way through the now quieter halls.

He noticed how easily she managed her crutches as they navigated the hallway. The rhythmic thud of the rubber bases and the soft creak of the aluminum were in sync with their steps.

"So," he began, wanting to fill the silence that had settled between them, "What's your specialty in the kitchen?"

"Brownies," she chuckled, "and before you say anything, not that kind of brownies. Just the regular, gooey, chocolaty kind."

He laughed, "I wouldn't have guessed. So, are you an aspiring pastry chef or is it just a hobby?"

She tilted her head, thinking. "A bit of both, I guess. I've always loved being in the kitchen. Baking is like therapy for me. It's easy; you follow the recipe, and if you do it right, you'll end up with something wonderful. Life, on the other hand," she gestured with a crutch to her current situation, "isn't always as predictable."

He nodded, absorbing her words. "That's a unique perspective, but I get it. In a world full of uncertainties, finding one thing you can control and predict can be comforting."

She glanced at him, her eyes reflecting a depth he hadn't noticed before. "It sounds like you speak from experience," she said.

Looking away, he considered how much he should say. "Let's just say I've seen enough to value the predictable moments."

Their path through the hallway was briefly interrupted by a parade of cheerleaders, their giggles and light-hearted banter echoing off the lockers. As they neared, one of them, Heather Langford, flashed a playful smirk at Jeremy.

"Hey Jer-bear!" she sang, with a teasing tone in her voice. Heather, with her polished preppy appearance, always reminded Jeremy of Kristen-lite.

"Kristen's been on the warpath looking for you," Heather said with faux concern, batting her eyelashes dramatically. "You stood her up at lunch. Not cool, Anderson."

Playing along, he raised an eyebrow, "On a scale from one to ten, how pissed is she?"

"Remember the gum incident with Dutch last year?" Heather quipped, referencing a well-known school saga.

He groaned, rolling his eyes, "So, she's super pissed. Got it."

Missy stood quietly beside him, holding back a laugh.

Heather winked at Jeremy, her warning clear. "You better watch out," she sang as she sashayed away, flanked by the rest of the cheerleading squad.

Missy looked at Jeremy, amused. "So, super pissed is?"

He sighed, "not good," he said before launching into the tale surrounding the "gum incident."

"I'm not sure if you know this, but Kristen's hair isn't just hair to her. It's her pride and joy. She makes sure that it is always meticulously cared for and always styled perfectly. I mean, she takes hours to get ready to go anywhere," he groaned.

"I see." she nodded with a smirk that showed that she knew exactly what he was talking about.

He continued, "Last year, right before school broke for the holidays, we were all on the bus after school, and Dutchie was in one of his moods— wanting to show off."

Her eyebrows furrowed, clearly picturing the scene, "Let me guess, Kristen was his unsuspecting victim?"

He nodded. "Yup, he thought sticking gum in her hair would be hilarious, hoping everyone would find it as funny as he did. But man, he couldn't have been more wrong.

When Kristen realized what he'd done, the entire bus went silent. She turned on him with a fury I haven't seen since, and I never want to see again. She tore into him with words I didn't know she even knew. For a moment, I thought Dutchie genuinely regretted being born."

She let out a low groan. "Ugh, Sounds like quite a scene. I'm almost sorry I missed it."

He chuckled, "Trust me, it was one for the ages. Dutchie learned the hard way not to mess with Kristen, especially not her hair."

She winced sympathetically. "Ouch. And those girls? They're part of your group?"

He laughed, "They're more like Kristen's entourage. I just happen to be in their orbit because of shared interests."

As the dust from Heather's dramatic exit settled, Missy's pace slowed. She turned to Jeremy with a vulnerable look in her eyes. "Can I ask you something without sounding too strange?"

Taken aback by the sudden change in tone, he nodded. "Of course. What's on your mind?"

She hesitated, steadied herself with her crutches, and took a deep breath before continuing. "What's Kristen really like these days?" she asked.

He blinked in surprise. "What do you mean?

She looked down, her fingers fidgeting with her crutch handle. "I guess what I'm trying to say is that Kristen and I were inseparable before high school. But when we both were here at Huxley, things changed. "I focused on schoolwork, getting good grades, and the debate team." Searching for the right words, she trailed off.

"Kristen chose the popular crowd, pep rallies, and well, you." Her soft voice revealed the complexity of her feelings. "She was my best friend, and she just let me go. I didn't change. I've always been this way, but to her, I became invisible."

He processed her words. He'd occasionally seen Missy in some of Kristen's old photos. They were usually brought out during family gatherings when Kristen's mom felt nostalgic. But he never knew the depth of their past friendship.

"Damn, Missy, I never knew any of that," he confessed, his eyes meeting hers again. "I'm really sorry. This must be so hard for you."

Her eyes held a distant sadness, "life's a journey, right? It's just hard seeing her become the life of the party while I'm left wondering where I fit in." She took a deep breath before continuing, a hint of bitterness creeping into her voice. "When I started at Huxley a year early, we drifted apart. I thought once she got here the next year, everything would go back to the way it was. But she had changed—new friends, new interests, she was a whole new person. I became a ghost from her past."

She looked away, struggling with her emotions. "It's more than her just moving on, Jeremy. Sometimes, it feels like she hates me. Earlier today, during lunch, I was sitting alone, minding my own business, and I felt this intense glare on me. I looked up, and there she was, across the cafeteria, staring at me with such hatred. We haven't talked in years, but I don't know. That look she gave me said it all.

"Missy, I've never heard Kristen say anything bad about you." He offered before continuing, "Though, honestly, she hasn't mentioned you much at all." He immediately regretted the last part, realizing it might not be what she wanted to hear.

She sighed, "That's the thing, being talked about negatively would be one thing. But being completely forgotten? That's even worse."

Chewing on his lower lip, he took in her words. "You deserve better than to be forgotten, Missy," he said, his voice sincere.

She gave a half-laugh, "That's easy for you to say. You're pretty much at the center of the Huxley High universe."

"That doesn't mean I don't see what's around me," he replied, looking into her eyes. "And for the record, high school isn't the universe. It's just a tiny speck in the grand scheme of things."

She tilted her head, considering his words. "You're right. This isn't forever."

His eyes stayed on her for a moment, the weight of his knowledge pressing heavily on him. As much as he wanted to brush off the high school drama and reassure her of the bright future she had ahead of her, he knew better.

He tried to find the right words, something comforting, but he knew he was on delicate ground.

"Sometimes people grow apart," he began carefully, "not because they want to, but because of the paths they choose or the pressures they face. Sometimes things just happen without explanation or any way to stop them."

She looked down, her fingers still picking at the handle of her crutch. "I know, I get it. High School is tough, but it doesn't make it any easier when it feels like our friendship never meant anything. I feel like I was so easily replaced."

He paused, taking a moment before responding, "Missy, no one can replace you. You have your unique qualities and strengths. Just because you and Kristen have drifted apart doesn't mean your friendship never meant anything."

She looked up, her eyes a mix of gratitude and sadness. "It's just hard sometimes, especially when it feels like our past never existed."

He paused, drawing from the insights of his many lifetimes.

"Missy, sometimes people make choices that seem right for themselves, but they don't consider how those choices affect everyone around them. When you skipped eighth grade, she probably didn't know what to do. Maybe she thought that she needed to find a new group to fit in, and when she did, it just fit a bit too well."

She nodded slowly, "But why did she need to leave me behind? We had so many memories together."

He took a deep breath, collecting his thoughts before speaking. "Sometimes, people reinvent themselves in high school. They're trying to figure out who they are and where they belong, and they make choices based on perceptions and the pressures around them. Maybe she thought being associated with the 'academic crowd' wouldn't fit into the new person she was trying to be. It doesn't make it right, but it might not be as personal as you think."

She looked thoughtful for a moment, "So you think she just got lost in this new version of herself?"

He shrugged, "Maybe— high school is a confusing time. We all get a little lost trying to find our way." He managed a weak smile, his heart heavy with the knowledge of what lay ahead for her.

She glanced at him, her eyes searching for understanding. "It's just hard. When we were younger, we promised each other we'd always be best friends, and then it's like she just moved on without looking back."

"I get it," he spoke softly. "But sometimes, people go on different journeys, and that's okay. Maybe Kristen is on her own path and figuring things out. And who knows? Maybe she'll realize what she left behind."

She bit her lip. "I wish I could believe that. It's just that every time I see her laughing with her friends, I wish I were a part of it. I guess I'm just not cool enough."

He looked at her intently. "You can't measure your worth by someone else's actions. You are incredibly cool in your own way, and just because Kristen's on a different path right now doesn't mean your memories and time together didn't matter.

The two continued walking, reaching the home economics room. As they approached the door, she turned to him. "Thanks, Jeremy," she said, "For listening. I guess my brother is right about you."

"Oh yeah, how so?" he inquired, half knowing the answer.

"Oh please," she groaned, coming back to her regular form. "You're his absolute hero; he never shuts up about you, follows all your sporting events, and hasn't missed a single game." She said, rolling her eyes. "He's positive you guys are going to win tomorrow night. "

He gave her a reassuring smile. "He's a good dude."

"He sure is," she responded, looking into the classroom awaiting her. "You should come to the game tomorrow night; you might have fun," he said, handing her the textbooks under his arm.

"If I do, will you score a home run for me?" she said, batting her eyelashes beneath her glasses.

Half shocked by the statement and half surprised to see the feisty version of Missy come back out for a jab, he shook his head, "You're not really a sports fan, are you, Missy?"

"No, not really," she chuckled.

He couldn't help but wonder again, "Who is this girl, and where has she been hiding?"

Today had thrown him for a loop. He'd seen a side of Missy that was totally new to him, and that meant something considering how many times he'd been through this life.

Usually, Missy was the girl everyone overlooked. The times he'd gotten to know her, trying and failing to play the hero in her story, she never showed any hint of this spark. It was like she'd been a black-and-white photo that was suddenly turned into this full-color version of herself.

It was weird. The fire she had when she ripped him apart for nearly running her over in his Jeep or when she shredded him for giving her a perfect form tackle that would make Lawrence Taylor proud.

It was real spirit, and these flirtations, is that what they were? he asked himself. He remembered her earlier comment, "Hey, Homecoming," replaying it in his head. This Missy was starting to grow on him.

"You should probably head in. It looks like class is starting," he said as he held the door open for her. "After you, chef."

She bowed mockingly as he gingerly handed her the books he'd been carrying for her.

"Why thank you, kind sir." As she entered the classroom, she turned, her playful demeanor switching to sincere gratitude. " Thanks for helping me out, Jeremy; today has been unexpected."

He smiled, "Anytime, Missy. Take care and save me a brownie."

"Only if you promise not to knock me over again," she said with a wink.

He chuckled, "Deal."

Walking away, he couldn't help but reflect on the day's events. Despite the chaos and unexpected turns, moments like these made it all worthwhile. As he headed to his next class, he felt a renewed determination to make a difference however he could.

18

BIG GULPS AND BIGGER GULPS

Sitting in seventh-period Biology, Jeremy's stomach growled ravenously, echoing his growing hunger pains. It felt like a beast straight out of a cheesy USA Up-All-Night horror movie was thrashing within him. The idea of enduring football practice without any nourishment was an unbearable thought.

"Didn't he have half of a Pop-Tart abandoned in his locker?" he thought. Even if he did, that was hardly a meal. He truly craved something substantial: food that would tide him over and get him through practice and the rest of the day. Jeremy pictured a quick dash to 7-11 before heading to the locker room. He couldn't shake the thought of nachos dripping with that golden fake cheese, paired with a couple of Big Bites and a Super Gulp filled to the brim with Mountain Dew. That was a feast fit for a king.

However, the end of class wasn't exactly a clear escape path. Students would be milling around, wasting time, and even worse, teachers would be looking for troublemakers in the break between the final bell and extracurriculars.

The clock seemed to crawl, but as the end of class neared, Jeremy made his move. He shot his hand into the air, disrupting the room's ambient noises.

Mr. Burns, engrossed in grading papers, looked up with surprise.

"Mr. Burns," Jeremy began, trying to keep his voice steady, "I was hoping I could leave a little early today." His request caused heads to turn and look at him. It wasn't often that someone requested an early dismissal, especially not someone like him, who was often at the center of things.

The teacher leaned back in his chair, studying his student. "What's the reason?" he asked.

Jeremy quickly offered his excuse: "I've been helping Missy Winston since she's on crutches. I need a head start to meet her at her class so I can help her get through the halls before they get too crowded." He explained, hoping his reasoning came off as sincere.

"You always seem to find a way to assist a peer, Mr. Anderson," the teacher responded, his mouth curling upwards in a slight smile. "Remember, actions speak louder than words, and yours often resonate."

Jeremy smirked, trying to hide his relief. "Thanks, Mr. Burns. I appreciate it!"

Quickly, he zipped up his bag while heading to the hallway, keeping his eyes peeled as he maneuvered through the maze-like halls of the school. As he walked, his mind raced back to Missy, the guilt gnawing at him for using her situation to his advantage.

Just as he thought he'd finally found a brief escape, he felt a force as strong as a hurricane blindside him. The sheer power of the blow almost sent him crashing to the floor, the weighty textbooks in his bag not helping his balance.

Gathering himself, he spun around to find the source of the ambush. Bathed in fluorescent light, casting a shadow on the lockers behind him, stood Del. His familiar smile was wide and cheeky, the mischief in his eyes unmistakable—it was the very expression that Jeremy had come to term as Del's signature 'shit-eating grin'."

"Well, look who it is," Del quipped, his voice dripping with fake sincerity, "the ghost of my best friend who's been playing hide-and-seek all day. What's going on, birthday boy?"

With a wince, Jeremy said, "Clean hit, man," rubbing the sore spot on his ribs where his friend's playful ambush had landed.

Del raised his hands in mock surrender, "Hey, my bad, I just felt like I owed you for not wishing you a happy birthday earlier; between you almost becoming roadkill thanks to Dutchie's Evel Knievel impression and the usual school chaos, it slipped my mind."

Jeremy waved him off, the corners of his mouth tugging into a slight grin. "Honestly, with the day I've had so far, I forgot it was my birthday too."

Del studied him for a moment, concern lining his face. "You okay, man?"

Jeremy nodded, glancing down the hall. "Yeah, it's just been one of those days. Speaking of which, I'm starving. I'm about to make a dash to 7-11 before McHale's drill session at practice. Wanna come with?"

A glint of excitement flashed in Del's eyes. "Hell yeah! You know that I'm always down for a snack run. Let's do it, my treat."

Jeremy grinned, "Perfect. But let's be quick about it. I'm trying to fly under the radar today."

"Why so stealthy today, Jer?" Del inquired as they walked out of the school and towards the parking lot.

Jeremy shot Del a sidelong glance, a smirk playing on his lips. "Let's just say it's been a day full of unexpected run-ins. I'm trying to keep a low profile for the rest of it."

Del, intrigued, raised an eyebrow, "Sounds mysterious. Anyone I should be wary of?" Jeremy chuckled, "Not wary, just prepared. You know Missy Winston?"

"Valedictorian Missy Winston? I saw her in Nurse McKinstry's office earlier. I wonder what happened?" Dell asked.

"I happened," Jeremy paused. It's a long story, not my best moment." He said, embarrassed. "Turns out she's full of surprises."

Del grinned, hopping into the passenger seat of Jeremy's Jeep. "Sounds like you've had quite a day."

Jeremy exhaled slowly, "Yeah, today's been—different."

Del tilted his head thoughtfully, "Speaking of different, it's weird, but Kristen— who I hear isn't exactly singing your praises right now…"

Jeremy cut him off with a raise of his hand, "Yeah, I've heard."

Del leaned in, his voice dropping slightly. "Well, at lunch, she was talking serious trash about Missy. It's wild because she'd never even acknowledged her existence before today. It was like she had it out for her or something."

Jeremy's brows furrowed, "Seriously? That's odd." He paused, remembering his earlier conversation with Missy and how she said that Kristen was glaring at her during lunch. "Missy mentioned something earlier about Kristen, but I didn't think it was that intense."

"Yeah, dude, watch out for Kris," Del warned with a half-serious tone. "You know what they say about a woman scorned. And if it's Kristen, multiply that by a thousand."

Trying to lighten the mood, Del quickly grinned, "So, for your big day, did Gregg decide to raid your savings as a birthday gift?" He laughed, not realizing just how accurate the joke landed.

Jeremy smirked, "Nailed it."

"Are you kidding me!" Del exclaimed, gripping the edge of his seat. "That's beyond messed up. I can't believe he keeps doing this to you."

As Jeremy rolled his Jeep through the winding suburban roads, he spilled the morning's events. The fight with his father, walking out of the house with no plans of returning, and the shock of the nearly depleted savings account. Each revelation had Del shaking his head in disbelief. He recounted the tale of the vile note and the solitary hundred-dollar bill but left out the part about the still-sealed envelope and its unknown contents.

"My college fund, Del – it's nearly wiped out." Jeremy shook his head, reliving the morning's events, "at the bank," he began with a heavy exhale, shifting his eyes to Del momentarily. "Gregg showed up, totally hammered, and made a scene. Honestly, it was a shitshow."

Del's eyes widened, a combination of shock and empathy reflecting in his gaze. "Dude, that's so messed up," he murmured, struggling for the right words. "But hey, you got a cool hundred bucks, right? Happy birthday indeed," he said with his tone dripping with sarcasm.

Jeremy hesitated, contemplating whether to mention the sealed document. He decided against it, figuring some secrets were best kept for now.

Del fixed Jeremy with a serious gaze. "Look, man, just put Gregg out of your head; he's not worth it," his voice firm but caring. "You know you've always got a place to crash at my house. You won't go hungry or be in anyone's way."

Jeremy gave a grateful smile. "Thanks, man. I'll try not to overstay my welcome. I'm going to fix up the cottage and make it livable; it could be a fun project. And hey, it'll be a cool hangout spot for us. I should be able to get it all set up by the weekend. I'll probably head up there on Saturday to get things started."

Del nodded, "Sounds like a plan, I'm there."

Jeremy's attention was suddenly diverted as they pulled into the 7-11 parking lot. Under the store's fluorescent lights, Kristen's cascading fiery curls were unmistakable. She was seemingly engrossed in the modest selection of greeting cards. The day's twists seemed to be far from over.

"What the hell is she doing here," Jeremy mumbled.

"Let's bail," Dell offered. "We can hit Arby's instead,"

"No, it's fine; I need to face the music; better to just get it over with."
Jeremy sighed as he killed the Jeep's engine, "Be a pal, grab me a few dogs

and a Super Gulp of dew if you don't mind," he said, looking back at Del. "I'll see what her damage is."

"You got it, dude." Del agreed as the two entered the store.

As he approached Kristen, Jeremy studied her. "God, she was stunning," he thought. Her body was lean; her clothes were a perfect combination of effort and fit. She was always so well put together.

This was the first time he'd seen her in ages. Memories from previous lives came flooding back. As he remembered their last split, the sound of her heartbreaking cries, the taste of her tear-streaked cheeks, a wave of melancholy hit him.

She had been his first everything, pure and unspoiled in the timeline of their initial meeting. However, he also remembered the emotional storm that came when she was upset, and he wondered if he was prepared to face that storm today.

With a gentle "Hey," he pulled her out of her thoughts, bracing himself as she turned to face him.

Her eyes showed a touch of mock anger when they met his. "Hey yourself," she responded with a playful pout. "Where have you been hiding all day, huh? You thought you could stand me up on your birthday?" She took a step closer, playfully poking him in the chest. "I've missed you, you big jerk."

Caught off guard by her light-hearted jesting, Jeremy couldn't help but chuckle. "Trust me, it wasn't on purpose. It's just one of those days, I guess. Missed you too."

With a twinkle in her eye, she teased, "Can I give the birthday boy a little birthday kiss?"

He glanced over to the soda fountain where Del was attempting, rather poorly, to hide and observe the two of them. "Sure," he grinned, "but make it quick. I wouldn't want Del getting too excited over there."

She followed his gaze and sang flirtatiously, "Hey, D.C.!"

Caught red-handed, Del replied with mock flirtation, "Hey, Kristen."

Jeremy turned back to face Kristen, his demeanor shifting to a more serious tone. "Listen, about today, I'm sorry. Things are complicated right now, and I didn't want to pull you into the middle of it."

Her eyes narrowed slightly, sensing the underlying tension. "Let me guess," she ventured, "Gregg?"

He sighed, running a hand through his hair, "Yeah, part of it involves him. But there's more; I'll tell you later."

She looked him over and asked, "Is any part of that 'more' related to our soon-to-be valedictorian?"

Caught off guard, he frowned. "What? No! Why would you even think that?"

She shrugged, trying to seem calm, though he detected a hint of genuine concern. "It's just... I saw the two of you in a heated conversation during the second period. And Heather mentioned she saw you guys again later on. I mean, should I be worried or something?"

He raised his eyebrows in surprise. "Missy and me? No way. It's not like that at all," he clarified, quickly recounting the day's mishaps. He detailed the near-miss with his Jeep and the staircase collision, emphasizing his genuine intentions to make amends for his missteps.

She shot him a pointed look, a hint of jealousy creeping into her voice. "You always have to play the hero, don't you? When will you realize, you're all mine? I'm not a big fan of sharing you with everyone."

"I can't help myself," he replied with a sheepish grin. "It's just who I am."

She narrowed her eyes, half in jest. "Just be sure not to play the white knight too often, especially around Miss Perfect. I wouldn't want to have to remind her of her place."

"What's your issue with her anyway, Kris? She's nice," Jeremy defended.

She sighed, looking for the right words. "I don't know, she's just a little too pristine for my taste."

Trying to keep the peace, he cautiously offered, "Maybe if you talked to her, you'd see a different side; she might surprise you; I think she might miss your friendship."

Her irritation flared. "So, now you're an expert on Missy Winston? You know everything about everyone?"

"No, it's not like that, Kris," He began, trying to calm the waters.

She cut him off, her voice rising with emotion. "Whatever. Just remember, don't leave me hanging for her again."

He looked deep into her eyes, hoping to convey his sincerity. "Honestly, Kris, you've got absolutely nothing to worry about. Cross my heart."

She playfully nudged him, her jealousy fading. "You better mean it." Then, checking the time, she groaned. "Oh, shoot! I had this whole plan to surprise you with a card and a treat after practice, but now I'm running late."

"Don't worry about it," he replied. "The thought alone is enough."

She brightened up a bit before demanding. "You are coming over for dinner then. I've got some gifts for you, and Mom's making her famous pot roast. You love it, right?"

He couldn't help but smile at the memory. Mrs. Ray's pot roast was legendary in his book; it was simple and hearty, everything a home-cooked meal should be.

"Sounds perfect," he agreed. "But hey, since I'm staying over at Del's tonight, do you think your folks would mind if he came too?"

Her voice took on a teasing tone. "You know I was hoping for some one-on-one time with you."

He hesitated, caught off-guard. There was a fragility to this situation, which he had always anticipated. He would've been thrilled at the prospect of a drawn-out make-out session with Kristen in his original life-time. But now, after countless cycles and having lived through so many adult experiences, the idea felt inappropriate.

He chose his words carefully. "Look," he started, his voice soft. You know I love our one-on-one time. But tonight, maybe it's not the best for that. Can I take a rain check?"

She let out a playful sigh. "Fine, if that's what the birthday boy wants," she teased, a mischievous glint in her eyes. "But don't be surprised if I can't help myself and pounce on you when no one's looking." She grinned, tapping her fingertips together in a sly rhythm.

"Fair enough." He said before pausing and drawing a deep breath. "After practice, Del and I need to swing by my house. We've got a covert operation to run," he said, his tone slightly whimsical to lighten the mood.

"Alright, but don't be late," she said playfully as she gave him a swift kiss on the cheek and darted out the door, calling back, "Love you!"

He leaned against the door frame and watched Kristen sashay towards her cherry-red Cavalier Z-24. The car, a recent 17th birthday present, was as vibrant and lively as she was. It had a certain youthful charm that reflected its owner perfectly. Just like her, the car was compact, sporty, and just the right amount of flashy. Her red curls fluttered in the breeze as she unlocked the car's door.

He took a moment, feeling the warmth of her kiss lingering on his skin. With a deep breath, he mentally ran through the checklist for the rest of the day. Football practice, a stealthy run home, and avoid another clash with Gregg, and, if all went according to plan, the evening would end with Mrs. Ray's pot roast.

Focused and determined, Jeremy called out to Del, "Let's get rolling; if we're late, McHale is gonna make us pay."

19

THIS IS PRACTICE

BACK AT HUXLEY, Jeremy and Del raced to the locker room. Around them, the hum of chatter and the rhythmic clacking of cleats on the pavement created a backdrop of familiar sounds as their fellow teammates moved in the opposite direction towards the practice field.

Just as they reached the door of the locker room, it flew open, revealing Coach McHale, his intimidating figure blocking the entrance.

The coach boomed, "So, my esteemed captains think they're too good to show up on time?" his voice echoed across the parking lot. Jeremy winced inwardly. The reprimand, though expected, stung.

Del stepped forward, his posture straight, "Sir, it's Jeremy's birthday today. He didn't get a chance to eat anything, and I thought it would be a good idea for him to fuel up before practice. We wanted to be in top form on the field," he explained, attempting to soften the coach's anger.

McHale surveyed them both, his eyes piercing yet not unkind. "Alright," he conceded, "But you've got five minutes to get suited up and out on the practice field or be prepared to run laps until the sun goes down, understood?"

The two exchanged glances, then nodded in unison, "Understood Coach." They replied, determination fueling their next steps.

After quickly changing into their practice gear, Jeremy and Del jogged onto the field as the patchy varsity group was in the middle of their calisthenics routines.

McHale's voice sliced through the air, "Anderson, D.C.! Laps until my whistle says otherwise." The coach's words left no room for argument, and the two began their steady pace around the field's perimeter.

Their feet pounded the grass in rhythm as Jeremy and Del fell into stride side-by-side. The sounds of their teammates counting off repetitions faded into the background as the duo circled the field.

"Alright, spill," Del panted slightly, "What went down with Kristen?"

Jogging beside his friend at a turtle's pace, Jeremy took a deep breath before speaking. "It wasn't anything huge. She's just a bit wound up about Missy, of all people. She thinks something is going on between us."

Del snorted, "Missy Winston? Seriously? She barely talks to anyone."

Jeremy rolled his eyes. "I know, right? It was just a couple of random run-ins, and now, suddenly, it's this whole thing. But look, more importantly, I need your help later."

"With Gregg?" Del asked.

"Bingo. I need to get some stuff from home, but I can't face another showdown. I thought you might be able to distract him," Jeremy proposed.

Del's eyes sparkled with mischief. "Ah, some good ol' diversionary tactics. Any ideas?"

"Well," Jeremy began, crafting a plan on the spot, "We'll stop by after practice. While I sneak in the back, you can knock on the front door, and when Gregg answers, you can ask if I'm back from practice. Play dumb, as if you don't know what he and I got into this morning. Then, go into some kind of nostalgic chat. You know that Gregg can't resist a trip down memory lane."

"Devious," Del grinned, appreciating the cunning behind the plan. "All that sneaking better be worth it."

Jeremy nudged Del playfully, "Oh, it will be; Mrs. Ray's pot roast at Kristen's is on the line."

Del's face brightened instantly. "Say no more. That roast is epic."

"Sure is," Jeremy replied with a smirk, the weight of the day's events feeling slightly lighter with a friend by his side.

As McHale's whistle pierced the air, Jeremy and Del fell in with the team. Positional drills flowed into a full team scrimmage. The varsity offense squared off against the JV defense, and vice versa. Due to the team's lean roster, the concept of rest was a luxury most of the team could not afford, especially players like Jeremy, Del, and a select few who practically never left the field. However, one glaring exception was Martin LaCroix, the self-proclaimed "star" quarterback.

In reality, Marty was the team's Achilles heel. While he had a decent arm, he lacked the grit and resilience that defined the rest of the squad. Injuries plagued him, often sidelining the quarterback in crucial games. And when he did play, his poor leadership led to a collection of broken plays, botched audibles, and blowout losses. It wasn't just his gameplay that annoyed Jeremy and Del the most; it was his attitude.

Marty's lack of commitment and leadership had earned him little respect, pushing him to the outer ring of the team's core. Had he not been in athletics, he would probably have found more in common with someone like Dennis Winston and other fringe groups.

Jeremy and Del, ever the leaders, often ramped up their efforts to compensate for Marty's shortcomings, but there was only so much they could do.

"Circle up team!" Coach McHale's authoritative voice echoed across the field, drawing the players together. As they knelt before him, the coach looked at his team with determination. "We've got a game within our grasp. This is our opportunity to shine, and our secret weapon is primed and ready." Jeremy and Del exchanged a glance, already guessing where this was headed.

"Isn't that right, LaCroix," McHale added, directing his attention towards Marty, who was trying his best to display confidence.

Without missing a beat, Marty replied, puffing out his chest, "Absolutely, Coach!"

Rolling their eyes discreetly, Jeremy and Del mimicked gagging gestures, trying to hold back their laughter.

"I've got some fresh plays for the game, and Marty's been studying them all week," McHale continued. "Offense, gather around him. He'll get you up to speed. Scout defense, follow me; we need to keep our offense sharp."

As the first-team offense huddled around Marty, it became clear that his grasp of the new strategies was shaky at best.

With his comprehensive knowledge of the team's playbook—gained from countless revisits of these exact moments—Jeremy didn't hesitate. He smoothly took over, explaining the new plays with clarity and precision. After all, he knew these plays better than anyone, even Coach McHale.

Jeremy's confidence and expertise were undeniable. He effortlessly navigated the playbook, the detailed maneuvers and tactics flowing from him as though they were second nature. Marty, Clueless, silently acknowledged his teammate's superior understanding and stepped aside to allow Jeremy to serve as the leader in the huddle.

Del was quick on the uptake and seamlessly backed Jeremy up, offering additional insights and direction. Together, they transformed the team's approach from half-speed walkthroughs, ensuring each player grasped the basics, to three-quarter speed drills emphasizing the importance of timing and synchronization. By the time they ramped up to full speed, with every collision and play executed with precision, it was evident that the team's performance had reached a level previously unseen under Coach McHale's direction.

From the sidelines, McHale observed the team's unity with a hint of surprise. In the back of his mind, he couldn't help but credit the newfound effectiveness to the introduction of his "new plays." This new scheme gave The Wildcats a fighting chance against Regional High, a chance they shouldn't have.

The Regional High School Rebels were neck and neck with Central High at the top of the league. A victory for Huxley would break that tie, causing Regional to lose its bid for the state title. Such a result would ripple across the fabric of time, with consequences Jeremy would not be able to course correct. The butterfly effect of this single game would build up over the years, and the outcome would be felt for decades in profound ways.

Making sure that Huxley lost wasn't going to be hard, given the gap in the two team's skill levels, but still, Jeremy wanted to leave a mark. He wanted to provide a sense of pride for his teammates that wouldn't drastically change the future. So, while he'd ensure that the game's final score resulted in a Rebel victory, he would also create moments of brilliance on the field for the Wildcats. He'd give them a moral victory while maintaining the destined outcome.

In each version of this game that Jeremy had played in, the Wildcats would be on the receiving end of a total thrashing. The far more skilled Regional Rebels would always burst out of the gates like a freight train, each play executed perfectly, allowing them to score at will.

On the other hand, the Wildcats, under Marty LaCroix's leadership, or lack thereof, would be easily stopped by the Rebels' defense.

The outcome would be utter chaos for the Wildcats. By halftime, they would be begging for mercy, their morale crushed under the weight of the scoreboard.

However, this timeline held the potential for a different story. "Why not introduce a dash of unpredictability, a sprinkle of hope, and perhaps spare the Wildcats from the usual demoralizing drubbing?" Jeremy thought.

With a playbook that he knew like the back of his hand and the vision of a captain who already knew Regional's every move, Jeremy intended to be the cornerstone in Huxley's defensive strategy. Having seen the play calls of Regional throughout countless lifetimes, he was primed to anticipate every move, every fake, every rush. Alongside Del, the duo could give the Wildcats a fighting chance.

His primary objective would be to shield his teammates from the embarrassment and physical pain of yet another blowout. One that he had participated in dozens of times. The plan was simple: maintain a close score, give the team a sense of hope, and keep spirits high. Yet, he would ensure the eventual outcome remained the same, preserving the integrity of the timeline. The game might end in a loss for Huxley, but it wouldn't be without its highlights for the Wildcats.

As the sun started to set and the team wrapped up their final preparations for Friday night's game, Coach McHale's whistle pierced the cold autumn air.

The coach gathered the panting players around him and launched into one of his textbook pep talks. His words overflowed with confidence, praising his methodically crafted strategy while gushing over his quarterback's supposed leadership prowess.

"Gentlemen," he began, passion evident in his tone, "under the precision of Marty's execution and the strategy we've drilled into this practice, we are on the verge of shaking off the label of 'the underdogs' and marking our first victory in this season's record book."

As McHale's words echoed across the field, a newfound life surged through the ranks of the Wildcats. The lingering feeling of past defeats faded away. For the first time, hope was in their hearts. They were united, ready to challenge fate and script a new chapter for their team.

After practice, Jeremy and Del found themselves called into Coach McHale's office. They had mentally prepared for a reprimand for being late to practice, but instead, they were met with an unexpected request. McHale leaned forward; his usually stern face was weary.

"Boys, you two need to step up," he began. "LaCroix might not be the strongest quarterback, but he's what we've got, and I need you two to support him on the field tomorrow night."

Both nodded in understanding. It wasn't news to them that Marty had his weaknesses.

"There's more," McHale added, taking a deep breath. "Sophomore Ben Jennings is out – his grades have tanked, and he's ineligible. We're at the bare minimum to field a team now."

Jeremy and Del exchanged glances, sensing the severity of the situation.

The coach continued, "I need both of you to call each player on our roster tonight. Tell them that lights out is at 11 pm, and everyone needs to be at school tomorrow before the end of first period. No absences, no tardies, both are grounds for game-day ineligibility." Jeremy felt the weight of the responsibility settle on his shoulders.

"Understood, Coach. We'll make sure everyone is here," Jeremy affirmed.

Del chimed in, "We got this, Coach."

McHale nodded, appreciative. "Thank you, boys, dismissed."

Once outside the office, Jeremy shared a determined look with Del. "Let's make sure everyone's ready for the game," he said, his voice carrying a blend of leadership and trust. "We'll set up shop at your place after dinner at Kristen's. We can split up the roster, divide and conquer."

They had a game to play, and they needed to make sure everyone was on board.

20

DIVERSIONARY TACTICS

JEREMY DISCREETLY PARKED around the corner from his house, and the two quickly got out. Del, exuding casual confidence, strolled towards the walkway to the house while Jeremy dashed into the shadows of the neighbor's yard.

Reaching the front door, Del hesitated before knocking with the forceful urgency of a cop on a late-night call. Silence. He rapped harder. Still, no response. His curiosity piqued, he inched closer to the window and peered inside. The sight that met him was something he'd never wanted to see. Gregg, sprawled out on his recliner, in nothing but his tightey-whiteys and a t-shirt, was passed out cold, snoring away.

"Oh man," Del muttered under his breath, disappointed, imagining Jeremy dealing with that constantly, "He's totally wasted."

With a renewed sense of urgency and a hint of mischief, Del rapped on the window. "Hey, Gregg!" he called, louder this time. Yet the man remained undisturbed, his snoring the only sound breaking the silence. Wasting no more time, Del glanced around, hopped over the porch railing, and darted around back, where he found Jeremy with a key poised to unlock the door.

With a hand on the doorknob, Jeremy looked up in surprise as Del vaulted over the railing and landed beside him.

"What the hell, man?" Jeremy whispered, his eyes darting to the windows to ensure there was no movement inside. "He's out cold," Del panted, pointing towards the living room window. "I knocked, banged, and even yelled. He didn't move an inch. He's passed out in his chair."

For a moment, the two stood there, weighing their options. Jeremy's grip on the doorknob tightened. "Look, if he's knocked out, we might have more time. But we need to be super quiet. Can you keep an eye on him while I grab my stuff?"

Del nodded, with determination in his eyes. "Yeah, I'll keep watch; I'll have a direct line of sight from the hall outside your room. If he gets up, I'll make some noise to distract him." Jeremy gave Del a grateful look, "Thanks man. Let's get this over with."

The two went inside, the stillness weighing heavily on them. Every creak of the floorboards and rustle of their clothes seemed to echo throughout the house, their senses heightened by the situation's tension. Moving swiftly but carefully, they set about their task, very aware of the unconscious figure in the living room, praying he'd stay that way until they were safely out.

Teaming up with synchronized precision, Jeremy and Del hurriedly moved through the dimly lit room. As Jeremy shoved handfuls of his clothing into large trash bags, the weight of the moment wasn't lost on him. This wasn't just a hasty departure but a step towards a new chapter in Jeremy's life.

Jeremy darted to his bedside table, snatching up his Discman along with a stack of CDs. Pearl Jam, Nirvana, and Stone Temple Pilots, amongst others, were all swept into a separate bag.

Meanwhile, Del, confident that Gregg would not be waking up any time soon, made a beeline for the shelves where Jeremy's Gameboy and cartridges were neatly stacked. "Man, can't leave these behind," he murmured, ensuring each game was safely tucked away.

The room was filled with the shuffling sounds of their hurried efforts, punctuated by Gregg's distant snores, which provided a comical background to their covert operation.

"Keep it down," Jeremy whispered.

Del nodded, pausing for a split second to listen for sounds in the living room. "You got everything?"

Jeremy took one final sweeping glance around his room. "Yeah," he whispered back, clutching the trash bags tightly, "Let's get out of here."

Tiptoeing down the worn-out carpeted stairs, Jeremy and Del could hear the telltale sounds of Gregg's deep, raucous snores echoing through the house. His mumbled words, slurred by both sleep and whatever alcohol had fueled him into this state, sounded distant yet eerily close.

Jeremy stood at the base of the stairs, his eyes locked onto his father, a flurry of emotions coursing through him. Anger and resentment, years, or perhaps lifetimes, of pent-up frustrations tempted him to act.

The desire to wake Gregg and confront him right then and there pulsed through his veins to release all the pain he had bottled up. But a wiser part of him, seasoned from experience, whispered words of caution in his ear. This wasn't the time or place. Not now. Not when so much was at stake.

With Del watching him intently, Jeremy took a slow, steadying breath. Leaning close to his snoring father, he murmured, "Sleep well, old man. May your dreams be as pleasant as you've made my life." The words dripped with icy sarcasm, each syllable measured and deliberate.

As they stealthily made their way to the exit, Jeremy couldn't resist a final act of defiance. With a smirk, he turned back to Gregg, flipping him the bird, a gesture that signaled the release of all the pent-up emotions he felt. Del's soft chuckle echoed in the still night as the two young men vanished into the darkness, leaving behind a house filled with bitter memories.

21

RAYS OF LIGHT

THE WARM LIGHTS of the Ray residence glowing from within greeted Jeremy and Del as they walked up to the house. Jeremy could feel a weight lifting from his shoulders with each step closer to the front door.

A waft of warmth met Jeremy and Del as the door opened, revealing Mrs. Ray. With her soft, rosy cheeks and ever-present apron, she was the epitome of a '90s mom, always with a welcoming smile stretched across her face, reaching her sparkling eyes.

"Hi, Mrs. Ray," Jeremy greeted, his voice filled with genuine affection.

"Come in, come in!" She ushered them inside, her voice filled with surprise at seeing Del. "I didn't know we'd have the pleasure of your company tonight, Antoine."

Del Groaned— "Please, Mrs. Ray, Call me D.C., or you can call me Del."

"No, you're Antoine and always will be for me," Mrs. Ray said with sweetness in her voice, "I always thought it was such a strong, handsome name."

Del groaned, rolling his eyes. "Mrs. Ray, you're about the only one that thinks that."

Jeremy, always quick to seize an opportunity to tease his best friend, said, "I don't know, Del, maybe we should start calling you Antoine at school. You never know; it might give you some extra sophistication."

Del shot Jeremy a mock glare. "You try it, and I'll personally make sure you run extra laps at the next practice."

For most people, he went by D.C. Only his closest circle, which included his family, Jeremy and, Stacy, referred to him as Del.

Del had a particular fondness for the nickname D.C. It felt cool and distinct to him, far more than his full first name, Antoine, which he associated with those goofy sketches from "In Living Color." Whenever he heard "Antoine," he inwardly groaned, "Hated it."

Yet, when Mrs. Ray used it, it felt different. Her voice had a warm, motherly affection, an endearment that softened the blow.

With Mrs. Ray, annoyance was replaced by a sense of belonging. She had the gift of making names sound like a sweet caress, even if they were ones you'd rather not be called.

The comforting aroma of home-cooked food that filled the house was delightful compared to the distant smoky scent of Mr. Ray's cigar creeping in from the back porch. As they walked through the familiar rooms of the Ray residence, memories from past visits flooded Jeremy's mind. The Ray's house always had a coziness about it, a combination of the people inside and their love for making it a home.

The screen door creaked as the boys stepped out onto the porch. Mr. Ray sat there; absorbed in his evening ritual. The soft rustle of the newspaper pages being turned and the periodic puffs from his cigar created a calm backdrop.

"Evening, Mr. Ray," Del greeted, nodding in respect.

Kristen's father looked up from his paper, his eyes crinkling into a familiar smile. "Ah, the birthday boy and his trusty sidekick," he teased, extending his hand for a handshake. "Good to see you boys. Grab a seat."

Just as the boys settled in, Kristen breezed onto the porch. "Her lively energy instantly changed the atmosphere." A couple of festively wrapped packages were in her hands, and her face was alight with a mischievous grin. Her signature curls were pulled up in a messy bun, and her makeup was flawless.

"Hey, birthday boy!" she sang with flirtation, approaching Jeremy."

Del chuckled, mocking her voice, "Hey, birthday boy!" He enjoyed getting Kristen flustered. She was always an easy target.

"Shut up, D.C.!" She sneered at Del playfully before turning her attention back to Jeremy. "Okay, close your eyes and hold out your hands," she instructed.

Jeremy, did as he was told, as Kristen gently placed the gifts in his hands.

"Okay, open 'em," she said, her eyes sparkling excitedly.

He opened his eyes to find two neatly wrapped packages. The larger one was soft and squishy, clothing of some kind, while the other was smaller and hard, a box of some sort.

"For someone who claims not to be good at surprises, you sure have a knack for keeping me in suspense," Jeremy teased.

The joke was on them because Jeremy knew exactly what was inside. He'd opened these two particular gifts more than twenty times in his existence— package one, a Nirvana T-shirt; number two, a key with a poem about how he'd now have the key to her heart forever.

He started to unwrap the box first, a little off script, but what was the harm in that?

"No," Kristen demanded, "the other one first."

"Alright, alright," Jeremy complied, tearing open the anticipated T-shirt and pulling it out. His surprise was genuine, and his expression was received well by Kristen,

Inside was a tee, and as expected, it was branded Nirvana, one of Jeremy's all-time favorite bands—the smiley-faced logo with crossed eyes was just as expected.

However, for the first time, the shirt was long-sleeved, and olive green, not the typical black short-sleeve tee that he'd received so many times before. He forced an excited expression to mask his confusion, "You remembered!" he exclaimed, genuinely touched.

Kristen beamed. "Of course I did. For the record, I had to look everywhere to find it in a long sleeve and everyone has the black one. I really wanted to get something different for you."

Jeremy thought to himself how strange this deviation from the timeline was. She'd have had to shop for this way before the start of this reset; nothing he'd done during the day could have caused this shift.

He laughed, "It's perfect, Kris. Thank you."

Then, he moved on to the smaller box. Opening it, inside, there was no key, no poem. Instead, he found a watch, intricately designed and clearly antique. The back was engraved with the words, "I will love you for all lifetimes."

"What the actual fuck!" Jeremy's internal voice screamed as his heart pounded in his chest.

Speechless, he inspected the watch. It was an exquisite and meaningful gift, especially given his unique circumstances.

"Kristen, this is—" he stopped, "I don't know what to say. It's beautiful."

She blushed slightly, "I just thought," she paused, "you love old things, I figured you'd appreciate it. Like how you always talk about The

Labrador, I just thought maybe the original owner might have stayed there, or at least we can pretend that they did."

Jeremy hopped up and gave Kristen a warm hug. "It's really great, Kris; I love it."

As they separated, Mr. Ray cleared his throat. "Well, now that we've had our touching moment, shall we head inside? I believe there's a pot roast waiting for us."

As Kristen and her father made their way to the dining room, Jeremy hung back, inspecting the watch in his hand, gliding his thumb across the inscription. His world was tilting off its axis. Something had changed in his life for the first time, without any ripple caused by his actions.

He wasn't sure how or why. The T-shirt's different color was unexpected, but the watch was truly unsettling. How could Kristen have chosen something so poignant and connected to his unique situation? Was it mere coincidence, or did she somehow know more than she let on?

Trying to keep his composure, Jeremy tucked the watch in his pocket.

"You okay, man?" Del asked, nudging him slightly.

"Yeah," Jeremy replied, forcing a smile. "Just a bit overwhelmed, I guess. It's a really nice watch."

Del raised an eyebrow but didn't press further. He knew Jeremy well enough to sense that something was off but now wasn't the time to get into it.

The dinner table chatter filled the room with a pleasant background hum, but for Jeremy, each laugh, each clink of a fork on a plate, seemed slightly out of sync. It was like watching a movie with the audio just a fraction of a second delayed.

Jeremy's fingers traced the contours of the watch in his pocket. Its presence gnawed at the back of his mind. He pulled it out just for a moment, glancing at the intricate design. The ticking seemed to drown out the chatter around the table.

Locking eyes with Jeremy, Del sensed the storm swirling within his friend. Their bond was forged from countless shared memories— from banding together against school bullies to the rollercoaster of emotions that came with every game day.

But at that moment, Del felt a shift in the air. Something intense was going on with his friend. Something that wasn't part of their usual high school drama. Del didn't have all the pieces to this puzzle, but the look he gave Jeremy made a silent promise: "Whenever you're ready to talk, I've got your back."

Jeremy put the watch away, but the weight of its presence remained. As dinner wrapped up, he knew that he'd need to address the elephant in the room. But for now, he wanted to bask in the warmth of the moment, surrounded by friends and family and the uncertainty of what lay ahead.

After dinner, Jeremy and Del, ever the gentlemen, helped clear the table. While Del stayed in the kitchen, helping wash the dishes, Jeremy followed Kristen toward her room.

"Door open, kids!" Mr. Ray's voice rang out, reminding them of the house rules.

"You got it, Daddy," Kristen playfully shot back, not missing a beat.

"Of course, Mr. Ray," Jeremy added, respecting the household boundaries.

While Kristen's parents had always trusted them, her father often felt the need to reinforce his position.

Reaching her room, Kristen left the door ajar just enough to appease her father's rules. With a twirl and a smirk, she faced Jeremy, hesitation flashing in her eyes for only a split second before she leaned in, planting a deep kiss on his lips.

Caught up in the moment, he kissed her back but then gently pulled away.

"I warned you," she said with a sly grin.

He met her gaze, searching for an answer in her eyes. "You did indeed."

"Is it okay if we just chat? It feels like ages since we've caught up." He said, leading her to sit next to him on her bed.

She pouted playfully, "Ugh, fine. But you're missing out."

"I think I can guess," Jeremy teased.

"So, what's up, Bear?" Kristen always had an assortment of nicknames for him, but 'Bear,' short for 'Jer-Bear,' was the one he found most tolerable.

"The gifts were amazing, especially the shirt," he paused, considering how to continue, "but the watch—"

Her face dropped, "You don't like it?"

"No, it's not that. I love it," he assured her. "I'm just curious about where you got it."

She rolled her eyes playfully, "Remember our trip to The Cape last summer? We saw it in one of those cute little shops in Provincetown."

A rush of memories flooded back to Jeremy. He recalled their Cape Cod adventure, their day trip to Provincetown, the whale-watching, and their lunch near the art gallery by the wharves.

"Oh, right," he said, smiling at the memory, "But how did you buy it without going back to P-Town?"

She smirked, "I called the shop a few weeks later, and Daddy let me charge it to his credit card over the phone. They shipped it to me, no problem. I've had it for months, and you can't imagine how hard it was to keep it a secret from you."

Jeremy often found his memories from multiple lifetimes blending, for better or worse. Sometimes, the experiences from one would spill into another, creating a kaleidoscope of emotions. But the watch, this deviation from the original gifts, struck a chord. It brought back memories of the genuine love he once shared with Kristen—a love that was pure and untainted by future disagreements over college choices or the pain of their eventual breakup. The weight of knowing their relationship's eventual end lingered heavily in his heart.

"Come on, let's have dessert," she said, pulling him from his thoughts. "We got you a cake, and I know you need to leave soon."

He nodded, standing up to follow her. "Hey, Kris?"

"Yeah, Bear?" She spun back to face him

"There's something I need you to know," sincerity in his voice.

Her expression was curious. "What's that?"

"No matter what happens in the future, no matter where our paths take us, always remember this moment, this night. And always know, I'll forever love you."

She blinked, her eyes glistening. "Promise?"

"I promise," he replied earnestly, "As long as I exist, I swear, you will always be in my heart."

She went to him and nuzzled against his chest. "I love you too, Bear. "

He held her tight, remembering how their bodies always seemed to fit together in an embrace.

She looked into his eyes and gave him a soft kiss, "Let's go see what everyone else is doing; you need some birthday cake before you go," she said.

He took a deep breath, savoring the moment. The weight of his lifetimes, of all the experiences and emotions, lifted, leaving him with just this beautiful moment with Kristen.

"Alright," he replied with a chuckle, "lead the way. Who can resist a good birthday cake?"

As they moved through the hallways, the laughter and conversations from the kitchen growing louder with each step, he felt a rare sensation – peace.

When they approached the dining room, hearty laughter echoed through the hallway. The door was slightly open, and through the crack, Jeremy could see Del, standing tall and animated in the center of the room, recounting a story with exaggerated gestures and comical expressions.

The Rays, typically a composed pair, were leaning back in their chairs, their faces flushed from laughing so hard. Mr. Ray's booming belly laughs complimented Mrs. Ray's delightful tinkling laughter. Their usually prim dining room had transformed into a makeshift theatre, with Del as the star performer.

Kristen's eyes twinkled with mischief as she took in the scene. "What on earth is going on in here?" she asked, feigning shock but enjoying the unexpected performance.

Without missing a beat, Del winked at her and continued his story, drawing Jeremy and Kristen into the world he was painting with his words.

"So, there I was, feeling like I'm on top of the world after acing that Geometry Mid-term," he recounted, puffing out his chest with pride. "You know, the one that even the valedictorian was sweating. Riding that high, I figured, why not celebrate with a slide down the banister in the main hall – a victory slide."

Mr. Ray, unable to contain his amusement, "Oh no, D.C., what happened next?"

Del adopted a look of mock seriousness. "Well, let's just say I didn't quite consider the freshly waxed floors waiting at the bottom. Instead of a smooth landing, I slid right into three freshmen and the janitor's 'wet floor' sign."

Mr. Ray's laughter erupted causing him to nearly spill his scotch. Tears streamed down his cheeks as he listened to Del's misfortune. "That's hilarious, D.C., but I have a feeling there's more to this story."

Del nodded with a mischievous glint in his eye. "Oh, there's more alright. When I finally came to a stop and got up, I felt this cool breeze from behind, my pants split wide open, and my whole ass was hanging out."

"Antoine! Language!" Mrs. Ray interjected with mock sternness, though her eyes sparkled with amusement.

Del quickly corrected himself, "Oh, sorry, I mean, my rear end was showing." He glanced at Jeremy, winking conspiratorially.

"But that's not even the worst part," Del continued with mock tragedy in his voice. "Right as I'm standing there, exposed to the world, Diane Westover walks by. She saw the whole thing!" He sighed dramatically. "I had been gearing up to ask her out, and there went my courage right out the window." He shrugged, "At least I lived to tell the tale.

Jeremy chuckled, "That you did, Del, that you did."

Kristen, still giggling, cleared her throat, "Alright, as much as I love story time with D.C., we have another event to celebrate." She beamed at Jeremy. "Birthday cake, anyone?"

The room cheered in agreement, the previous laughter mingling with excited chatter. Del, ever the center of attention, took a theatrical bow, setting the stage for the birthday festivities finale.

After enjoying a generous slice of cake, Jeremy caught Del's eye and subtly indicated it was time to leave. As he got up from the table, Kristen immediately piped up, "Why don't you let D.C. drive your Jeep home, and you can stay here? We could cozy up with a movie. Mom, Dad, can't he stay?"

Jeremy interjected before the Rays could respond, explaining the significance of the night before a game. "You know we have strict rules, Kris. Plus, Del and I have this captain's responsibility to make sure everyone's in line for tomorrow. If we don't, we risk forfeiting the rest of the season."

Kristen pouted, letting out a playful, "Oh poop!" She then crossed her arms and gave Jeremy a mock bratty look. "Alright, fine, I get it, sports stuff. But you're not off the hook. You better carve out some time for me after the game. And don't you dare stand me up for our lunch date tomorrow, mister?"

Jeremy raised his hands in a surrender gesture, smiling. "I promise, no more ditching on my part."

The two boys got up from their seats, with Jeremy turning to address Mr. and Mrs. Ray. "Thank you both, truly. This evening has been great. It's easily one of the most memorable birthdays I've ever had."

The cool night air greeted them as Jeremy and Del stepped outside, but the warmth from the Ray household lingered, wrapping Jeremy in a cocoon of happiness. He replayed his recent statement, comparing this birthday to all the others he'd lived through.

Yes, he'd had extravagant celebrations in all the posh locations. The yacht party for his 21st birthday in Life 5 was something out of a movie. In that life, he'd quickly turned his college trust into a fortune and even tried to win Cassandra's heart with it. That had been a lesson in the perils of trying to buy love. Those lavish celebrations lacked the genuine warmth and intimacy of tonight.

This birthday, surrounded by friends and loved ones, grounded in authenticity and laughter, had a charm that no amount of wealth could ever match.

"See you tomorrow, Kris," Jeremy called out, waving to the silhouette by the window.

"Hey, Mr. Ray," Del shouted as he walked backward down the path to the driveway, "how about coming to the game tomorrow? I'll even get you VIP box seats."

Mr. Ray chuckled from the doorway, his eyes twinkling with amusement. "Oh, D.C., I've been to enough of those games to know you boys don't have 'box seats.' But I appreciate the offer. I'll be right here, enjoying my stogie and scotch. You can regale me with tales of your heroics the next time you come for dinner."

Del laughed, giving Mr. Ray a mock salute. "Will do, sir. Just send word the next pot roast night!"

With that, the two boys walked down the path and disappeared into the night.

22

THE BOILER ROOM

IN DEL'S BASEMENT, the two team captains set up their command center. Everywhere you looked, the décor screamed 'Del'. Posters of his favorite bands covered the walls: his newest favorite, The Spice Girls. His most prized piece had Sporty Spice frozen in a mid-air kick. For additional flair, Del had added a voice bubble to make it look like she was declaring, "D.C. kicks ass!"

Del's unapologetic individuality was infectious. He celebrated his unique tastes, never shying away from his love for female pop idols or any other part of his eclectic personality. In a world that constantly tried to fit everyone into boxes, he built his own box and reveled in it.

While some might have found the basement juvenile or cluttered, to Jeremy, it represented their adolescence. It was a safe and familiar space where they'd spent countless hours laughing, debating, and planning.

The two quickly got to work, spreading out their team roster and playbooks on an old coffee table. They began dialing their teammates, making sure each one was on track for the next day. With the threat of the game being forfeited due to an undersized roster, they couldn't afford to take any chances. After a couple of hours, with most of the calls done, they leaned back, satisfied.

Del sighed, "Double-check the list. Is there anyone we missed, that might be a risk?"

Jeremy scanned the roster, "Shit! Give me the phone!"

Del tossed the clear, neon corded phone to Jeremy; catching it with one hand, he dialed, "Hi, ma'am, this is Jeremy Anderson, Huxley High football co-captain. Is Tomo around?"

Del dropped his head, "Tomo," he groaned.

I see, uh-huh…yes, Jeremy responded to the angry voice on the other end. "I'm sorry but" …he was interrupted, "yeah… can you just… okay." Jeremy looked at the handset, the dial tone buzzing. "She hung up."

What'd she say? Del asked.

"I'm not sure. I think she was pretty pissed. There's quite a language barrier there, you know," Jeremy shrugged.

"I guess that's the best we can do; maybe we can cruise by Tomo's house on the way to school and make sure he's up," Del suggested.

"Sounds like a plan," Jeremy chuckled, looking around the room, his eyes landing on the Spice Girls poster. "Hey, if Sporty Spice believes in you, who are we to doubt her?"

Del laughed, "You got that right, man. Mel C. only speaks the truth."

As they finished their captain duties, they took a moment to relax. Jeremy chuckled, "You had Kristen's parents dying with that story after dinner. I seriously thought Mrs. Ray was going to pee in her pants."

Del grinned, pushing his hair back, "Yeah, I gave that one a little extra flair tonight. I was trying to buy you some time with Bubblelicious for your birthday.

Jeremy glared at him with a smile, "Bubblelicious? Is that what you're calling her now?"

Del shrugged with a mischievous grin, "It's either that or Ginger Spice. Take your pick. Speaking of which, what was with that watch she gave you? "You seemed really surprised by it."

Jeremy's fun-loving expression turned serious for a moment. "Honestly, I don't know. It caught me off guard. We had a moment this summer when we saw it in a shop; she remembered and got it for me; it's strange."

Del leaned in, curious, "How is it strange?"

"It's just—," Jeremy trailed off, searching for words that would not reveal his secret. "Different from what I had expected, I guess. But it's a good kind of different. It makes me feel like maybe things aren't as set in stone as they seem."

Del thought for a moment before breaking into a grin, "Well, one thing is for sure; whatever the universe has in store, we'll tackle it together, just like we do with everything else."

Jeremy smiled, comforted by the bond they shared. "Thanks, man, I appreciate it."

Del gave a mock salute, "Anytime, Captain. Now, how about a game of Mario Kart?"

Jeremy grinned, "You're on. Prepare to eat my dust."

As Del got up to turn on the TV, Jeremy asked "Can I ask you something?"

Del looked up, a hint of curiosity in his eyes. "Shoot."

"How do you always seem to have everything under control? Honestly, I can't remember the last time something didn't go your way. What's that like?"

Del paused for a moment before leaning back in his seat and considering the question before responding. "It's not that I always have everything under control. It's more that I try not to let things throw me off balance. I guess I believe that if I stay positive, good things will happen."

Jeremy tilted his head as he looked at Del. "It's just that, from the outside looking in, it seems like you're the luckiest guy alive."

Del chuckled softly, "Trust me, my life isn't all rainbows and unicorns. I've had my fair share of shit-storms, for sure. I guess I just choose to move forward instead of beating myself up when things don't go my way."

Jeremy raised an eyebrow, "So, what? You just shake it off and move on?"

"I guess so," Del replied with a reflective note in his voice. "It's all about perspective, man. Instead of seeing things as bad luck, I try to find a lesson or a silver lining. It's not always easy, but it helps."

"So, each week when we take a beating on the field, you just let it roll? Jeremy asked.

Del sighed and leaned back, locking his fingers behind his head. "It's not as simple as just letting it roll, Jer-. Football, like life, is full of ups and downs. Sure, we've had more downs than ups, but it's not about the score at the end. It's about the lessons we learn, and how we grow as a team."

Del shifted in his seat, his playful demeanor momentarily replaced by a serious one. "Look, I won't pretend that losing doesn't suck, it does. Honestly, it eats at me sometimes. But I refuse to let it define me or our team. We've got heart, Jer. That means something."

Rubbing his temples, Jeremy sighed, "It's just hard, man. Every week, it feels like we're just out there for another round of punishment."

Del nodded sympathetically. "I get it, I really do. But let me ask you something. After every loss, every rough game, why do you show up for practice the next day?"

Jeremy paused, thinking, "Because I made a commitment to this team —to you, to the guys."

Del smiled, "Exactly. And that's the spirit we need. Wins and losses come and go. But commitment, perseverance, and passion? Those stay. And that's what we'll be remembered for."

So, if we go out tomorrow and get demolished, you're cool with that, so long as we get smoked as a team?

Del took a moment before answering, looking deep in thought. "It's not about being 'cool' with losing. I hate losing just as much as the next guy, probably even more. But here's the thing— you can't control every outcome in sports or even in life. But you can control how you respond to it."

Jeremy raised an eyebrow, skeptical. "That's pretty philosophical for a guy with a Spice Girls poster in his basement."

Del laughed, "Hey, Sporty Spice has some deep thoughts, okay? But seriously, I'd always rather win. Who wouldn't? But if we get out there, give it our best shot, have each other's backs, and play as a team, I can live with whatever happens.

Jeremy thought about Del's words, appreciating the genuine emotion behind them. "You believe that, don't you?"

Del nodded, "Every word of it.

"So that's football. What about other stuff?" Jeremy probed carefully. Del tilted his head, his brow furrowing slightly, sensing the depth behind Jeremy's question.

"Like life stuff, you mean?" Del asked.

Jeremy nodded, taking a deep breath before continuing, "Yeah, you know, choices, paths we take or don't, things we say or leave unsaid. Have you ever wished you could go back and change the past?"

There was a heavy pause. Del seemed to contemplate the gravity of the question, his eyes drifting as he got lost in thought. The room was silent except for the humming furnace on the other side of the basement.

Finally, he spoke. "Everyone has those moments, those 'what if' scenarios playing in their minds. I mean, I've definitely had my share of regrets. But if I walked around worrying about all those things, I'd never be happy." He leaned back, running a hand over his head. "But if you're asking if there's something major that I wish I could change, there is one thing." His voice grew softer, almost hesitant.

Jeremy leaned in; his curiosity piqued. "What is it?"

"It's about my mom," Del sighed. "Right before she passed, we had this huge fight. It was just stupid teenage stuff, you know?" I said some really shitty things, and, well, she died before I could apologize. Before I could tell her how much I loved her."

He looked down, taking a moment to compose himself. "If I could go back and relive that day, I'd hug her tight and tell her how much she meant to me."

Jeremy's heart broke for his friend. The loss of his mother was a rare tragedy in a lifetime of blessings for Del, one that he'd never open up about.

"I'm sorry, Del. That's really tough. I had no idea that happened." Jeremy consoled.

Del gave a weak smile. "Yeah, I don't talk about it much— It's tough. But it's also a constant reminder of what life's all about. We need to cherish the time we have. Don't let yourself get caught up in all the negative energy out there. If you do you'll no doubt end up with regrets."

"Regrets, huh?" Jeremy echoed, locking eyes with Del. "I have one. One I think we both have."

Del's jovial expression faded, replaced by concern. "What's that, Jer?"

"Dutchie," Jeremy whispered with a sigh.

"Fucking Dutchie," Del's brow furrowed. "Man, he's a lost cause. It's been a long time since he was the Dutchie we knew."

"But he's still in there, Del. Our Dutchie." Jeremy's tone was insistent, almost pleading.

Del sighed, leaning forward. "Look, man, it's been years. Who he is now," he paused, "I don't know, he's way out there, man."

"But think about it: when did it all start?" Jeremy pressed. "I'm not talking about the family tragedies, but the day he really changed."

Del's face widened with realization. "You're talking about eighth grade, aren't you? That year, everything went sideways. And yeah, we had just won the Pop Warner title. So, springtime, I guess."

Jeremy nodded. "And Dutch's passion for science. Remember that?"

Del's eyes grew distant as he remembered, "Oh yeah. He loved everything about it. Stars, animals, rocks— He was such a science geek." He paused, his expression darkening. "Wait, are you talking about...?"

"The Science Fair," Jeremy affirmed, his voice heavy. "That's when Dutch lost himself."

Jeremy leaned forward, catching Del's eye. "Remember his project?"

Del blinked, processing the information. "The baby chicks?"

"Yup!" Jeremy exclaimed, "Dutch was so excited about it. He wanted to show off the hatching process."

Del smirked, "Oh man, I remember. He wouldn't shut up about it. He was always going on and on about the chicks hatching and growing."

"Exactly." Jeremy nodded, "he had it all planned out. After they hatched, he was going to raise them. Even talked about building a coop behind his aunt's place."

"Yeah, especially after he had to move in with her," Del added with a somber tone, remembering the tragic loss of Dutch's mom. "It was something positive for him.

"A distraction within the chaos." Jeremy sighed, "It was more than just a project, Del. It was hope for him. A new beginning. And then—Jeremy's expression darkened, "After all that work, his aunt would always turn off the heat lamps because she was worried about the electricity bill."

Del shook his head, "Yeah, I remember. It messed up the whole thing."

Jeremy interjected, "Only a few hatched, right? Three, I think."

"Something like that," Del confirmed, his face grimacing. "They were weak, barely clinging to life. Yet Dutchie still brought them to school, holding onto a glimmer of hope."

Jeremy's voice grew softer, "He thought Mr. Green could help nurture them back to health."

Del's eyes clouded with the memory, "He was completely shattered. He told me he'd even prayed, hoping they'd pull through."

Jeremy nodded slowly, "Yeah, he told me that, too. Those chicks meant more to him than just a project. They represented a chance at something better, something pure among all the pain he was going through." Jeremy rubbed his temples, "You think it was just about the project grade, Del? It wasn't—it was what Mr. Green did."

A shadow passed over Del's face, darkening his features. "That day— I've tried so hard to forget it. It's still one of the most horrifying things I've ever witnessed."

Jeremy's voice dropped to a whisper, "We were right there, right next to each other, watching as he took those fragile chicks—"

Del cut him off, his distressed voice heavy. "Don't! I still hear the noises that they made—the sound of innocence being snuffed out."

Jeremy continued, his voice full of emotion, "But even worse than that was the look on Dutch's face.

Watching each of those tiny lives being taken away, it was as if he was reliving the loss of his family all over again, right there in front of the whole class."

Jeremy took a deep breath, "Remember how Dutchie reacted? It was like each chick was someone he lost - his dad, his sister, and his mom."

Del looked away, his eyes tearing up, "Yeah. I remember. He just froze, didn't he? Like he couldn't believe what was happening right in front of him."

Jeremy nodded, "Exactly. His face went blank. There was no emotion, just emptiness. It was like all the life was drained out of him."

Del swallowed hard. "After that day, he wasn't the same. It's like he just shut down and started pushing everyone away, even us."

Jeremy sighed, "I think that's when he gave up on everything. I just wish—I wish we could've done something more," he paused— "Sorry to be such a downer, but I saw him today, and it just brought everything back."

Del's tone shifted from somber to curious. "I heard about how you played superhero for Dennis Winston again before first period."

Jeremy rolled his eyes. No, it was after that. And for the record, bailing out Dennis has become a full-time job. I ran into Dutchie in the restroom and had a chance to really talk to him."

"Really? What about?" Del inquired, his interest piqued.

"I just talked to him about why he acts like he does. How he's always such a dick all the time."

Del looked at him, intrigued, "And?"

"He gave the usual defensive spiel. But here's the kicker," Jeremy said, leaning in. Just as he was leaving, he gave me advice about covering Tony Jefferson tomorrow night. It's like he still knows football like he's been keeping track or something."

Del leaned back, a smirk appearing on his face. "So, you're telling me Mr. Tough Guy Dutch is secretly our football spy?"

Jeremy laughed, "I wouldn't go that far, but yeah, he gave me a tip. It was pretty specific, too. Why would he do that unless he'd been paying attention?"

Del arched an eyebrow, "Maybe he's not as far gone as we think. Or maybe, deep down, he still cares about the team. Maybe underneath all that armor, our old Dutchie is still in there, cheering us on from the shadows, wishing he never quit."

Jeremy sighed, gazing off into the distance. "Do you remember that game in seventh grade when he ran the entire length of the field, dodging every tackle, scoring that winning touchdown?"

"The crowd went nuts." Del chuckled, "And remember his arm? He could've been our star quarterback. The passes he made were insane. Tight spirals, always on target. He's a million times better than Marty could ever be."

Jeremy chuckled with a hint of sadness in his eyes. "Yeah, he sure is, but after everything he went through, it's like he lost his passion for the game—like he lost his passion for a lot of things."

Del nodded solemnly. "Life took a lot from him, but you're right; he was naturally gifted. Sometimes I wonder if things had been different, he'd be the one leading our team to victory instead of, you know, where he is now."

Jeremy leaned back, thinking. "You know, maybe talking to him today was a sign. Maybe we can bring him back. Maybe we can help him find that passion again."

Del looked hopeful, "That would be amazing, wouldn't it? Getting the old Dutchie back, even if just a glimpse."

"Yeah," Jeremy agreed, "It's a long shot, but it's worth trying. Everyone deserves a second chance."

Jeremy looked intently at Del, "Maybe we don't necessarily need to get Dutchie back on the field, although, yeah, that would be great. But what if we could just get him a win off the field? Help him out in some way?"

Del shook his head, "You know Dutchie, he's too proud. He won't take any charity from us."

Jeremy sighed, "I know he wouldn't want a handout, for sure. But I'm not talking about that. I'm talking about just genuinely being there for him."

Del paused, reflecting, "That's a tall order, man. But you're right. Maybe we keep an eye out, and if a chance comes up to help him without making it seem like charity, we go for it."

Jeremy nodded, "Exactly. We'll just be there when he needs us."

Del clapped his hands together before hopping to his feet, "I'm with you, man. You know that I'm always up to lend a hand to anyone who needs it."

As he got up, he momentarily lost his balance, almost tripping over the ottoman. Regaining his composure, he reached for his movie collection, grabbing his copy of Nightmare on Elm Street 2.

"After that heavy talk, I need something a bit lighter," he said, sliding the tape into the VCR. "We're watching this."

23

ANYTHING BUT ROUTINE

THE EARLY MORNING sky was painted orange and pink as Jeremy's Jeep made its way through the quiet streets. The town was still sleepy, and it was clear that their mission that morning was out of the ordinary. But with the game on the line, every move mattered.

"Man, if Tomo sleeps in again, I swear—"Del began, adjusting the rearview mirror.

"He just doesn't get it, does he?" Jeremy replied, taking a turn toward Tomo's street. "I mean, the guy's an absolute beast on the field. We need him."

They both remembered Tomo's arrival at Huxley. He was an instant sensation. Being an exchange student in a small town always drew attention, and Tomo was no exception. Despite his large and intimidating build, those who took the time to get to know him discovered a gentle giant. He was kind, considerate, and always eager to help, even if it meant putting himself out there. However, not everyone understood. Some classmates would make fun of his accent or laugh when he struggled to find the right English words. It was a cruel reminder that while he was a hero on the football field, off it, he was still trying to find his place.

Pulling up to Tomo's house, the two boys hoped their teammate was ready and raring to go. Today was crucial, not just for the game but for Tomo's confidence and his place within the team. Sitting in the driveway, Jeremy's mind flashed back to the scolding he received from Tomo's mother the night before. Conversations with Ms. Matsuo were always tricky due to the language barrier, and he often found himself unsure of her tone.

As they approached the porch, the door swung open before they could knock, revealing Tomo. His size might have intimidated some, but his warm smile gave away his gentle nature.

"Hey, D.C!— Hey, Jack!" he greeted, his voice filled with genuine cheerfulness.

His towering presence dwarfed the entrance, yet his broad smile and excited eyes softened his appearance.

Del, momentarily caught off-guard by Tomo's correct punctuality, chuckled and nudged Jeremy." Look who's awake for once!" he remarked, grinning.

"Morning, Tomo. Looks like we didn't need to get you out of bed today," Jeremy added.

Tomo's hearty laugh echoed on the porch. "Mom woke me up early. She said you guys called late last night. She was really pissed off. Big game tonight. I'm ready!"

The boys exchanged amused glances."That's the spirit, big guy!" Del responded, giving Tomo a friendly pat on the back.

"Hop in, and we'll give you a lift," Jeremy added.

"Shot-gun!" Tomo exclaimed as he sprinted to the Jeep

"You can have it," Del chuckled, "All yours, big guy."

In the jeep, the energy was electric. With Tomo's infectious enthusiasm setting the tone, the boys eagerly discussed strategies and expectations for that night's game.

As the Jeep approached the fork in the road leading to the high school, the boys spotted a familiar pair making their way on foot. Missy, with her younger brother, Dennis, walking cautiously beside her, was navigating the sidewalk with difficulty due to her crutches.

"Jesus, Jeremy! What did you do?" Del yelled out from the back seat.

"It was a total accident, alright? Just be cool," Jeremy replied defensively as he pulled up alongside them. "Hey, you two," he greeted.

Caught off guard, Dennis's eyes widened in admiration. "Hey, Jeremy! Hey Tomo! Hey D.C.!"

Missy, always composed, responded politely, "Hey boys."

With his characteristic straightforwardness, Tomo asked, "Why are you walking?"

Missy sighed, "Mom had an early shift today, and Dad's working overnight. We had to walk since we're too close for the bus route."

Mr. Winston, a police officer, and Mrs. Winston, a nurse, often had conflicting schedules. They consistently took on extra hours, determined to save for their children's college educations.

While they were confident that Missy's academic achievements would lead to scholarships, Dennis was a different story. A dreamer at heart, his unexceptional grades weren't likely to attract significant financial aid. The dedication of the Winston parents to their children's futures was unrivaled. They were a close-knit family, bound by love and shared aspirations.

"Hop in, we can take you," Jeremy offered.

Before Jeremy could finish his sentence, Dennis eagerly clambered over the Jeep's open side, settling himself next to Del in the back seat. Tomo, always the gentleman, stepped out to assist Missy. "Ladies sit in the front. You get shot-gun," he said with a smile. After taking her crutches and ensuring she was comfortably seated, Tomo climbed into the back. His substantial weight caused the Jeep to shudder slightly, comically squishing Dennis into Del's lap.

As Jeremy drove towards the school, Tomo shouted over the rush of the wind, given the Jeep's top was down. "Lucky, we saw you guys! Jack's a good guy for stopping," he added with a thumbs-up towards Jeremy.

Wedged between Del and Tomo, Dennis turned to Del with a puzzled expression and asked, "Who's Jack?"

Del, gesturing towards Jeremy in the seat in front of him, replied, "That's Jack."

Missy chimed in, her voice playful, "Yeah, Jeremy owes me a lifetime of servitude, so this will just help chip away at his debt."

Jeremy shot her a soft, appreciative smile. "It's the least I can do," he replied, their eyes momentarily locking.

As he navigated the road, Jeremy couldn't help but steal glances at Missy. Her hair danced wildly in the wind, occasionally tangling with her glasses. With every glance, a new realization dawned on him, one he'd never felt before in any of his lifetimes.

Missy was genuinely beautiful. The fact that most boys overlooked her and the idea that she wasn't frequently considered as 'girlfriend material' puzzled him now.

Tomo playfully slapped Jeremy on the shoulder from the back seat. "Jack, always helping people. I'm so happy he's my friend."

Dennis, still confused, turned to Del. "Jack?"

Del responded with a light chuckle, "Tomo has a bit of a translation mix-up now and then."

Dennis's brow furrowed in sympathy. "It's rough how some people mock him for that."

"I agree," Del nodded. "Ever watch 'Saved by the Bell'?"-

"Of course!" Dennis said enthusiastically.

"Tomo's a huge fan," Del began, "He used to watch translated versions of it back in Japan. So, picture this: Tomo's first day at Huxley High, and he meets our very own golden boy here," he gestured toward Jeremy, "who could easily be the star of his own high school series."

Dennis tried piecing it together, still somewhat lost. Del, noting his confusion, explained,

"So, on that first day when Tomo was having a hard time finding his way, Jeremy, being his usual helpful self, stepped up to help him find his class. As Jeremy showed Tomo around, Kristen, in her cheerleader uniform, walked up and introduced herself."

At the mention of Kristen's name, Dennis's pulse quickened.

Del grinned, starting to see the realization dawn on Dennis's face. " Are you Putting it together now?"

"You mean Tomo thinks Jeremy is Zach Morris?" Dennis asked, astonished.

"Bingo!" Del exclaimed.

"And Kristen is his Kelly Kapowski!" Dennis continued, the complete picture now clear to him.

"But the name 'Jack'? What's that about?" Dennis asked, still confused.

Del leaned in with a mischievous glint in his eye. "That's the best part. The bootleg episodes of 'Saved by the Bell' Tomo watched subtitled 'Zach' as 'Jack.' So, for Tomo, it's always been Jack Morris."

Dennis couldn't contain his laughter. "Oh my god!—That's hilarious!"

Catching the infectious laughter over the rushing wind, Tomo asked, "What's funny?"

Del glanced at Dennis before responding, "Dennis here was just telling me about this episode of 'Saved by the Bell.' He has a huge crush on Kelly Kapowski."

Dennis, flustered, retorted, "No, I do not!" Dennis looked at Jeremy's eyes in the rearview mirror and shook his head vigorously.

Tomo's face lit up with a smile. "Ah, I love that show!" He gave Jeremy another playful slap on the back. "Jack Morris— He's the best."

"Sure is," Del agreed, looking at Jeremy, "he certainly makes the show worth watching."

As the Jeep made its way to Huxley High, Jeremy's thoughts lingered on the conversations of the night before, on Dutch, on Missy, and the impending football game.

Arriving at school, Jeremy felt a sense of normalcy. There were no sudden shifts or unexpected turns; everything was right where it should be. Before he could help Missy out of the Jeep, Tomo was already in action, hopping out from the back with grace. With his characteristic enthusiasm, he opened her door and effortlessly lifted her from the passenger seat.

Taken aback by Tomo's surprising strength, she let out a startled squeal, her cheeks turning pink.

"Thanks, Tomo," she said, trying to regain her composure, "You can put me down now."

Caught in the wave of his enthusiasm to help, he froze, embarrassment washing over him. "Oh, sorry," he mumbled, carefully easing her down.

Having wriggled out from the Jeep's back seat, Dennis quickly fetched Missy's crutches, passing them to Tomo. "Here you go."

Tomo took the crutches and positioned them so Missy could comfortably step in.

Del, getting out from behind the passenger seat, approached Jeremy. "Fun ride, big guy. Seems like there's always an adventure with you, huh?"

Jeremy nodded in response, "I guess so."

Suddenly, as if materializing from thin air, Stacy joined the group. Her eyes took in the Winstons and Tomo. "Looks like our gang's expanding," she remarked, a hint of amusement in her tone. Turning her gaze to Tomo, she teased, "Hey, Tomo! Good to see you awake for once."

Stacy's eyes darted to Missy's crutches. "What happened to you!" she asked, her tone mixed with genuine concern and playful teasing. "What's with the bum wheel?"

Exchanging glances with Jeremy, Missy tried to play it off, "Oh, it's nothing. I just tripped. I can be such a klutz sometimes."

Knowing there was more to the story, Del chimed in with a hint of sarcasm, "That's not what I heard."

Missy shot him a sharp look, "That's my story, and I'm sticking to it."

Jeremy's face paled slightly, taken aback by how Missy's response sounded so much like something Colin Quinn would say when he'd wrap up his weekly SNL Weekend Update. But that was impossible; Quinn wouldn't take over those duties for years from now.

Shaking off the uncanny resemblance, Jeremy admitted, Let's just say I was rushing to class, and she got caught in the crossfire; it was a total accident.

Stacy, always up for playful teasing, joked, "Running late for class, huh?" I'll bet you were too busy sucking face with Strawberry Shortcake."

Jeremy's face reddened as he interjected, "Stacy, that's not very nice!"

Stacy sarcastically suggested, "Well, whatever did happen, I bet he said he was sorry and has now committed his life to serving you for the rest of yours." She didn't know how much truth was behind her playful words.

Missy played along with a grin, "You know, that doesn't sound too bad. Having Homecoming here at my beck and call? I could definitely put him to good use. Maybe have him carry out all my nefarious plans," she concluded with a dramatic, almost theatrical, evil laugh.

Stacy threw her head back, laughing genuinely this time. "I've gotta say, I like this girl. Who knew you had such a wicked sense of humor?"

The truth was, in all of Jeremy's lifetimes, Stacy and Missy had never even been on the fringes of the same social circle. They were always, in every sense, perfect strangers.

The novelty of this newfound interaction between them made Jeremy wonder if such encounters might lead to significant changes or ripples in the future. He mentally bookmarked the moment, knowing he'd need to keep an eye out for any potential consequences.

As the group gathered to head into the school, the unmistakable roar of Dutch's Turismo echoed through the parking lot.

"Fucking Dutchie," Dennis groaned as he stepped behind the group, instinctively seeking a place to hide.

Jeremy reassured Dennis by wrapping his arm around him and saying, "Don't stress, man, everything will be fine."

Stacy, always protective of her friends, stepped forward with a warning edge to her voice, "He'd better keep his distance. If he so much as looks at me the wrong way, I will tear him a new one." No one doubted her.

Del smirked, "Honestly, I'd pay to see that."

Tomo, ever the peace-loving soul, shook his head. "I wouldn't want that. We need more love, more hugs."

Del grinned from ear to ear, slapping Tomo on the back, "Tomo, you big softy, I love you, man."

Tomo's cheeks reddened slightly, "Really?" he replied, "Anata wa Watashi no shin'yūdes."

Del, taken aback and fumbling over the unfamiliar words, "You wanna washy my what? Whoa there, buddy! That's not exactly what I had meant."

Tomo chuckled heartily, "No, no! Anata wa Watashi no shin'yūdes means 'you are my best friend.' All of you are!— You, Jack, little Stacy, and now Missy, and—um," he stammered, looking at Dennis.

Dennis raised his eyebrows, prompting Tomo, "Dennis?"

"Yeah, yeah! Dennis, you're like *Screech*, the funny guy who likes to laugh. You are my best friend too."

The conversation stopped as everyone's attention shifted to watch Dutch slowly approach. The sound of the Turismo's exhaust rumbled in the background. But Dutch cruised calmly past them instead of the antici- pated dramatic entrance or aggressive near miss. His arm casually rested out the window, forming a gesture that was somewhere between a point and a peace sign. Without directly looking at them, he gave a nod of acknowledgment as he passed by.

The car's engine rumbled softly, indicating he was headed to the back of the school, towards the vocational wing.

Stacy rolled her eyes dramatically, "What a sweet moment," she said, pretending to gag. "Can we move along? I'm not really up for a love circle, especially since," she glanced at Missy while gesturing at Jeremy, "What did you call him?"

"Uh, Homecoming?" Missy replied with a smirk.

"Right, 'Homecoming' over here was supposed to hang out with me for his big 18th birthday but he totally stood me up."

Jeremy frowned, his hand flying to his forehead in frustration. "Stacy, I totally forgot. Del and I—"

Stepping forward, Del cut him off, "Shh, I've got this." Slipping his arm around Stacy's shoulders, he steered her towards the school. "C'mon, let me fill you in."

Dennis and Tomo watched, amused. Del turned toward them and asked, "You guys coming?"

"Yeah, yeah!" Tomo replied with his signature enthusiasm. Without warning, he scooped Dennis up, tossing him over a shoulder. "Come on best friend!" he called out as they made their way up the hill. "I'll keep you safe from that evil Dutchie!"

Behind them, Jeremy called out, "We'll catch up!"

Dennis squirmed and wriggled, attempting to escape Tomo's playful grip, mortified by the giggling and glances of the passing students.

Jeremy and Missy followed behind them as they walked toward the building. Her crutches clicked rhythmically against the pavement; she turned to him with a curious head tilt. "Your birthday was yesterday?" she asked.

"Yeah," he admitted, scratching the back of his head, "It was."

"Why didn't you tell me?" she asked genuinely.

He shrugged, "It just didn't come up."

Sighing heavily and with guilt evident in her eyes, she said, "I was so mean to you. I feel awful now. I'm so sorry."

He waved off her apology, "It's no big deal. I promise."

She tilted her head thoughtfully, her earlier curiosity returning, "So, was the rest of your day any better after our run-ins'?" She used air quotes, emphasizing their accidental encounters.

He chuckled, "You mean our collisions? Yeah, it turned out alright, I guess."

She arched an eyebrow, "Yeah, what did you end up doing? Besides standing up, Stacy, that is. Is ghosting girls something you do a lot? I remember Heather talking about how you ditched Kristen at lunch, and now Stacy?"

His face flushed, as he searched for the right words, "Uh, no—it's not like that." He stumbled over his response, caught off guard by her line of questioning.

They walked side by side in reflective silence for a few moments. Eventually, she spoke up, cutting through the quiet, "I'm sorry for the teasing. You were going to tell me how you spent the rest of your birthday?"

He hesitated, wanting to deflect. "Oh, nothing super special," he tried to gloss over the topic.

She raised an eyebrow, her gaze curious. "You mentioned it turned out to be a pretty decent day," she reminded him. She narrowed her eyes, challenging him. "Come on, spill it. I'm interested."

Reluctantly, he began, "Well, there was practice," he hesitated, deliberately omitting the part about his covert trip home and the sight of Gregg passed out in his undies. No one needed that story. "Then Del and I went to Kristen's for dinner."

Her face lit up, "Oh, the Rays are incredible! What did you guys have?"

"Pot roast," Jeremy replied, with a hint of nostalgia in his voice.

She let out an appreciative moan, "I've had that before! Donna is such a good cook."

He looked at her, puzzled, "Donna?"

She smiled, "Yeah, Kristen's mom. The Rays, Donna, and Ed were always so nice to me."

His thoughts buzzed. He'd always addressed them as Mr. and Mrs. Ray, even though he felt like a part of their family.

She continued reminiscing, "I had so many sleepovers at Kristen's when my parents had to work nights." A smirk played on her lips, "Let me guess, scotch on the rocks and a cigar for Ed before dinner?"

Jeremy chuckled, tapping the tip of his nose, "Exactly."

She sighed wistfully, "Sounds wonderful."

Jeremy changed the topic slightly and said, "You know, I talked to Kristen about you. She doesn't hold any grudges, really."

Her eyes widened in disbelief, her tone sharp, "You talked about me?"

He tried to soothe her, "Look, it was no big deal. I think she saw us arguing in the parking lot and heard from Heather that we were together in the hall. She was, maybe, a little jealous?"

Her voice dripped with sarcasm, "Jealous— of me possibly 'stealing' her precious quarterback?"

He corrected her, "I'm not a QB, Missy; I'm a linebacker and tight end."

She shot back, clearly infuriated, "I don't care about how 'tight' your end is. You shouldn't have talked about me. Now, she'll probably hate me even more." Her voice wavered.

"Missy, I'm sorry," he began, "She doesn't hate you."

She interrupted, her voice filled with hurt, tears filling her eyes. "She hasn't tried to be my friend in years Jeremy, and now, suddenly, here you are gossiping about me with her. It's just too much!"

"Missy, it wasn't like that—" he tried. But she wasn't having any of it.

"You know what? I thought you were different. But it turns out you're just like I thought—shame on me. Just give me my books and leave me alone," she demanded, snatching her belongings from him.

As he watched her struggle her way into the school, Jeremy felt conflicted, torn between relief and regret. He knew that having Missy out of this life might be for the best, but he couldn't shake the feeling that giving up on helping her would be a mistake.

24

BUBBLICIOUS

When Missy entered the school, she was immediately confronted by a flight of stairs. With her books in one hand and crutches in the other, getting to the top seemed impossible. Determined, she started her careful climb: left crutch, right crutch, left foot, right foot.

As her classmates hustled around her, she maintained her rhythm, proving to herself and others that she could overcome the obstacle.

By the time she reached the main floor, she was feeling a mix of exhaustion and pride. However, her victory was short-lived. A group of energetic freshmen, caught up in their morning rush, brushed past her, accidentally knocking a notebook from her grasp and sending it skidding across the floor.

She wobbled, nearly losing her balance, before stabilizing herself. Taking a deep breath, she let out a weary sigh. She stepped toward where the notebook had landed and felt a sticky sensation under her crutch.

"Ugh, what is this, gum?" She groaned, observing the over-chewed substance stretching between the floor and the rubber tip of her crutch.

"Forget this," she muttered to herself. Setting the crutches aside, she began a slow limp toward her fallen notebook, feeling a slight improvement in her ankle from the day before. "Stay strong," she whispered to herself as encouragement.

Just as she started to regain her composure, the day took another turn, stopping her dead in her tracks.

Kristen, impeccable in her game day cheerleader outfit, was bending down to pick up the notebook, inspecting it closely.

"Hey! Anyone drop this?" she called out as she held it over her head. Missy's heart raced.

"That's my favorite notebook. I can't just leave it," she thought to herself. The idea of facing Kristen was intimidating. However, the notebook's contents, her notes, and her carefully drawn-out plans were invaluable. She had to get it back.

With each step, Missy's limp improved a little. Her momentarily forgotten pain was masked by the need to get her notebook back.

By the time she reached her, Kristen, ever the nosey one, was already flipping through the notebook's pages.

Missy took a deep breath and said softly, "That's mine, Kristen."

When their eyes met, a mix of old memories and silent tension filled the space between them.

With a guilty look and a nervous giggle escaping, Kristen offered, "Sorry, I was just trying to figure out who it belonged to."

"Thanks," Missy replied with a hint of coolness, taking the notebook as Kristen held it out.

"Didn't I see you on crutches in the parking lot? What happened to them?" Kristen asked.

"They were just slowing me down," Missy responded.

Missy's mind began to spiral. "She saw me in the parking lot. Did she see me with Jeremy? Is she mad that we were together? Is she moments away from ripping my eyes out with her flawless French manicure?" She could feel a bead of sweat forming on her forehead.

Kristen looked at her, squinting slightly, "Are you okay, Missy? You seem a bit distracted."

"Yeah, I'm fine," Missy said as her mind continued to race, "Why is she talking to me? Is it because of the conversation she had with Jeremy? This is all too much. Everything was fine before Jeremy Anderson came crashing into my life— now, all this chaos, I can't handle it."

Kristen snapped her fingers in front of Missy's face, "Missy? Earth to Missy?"

Shaken, Missy responded, "Sorry, what?"

"Let me help you with your books. Where's your next class?" Kristen offered.

Coming out of her rush of thoughts, Missy responded, "English, with Pritchett."

Reaching out her hand, Kristen demanded, "Hand them over. I'm heading that way for Bio anyway. And word on the street is a certain blonde hunk might be the reason for your limp."

Missy sighed, "Jeremy? Yeah, he's not my favorite person right now."

Kristen's eyes softened a bit, and she felt a bit of relief. She never truly considered Missy a threat to Jeremy, but there was an undeniable natural beauty about her that made Kristen jealous.

"Let's wait until it's less crowded," Kristen suggested, trying to lighten the mood.

"Good idea," Missy agreed, but the atmosphere remained tense.

Trying to ease the awkward silence, Kristen started rummaging through her purse, searching for something to talk about.

"Want some gum?" she asked. "I need to switch out this piece. This new sugarless stuff is the worst. It doesn't last at all." She continued rummaging through her purse, her fingers navigating a labyrinth of cherry lip gloss, scrunchies, and an assortment of cosmetics Missy had never seen before.

"Aha! Found it!" Kristen exclaimed triumphantly, pulling out a crushed gum wrapper from her bag. She tore it apart, revealing two final pieces. "Two left. Perfect." She said as she handed one to Missy and popped the other into her mouth, savoring the flavor. "Mmm—Watermelon Bubblelicious. The good stuff."

Missy, not as enthusiastic but not wanting to disappoint Kristen, chewed thoughtfully. "Yeah—it's pretty good."

"Pretty good!" Kristen exclaimed. "This is from my secret stash! You have to appreciate it more than that." She teased.

Missy played along, closing her eyes and exaggerating her enjoyment. "Oh, there it is; I can taste it now; it's like I'm at a summer picnic," she said.

Kristen giggled, playing into the fantasy. "Right? Can't you actually taste it?" She closed her eyes, letting the flavor transport her. "Hear those birds? And there's a squirrel over there; get that nut little buddy!"

Missy continued, "Oh, the smell of freshly cut grass. And those burgers on the grill? No cheese on mine!" She sang to a fictional grill master in the distance.

Kristen laughed heartily, "So now it's a cookout? I'm in!"

She opened her eyes, catching Missy's amused gaze. "Okay, this gum is something. We have to keep this a secret, or else there'll be Watermelon Bubblelicious parties everywhere."

"Definitely," Missy agreed, chuckling at the thought. "Just imagine the burnouts tripping out on all this flavor."

Kristen placed a finger over her lips. "It'll be our secret." She glanced around, "Looks like the coast is clear. Let's get you to class. And don't stress about being late—Pritchett loves me."

Missy and Kristen made their way to the first period. Their steps were light, and their conversation was easy. The school's social hierarchy melted away, and they were transported back to their middle school days.

"Do you remember those 90210 marathons we used to have?" Missy giggled. You were all about David Silver!"

Kristen scoffed playfully, "Oh, come on! David was so cute, and what a dancer, but admit it, you were totally in love with Brandon."

Missy grinned, "Okay, okay, guilty.—his blue eyes? So dreamy."

They laughed, reminiscing about the TV shows they'd binge-watch and the late-night snack attacks. "Remember our Blockbuster runs? Every time we rented something, no matter what, we always had to get Dirty Dancing," Missy recalled.

Kristen smirked, dramatically deepening her voice to imitate Johnny Castle, "*Nobody Puts Baby in a Corner.*"

"We must've watched that final dance scene a million times." Missy laughed.

As the two girls strolled through the hallways, they reminisced about all the sleepovers, dance routines, and silly dramas they once shared. In those moments, they weren't the overachieving star student and the popular cheerleader; they were just Missy and Kristen.

Kristen handed Missy her books outside Mrs. Pritchett's English class as students shuffled about, settling into their desks. The muffled sounds of chatter echoed softly, punctuated by the occasional laughter.

"Thanks for helping me, Kris," Missy began, her voice sincere. "It was nice catching up with you."

Kristen's lips curled into a smile. She peered past Missy into the classroom, her eyes darting from face to face. "Who's in this class with you?" she asked absently.

Just as Missy was about to answer, Kristen's attention shifted. "Hold on a sec," she said, her voice singing as she called out, "Hey Bear!"

Jeremy looked up from his desk, spotting his girlfriend. When their eyes met, he offered a casual wave in response. As Kristen moved slightly, he noticed she wasn't alone. "Missy?" he thought, as he reached for the journal in his bag. Deciding it would be best to wait and let the situation unfold, Jeremy shifted his focus back to his journal.

Kristen returned to Missy, "Gotta run," she said hurriedly.

"Yeah, sure," Missy responded, slightly disappointed.

But as Kristen started to leave, she stopped and turned back. "Hey, Miss? How about hanging out after the game tonight? A few of us are going out for pizza. We usually have to cheer up the boys after a loss, and tonight's game against Regional will be rough. We will probably need an extra nurse," she teased.

Missy was caught off guard. She'd always wanted to be part of Kristen's crowd. But now, she was uncertain. Was Kristen inviting her out of genuine interest or was it because of something Jeremy had said? "I don't know, Kristen. Football is really not my thing," Missy replied cautiously.

Kristen's eyes pleaded with her, "Come on, Miss! It'll be fun. Just come to the game, and we'll all go out afterward."

Missy hesitated, her expression a mix of hope and uncertainty.

"It will be a good time, I promise!" Kristen reassured, noting Missy's reservations.

Missy took a deep breath, "Did Jeremy mention anything to you about me? Did he put you up to this?"

Kristen seemed genuinely taken aback. "Why would you ask that? I'm inviting you because I want to. Honestly, it's nice to talk to you again. I feel like I can be myself with you. Believe it or not, none of my friends understand my love for 'Dirty Dancing'; they think it's ancient. And their music taste? Total garbage! They always hijack the radio in my car, and I have to put up with it. It gets super annoying sometimes." Kristen chuckled, trying to diffuse the tension, "I could seriously use someone in my corner."

"Okay, I'll come," Missy agreed.

Kristen's face lit up. "Awesome! How about I pick you up? I'll have to be at the field early since I'm cheering, but you're okay with that, right?"

Missy hesitated before agreeing, "Yeah, sure, I'll just bring a book to pass the time."

Kristen raised an eyebrow playfully, "Missy, leave the book at home. Try to mingle and be social, alright? Trust me, it'll be fun."

Feeling a mix of apprehension and excitement, Missy responded with a slight chuckle, "Alright, alright, I'll give it a shot."

With an energetic and bubbly "Hooray! "Kristen waved a flamboyant goodbye to Missy, her cheerleader spirit shining through.

As Missy walked to her desk, she felt the weight of Jeremy's gaze. She glanced over, and their eyes met. Instead of words, a meek smile crossed her lips, filled with sadness and regret for how she had lashed out at him earlier.

Jeremy nodded back, the faintest hint of a smile touching his lips, acknowledging the silent truce. As she settled into her seat, the room fell quiet under Mrs. Pritchett's stern gaze. "Alright, class," she began, "let's get started."

25

SAVED BY THE BELL

AFTER THE ROCKY start with Missy, Jeremy's day unfolded uneventfully. It was an ordinary Friday in 1996. He'd lived through this exact day countless times, but each repetition had nuances. Today, however, everything was precisely as he remembered.

In classes, he effortlessly answered questions when called on, occasionally giving wrong answers, deliberately playing down his extensive knowledge. This was a skill he'd perfected over countless lifetimes. After all, blending in was critical.

Sitting in the lunchroom, Jeremy was deep in thought. Seeing Kristen and Missy together outside of English class weighed on him, and a continuous loop of questions and possible scenarios played out in his head. He needed clarity.

"Hey, Kris," he said suddenly, "Can we take a walk before the next period?"

She looked at him with a flash of surprise filling her eyes, which was quickly replaced by excitement.

"Absolutely!" she said enthusiastically, likely thinking he wanted a more private, intimate setting.

Ignoring the group's catcalls and playful taunts, Jeremy took Kristen's hand and led her out of the noisy cafeteria. The hallway outside was quieter, offering them a chance to talk away from the crowd of prying eyes and ears. The two walked together, with her taking the lead, heading towards a secluded spot they both knew well. Yet just before they got there, he hesitated, tugging her arm gently to stop her.

"What's up?" she asked, glancing towards the corner they were about to turn into. "C'mon, we don't have much time before the next bell."

He exhaled, trying to gather his thoughts. "I need to ask you something."

She rolled her eyes half-teasingly. "Seriously? More talking? That's all you want to do these days."

He bit his lip, knowing he had to tread carefully. "It's just that, I saw something weird this morning, and it involved you."

She raised an eyebrow, clearly intrigued. "Weird? What do you mean, weird?"

Taking a deep breath, Jeremy finally said, "You and Missy."

Her reaction was immediate. "So? What's so weird about that?"

He shifted his weight from foot to foot. "Well, you two seemed— close. I mean, you were helping her. It's just unexpected."

She chuckled. "Yeah, I was helping her to class. She looked like she was having a hard time after ditching her crutches." Her playful demeanor shifted slightly as she added, twirling one of her curls, "By the way, someone mentioned that you had something to do with her injury. That you accidentally knocked her down the stairs or something. Smooth move, Bear."

He looked away, as she stared at him, awaiting an explanation. He dropped his head. "I don't know what to say. I didn't knock her down the stairs. It wasn't that bad." He looked back up at Kristen, searching her eyes for answers. "But why were you two together? That's what caught me off guard."

She responded with a nonchalant shrug. "She dropped her notebook. I picked it up. She needed help, so I helped her. Isn't that what people do?"

"Yeah, I guess," Jeremy replied, somewhat unconvinced.

Her face softened. "Honestly, it was refreshing. We only chatted briefly, but it was like we were back in middle school. She wasn't all serious like I thought she'd be."

He nodded, thinking back to his interactions with Missy. "The few times I've talked to her, she's been pretty cool and way funnier than I expected."

Kristen let out a laugh. "Oh, she's funny. At least she was back in the day. Look, Jeremy, I've got to come clean about something."

His brows furrowed in confusion. "What's that?"

She took a deep breath. "I was really upset when I saw you two together yesterday. I was jealous, and yes, I was scared."

"Scared?" he repeated, trying to grasp her meaning.

She nodded, "Yeah. For a moment, I convinced myself that you and Missy had some secret thing going on. I half-joked about it yesterday when we were at 7-11, but deep down, I was genuinely worried it might be true. So, when I had her book in my hands this morning, I couldn't resist the opportunity to snoop and see if I had anything to worry about."

His anticipation grew. "And?"

Using her fingers to emphasize air quotes, Kristen mimicked Missy's earlier statement, "'Not my most favorite person right now.'"

He exhaled deeply. "That sucks. But why would you think there's something between Missy and me?" he asked.

She hesitated for a moment, searching for the right words. "Because we have history, Bear. Missy and I were inseparable once. She was my best friend, my only friend really. And then, when she came here to Huxley a year early, we drifted apart, and things changed.

When I saw you two together, I felt jealous and, I don't know, regret. fear?" She took a deep breath, "And it's not just about me and Missy. It's about me and you. You're important to me, Jeremy. I thought maybe she was offering something I couldn't or that you'd see how great she really is, and you wanted someone with a bit more brains than me."

Jeremy looked at Kristen, noticing a vulnerability he hadn't seen in her in any previous lifetime. "Missy and I just happened to cross paths a few times," he said, choosing his words wisely. Honestly, that's it. I had never really spoken to her before yesterday. She's nice, but I promise you have nothing to worry about."

"I know, but she's so put together, I was afraid you'd like that. She's so bold, and, let's face it, she's so much prettier than me," Kristen offered timidly.

His face dropped; this insecurity was totally out of character for her. Sure, he'd taken note of Missy's looks while driving her to school that morning, but that was a simple observation, "What are you even talking about, Kris? "

"Oh, Come on, Bear," she said, her face draining of expression. "Seriously? —You've never checked her out? She's flawless."

"Kris, I am confused. You are the prettiest girl in this school, and you were Junior Prom Queen as a sophomore! Where is this coming from?"

Jeremy was puzzled by this side of Kristen, something he'd never known; insecure Kristen was a new experience for him.

"All of us girls always talk about how clean and effortless her look is," Kristen confessed, "She never has a single pimple, which we know because she hardly wears any makeup. She drives us all crazy. The way she rolls in day after day, looking like a perfect news anchor with the leading story for the night, it can be infuriating."

Kristen's face was fueled by frustration as she continued. "Like, just this morning, there she was, hobbling up the stairs with her perfect hair and every piece of clothing all tucked and pressed; I swear to god, I wanted to kick her in the other ankle," she joked.

"I've honestly never noticed Kris, I swear." Jeremy injected trying to soothe her.

"But what's worse', she continued, snapping her gum furiously, "seeing you with her in the parking lot made me question how I'd treated her. Pushing her away just because she wanted to reach her potential," she paused to blow a curl out of her face."And I'm over here getting so caught up in high school popularity contests. I mean, who even does that? "How will being head cheerleader help me be a good person in the future? Missy has it all figured out. I thought about what it would be like if we had stayed friends this whole time."

He reached out, tucking the pesky stray curl behind her ear. "High school makes us all do crazy things. It's a mess, but we can't let it define us or our relationships."

She nodded, taking in his words. "I know. So, I decided to do something about it. This year will go by in a flash, and soon Missy will be off to college, and she will be out of our lives forever, so, starting today, I gonna try to be her friend again."

He wondered if his words could have swayed Kristen's decision. "Did our conversation yesterday have anything to do with this new mission?" He asked.

"Not really," she paused, "maybe a little. Honestly, every time I see her, I can't help but think about the possibilities, the what-ifs. Maybe seeing you two together was just the little nudge I needed to swallow my pride and do something about my guilt."

He made a mental note of what she'd just said. His actions caused a ripple, and he'd have to stay close to it to see how far it would go. He smiled gently, "That's great, Kris. I think she'd really like to be your friend again."

Kristen hesitated, then began in a rhythmic tone, "I also hope you're okay with this, but—" She took a deep breath before speaking hurriedly, "I invited her to the game and to hang with us afterward. Please don't be upset! I swear I won't make it weird." She closed her eyes tight, preparing for a reaction she was used to when dealing with Jeremy from lifetime number one.

He looked at her, his brow raised in genuine curiosity. "So, is Missy meeting you after the game? What's the plan?"

She exhaled a massive sigh of relief before outlining her idea, enthusiasm evident in her voice. "Well, I thought I could pick her up, and we'll head to the game together. I told her we'd have to be there early because of game day prep. And guess what? She said she'd bring a book! Can you believe it? She's such a nerd— it's kind of adorable. I told her to ditch the book and try mingling, you know, get to know some people."

He leaned against the wall, crossing his arms thoughtfully. "Kris, I get where you're coming from, but that might be asking a bit much, don't you think? Seriously, she's never been to one of these games. You'll be busy cheering, and she doesn't know the first thing about football. It's a lot to expect her to sit there alone."

Kristen bit her lip, her enthusiasm dimming. "I hadn't thought of it that way. I want her to have a good time. I really want this to be a restart for us."

He nodded, trying to find a solution. "Well, what if she brought along a friend?"

She gave him a dry look. "Jeremy, Missy doesn't really... you know, have 'friends' like we do."

"I was thinking more along the lines of—" Jeremy hesitated, trying to find the right words as Kristen's eyes widened in realization.

"No way! Not that little weenie!" She groaned in exasperation.

He couldn't help but chuckle at her reaction. "Come on, Kris. Dennis is a good kid." But Kristen wasn't having any of it, launching into a passionate rant.

"Every time we'd have a sleepover at Missy's, Dennis would be there. Every—single— time. He'd be lurking around, doing his awkward Dennis thing." She deepened her voice, imitating Dennis, "Hey, Kristen, are you a Star Wars fan? Or, hey, listen to this new tape I got!" She rolled her eyes dramatically, "It was always some weird synth-pop nonsense from the 80s. I swear, it made me want to rip my ears off. God! He's such a dork!"

"I get it, Kris—Dennis is unique," Jeremy began cautiously. But wouldn't it be worth enduring his dorkiness just for one evening? How about this— Let Missy bring him to the game if she wants. Afterward, I'll take him home and catch up with you later."

She looked at Jeremy, staying silent.

"Kris, it's just one car ride to the game; that's all I'm asking for. That's fair, right?"

Pouting in her signature overdramatic manner, she finally gave in, "Fine!"

With a sense of urgency, she tugged at his arm. "Come on, Bear, we might have a few minutes. Let's go to the stairwell." But just as she began to pull him in her direction, the bell rang, interrupting their moment.

"Ah, Poop!" Kristen exclaimed with a mix of playfulness and frustration. "You owe me some quality time, big guy." She poked him in the chest, and he knew all too well that when Kristen used the term "big guy" she wasn't thrilled.

He exhaled deeply, hoping the rest of the day would be free from any more unexpected turns. The evening's game was what he eagerly anticipated.

Jeremy had played this game against Regional High many times before and knew tonight would be exciting in its own way. There was nothing to lose except the game itself, and losing was the only option.

26

SPICE UP YOUR LIFE

As THE SCHOOL DAY ENDED, Jeremy weighed his options for the next couple of hours. Kick-off was at 7 pm, and it was only 3 o'clock now. He had some time to kill.

Del would be spending this precious time with his dad. Game days had taken on a sacred aura for the Del Coronado family since Del's mom passed. It was their time to bond, to share quiet moments before the game.

Kristen would be wrapped up in her pre-game rituals. Their schedules on game days were like two ships passing in the night, never quite meeting until after the game.

Then there was Stacy, their theatre queen. She would be immersed in rehearsals, preparing for the starring role she had landed in the upcoming fall production of *"The Grapes of Wrath."*

When the school's final bell rang, it forced Jeremy's thoughts back to the present. "Guess it's some "me" time," he mused, the memory of the mysterious contents in his backpack. Specifically, Gregg's envelope, as he referred to it in his mind with disgust. He had forgotten about it in the whirlwind of the past day's events. With a deep breath and a reluctant nod, he whispered to himself, "Alright, I guess it's now or never."

Making his way to the exit, Jeremy was pulled from his thoughts by a familiar voice calling out behind him.

"Hey, Homecoming! Wait up!" He turned around, a smile tugging at the corners of his mouth, recognizing that playful jab. Missy was hurrying towards him.

"Hey Missy," he greeted warmly, "How's the ankle?"

"Much better, thanks," she responded, pausing momentarily to catch her breath. "Look, I just want to say I'm really sorry about this morning."

He offered a reassuring smile. "It's cool, don't worry about it. You aren't the first person to put me in my place. You told me something in confidence, and I betrayed your trust. I shouldn't have shared what you said with Kristen."

Missy, a little surprised by his humility, nodded. "Thanks for understanding. It's just that a lot has been going on at the moment— sometimes I snap without thinking."

He locked eyes with her, a sincerity reflecting on his face. "I really appreciate that, Missy," he said with genuine warmth.

Seeing the depth of honesty in his response, Missy was momentarily taken aback. Nodding, she replied, "I mean it. I shouldn't have snapped at you."

Digging into her backpack, she pulled out a small item wrapped in tin foil. "Here," she offered, extending the mysterious gift towards him, "consider this a peace offering."

"What's this?" he asked as he peeled back the foil layer, revealing a gooey chocolate brownie. "No way!" he exclaimed with genuine surprise.

Giggling and a bit flushed, she took a playful bow. "Courtesy of Chef Winston."

Grinning, he asked, "Should I eat it now?" Being 18 again had its advantages, not least of which was being able to indulge his sweet tooth without repercussions.

"Of course, it's all yours; go for it," she replied, her eyes twinkling with anticipation.

When he bit into the brownie, he was immediately taken with its deep, chocolatey flavor. But there was something else, a distinct taste he couldn't quite put his finger on.

"This is incredible, Missy!" he marveled, "but there's a twist to this. What is it? It's almost—spicy?"

She smirked, her playful nature surfacing. "I'd share the secret, but the last time I confided in you, word got out pretty quickly."

He shot her a mock, offended look. "Come on, Missy. I've never had a brownie quite like this," he said, popping the other half of it in his mouth.

Sighing dramatically, she relented. "Alright, but you can't tell a soul."

Seeing his sincere nod, she whispered, "It's cayenne pepper. I like a little kick in my treats."

His eyes widened in realization. "That's amazing, Missy. It's truly a unique touch."

She giggled, pleased with his reaction. "Thanks, I'm glad you enjoyed it."

"Enjoyed? I could kill a whole batch of these. My compliments to the chef!" he replied, chuckling.

Missy's cheeks turned a light shade of pink. " I just wanted to make it up to you," she admitted.

His expression softened as he looked at her, a gentle smile forming. "You didn't have to do anything but, thank you. It means a lot. And honestly, you've got some serious baking skills."

She chuckled, playfully tucking a stray hair behind her ear. "Thanks. It's a bit of a hidden talent, everyone has their secret passions, right?"

He nodded in agreement, "They certainly do. But thank you. Not just for the brownie but for taking the step to make things right. It isn't always easy, but it's always worth it."

Hesitating, he asked her, "Um, what are you up to now?"

She shrugged, "Nothing, just waiting for Dennis to walk home."

"And after that?" he inquired further.

She raised an eyebrow, amused, "Well, I guess you've heard by now. I'm suddenly a football fan. Your girlfriend invited me to the game tonight. I just need to be back home by around 5:30 to get picked up."

Seeing an opportunity, he quickly asked, "So, you've got a few hours to kill then. How about going for a ride? Nothing weird, I could just use some company; Dennis can come along, too. Actually, I need to catch up with him."

As if on cue, Dennis began to approach them. When he saw his sister talking to his hero, he picked up his pace.

"Speak of the devil," Jeremy said noticing Dennis strolling down the hill towards them.

Missy turned to see her brother approaching them with an enthusiastic bounce in his step. As he neared, his face lit up with excitement and curiosity, clearly wondering why his sister was in a one-on-one conversation with Jeremy.

"Hey, sis," Dennis greeted as he approached, giving Jeremy a slightly awkward wave. "What's up?"

Jeremy offered him a friendly nod, "Hey Dennis. Good timing. I just asked Missy if you two wanted to join me for a drive. Nothing major, just a chance to hang out and maybe grab a snack."

Dennis looked at the two of them, surprised but trying to keep his cool."Uh, sure? I mean, yeah, that sounds good."

The opportunity to spend time with his idol was not something Dennis was going to turn down.

Missy smiled, "Alright then. A drive sounds nice. Just let me grab my things." She said, gesturing to her bag on the hill a few steps away.

As she grabbed her backpack, Dennis leaned closer to Jeremy, "Is everything okay? I mean, it's not every day you invite me and Missy for a drive."

Jeremy chuckled, "Everything's fine. I just felt like it'd be fun to hang out, you know? There is usually a certain long-haired thug at the center of our interactions; I thought it'd be cool to just hang out, no stress."

Dennis nodded, "Got it. Where are we going?"

"You'll see," Jeremy said, climbing into the Jeep. Before Dennis could claim the passenger seat next to him, Jeremy added, with a hint of playful authority, "Remember Tomo's rules; ladies ride 'shotgun.' Get in back."

27

THE COTTAGE: PART TWO

THE LABRADOR'S history was everywhere you looked. Overgrown with weeds and wildflowers, stone foundations marked where guest rooms and the grand ballroom once stood. The cottage stood tucked deep behind the ruins, nestled amongst the trees.

It had a homely aura, with its slightly tilted chimney and wild roses growing along its sides. It stood as a silent guard, bearing witness to the many stories that had unfolded on the grounds.

Dennis was the first to break the silence as the three sat in Jeremy's Jeep, parked in front of the worn-down building. "This place is creepy. Do you guys think it's haunted?" he remarked, looking out the window.

Missy's gaze fixed on The Cottage. "I think there's a certain charm to it. It feels like it's holding onto memories. Like if you listen closely, you might hear echoes of the past."

Jeremy smiled, "That's what makes places like this special. They keep stories alive, even if the rest of the world has moved on." Oh, and Dennis, he paused, giving him a devilish look; it's definitely haunted."

As Jeremy and Missy got out of the Jeep, Dennis attempted to imitate Tomo's earlier smooth exit from the backseat. But his movement lacked grace, causing him to tumble and crash on the ground before quickly getting to his feet, hoping no one saw his clumsiness. He took a moment to inhale the crisp autumn air deeply, trying to regain his composure. Ever the daydreamer, he looked around and mused, "You know, if this place is haunted, you have to wonder about what kind of people stayed here. Who were they?" he asked as he traced his fingers on an old sign at the entrance.

Missy, following suit, walked over to the edge of the lake. She stared at the cottage's reflection in the still water. "You think they were happy here?" she asked softly. "Before whatever happened, you know, happened?"

Jeremy looked intently at the cottage. "Every spot has tales of good times and bad times. But I like to think that most of the days here were filled with only good times," His hand motioned toward a majestic oak, its limbs sprawling wide as if cradling memories of a long-forgotten past. "I'll say this— If the legends about my grandfather are true, he knew how to throw one hell of a party. This place must've seen some incredible nights."

Dennis walked over to an old stone bench, brushing away some leaves and taking a seat. "It's funny, isn't it? How life goes on, yet these places remain, holding onto the memories."

Missy nodded in agreement as she sat down next to him. "It makes you appreciate the moments, knowing they become a part of a bigger story."

Feeling the weight of countless lifetimes and memories of his own, Jeremy added, "It's a reminder that while we might move forward, it's important to remember the past. It shapes us, teaches us, and in places like this, it waits for us."

The three sat in quiet contemplation, each absorbed in their thoughts. The silent ruins of Labrador and the ever-watchful Cottage bore witness to their reflections on time.

Jeremy, gesturing towards the cottage, asked. "You guys want to go inside?"

"Are we allowed? And, um, is it safe in there?" Dennis questioned; his adventurous side was replaced with caution.

Jeremy nodded reassuringly. "It's sturdy. It might have a few creaky spots and a lot of dust, but it's held up for years. I was just here yesterday, checking it out. I promise it's safe."

Missy's curiosity bubbled up, overshadowing her reservations. "I've always wondered about places like this, the stories that they hold. Let's go in."

Jeremy's hand rested on the weathered wood before pushing it open. The air that greeted them was musty, carrying tales from another time. He spread his arms wide, showcasing the cottage's interior. "Well, here it is. Mi Casa Su Casa."

Dennis looked around, puzzled. "Wait, you live here?"

Jeremy chuckled lightly. "Not yet— But soon, this will be home sweet home. My dad owns this piece of the property; he never comes up here."

Missy tilted her head, trying to make sense of his words. "So, you're planning to move in after college?"

"No, not after college," Jeremy clarified, "More like after tonight's game."

Their expressions shifted to a mix of surprise and concern. Missy spoke up first, "Are you sure about this? This place doesn't even have electricity."

Jeremy smiled confidently. "It's got power. I just have to turn it on. I've been in tougher spots. I've got lanterns and some blankets. The first few nights sleeping here might be rough, but by Sunday, this place will feel like home, you'll see."

"Why?" Missy questioned, her voice laced with concern. "This just seems dangerous, Jeremy. Why would you want to live up here? Did something happen at home?"

Dennis piped up, deflecting Missy's inquiry. He'd heard tales of Gregg, and for once, he wanted to shield his frequent protector from explaining a source of pain, "I've heard of squatter's rights. If he stays here long enough, he might be okay."

Missy gave Dennis a sidelong glance. "Oh, so one documentary on cable and suddenly you're a legal expert?"

Dennis just shrugged, but before the argument between the siblings could continue, Jeremy stepped in. "It'll be fine, really. My dad never comes up here, and if he ever does, he and I will just have a little chat. It's safe enough, I promise. Plus, I may have the upper hand if he ever does show up." His voice was confident and reassuring.

"What kind of upper hand?" Dennis asked.

The atmosphere grew somber as Jeremy unraveled his tale. He spoke about the version of his life that existed before resets, all the abuse and disappointment. He talked about his family's history, explaining how they once owned the grounds they stood on.

Jeremy then brought them back to the events of the previous morning — the fight with his father, the revelation about his college account, the horrible note, and the sealed document, its contents still a mystery.

Missy and Dennis stood silent for a moment, absorbing the gravity of what Jeremy had just told them. The playful mood from earlier had shifted to one of understanding and empathy. The ties of friendship deepened as they stood together in the shadow of the old cottage.

Dennis, ever curious, asked, "So, any guesses on what's inside that envelope?"

Jeremy shook his head slowly, "Honestly, I have no idea."

Missy asked with a curious tone. "Where did you leave it?"

"It's in my backpack, in the Jeep," Jeremy replied.

Dennis's eyes sparkled with excitement and intrigue. "Come on, man! You can't just leave us hanging like that. I'll go get it, and we can open it and see what's inside!"

Jeremy exhaled deeply, "I'd rather not right now. With the game coming up, I need to keep my mind clear. The last thing I need is another curveball today."

Dennis sighed, "Yeah, it's a big game tonight. Everyone expects Regional to crush you guys." He paused, apologetically glancing at Jeremy, "Sorry, man."

Jeremy gave him a forgiving look. "It's okay, Dennis. We're the underdogs. I'm well aware that Regional has the upper hand. All we can do is play our best and maybe catch them off guard."

Trying to understand the stakes, Missy asked, "So, this is like a super-important game?" Before Jeremy could respond, Dennis jumped in with his usual enthusiasm. "For Regional, absolutely, if they win tonight, they're in the championship.

Missy's eyebrows furrowed, "And if we win tonight?"

Dennis hesitated, "Well, it wouldn't mean anything, and realistically speaking, it's a long shot. The Wildcats haven't had the best season. It's a shame, too. We have some serious talent on our team." He looked at Jeremy with admiration in his eyes. "Take Jeremy here, for instance. He's scored five touchdowns as a tight end in the last four games. But where he truly stands out is on defense; he is so versatile. He can play just about anywhere."

Feeling embarrassed by Dennis' admiration, Jeremy shifted uncomfortably. "Thanks, Dennis, that's some high praise."

Undeterred, Dennis continued, "Don't get me started on D.C. That guy has a future ahead of him. With the right exposure in a division-1 school, I could totally see him going pro."

Jeremy chuckled, "You're really high on Del. He is good, no doubt."

"Good?!" Dennis sounded almost offended. "Jeremy, if D.C. played for any other team, he'd be breaking records left and right. Rushing, receiving, you name it. Imagine if you guys both played for Regional, with you and D.C. on that team," He paused, daydreaming, "Man, you guys would probably be able to beat Westfield State as a high school squad." As he rattled off names and stats, Missy observed the passion with which he spoke about the Wildcats. It was obvious he cared deeply about the team and its players.

"We're loaded with talent. The issue isn't with the players. It's the leadership or lack thereof," he said, clearly frustrated by the season's missed opportunities.

Jeremy raised an eyebrow and smirked, "So you think leadership is our problem, Dennis? I hope you're not pointing fingers at me since, you know, I'm a co-captain with Del."

Caught off guard, Dennis's eyes widened. "No, I didn't mean it like that. I think both you and D.C. are great captains. My point is more about overall guidance—the play calls made during games and strategies set by the coaches; those are out of your hands."

Watching the exchange, Missy had to hold back a smile. "From the bleachers, everything looks simple, huh?"

Dennis exhaled, frustrated. "It's just that I love our team. More than The Pats, The Sox, or any other team you'd see on T.V.— I just feel like there's a missing piece."

Jeremy leaned in, "So, are you saying it's Coach McHale's fault we aren't winning?"

Dennis straightened, taking a moment before he responded. "Pretty much. His coaching decisions have a ripple effect."

That choice of words made Jeremy's ears perk up. "Ripple effect? Now, that's an interesting way to put it," he said, hiding his deep familiarity with the concept of cause and effect.

Dennis nodded, gathering his thoughts. "Look, McHale was an amazing player. I've seen his old game footage. He had talent, just like you, Jeremy. But that doesn't necessarily mean he's a great coach. You know the saying, 'those who can, do; those who can't, teach'?"

Missy jumped in, "Dennis, that's not true."

Dennis continued, "Well, in McHale's case, it is. He certainly could 'do,' and he definitely can't teach. I have him for gym. It's not fun."

Jeremy leaned back, nodding slowly. "Dennis, I get where you're coming from about Coach McHale. And you might be interested to know he's introduced some new schemes for tonight. We've got some simplified plays with streamlined strategies and more direct calls."

Dennis sat up, visibly excited. "A new playbook? That's huge! And you guys have been drilling these plays all week?"

Jeremy hesitated for a second."Well, not all week. Coach McHale handed them out during yesterday's practice."

Dennis groaned in frustration, shaking his head. "That's what I'm talking about. Who waits until the day before a game to change the playbook?"

Curious, Missy asked, "Is it that difficult to adjust so quickly?"

Dennis turned to look at her, "Think about your last major exam. One that really stressed you out."

She thought about the question, "Definitely my first stats test at WNEC. I spent weeks preparing. I studied for hours every night, trying to make sure I knew the entire study guide inside and out."

"I remember," Dennis interjected, "You were a bit of a nightmare."

Missy shot him a playful glare before sharing, "I got a B+. I was crushed. It was my first B, ever. I had to beg my professor for extra credit."

Dennis nodded, drawing a parallel, "Now, imagine if you had to retake that test, but this time, you only got the textbook the day before. That's what Jeremy and the team are dealing with.

"It's far from ideal," Jeremy admitted, running a hand through his hair. But we worked late into the night yesterday. I truly believe we're in a good spot right now. Some of the guys even seem more confident. Who knows? We might pull off a surprise or two."

Dennis looked skeptical, "You think LaCroix is up for it? Honestly, he hasn't been the team's shining star."

Missy looked at Dennis with a puzzled expression. "You mean Martin LaCroix? He plays football?"

"He's our quarterback, Missy," Dennis said with a roll of his eyes.

She raised an eyebrow, "Really? He's in my Honors Chemistry class. He always struts around like he owns the place. I never pegged him for the athletic type."

"He's not," Dennis snorted.

Jeremy quickly defended his teammate, saying, "Come on, he has his moments. The kid's got a decent arm."

Dennis shook his head, "Yeah, but he's not a leader. I can't see how you guys respect him. He's a total jerk. He's tried to pick on me a few times. And honestly, after dealing with Dutch every day, Marty's attempts at bullying are a joke."

Jeremy took a moment to consider Dennis's remarks about Marty and decided not to discuss it any further. He was confident Dennis could handle himself.

"I've mastered the new playbook," Jeremy confidently stated, returning the conversation to the game. "It's pretty straightforward. The main challenge is ensuring Marty remains unshaken during the game. If we can do that, I think we'll be okay."

Jeremy met Dennis's eyes, "I'm going to need you cheering especially loud for us tonight, buddy."

Dennis's chest puffed up with pride, "You can count on me," he assured with a nod. "I knew you'd say that," Jeremy grinned, "Which is why you're going to be a VIP tonight, complete with a personal escort to the game."

Dennis's eyebrows shot up, "VIP?"

Missy, slightly puzzled, also glanced at Jeremy, trying to understand what he meant.

"I spoke to Kristen," Jeremy explained, "She made plans with Missy to go to the game, so I asked if you could tag along." Turning to Missy, he added, "I hope that's alright?"

Missy gave a grateful smile, relieved that she wouldn't be attending the game solo, "Of course it is."

Dennis felt a flutter in his stomach; the prospect of being near Kristen was both exciting and terrifying, "Oh, um... what should I wear? How should I act? Do I need to bring anything?"

Jeremy chuckled, aware of Kristen's less-than-stellar opinion of Dennis, "Just relax and be yourself. You'll be fine," He added with a playful wink.

Wanting to steer the conversation in a lighter direction, Jeremy rubbed his stomach theatrically. "On another note, I'm starving. What do you say we grab some food? I don't think one brownie will fuel me through a full game," he teased, giving Missy a playful wink.

"Well, in that case," Missy began with a mock stern voice, "let's find you something that'll sustain you through all three periods, shall we?"

Dennis groaned, shaking his head. "Sis, you are the dumbest smart person I have ever met. Football has four quarters."

Jeremy chuckled, "Easy there, Dennis, she's trying."

"Yeah, yeah, whatever," Dennis muttered, but there was a grin on his face.

Leaving The Cottage, the late afternoon sun washed the ruins of The Labrador in a warm glow. Jeremy's mind was focused on the night ahead and a game that he couldn't afford to win.

28

FRIDAY NIGHT LIGHTS

AT THE END of the first half, the score was tied:

Wildcats 21- Rebels 21.

Inside the Wildcats' locker room, the atmosphere was thick with tension. The team had shown glimpses of brilliance during the first half, but consistency eluded them. Coach McHale broke down plays, pointing out areas for improvement, while Jeremy and Del took it upon themselves to fire up their teammates, reminding them that there was still another half to play.

"The game isn't over, gentlemen," Del rallied, "we have two full quarters of football left. They may be stronger than us, but no one ever thought we'd be able to hang with them, let alone have a chance to win."

"He's right," Jeremy added, "I am proud of you all; everyone is doing a great job out there. Let's put some of that magic from the first half back together and finish this game with pride."

Just as they were reigniting the team's spark, Marty shouted from the back of the locker room, where he was icing on his legs, "I'm getting crushed—the offensive line needs to step up; you guys are pitiful!"

"Whoa!" Jeremy shouted, glaring at Marty. Uncalled for LaCroix! These guys are laying it all out for you; everyone is playing both ways. Have some appreciation."

"Appreciation? "Marty chuckled; these guys couldn't block my sister., The pass rushers are coming through the line like freight trains."

Del, infuriated, yelled, "You're our Quarterback! Where's your leadership? Look at Tomo," Marty's eyes didn't move, keeping them fixed intently on Del.

"I said, look at him!" Del shouted, his voice echoing as his teammates' murmurs fell silent. His voice was filled with passion: "This guy is facing double teams on every single defensive play, and he's still managed to get a pair of sacks. After that kind of effort, do you expect him to switch gears and provide perfect protection instantly? Maybe you should try and adapt, move around in the pocket, create some space."

With frustration, Marty shot back, "It's Tomo. It's his fault I'm taking a beating. He's just not keeping up out there."

Tomo's shoulders sagged at the accusation. Marty continued, "You need to step it up, Sumo."

Tomo clearly understood the derogatory undertone. However, showing resilience, he responded, "I'll do better."

"That's enough!" Jeremy's voice boomed, commanding attention. "Composure!" The intensity of his voice made the room fall silent. "We are a team. We're in this together. We know what needs to be done, and we need to execute. Coach McHale will guide us through the necessary adjustments. Listen to him, trust his direction, and take it as gospel."

The atmosphere grew tense as the halftime show ended and the marching band left the field. Jeremy instructed Tomo to bring the team out with Del for the second half, "Take my captain's spot and lead the guys back onto the field."

Tomo's gloomy demeanor instantly shifted, his face lighting up with excitement. "You got it, Jack!" Seeing Jeremy's approving glance, Del rallied the team, "Let's move out, boys!"

As the Wildcats made their way out of the locker room, Jeremy made it a point to encourage each player, enthusiastically patting their shoulder pads and helmets, instilling a sense of motivation and confidence.

However, the last in line, donning the jersey with the number 16, received no such encouragement. Jeremy gripped Marty's jersey, pulling him aside. "Hold up a second, Martin," Jeremy's tone was sharp.

Already exasperated, Marty snapped, "I don't have time for your drama, Anderson. And if you dare undermine me in front of—"

Jeremy cut him off swiftly, "No! You listen to me! Your attitude, both on this team and in life, needs an overhaul. If I ever hear you belittling

Tomo again, or anyone for that matter, you'll no longer be any part of this team."

Marty scoffed dismissively, "What are you planning Anderson?—a Nancy Kerrigan special?"

Jeremy locked eyes with Marty, his voice cold and direct. "Listen, Martin, there's no room for your arrogance here," he paused, ensuring every word sunk in, "I hate to break it to you, but if you continue down this path, your life will be a string of disappointments and failures; you'll be nothing more than a forgotten memory."

Jeremy's expression remained stonefaced as he continued, "I can see it now: years from today, you'll be alone, riddled with regrets, wishing for a way out of the miserable existence you've created for yourself." The energy between the two was intense. Marty's eyes locked on Jeremy's, whose words were unnervingly precise. "And as for friends and loved ones? They'll all drift away, tired of your antics. You'll find yourself isolated and alone."

Marty scoffed, attempting to brush off Jeremy's chilling prediction. "Whatever, Anderson. Your little pep talk won't work on me. And as for Tomo, he needed someone to put him in his place."

Jeremy took a deep breath, maintaining his cool, "Alright, LaCroix, just remember, actions have consequences, and Karma is a bitch." Giving Marty a firm glare, "Now get your ass on the field and lead. I'll be watching."

Marty sneered, "Sure, whatever," and pushed past Jeremy to rejoin the team.

As Jeremy hustled to catch up with the rest of the Wildcats, a figure lurking under the bleachers caught his attention, the dim stadium lights barely outlining the silhouette. Curiosity slowing his pace, He tried to get a closer look. The mysterious individual seemed intensely focused on the players warming up on the field. Jeremy shouted, "Who's that?" causing the figure to stiffen and turn.

Emerging from the shadows, it was Dutch, his eyes filled with intensity.

"Dutchie, what are you doing here? " Jeremy called out, his voice a mix of surprise and suspicion.

"Just watching the game," Dutch replied dismissively, "Forget you saw me."

"But why here? Why are you hiding?" Jeremy pressed.

"I just like watching from here; don't worry about it," Dutch said with a hint of annoyance.

"Alright, Dutch. Just stay out of trouble," Jeremy advised.

Dutch's eyes stayed on Jeremy. "Good luck out there," he murmured, disappearing back into the shadows.

Jeremy sprinted across the field, heading towards his teammates. With every stride, the cleats on his shoes bit into the turf.

Del and Tomo stood near the 40-yard line, deeply engrossed in conversation. Going over plays, their hands moved animatedly as they simulated various scenarios. Holding a football, Del acted out a maneuver while Tomo nodded, occasionally interrupting with a pointed finger to emphasize a different approach.

Drawing closer, Jeremy could catch snippets of their conversation.

"Just remember to cut in when you see the guard pulling," Del instructed, his voice assertive yet encouraging.

As Jeremy's eyes drifted toward the bleachers, he found Missy. When their eyes met, a gentle smile played on her lips, and she gave a subtle, almost coy wave. Beside her, Dennis was a bundle of energy, his every movement radiating excitement. He seemed to be breaking down the game's first-half highlights to anyone who would listen, his hands flying around as he reenacted pivotal moments.

Making his way back to the team, Jeremy was immediately drawn to a heated exchange on the sideline. Coach McHale, usually composed, was visibly agitated, his face red and voice elevated. Marty stood toe-to-toe with the coach, his body language conveying defiance as he crossed his arms defensively.

"Marty, those plays were specifically designed for situations like this. You need to execute them as they're drawn up!" McHale's voice was stern, and the weight of the game's importance was distinct in his tone.

"Maybe if I had more protection in the pocket, I could!" Marty scoffed, his voice dripping with defiance. His eyes darted pointedly to Tomo, laying blame without saying it. "Some guys aren't pulling their weight."

Approaching his teammates, Jeremy could see the raw emotion in

Tomo's eyes. The sting of Marty's words was unmistakable, but Jeremy knew that rallying around each other was the key.

"Let it go, Tomo," Jeremy reassured his teammate. "You're playing out of your mind out there. We all see it."

Tomo looked up, his eyes red-rimmed but determined. "He's not a good person," he mumbled, shaking his head in disbelief at Marty's audacity.

Del, always the peacemaker, added his own words of encouragement. "We've got your back," he said, offering a firm pat on Tomo's shoulder. "We're a team, and we stick together. Forget Marty— let's show him what we're made of on the field."

The three shared a moment of unity, knowing that no matter what happened, they'd face it together.

The second half of the game was an intense back-and-forth battle. The stadium vibrated with tension as the teams fought for control, both moving the ball with determination, but ultimately, neither team was able to score.

With the clock ticking, the Wildcats got themselves back into scoring position. The atmosphere was thick with tension as the end zone became within reach, placing them just yards away from a potentially game-winning score.

The crowd's cheers were deafening, and the weight of the moment was intense. Jeremy knew that in these moments, heroes were made, but he had a different plan. He was going to keep his team from winning.

As the Wildcats gathered in the huddle, Marty quickly took charge. "Listen up!" he shouted, trying to be heard over the roaring crowd. He relayed the play: "I-right 22 blast, on two. Let's punch this in!"

They broke the huddle and lined up quickly. Jeremy, knowing what he needed to do, took a deep breath. As the ball was snapped, the play went as designed, with Del taking the hand-off from Marty. However, he was met with a wall of defensive linemen, stopping him after a short gain of two yards. Without hesitation, Marty called a timeout.

The Wildcats regrouped on the sidelines. Coaches shouted, and players gasped for breath. Jeremy tried to appear as invested as everyone else, but his mind was on a different track. He had been playing a delicate chess game, balancing the Wildcats' success with his ultimate goal: ensuring the Rebels got their championship birth.

Under the bleachers, Dutch fixed his eyes on the Wildcat offense, trying to anticipate their next move as they took the field after the timeout. He watched in disbelief as Marty scanned the defensive formation and called an audible, changing the play.

"Is he seriously calling a pass play?" frustration evident in Dutch's tone. "Just run the damn ball and take time off the clock, kick the field goal, take the win!" he exclaimed.

Lined up at Tight End, Jeremy took in the play adjustment with a surge of disbelief. The original strategy to run the ball would have been easy to sabotage. He could easily miss his blocking assignment, allowing Del to be tackled for a loss and keep the clock running. However, Marty's sudden switch to a pass play made Jeremy the primary receiver, complicating things significantly. He had to run a convincing route and drop the pass without making it obvious.

As the ball was snapped and the play began, time seemed to slow down. Running his route, Jeremy felt the defense closing in on him. Just as he turned his head back to the line of scrimmage, the ball flew towards him in a perfect spiral. Without thinking, his hands instinctively caught the pass just before a Rebel defender pushed him out of bounds, stopping the clock and keeping a Wildcat victory within reach.

Dutch's heart soared as he watched the play unfold. "Yes!— Great hands, Anderson!" he shouted, pounding on the underside of the bleachers.

On the sideline, the Wildcats erupted in cheers. They were now in prime position to snatch victory from the jaws of defeat. Jeremy, meanwhile, tried to conceal his inner turmoil. As he got up, brushing off the grass from his uniform, he locked eyes with Marty. There was a brief nod of acknowledgment, but layers of unspoken tension remained.

The next play would be critical, and Jeremy knew he had to tread carefully to maintain his deception. The situation was tense. The Wildcats huddled up, waiting for their coach's call. Every eye in the stadium was on them, and every heartbeat echoed the same thought—"Can the Wildcats pull this off?"

McHale quickly signaled the play from the sideline. As anticipated, it was a running play. The plan was simple: chew the clock, kick a field goal, and win the game.

Still in his hideout, Dutch crossed his fingers and whispered to himself, "Come on, boys. We need this."

As the ball was snapped, the offensive line surged forward, trying to create a path for Del. Jeremy, playing his part, acted as a decoy, drawing a couple of Rebel defenders with him. Taking the handoff from Marty, Del darted forward, squeezing through a narrow gap in the defense. He churned his legs, pushing, fighting for every inch. After what felt like an eternity, he was brought down after a 5-yard gain.

The Wildcats were now on the Rebel's 15-yard line. With just 20 seconds left, Coach McHale signaled for a timeout.

The stage was set— Alex Knight, the Junior sensation, was about to be called into the spotlight. Having transferred to Huxley at the beginning of the year, Alex was known for his nerves of steel, especially when it came to game-winning kicks. He'd won multiple games at his previous school, tallying more points than any kicker in Western Massachusetts High School football history. The buzz around him wasn't just talk; Alex had proven himself time and time again.

As the seconds on the clock ticked away, Alex confidently began strapping on his helmet, mentally preparing himself for the kick that could seal the Wildcats' first victory in years. However, to everyone's surprise, Coach McHale waved the kicker off.

Marty, returning to the huddle, relayed the call to the team. The play was something they hadn't practiced before.

"What the hell, LaCroix!" Del exclaimed, clearly frustrated. "Another pass? We've never even run this play in practice, and with your two interceptions, this is a bad call."

"Listen up, gentlemen, Coach wanted to kick; I told him winners want the ball. This is my game to win. Just pick up the blitz, D.C., let me worry about the rest," Marty retorted sharply.

Tomo, usually quiet in the huddle, interjected, "Why not let Alex kick? He can win it for us."

Marty wasn't having it. "This is my victory—Sumo, you just shut up and block. I'll get us in the end zone," he barked back, using the derogatory nickname he knew hurt Tomo.

Jeremy wasn't worried about the play's potential failure or McHale's decision to put the game's fate in the quarterback's hands. He was boiling with anger over Marty's remarks toward Tomo. He would have to deal with that after the game.

Marty, gathering the team, broke down the play. "Jeremy, get open on the fade; I'll find you in the back corner of the end-zone." And with a menacing grip on Tomo's face mask, he added, "If you screw this up for me, I swear, you'll regret ever coming to this country."

Tomo's eyes, which often emanated tranquility, now radiated a fury Marty had never seen. With a swift motion, Tomo forcefully removed the quarterback's hand from his face mask, sending a clear message of his disdain.

"Ready, Break!" Marty ordered, trying to regain control of the team.

As the Wildcats took formation on the line of scrimmage, it was as if time had paused in anticipation of the next play.

Dutch anxiously watched the unfolding drama, each second feeling like an eternity.

As Marty barked out the cadence, the Rebels anticipated the snap, launching into an all-out blitz. Del, showcasing his versatility, managed to block a defensive end who was hell-bent on disrupting the play.

Jeremy burned past his defender, making a beeline for the end zone. While every muscle in his body was trained to catch any ball thrown his way, he found himself hoping for a misfire or, better yet, another LaCroix interception. He knew every play in the book, but this surprise audible was a wildcard he had never seen in any football scenario he'd ever been a part of.

Within the chaos, Tomo, the usually dependable lineman, had a different endgame in mind. After holding his block for only a few seconds, Tomo let the Rebel nose guard break free. The opposing player didn't need a second invitation and charged full steam ahead at Marty.

Jeremy turned back just in time to see the horror: Marty toppled to the ground, his leg bending at an unnatural angle, the ball fumbling out of his grip.

As a gut-wrenching scream filled the air, Tomo towered over the injured quarterback, his expression cold and unyielding. "Karma," he sneered.

During the chaos, a Rebel player swiftly picked up the loose ball. Dodging and weaving, he ran the length of the field, crossing into the Wildcat end zone just as the clock ran out.

As the final play unfolded, Dutch's suppressed rage erupted. "Damn it, McHale! What the hell was that?!" he roared. "What a stupid fucking call!" he screamed, shaking his head in disbelief as the emotions of the entire season crashed down on him.

The stadium was blanketed in silence, broken only by the distressing sounds of Marty's agony as he lay on the turf. A chilling stillness had taken over, and the euphoria of the game and the tension of the final moments had been forgotten in the wake of the quarterback's injury.

"Trainer!" Del's voice rang out, his call echoing across the field. But the medical team was already sprinting onto the field.

A commendable calmness had settled upon the Rebels despite their recent triumph. As if guided by a shared, unspoken understanding, each player took a knee, hands together in unified respect for their opponent.

The Wildcats gathered around their teammate, forming a protective circle, heads bowed, each player deep in prayer. Whatever differences they had with Marty, the present moment transcended them all. Concern, fear, and hope-filled their hearts as they witnessed the agonizing aftermath of the play.

Jeremy, however, was lost in his emotions. On the one hand, he was genuinely concerned for Marty's well-being; on the other was the uncertainty of how this ripple would affect his plans. As guilt gnawed at him for such thoughts, his eyes shifted to Tomo. The usually gentle giant now stood with a steely look, his face without expression. The weight of his action, leading to this tragic outcome, hung heavily in the air.

As Jeremy slowly approached Tomo, their eyes met. Words weren't necessary; the subtle nod they shared spoke volumes. Both of them, in their own way, had tried to influence the game's outcome, but where Jeremy had been discreet, Tomo's actions were direct and unapologetic.

29

FRIDAY NIGHT FIGHTS

As JEREMY FOLLOWED the pack of Wildcats toward the locker room, his eyes instinctively darted to the shadowy area beneath the bleachers, hoping to catch a glimpse of Dutch. But the spot where he had been hiding earlier was now empty. His heart sank, as he had hoped to see him after the game.

When they neared the gates of the football field, Jeremy, Del, and Tomo, who were bringing up the rear, were met with a pair of familiar faces. Missy and Dennis stood there, waiting patiently. Missy's eyes were filled with concern while Dennis tried to mask his excitement with an artificial look of gravity.

"Hey," Missy began, her voice gentle, "That was intense. How's Marty?"

Jeremy sighed, "He's in a lot of pain, but he's in good hands."

Dennis chimed in, "Wild game, huh? I've never seen anything like it.

"Tomo, clearly spent and not in his usual jovial form, added, "Football is unpredictable."

Del, placing an arm around Tomo's shoulders, responded, "Life is unpredictable, Big Guy, but we look out for each other, right?" They all nodded in agreement. The day's events had tested their bonds, but ultimately, their unity and mutual respect for one another prevailed.

"Hey, we're gonna head to the locker room," Del said, gesturing for Tomo to join him, giving Jeremy a knowing glance.

"You up for carrying my gear, Screech?" Tomo asked Dennis, his eyes shining with mischief. Dennis, eager to fit in, replied, "Sure thing!"

"We'll see you in a bit then," Jeremy said, nodding toward Del and Tomo. "I'll drop you home later, Dennis," he added as the three strolled up the path toward the school building, leaving him alone with Missy.

Missy hesitated before saying, "Tough game, huh?"

Jeremy sighed, "Yeah, but it's just high school football." He trailed off, unable to stop thinking about Marty's injury and the ripple effect it might cause.

Trying to brighten the mood, Missy offered, "I may not get all the rules, but you played great out there! Dennis couldn't stop talking about every play you were involved in, especially that— what did he call it? An interception?"

He chuckled, "Yeah, when I caught the pass meant for the other team."

She smiled, "That's the one. That was really something!"

"So, what are you up to now?" He asked.

"We were just waiting for Kristen." She said, "I guess we're going to head to Frankie's?"

His face brightened instantly. "Frankie's? That place has the best pizza. It's been years since I've had it."

She looked at him, puzzled. "Really? I could've sworn I saw you there last week. I was picking up some takeout with my mom, and you were there with Kristen and the rest of the cheer squad."

Caught off guard, he tried to backpedal. "Oh, right—I guess it just feels like longer. Time's been a blur lately." Swiftly changing the subject, he asked, "How was Dennis on the way over? He didn't creep out Kristen too much, did he?"

Missy amusedly replied, "Not really. He was pretty quiet but he did take an hour-long shower after you dropped us off." She put her palm to her forehead. And I'm almost positive he's wearing my dad's cologne. What a weirdo." She said, shaking her head in disbelief. I think my little brother has a major-league crush on your girlfriend." She ended with a giggle.

"Is that so? Well, at least he has good taste," He chuckled.

She quickly added, "Please don't give him a hard time, okay?"

He looked sincere as he responded, "Don't worry, I'd never tease him about it. Everyone has their crushes."

"Yeah, I guess that's true," she sighed. "Thanks for being cool about it."

He extended his arm toward the hill, "Want to walk with me up to the locker room? Kristen usually comes out there to meet up after the games. That way, you won't have to wait down here by yourself."

She smiled, "Sounds good."

Walking up the hill, the distant rumble of an engine and the blaring sound of Man in the Box by Alice in Chains emanated from a car's speakers, interrupting their conversation.

"Is that Dutch Wyatt?" She asked, her eyes narrowing at the vehicle parked in the distance.

"Looks like it," Jeremy replied with a nonchalant shrug. I guess he's been showing up at games lately."

Her voice wavered with a hint of anxiety, "I hope he's not here to cause trouble."

Jeremy reassured her, "I'm sure it's fine. He used to play on the team with us. I think he misses it."

As they neared the locker room, they spotted Dennis perched on the steps. His earlier animated expression was replaced with one of anxiety. His eyes were fixed intently in the direction of Dutch's car; a storm of emotions was all over his face.

Suddenly, the locker room door burst open, revealing Kristen and Heather. Kristen's eyes lit up the moment they landed on Jeremy. "Bear!" she exclaimed, not wasting a moment before jumping into his arms and bombarding him with enthusiastic kisses. "Tough loss, babe, you guys should've won," she consoled, looking up into his eyes.

Feeling the weight of the public display, Jeremy blushed, trying to gently untangle himself from her embrace. "Thanks, Kris," he mumbled, with embarrassment in his voice.

Kristen, always one step ahead with plans, announced, "Heather and I are bringing Missy to Frankie's. Del said he and Tomo will meet us there." She then turned her focus sharply to Jeremy, her tone taking on a more serious edge, "You're still dropping Dennis home first, right, Bear?" Her gaze was unwavering, ensuring that she'd get a commitment.

Knowing better than to argue, Jeremy responded instantly, "Yes, of course." Sensing Dennis's discomfort due to Dutch's presence, Jeremy added, "Dennis, why don't you hang in the locker room while I change? I'll drive you home, and then I'll meet everyone at Frankie's." He glanced at Missy, seeking her approval.

She responded with an understanding nod, grateful for Jeremy's thoughtfulness.

As the girls said goodbye and Jeremy and Dennis made their way into the building, the eerie rumble of the Turismo's idling engine combined with Lane Staley's hauntingly powerful vocals cast an uneasy vibe over the quiet night air.

The tension from the car was deep, and Dennis's unease was obvious. "I don't like this," he mumbled under his breath.

Jeremy, always protective, turned his attention to the girls as they headed towards Kristen's car. "You girls sure you're going to be okay with Dutch around?" he questioned, concern in his voice.

"Oh, don't worry about him," Kristen exclaimed with a smirk, playfully clenching her fist. "I know how to handle Dutch Wyatt."

Jeremy gave a relieved chuckle, "Alright, be safe, girls. See you in a bit."

With that, he and Dennis disappeared into the building, leaving behind the rumbling car and its ominous aura.

Inside the locker room, the Wildcats moved with a mix of fatigue and disappointment, storing their equipment and making minor chit-chat. The weight of their near-miss at victory and concerns over Marty's condition hung in the air. Tomo sat on the bench in front of his locker, peeling the white tape away from his wrists. Every strand that came off seemed symbolic of shedding the game's weight.

Del, always one to uplift his teammates, approached Tomo, attempting to ease the weight of the game's outcome. "Look, about that block," he began, "Everyone misses one now and then. Besides, you gave everything you had out there tonight."

Tomo looked up, his deep-set eyes meeting Del's, pausing before he responded, "I'm not torn up about it." A sly grin crept onto his face. "Honestly, I could've held that guy back all day. It just—didn't seem that important at the time." Del raised an eyebrow, absorbing Tomo's words. The message was clear: Tomo had made a conscious choice, and he was standing by it.

Jeremy stepped through the swinging double doors of the locker room just in time to see Coach McHale signal for everyone's attention. The familiar drone of the post-game shower and gear rustling ceased as every Wildcat turned towards their coach.

McHale's face was drawn, showing the weight of not only the evening's loss but of something far more profound.

The coach cleared his throat, the team anticipating his words. "Boys," he began, his voice steady. Losses in life and on the field are inevitable. They hurt, but they also build character." He paused for emphasis, "and character is what defines a man."

The room remained silent, each player absorbing the wisdom,

preparing themselves for the inevitable talk of how they'd regroup for the next game.

"I've gotten an update from the trainers about Marty," he continued, taking a deep breath. "He won't be playing again this year. It's possible," he paused, letting out a weary sigh, "he may never play again." A collective gasp echoed around the room. Marty, with all his flaws, was a key player. The gravity of his absence was not lost on anyone.

McHale's gaze swept the room, landing on each of his player's faces. "And there's more. Due to Marty's injury, we are below the minimum roster requirement. We won't be able to field a complete team for the rest of the season." The words sank in, and a cold realization spread across the room as the coach continued, "We have to forfeit our final games," McHale confirmed. Whispers of disbelief spread; players exchanged bewildered looks. The implications were massive.

Jeremy moved further into the room, sitting next to Del and Tomo. They'd faced challenges together before, but this, this was different. The path ahead was uncertain, but one thing was clear: the Wildcats' story for the season had taken an unexpected turn.

Desperation flooded Jeremy, his mind racing to calculate the consequences of this altered timeline.

The game next week against Truman Tech was not just any game; it was the centerpiece of the entire season. Its historical and emotional significance for the town, the players, and Jeremy's mission was enormous.

Jeremy glanced around the locker room, surveying his teammates' disappointed faces. The game against Truman was more than just a game. The event shaped the community with historic rivalry, passionate fans, and electrifying anticipation.

The more Jeremy thought about it, the more he realized that countless moments of connection, celebration, and even confrontation would never happen without that game. Relationships might never be forged or mended, opportunities could be missed, and the future as he knew it might diverge irreparably from its intended path.

Gathering his thoughts, Jeremy stood up. "Coach," he began, his voice resonating with an authority that silenced the room. "I understand our situation, and I respect your decision. But is there any possibility that we could find a way to play that game?— not just for us but for the school and the community, for all the tradition and history that comes with it."

Coach McHale considered Jeremy's question aloud, "The Athletic Department has stringent rules about this kind of thing. We have to field a minimum of 35 players to be eligible."

Alex Knight piped up from a corner, his voice echoing in the tense silence. "What if we just found someone to suit up? They wouldn't have to play." His eyes shifted towards Dennis, a hint of a plan formulating. Dennis' eyes widened in disbelief.

"No way!" he protested, shaking his head wildly.

Sharing a momentary glance, Del, Jeremy, and Tomo exchanged a look of understanding. Del spoke up with excitement, "That might work, Coach. Dennis has decent grades; he's academically eligible. We can suit him up, and I can step in as QB."

Jeremy quickly added, "It's an option. He could stay on the sidelines, safe and sound."

McHale seemed to mull over the proposition, stroking his chin thoughtfully. "If you get him to Monday's practice, I won't involve the Athletic Director. However, we'd need a consent form signed by his parents. Can the kid manage that?"

All eyes turned to Dennis. He hesitated, then sighed, "I don't want to be involved in this."

Sensing his apprehension, Jeremy tried to ease his worries. "Dennis, just trust us— we won't let anything happen to you. At practice, you'll just watch, no contact. It'll be like having front-row seats on the 50-yard line." After a long pause, Dennis surrendered, "Alright, fine, but I'm not stepping into that game."

Coach McHale looked intently at Dennis and then at the team. "This stays between us. The Athletic Department can't catch wind of this until game day. Is everyone clear?" Nods of agreement rippled through the room.

"We got it, Coach," Del said, affirming his understanding.

McHale leaned back against a locker, his expression thoughtful. "We'll keep Dennis off the field. He'll be there purely to meet the numbers. But if word gets out, the season is over. Are we clear?"

Jeremy stepped forward, a determined look in his eye. "We're clear, Coach. We've got a week to prepare. We'll keep Dennis safe and give Truman a game they won't forget."

The atmosphere in the locker room shifted from despair to determination. The Wildcats were united, each player aware of the stakes and each ready to step up for the team.

Though apprehensive, Dennis seemed somewhat comforted by Jeremy's words. "Fine," he sighed, "I'll be there on Monday. But remember, not one foot on that field."

McHale clapped his hands, bringing the room to attention. "Alright,

Wildcats. Let's get ready for next week. We've got a game to prepare for, and it starts Monday. Dismissed!"

As Del and Tomo left the locker room, their footsteps faded, leaving Jeremy and Dennis in a cocoon of eerie silence. The overhead fluorescent lights flickered intermittently, casting odd shadows on the lockers and benches.

Dennis sat in front of Jeremy's locker, his unease evident. The weight of their plan pressed down on him. "Jeremy, this doesn't feel right," he whispered, avoiding eye contact.

"Hey," Jeremy approached, bending down to Dennis's level, "you trust me, right?"

Dennis nodded hesitantly. "It's just— the spotlight. I don't want it."

Jeremy's hand reached Dennis's shoulder, giving it a comforting squeeze. "No one will know it's you. We'll keep it between us."

Just as the uneasiness within Dennis began to fade, the door to the locker room flew open, and in stormed Dutch, his face contorted with rage. His voice boomed across the room. "McHale! You worthless piece of shit!"

In the far corner, Coach McHale stood up from his desk, his face pale. His usual air of authority was replaced by shock. "Now, Dutch, calm down!— he pleaded.

Dennis instinctively ducked behind a locker, his eyes wide with terror. Jeremy's senses sharpened. Without hesitation, he sprang into action.

Dutch's roar echoed as he lunged at McHale. "You couldn't let them get one damn win!?" His fingers curled into tight fists, ready to strike.

Jeremy's feet pounded against the tiled floor. "Dutch, stop!" He tackled him from behind, locking him in a bear hug, his muscles straining to hold him back. Dutch struggled, his anger making him even more formidable. But Jeremy dragged him back using all his strength, desperation evident in his voice.

"Dutch! It's not worth it!" Jeremy demanded as their combined weight threatened to bring both of them crashing to the ground.

McHale's voice echoed like a thunderclap. "Anderson! Get him out of here!" he commanded with newfound authority. Jeremy tightened his grip on the raging Dutch. With unwavering determination, he grunted, "Time to go, Dutch," steering him forcefully but steadily toward the exit.

By the time they reached the locker room doors, Dutch's intense anger had simmered into a low growl of resentment.

"What the hell, Dutchie?" Jeremy's eyes were fierce and challenging. "You know they could expel you for this, right?"

Dutch's nostrils flared. "He's a joke, Anderson. McHale blew it with that shitty fucking call. The loss is on him, not you. It's all so screwed up."

"Dutchie, it's just a high school football game. It doesn't matter; life goes on," Jeremy tried to reason, his voice a calm contrast to the storm raging in Dutch's eyes. But Dutch was in no mood for reason.

"You guys had it, a win, finally!" Dutch shouted, pacing back and forth like a caged animal, his every word filled with a mix of disbelief and anger. "But because of Coach Dickhead in there pulling that ridiculous stunt at the end of the game?" He yelled while pounding on the locker room door, ensuring the coach inside could hear him.

"You guys had a clear shot at winning. That new kid Knight, from Central? He can boot the ball from 50 yards out, easy." He stopped pacing and fixed Jeremy with a pointed look, his voice lowering but intensifying. "Why didn't McHale just take the three points and the win?"

Now, I'll bet you guys might not even finish the season! McHale is the one who let Marty get hurt! He should've just taken the easy points and the win. It could've been different now." There was a genuine pain in Dutch's voice, mixed with frustration. "We should all be partying right now."

Jeremy's eyebrows furrowed in confusion. "What do you mean, 'we'?— Since when do you care so much about our losses?"

"You know what I mean, it's just— bullshit," Dutch lunged to get past Jeremy and back into the building,

"No, Dutchie! Stop it! We aren't giving up. We have a plan. We've got someone to dress in Marty's place," Jeremy said firmly.

"Oh yeah? Who?" Dutch scoffed.

The question forced a defeated expression to take over Jeremy's face.

Dutch burst out laughing. "Let me guess—the nerd?" his words echoed through the chilly evening air.

Jeremy dropped his head, realizing how insane of an idea it was.

"Oh, that's great, he's gonna get murdered," Dutch groaned sarcastically.

Jeremy sighed, regret evident in his eyes. He lifted his head and regained confidence, "He won't play, Dutch. He's just going to fill a roster spot."

Suddenly, his attention was clear, his eyes sharp. "So, you'll have the little worm dress up for Marty? That'll help." He said, his voice filled with sarcasm.

"He won't see the field," Jeremy defended, thinking of Dennis's vulnerability. Dutch's eyes narrowed, "With McHale? He's going to get that kid killed. It's not right."

"We need to play the game, Dutch. It's more than just a win or a loss. If you have a better plan, I'm all ears."

As Jeremy's words hung in the air, they knew the stakes had never been higher.

Dutch's eyes took on a distant, reflective quality as though he was diving deep into memories of days long past.

"You want a better plan?" he said with a smirk. "You got it. I'll see you at practice on Monday. It's time for a change."

Jeremy blinked in surprise. "What are you talking about?"

Without looking back, Dutch continued his stride into the shadows, his Turismo waiting at the path's end.

"Monday, after school, Anderson, I'll be there," he shouted over his shoulder.

Frozen in place, Jeremy watched a mix of bewilderment and hope bubbling inside him. The roar of the Turismo's engine punctuated a dramatic exit, shattering the stillness of the evening.

As the dust from Dutch's speedy departure settled, the locker room door creaked open, revealing a hesitant Dennis clutching Jeremy's jacket. "Is the coast clear?"

Jeremy managed a weak smile."Yeah, he's gone."

Dennis exhaled a sigh of relief. "Seriously, that guy's a ticking time bomb. Why won't he just leave us alone?"

Jeremy draped an arm around Dennis's shoulder. "Sometimes, people just need a chance to find their way. And I have a feeling Dutchie is about to surprise us all."

30

FRANKIE'S

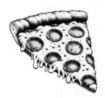

WITH ITS INTERIOR dripping with '80s nostalgia, Frankie's Pizza was a tribute to Huxley High School's glory days. Stepping in, you were greeted with an explosion of Huxley blue and gold. Pennants and championship memorabilia were plastered over every inch of the walls.

Kristen, Heather, and Missy occupied a booth, their laughter punctuating the air as they chatted and sipped their diet cokes. When Del and Tomo walked in, smiles and greetings replaced the girls' conversation.

"Have you girls ordered yet?" Del asked in his characteristic playful tone.

Frankie, ever the gracious host and every bit as charming as he was in high school, approached them and asked, "What can I get for my favorite Wildcats tonight?"

"A large cheese and a large pepperoni for starters," replied Tomo, his eyes skimming the menu for more. "What do you guys want?"

Missy raised an eyebrow, "Two pizzas just for you, Tomo?"

With a hearty laugh, Frankie responded, "Ah yes, the 'Tomo Special'— one of each, a favorite indeed."

But Kristen quickly added, "Better make that two Tomo Specials, Frankie. Jeremy will be here any minute.

Just then, the entrance bell jingled, announcing Jeremy's arrival. "Hey, sorry for being late. McHale held me back," he announced as he grabbed a seat beside Kristen.

Del whispered loud enough for the group to hear, "All set for the plan with Big D next week?"

Jeremy looked at Missy, signaling Del to keep the plan a secret, but Del missed the hint.

"What plan?" Missy asked, her curiosity piqued.

Despite Jeremy's request for secrecy, Del enthusiastically shared what happened in the locker room after the game. He told them about how Marty's injury put the rest of the season in jeopardy, and the plan was to have Dennis suit up against Truman.

Kristen's eyes widened in disbelief. "Wait, what?" Before Missy could articulate her shock, Kristen continued, "Dennis? The dork—?" She quickly cast a regretful look at Missy. "Sorry, I didn't— it's just, I mean," she stumbled." What is this, some kind of 'Lucas' situation?" The atmosphere in the room grew tense.

Jeremy could feel the weight of the situation pressing down on him. "It's not like that, he began, attempting to clarify, "We're not trying to make Dennis the next star quarterback or anything. We just need him on the roster to fulfill the team's requirements. He won't see any action."

Missy, visibly concerned, added, "And what if something happens? What if there's an accident or— I don't know— what if he gets hurt?"

Del interjected to lighten the mood, "Come on, we're talking about Dennis here. He's more likely to get hurt tripping over his shoelaces than from anything on the football field."

Kristen, though still skeptical, tried to find humor in the situation. "Well, I never thought I'd see the day. Dennis Winston in football pads, that will definitely make the yearbook."

Sensing the need to wrap up the conversation, Jeremy added, "Look, we're doing this to save the season. We have a plan, and we're sticking to it. Dennis is on board."

Missy leaned back in the booth, still processing the news. "Okay, but promise me one thing," she said, locking eyes with Jeremy, "Promise me you'll keep him safe."

Jeremy nodded solemnly. "I promise." He leaned forward, lowering his voice for added emphasis. "Plus, there's a chance we might not even need him to suit up after all," he hinted with a mysterious tone.

Del's eyebrows knitted together in confusion, a question forming on his lips. "What do you mean? What's going on?"

"Bedtime story," he whispered to Del, an inside term the two used to preface the need for a late-night confidential conversation.

The aroma of the freshly baked pizzas filled the air as Frankie placed them on the table. Without a second's hesitation, Tomo reached out and grabbed a slice, taking a large bite.

Kristen, twirling a curl, looked at Jeremy with playful eyes. "So, what's the plan for the weekend? I could use some quality time with my Bear," she said, casting a flirty glance in Jeremy's direction.

Jeremy cleared his throat. "I've got some things to do, but I'll make sure to carve out some time for you."

Missy's eyes sparkled with curiosity as she piped up. "Speaking of which, you mentioned doing something with the cottage, right? I'm excited to see what you have planned for it."

Del's eyes widened in realization. "Oh, man! That's right, the cottage! It's been ages since I've been out there. What's the plan, Jer?"

Looking around the table, Jeremy outlined his plan. "I think it'll be a cool place for us to hang out. I'm going to start cleaning it up this weekend." He met Missy's eyes, silently communicating a shared secret.

Kristen, always enthusiastic about new adventures, added, "That sounds like a blast! We can all help out. Maybe even have a picnic."

Heather frowned. "Can't. I have to go to my stupid brother's piano recital. Trust me, it's going to be a total drag."

In between bites, Tomo chimed in, "I'm out too. Moms on my case about my English grade. Wants me to get a B average by the end of the semester. I need to study."

Kristen groaned. "Missy, you in? It'll be a total sausage fest without you."

"Can Dennis come too?" Missy looked at her with puppy-dog eyes.

Sighing, Kristen conceded, "Fine, Dennis can tag along."

"Thanks, Kris." Missy's smile brightened. "I just need to wait until after I see my parents in the morning. They are both working nights this weekend."

Del's hands met in a single, excited clap. "Perfect! Jer, you can crash at my house tonight. We'll hit the road after breakfast."

As the night drew to a close, the group left Frankie's; their stomachs were full and their spirits high.

Outside, the gentle hum of the neon sign and the faint echo of the jukebox inside served as the backdrop to their farewells.

Kristen hopped into her car, with Heather already settling into the passenger seat, fumbling with the radio.

Tomo adjusted his jacket and looked up the road. "I'm just gonna walk from here. It's not too far." He waved and started on his way.

Del jumped into Jeremy's jeep, adjusting the seat for his tall frame. He gave a mock salute, leaving Jeremy and Missy standing side by side.

Jeremy turned to Missy, a soft smile on his face. "Did you have fun tonight?"

She nodded as her eyes met his. "Kristen has been a real sweetheart. Now I see why you're with her."

Jeremy chuckled, "She has her moments, especially when you get past the surface."

From her car, Kristen's voice sliced through the night. "Missy! Hurry up! Heather's torturing me with Dave Matthews. I need backup ASAP!" Her tone was playful, filled with pretend horror. Missy laughed, rolling her eyes. "I'm coming!" She shouted back, then turned to Jeremy. "See you tomorrow?"

"Definitely," he replied with a nod.

Missy's silhouette was lit by the soft glow of the parking lot lights as she walked away and got into Kristen's Z24. Jeremy watched as they slowly pulled away, leaving him in the quiet stillness of the night.

31

DAYTRIP TO THE PAST

THE MORNING AFTER THE GAME, colorful cereal boxes lined the counter of the Del Coronado kitchen.

Del, spoon midway to his mouth, paused. "So, about last night at Frankie's, what did you mean we might not need Dennis? I never got to ask you when we got back here. You fell asleep a half hour into Friday the 13th: Part 3."

Jeremy laughed softly. "Man, I was so tired, I totally zonked out, huh? Sorry about that."

Del grinned with a hint of mischief in his eyes. "You sure did. By the way, who's Cassandra? You kept mumbling her name in your sleep. Someone you're dreaming of?" He teased, wiggling his eyebrows suggestively.

A flush crept up Jeremy's neck. "Uh, yeah, I don't remember," he mumbled, trying to deflect Del's questions.

"Anyway, what's your secret plan for Truman? You've got someone to help us fill the roster besides Dennis?" Del asked, returning to his original question.

Jeremy leaned in. "Not a plan. A weapon." He said before telling Del about the locker room incident with Dutch, his anger, the confrontation, and his promise to join the team on Monday.

Del, wide-eyed, asked, "You think he's going to show?"

"I'm going to make sure of it. We're taking him to the cottage with us. It's time for a little heart-to-heart with our old pal Dutch." Jeremy said as he got up to rinse his bowl. The running water sounded loud in the otherwise silent room. Turning to Del, he asked, "Remember that time we found that old box in the cottage's attic? The one with the old photos of all the maintenance workers' families?"

Del laughed, "Yeah! We made up those wild stories about them being the ghost families that haunted the woods up there. Man, "those were some of the best times of my life."

Reflecting on the past, Jeremy added, "Yeah, it really was an awesome time, and I think Dutch would agree. Think about it: in those days, he had his whole family and a bright future ahead of him. I hope that taking him back there will remind him of the good times and bring the old Dutchie back to life."

"I don't know, man. Del said, remaining unsure of the plan. "You really think bringing him up there is going to magically change his perspective? —Sounds like a stretch; I am telling you, man— the guy is lost.

Jeremy stayed firm, "It's worth a try, don't you think?— He was our best friend; we owe it to Dutch to try to bring him back. Who knows, it could turn out really great. remember last night we agreed that we'd try to look out for him? This is our shot."

"Okay, you're right," Del finally agreed, "We'll take him to the cottage and see what happens. But you have to promise me one thing." Jeremy raised an eyebrow, "What's that?"

"If things go sideways and Dutch starts acting out or goes wild in any way, we drop the whole thing and go back to Dennis and the original plan — Deal?"

Jeremy held out his hand, "Deal." The two locked eyes, sealing their pact. They were in this together, no matter what happened.

The Jeep's tires hummed on the pavement as they turned onto the road leading to the section of town known only as "The Mills."

They spotted Dutch's aunt as they pulled up outside a particularly weary-looking house. Her wrinkled face and graying hair told stories of years filled with hardships. She sat in a creaky rocking chair, a half-smoked cigarette dangling from her lips.

"I ain't buying whatever you're selling!" she called out defiantly, even before Jeremy could kill the engine.

Del raised his hands in a non-threatening gesture. "We're not here to sell anything, ma'am. We're here to see Dutch." She squinted at them, recognition dawning. "You're the Anderson kid, aren't you? What do you want with Dutch?"

"We just want to talk, that's all," Jeremy replied gently, stepping out of the Jeep.

Dutch's aunt took a long drag from her cigarette, exhaling the smoke slowly. "He's inside. But no funny business. You hear me?"

Jeremy nodded. "Thank you, ma'am."

The door swung open abruptly, revealing Dutch. His broad frame filled the doorway. His hair was a tousled mess, and the lines on his face seemed deeper, making him look older than his years. There was a weariness in his eyes but also a flash of defiance.

"What do you want?" he demanded, his voice gravelly. "I said I'd be there Monday, didn't I?"

Jeremy held his ground, keeping his tone even. "We know. We just thought—well, if you're serious about this, we should get started right away. The playbook isn't light reading, and with the game coming up, there's not much time."

Del jumped in, trying to add weight to the pitch, "We're headed up to the cottage. We thought you might want to come with us, get away from here for a bit, and we could go over the playbook."

Dutch looked at him with a raised eyebrow, then glanced at Jeremy as if sizing them both up. "The cottage, huh?"

"Yeah," Del continued, "We thought it'd be a good spot to get you up to speed—you know, away from all the distractions. Plus, it'll be cool to take a trip down memory lane. The three of us haven't been up there together in years."

A hint of a smile tugged at the corner of Dutch's mouth. His head filled with memories of simpler times when the world's weight hadn't quite settled on his shoulders. "You guys don't quit," he finally said with a sigh.

No, we don't; we need you, Dutchie," Jeremy replied earnestly. "The team needs you."

Dutch took a moment to mull over their words. Then he gave a short nod. "Alright, give me a few to pack some stuff. But this doesn't mean I'm playing for sure, got it? We'll see how this 'study session' goes."

Jeremy and Del exchanged a hopeful glance. "We'll wait for you in the jeep," Jeremy offered, backing away from the door.

They couldn't help but think about the road ahead as they waited. Convincing Dutch to return to the team was one thing, but ensuring he was game-ready was another. They hoped that the bond they once shared, combined with the tranquil backdrop of the cottage, would pave the way for a successful reunion.

The journey to the cottage was always memorable, but today, it had a different energy. The trees surrounding them felt thicker, and the sounds more muted, as if nature was aware of their critical mission.

Del pointed out the window at the old wooden sign marking the entrance to the grounds where The Labrador once sat. "Looks like we're almost there,"

The sign was covered in graffiti prominently featuring the letters D.W. —the intricate patterns showcasing the artist's skill.

"Your work, Dutch?" Jeremy asked, looking in the rearview mirror.

Dutch leaned back, glancing casually at the sign as they passed it. "Yeah, not my best work," he said with a shrug.

Del chuckled, "Still, it's impressive that it's lasted this long. When did you do it?"

"Beginning of junior year," Dutch replied, his voice taking on a hint of regret. "I used to ride my bike up here to clear my head, and one night, I felt the urge to leave a mark."

As they pulled up, the cottage seemed to anticipate its visitors. After years of neglect, fixing it up wouldn't be easy.

With determination, the three young men sprung into action. Del and Dutch tackled the insides, hauling out garbage and sweeping up years of dirt and dust, while Jeremy took on the outside tasks, patching up holes and ensuring the place was safe from critters. As they worked, the sound of gravel under tires told them that one of their friends had arrived. A bright blue VW bug approached the cottage with Stacy at the wheel.

"What's she doing here, Jeremy asked aloud.

"I called her before you got up this morning and invited her. You were still dreaming about mysterious babes named Cassandra" he quipped, winking at Dutch.

Dutch smirked in reply. "Who's Cassandra? She sounds hot."

Stacy's entrance cut the banter short. Balancing a tray of drinks, she looked around with surprise and skepticism when her eyes landed on Dutch. "I brought some drinks. I thought you might be thirsty," she commented, her tone casual and her eyes sharp. "Didn't expect to see you here, Wyatt."

Jeremy, sensing the need for mediation, quickly intervened. "Stacy, look, it's all good— Dutch is helping us out. He's joining the team."

Stacy raised her eyebrows. "Is that so? Just make sure you stay in line, Wyatt. I've got my eyes on you."

Dutch nodded, an air of indifference around him.

Stacy, meanwhile, moved to the porch, taking a moment to appreciate the scenic beauty around her. "It's a perfect day to be out here," she remarked, settling down comfortably.

Stacy grumbled as the tab on her Coke can snapped off. "Dammit," she muttered, staring at the unopened drink in frustration.

"Dutch noticed her dilemma and offered to get the opener from the kitchen. As he left, he shot a meaningful glance towards Jeremy.

Surprised by Dutch's behavior, Stacy mouthed, "What the hell?" at Jeremy, who just shrugged."

The sound of gravel crunching once more signaled the arrival of Kristen's Z24. Missy was seated confidently in the passenger seat, with Dennis squished in the back.

"Hey, boys!" Kristen sang, her gaze moving across the group, only to freeze as it met Stacy's. "Stacy," she acknowledged with a restrained nod.

With a mischievous grin, Stacy replied, "What's up, Red?"

Missy and Dennis, seemingly content to let the two have their moment, followed Kristen's lead towards the cottage.

Stacy leaned towards Del, her voice dripping with irony. "First the school's bad boy, and now the Winstons? What is this, the Twilight Zone?"

Del chuckled, wrapping an arm around Stacy's shoulder. "Be cool, Stace. You know we're equal opportunity."

The atmosphere on the porch grew tense as Dutch appeared, holding out the can opener to Stacy. "Here you go," he said, his tone neutral.

"Thank you very much."She replied, taking the can opener, her voice dripping with sarcasm.

Dennis, who had often been at the receiving end of Dutch's bullying, stopped in his tracks, his eyes widening in surprise.

Beside him, Kristen murmured in disbelief, "Fucking Dutchie."

Jeremy, sensing the rising tension, quickly stepped in. "Everyone, listen. Dutch is helping get the cottage in shape, and, more importantly, he's a Wildcat now—really, he always has been; he's just been away for a while, but now he's back. Honestly, I'm tired of explaining the whole situation."

Catching Dennis's eye, Jeremy added, "Dennis, you should be grateful.

You won't need to suit up with Dutch on the team.—Let's all just get along." He said, sweeping his hand over the gathered group.

Losing interest in the drama, Kristen tried her best to deflect. "Whatever, I have sandwiches; let's all eat. I wasn't sure if Tomo would change his mind and come; you can never tell with that guy, so I made a ton. I figured it's better to have too much than not enough," she remarked.

Each person found a spot to settle in with a sandwich in hand. The atmosphere lightened as they ate, laughter floated in the air, and it was easy to forget any previous tension.

Jeremy rose from his spot once the last crumbs were brushed away and the empty wrappers were collected. "Alright, Del, Dutch," he called, waving them over. Time to hit the books. Let's get to it."

The three of them headed down a worn path, with Jeremy leading the way with a playbook tucked under his arm.

The girls, along with Dennis, made their way inside. They found a series of mismatched chairs and a couch that had seen better days. As they settled, Dennis was first to break the silence.

"I still can't believe Dutch Wyatt's here. I mean, I'm glad I don't have to suit up against Truman and all, but putting our future in the hands of such a loose cannon makes me nervous."

With a glint in her eyes, Kristen added, "You know, there's a story about the Wyatts. They say Dutch's great-great-great-grandmother was a witch in the 1700s. Legend has it that she was burned at the stake.

Stacy rolled her eyes and groaned, "Ugh, that's just an old wives' tale. From what I've heard, the Wyatts have always been trouble. They're just bad people with bad karma that caught up to them.

Dennis, exasperated, interjected, "None of that's true. All those ghost stories about the Wyatts and their centuries-old curse are just tall tales. The real story is way more tragic.

Kristen sighed as her eyes wandered to the window. "Oh, not another sob story. We've all heard about the boiler room accident in "The Mills."

"Dennis nodded solemnly, "Yeah. Mr. Wyatt was among the most skilled workers there, respected by all. One day, a malfunction caused an explosion in the Mill on Mechanic Street. He was in there, doing routine checks. They couldn't get him in time. He didn't make it."

Missy's eyes reflected the gravity of Dennis's story, her face tense with attention.

Dennis continued, "But what came next was much worse. Just a year later, Dutch's younger sister drowned in a town pool."

Stacy's hand flew to her mouth, her eyes wide with shock. "Oh my god. This is— it's just too much," she whispered, her voice shaking, barely holding back tears. "Two tragedies right after one another. How did the family deal with them?"

Dennis's voice wavered slightly, "They didn't. In the spring of the following year, overwhelmed with grief, Dutchie's mother committed suicide, leaving him orphaned. He was sent to live with his aunt, who barely could take care of herself, let alone Dutch."

Missy felt pain in her heart. "Oh my god. We all judge him and see him as the bad guy. But he's just a kid who's seen too much tragedy."

Stacy, tears now streaming down her face, said, "All this time, I thought he was just a bad guy who did bad things. But now, knowing this, how can we judge him?"

Missy sat beside Stacy, putting an arm around her, "It's a reminder. Everyone we meet is battling something we know nothing about. We need to be kinder."

Dennis took a deep breath, "It's easy to judge from the outside. But everyone has a story. That's why I brought this up. Dutch doesn't need any more judgments; he's had enough of that. What he needs is some friends."

Stacy, wiping away a tear, tried to imagine Dennis's torment, torn between standing up for himself and empathizing with his bully.

He smiled softly, "I've always been thankful for Jeremy. Somehow, he has a way with Dutch. He can put him in his place. Maybe that's what friendship is – understanding and being there, even when it's hard."

Kristen uncomfortably shifted in her seat," Look, I'm all for a sad back-story, but that doesn't give someone the right to terrorize others. We all have our struggles." Her face flushed with a mixture of guilt and anger.

Stacy interjected sharply, "Red, It's not about giving him a pass. It's about understanding why. All this time, I've judged him, labeled him. And now I feel awful." Tears welled in her eyes as she considered the judgments she'd so readily heaped on Dutch without truly knowing his story.

Missy offered, "We all make judgments, Stacy. It's part of being human. What's important now is that we move forward. We can't change the past, but we can change our attitudes from now on."

Stacy took a shaky breath, nodding. "You're right—I just wish I had known sooner. If I did, I would have been nicer to him."

Kristen huffed, clearly still not convinced. "Understanding is one thing. But he still needs to be held responsible for his actions."

The group sat in silence, grappling with the revelations and their feelings about Dutch.

The three boys made their way to a large rock that overlooked the lake on the grounds of what used to be The Labrador estate.

Del kicked a stone into the water, watching the ripples spread. "Do you guys remember that time we played hide-and-seek here, and Jeremy got stuck in that old tree trunk? Jeremy laughed. "I thought I'd be there forever. You two took your sweet ass time to find me."

Dutch, a faint smile playing on his lips, interjected, "How about when we all jumped into the lake without permission? Man, my mom was so pissed at me when I came home drenched head to toe."

Jeremy chuckled. "I remember your face when she opened the door— looked like you'd seen a ghost.

Del laughed, "She was so steamed. Didn't you get grounded for two weeks?"

Dutch sighed, "Yeah, and I had to do extra chores for a month. But it was worth it." He looked out over the water, the glint of the sun reflecting in his eyes. "Those days, before everything went to shit, that was the best time of my life. I wish I could go back and do something about it. All of it."

Jeremy looked at Dutch, his heart heavy with the weight of knowing his friend's fate. He knew he couldn't change it; the universe had rules, and as much as he wanted to, he couldn't save his friend. However, there was a silver lining. He could ensure that Dutch's remaining days were filled with the happiness they once felt as young boys on that rock.

It was about rewriting Dutch's story, shattering the myth of the Wyatt curse, and creating a legacy that wouldn't remember him as the tormented bad boy but as a hero—a testament of hope and resilience for everyone in town.

Clearing his throat, Jeremy switched gears. "Alright, let's dive into this playbook. We need to get our strategy on point." He said as he opened the playbook.

Dutch leaned in, his eyes scanning the pages with an intensity contradicting his laid-back demeanor. His insights and understanding of the game, each play, and positioning were astonishing. It was as if he'd never left the field, his football intellect shining through.

Del, equally impressed, said, "Man, Dutchie, you've still got it. Why did you ever quit?"

His eyes distant, Dutch responded, "You know what, man, I used to brush off the talk about the 'Wyatt curse.' I thought it was just superstitious bullshit. But after everything that happened with my family," He swallowed hard, "I couldn't bear the thought of you guys getting caught up in whatever dark cloud hangs over my family. I didn't want any of you sucked into it. I figured if I stepped away, it might keep you guys safe. That's why I try so hard to get everyone to hate and fear me. I'm giving everyone a reason to stay away to protect them from any curse that might come for me."

Del blinked, taken aback by Dutch's honesty. It was heartbreaking to think that Dutch carried such a heavy burden, sacrificing his love for football and any real friendship to protect those he cared about.

Dutch squared his shoulders and met Del's eyes with determination. "But you know what, man? I'm tired of running from ghosts. I can't keep blaming a curse for everything that goes wrong in my life. If I want to beat it, I've got to face it head-on."

He looked at Jeremy, "Thanks to you guys, especially Jeremy; I've realized that sometimes the best way to challenge fate is to lean on those who've always had your back. You guys are my brothers. I've been away for way too long, and it's time I changed that."

Del, moved by Dutch's words, grinned. "So, you're saying you're back?"

Dutch nodded firmly, a hint of his old mischievous smile playing on his lips. "Oh, I'm not just back, Del, I'm all in, one hundred percent a Wildcat. We started this journey together in 7th grade, time to see it through."

Jeremy slapped Dutch on the back, his grin mirroring Del's. "Welcome back, Dutchie. We've missed you."

The atmosphere was electric with anticipation and hope, and for the first time in a long time, Dutch felt like he was exactly where he belonged.

32

SLUMBER PARTY

INSIDE THE COZY COTTAGE, Kristen sat surrounded by a medley of cosmetics. As she expertly applied a touch of blush, Missy watched with fascination.

"Kris," she began curiously. Why do you use all those products?"

Kristen looked at Missy with a hint of vulnerability. "Not everyone has that effortless beauty like you do, Miss. I need a little—well, a lot of help."

Missy's expression shifted to disbelief, and her cheeks took on a soft blush. "Come on, Kristen. I'm not pretty."

With a bewildered look, Kristen set down her mascara. "You're joking, right?" she deadpanned. "Miss, you are so pretty. There's this elegance about you, a natural glow. Seriously, it's kind of disgusting." She chuckled.

Missy raised an eyebrow, genuinely surprised. "Me, elegant?—No way. I'm just average at best. You have this magnetic charm, Kris. When you walk into a room, heads turn. You are total confidence."

Kristen bit her lip, taking a deep breath. "Look, if I am being honest, what you just described is exactly why I use all this stuff," she said, picking up her mascara and shaking it at Missy.

Kristen bit her lip, taking a deep breath. "Look, if I am being honest, what you just describe is why I use all this stuff," she said, waving her hands over the pile of makeup in front of her. "Seriously, it's exhausting trying to keep up this appearance. Sometimes, I wish I could be more like you. You have this natural aura —a mystique. Honestly, I think people might be a little intimidated by you."

Missy's brow furrowed, her surprise evident. "Intimidated? By me?"

Kristen nodded gently, "Yeah— Sometimes, you can come off a bit overconfident, like you think that you're better than everyone. Maybe, if you'd just— I don't know, open up a bit more and be yourself, people will see the warm-hearted Missy that I know you are."

Missy sighed, dropping her head. "I never realized I came off that way."

Kristen reached over, gently lifting Missy's chin. "But that's the thing; you shouldn't have to change anything for anyone. Maybe just let them in a little? Show them the Missy I used to know, the Missy I am glad I am getting to know again."

Missy's eyes shimmered, gratitude evident. "I wish I had your courage and poise, Kris," she whispered.

"And I wish I had your kindness, Kristen replied with a soft smile.

In the quiet that followed, Kristen and Missy discovered the friendship they thought was lost was still there. In the safety of each other's company, they could be themselves, a rare gift they hadn't found with anyone else.

Del's signature playful smirk appeared as the three boys approached the cottage's front porch. He interrupted a deep conversation between Stacy and Dennis, "What's going on here— you two trading beauty tips?" he quipped, raising an eyebrow. On the other hand, Jeremy was eager to check in on Missy and Kristen. But before he could reach the door, a tense moment unfolded behind him.

With a heavy presence, Dutch fixed his eyes on Dennis, who ducked his head, trying to avoid making eye contact. Breaking the silence, Dutch declared, "Dennis, I've got something to say to you."

Stacy, always the protector, straightened up, her eyes cautiously narrowing. But before she could react, Del raised his hand, signaling her to hold back.

Dennis, apprehension evident in his voice, replied, "Whatever it is, Dutch, I'm sorry, okay? Let's just keep the peace today."

Dutch interrupted, his voice assertive yet layered with regret, "No, Dennis. I'm the one who's sorry."

Dennis, taken aback, hesitantly raised his eyes to meet Dutch's. The once menacing figure now stood vulnerable in the dimming light. "All the shit I've given you, all the times I've made you the target—it wasn't right. I apologize. It stops now."

Stacy and Del exchanged a glance. Del's chest swelled with pride, a broad smile playing on his lips, clearly pleased by Dutch's gesture.

Stacy, initially prepared for confrontation, seemed to be processing the situation. She slowly rose from her seat, taking tentative steps towards Dutch. The stark difference in their heights became more pronounced as she stood before him. Her initial stern expression melted away as she looked up, searching his face for sincerity. Without a word, she reached up and wrapped her arms around him in a heartfelt embrace, signifying a new beginning.

Jeremy gently pushed open the cabin door, pausing to gather himself before stepping in. There, bathed in the soft light filtering through the curtains, sat Missy and Kristen, engrossed in their own private world. He leaned against the doorframe, silently watching, his heart a storm of emotions.

The weight of these past days and the ripple effect of the choices he made in life twenty-six weighed heavily on him. Before him were two vibrant young women, both holding unique places in his heart. But he knew deep down that neither had a permanent place in his future.

Memories of Cassandra flooded his thoughts. She was the missing piece, the one who truly completed him.

Kristen was right for him now, but she would never be his soulmate. Their relationship would soon become strained, marred by disagreements and clashes over ambitions and expectations.

His eyes drifted to Missy. Her soft features held an innocence that drew him in. She was like a fresh page in a book he hadn't read. He felt a bitter realization that she'd never be a permanent part of his story. Was he developing feelings for her? The mere thought made him recoil internally, trying to bury the emotions that threatened to surface. He was so consumed in his thoughts that he failed to notice the girls had spotted him.

Missy's bright and playful voice broke his trance. "Homecoming!" she exclaimed before turning towards Kristen. "He does that zoning-out thing sometimes. It's so weird."

Sensing something deeper behind Jeremy's distant look, Kristen nudged him gently. "Everything okay, Bear? Did things go smoothly with Dutch?"

Jeremy blinked back to the present, shaking off his introspection.

"Yeah," he replied, his voice steady. It's more than okay. Dutchie is all in. He even apologized to Dennis and promised to stop the bullying."

Missy's eyebrows shot up in surprise. Her gaze flitted between Jeremy and Kristen, a hint of admiration shining in her eyes.

Jeremy stretched, feeling the cool evening air on his skin. "It's going to get dark soon, Kris," he said, looking at her. You mentioned quality time earlier. Do you have any plans in mind?"

With a trademark mischievous twinkle in her eyes, Kristen surveyed the refurbished cottage and surrounding area. "You know, now that we've got this place all spruced up, it's not going to get that cold tonight. How about a camp-out? I can run home really quick and grab some camping gear. Do you think everyone would be game?"

Del, who had just entered the scene, raised an eyebrow curiously. "Game for what?"

Hearing the mention of a camp-out, the rest of the group on the porch joined the conversation, curious expressions painted on their faces. Kristen explained her idea, and it was immediately met with excited agreement. Stacy began listing out things they'd need.

"Alright—Dennis, you can hop in with me and make a supply run. We'll need food, drinks, and the essential s'mores, and Dennis," she winked at him, "Prepare for the musical education of your life."

Missy said with her usual thoughtful demeanor, "I'll go with Kristen to grab blankets and pillows. I might need to swing by my place first to check in with my parents, but they should be cool."

Dutch, who had been silent till now, cracked his knuckles and said, "If we're doing this, we'll need some epic tunes. Can someone bring me back home so I can grab my car? I'll pick up my boombox and CDs."

"I can take you Dutch," Stacy offered; one condition: try to bring something other than just metal, alright? Let's mix it up a bit. If you can't, no biggie. I've got some of Del's CDs in my car, and I'll bring them up when I get back."

Del's eyes sparkled with anticipation. "Awesome, Stace. Tonight's shaping up to be legendary!"

Missy raised an eyebrow at the boys, teasingly asking, "So while we're out doing all the running around, what exactly will you guys be up to?"

Jeremy grinned, striking a mock salute, "Fire duty. Del and I have got it covered. Remember, we were in Boy Scouts together; trust us to handle the flames."

With responsibilities set and the anticipation mounting, the group set off to gather what they needed, looking forward to an evening bursting with good tunes, heavy laughter, and lasting memories.

Dutch's return marked the start of the evening, his arms cradling a boombox and a selection of CDs echoing the vibes of 90's grunge, metal anthems, and 80s power ballads. The boys briefly debated the musical kickoff for the night, eventually settling on Guns N' Roses' "Use Your Illusion II" album. However, an unspoken agreement hung in the air: the playlist would shift to a more party-friendly groove once the girls and Dennis returned.

The distant rumble of an approaching car soon followed, revealing Stacy and Dennis. But the real surprise was the recognizable face that emerged from the back seat.

"Guess who we found on the way?" Stacy exclaimed, pointing to Tomo with a wide smile.

Dennis chuckled, adding, "He figured he wouldn't let us have all the fun."

Tomo raised his arms dramatically, proclaiming, "There's no way I'm missing out on a night with my best friends!"

Lastly, Kristen's car pulled up, visibly packed with all the comfort essentials. As she popped the trunk, a cascade of blankets, comforters, and pillows tumbled out. With what appeared to be a well-practiced routine, Missy and Kristen transformed the Cottage's interior into a plush sleep-over haven. Once their cozy masterpiece was complete, the duo headed outdoors to join the group.

The campfire was roaring, blazing majestically, sending playful shadows dancing into the night and cloaking everyone in its comforting warmth.

Stacy wrinkled her nose as the familiar strains of "November Rain" drifted through the air. "Ugh, Guns N' Roses? Really, guys? Could we be any more cliché?" she groaned, flopping down on one of the blankets.

Tomo immediately jumped to the defense of the classic rock choice. "Come on, Stacy! It's great. He began, leaning in with a gleam in his eye, "Axl Rose, he's so small, but his voice? So big!" He then belted out the world's worst imitation of Axl's unique vocal style, causing a round of laughter from the group.

Kristen, looking to avoid a potential musical standoff, quickly intervened. "Alright, alright! We can switch it up later. Let's just enjoy the fire and each other's company. Who's up for some s'mores?"

The mention of the beloved campfire treat seemed to unite the group, and soon, everyone was engaged in the age-old debate of how to roast the perfect marshmallow.

Surrounded by the enveloping embrace of the night, they sat huddled around the fire. The gentle pops and crackles from the burning wood and the stars overhead created an atmosphere of connection.

Dennis, always the strategist, turned to Dutch, "We don't have much time to prep for the game; think you'll have the playbook down in time?"

With the golden glow of the fire reflecting off his eyes, Dutch answered, "If Coach McHale gives us some freedom on our plays, I think we've got a shot."

"Yeah, it'll be great to have a real quarterback for once," Del shot, "Sorry, Marty he said, raising his coke to the air in respect; get well soon," he mused, taking a sip.

Before football could further dominate the conversation, Kristen playfully interrupted, "Guys, come on! We didn't decide to have this sleepover to obsess over football all night. There has to be something else to talk about!"

With her typical wit, Stacy added with a dramatic eye roll, "Ginger Snaps over there is right. I mean, I'm all for chalk talk, but there's a world beyond the gridiron."

A hush settled on them before Jeremy's voice laden with curiosity broke the silence, "Have you guys ever wondered about the bigger picture of life? Like, what if we're on a cycle, living life after life?"

Dennis' eyebrows shot up in intrigue, "So, you mean like reincarnation?"

With a thoughtful nod, Jeremy continued, "Yeah, what if every lifetime is a chance to learn, love, and evolve? Maybe our paths cross time and time again."

Always curious about cultures, Missy turned to Tomo to ask, "I hope I'm not overstepping, but is there a Japanese belief about rebirth?"

Tomo pondered a moment before replying, "Many do believe in reincarnation, but I'm more about living for today. I try to treasure every moment and spread kindness."

Del, grinning, chimed in, "That's the spirit! I mean, why worry about past or future lives? I'm focused on being the best dude I can be every day."

Dutch's voice dropped a tone, "Given my past, I often think about what comes after life. I think, once you're gone, it's just— dark, empty, nothing."

Moved by his admission, Missy spoke softly, "Dutch, I can't even begin to understand what you've been through. But I truly believe there's more to our existence after this life. I hope, for all our sakes, none of us find out the answer for a long, long time."

Jeremy found himself captivated by Missy's words but even more so by his profound connection with her. There was an undeniable pull, an attraction he couldn't quite explain. In his previous lives, Missy was nothing more than a momentary presence. She had never been this close to him.

In this 26th life, from their unexpected first meeting in the parking lot to their unforeseen collision in the school's stairwell, Missy had become an irreplaceable part of his journey. Why now? Why her? What had shifted in this cycle?

While he had accepted the tragic fate that awaited Missy and resolved to ensure her remaining days were filled with joy, Jeremy hadn't anticipated the depth of emotions he'd come to feel for her. The sudden attraction was intense.

He couldn't help but analyze the decisions he'd made so far in life 26. He wondered where he might have inadvertently shifted this cycle's path and pulled Missy irresistibly into his world.

Snapping Jeremy from his thoughts and in her ever-dreamy way, Kristen voiced, "I want to believe in an afterlife filled with love, where souls meet and mingle eternally."

Missy smiled, "That sounds beautiful, Kris. Here's hoping."

With her characteristic realism, Stacy offered, "I like to think there's something beyond this life. But I also feel there's a touch of fate or destiny, guided by some higher force." She scanned her friends' expressions, adding, "I just believe there's a greater power watching over us."

With newfound confidence, Dennis added, "Whatever lies beyond, I'm just grateful for right now. he said with sincerity. "Being here tonight, with all of you, I feel truly accepted for the first time."

As the night deepened, their conversations took them through the winding paths of life, existence, and the bonds that united them.

With every passing hour, their connections grew stronger, and the air around them became thick with the mysteries of the universe and the warmth of true friendship.

33

THE DAWN OF THE WILDCAT

As the group woke up from their sleepover, they found themselves surrounded by evidence of their festivities. Empty snack bags fluttered in the breeze, discarded cans littered the ground, and various personal items were strewn about—someone's sweatshirt here, another's sneaker there—all silent witnesses to the previous night's events.

"Has anyone seen Dutch or Dennis?" Jeremy inquired, his tone a blend of concern and curiosity. He began rummaging through the litter, wondering if they might've left a clue behind.

Still trying to wake up, Missy responded, "The last I knew, they were talking by the fire when I dozed off.

Kristen groaned, snuggling deeper into a blanket, "It's way too early for this. Bear, come over here and cuddle with me. The others can go look for them."

Stacy grumpily shot back, "Rise and shine, Red. We're all in this together. They're our friends."

Del, already on his feet and stretching, pointed to a faint trail of footprints leading toward the woods. "Relax, I think I know where they are."

Tomo, trying to lighten the mood, chuckled, "Maybe they went to catch the sunrise together."

Stacy smirked, "A sunrise date? How romantic." She chuckled, batting her eyes.

Jeremy's eyes locked onto Missy's anxious expression. Trying to reassure her, he said, "I'm sure they're fine. We'll find them."

Looking outside, he caught sight of the haunting grill of the Turismo staring back at him. "Dutchie's car's still here and in one piece. That's a good sign," he thought, trying to soothe his worry.

Del, asserting his leadership, declared, "Okay, team, let's move out and stick together." Motivated by his decisive tone, the group gathered their wits and headed out into the early light to find their friends.

Their feet crunched on the forest floor, occasionally snapping twigs, as they made their way toward the familiar rock overlooking the lake. Breaking through the last of the shrubs, their anxiety was replaced by a mix of amusement and disbelief.

With vibrant energy, Dennis was sketching out football plays in the dirt on the sandy shores of the lake, using a long stick as his pointer.

It appeared that he was drafting up a play of his own design. As he did, Dutch nodded, confirming his understanding of the strategy, occasionally asking questions and suggesting his own ideas.

Stacy chuckled, covering her mouth to hold in her laughter, "Of all the places—they're here, plotting football moves?"

Kristen shook her head, smirking, "So much for our dramatic search! They're just lost in their own football world."

With a hint of a smile touching his lips, Jeremy observed, "Dennis is definitely getting into the game spirit."

Missy's relief was evident. Racing over to Dennis, she exclaimed, "Seriously? You had me worried! What's going on here?"

As the rest neared the duo, Del, never one to miss an opportunity for banter, teased, "Look who we have here, the gridiron masterminds getting ready to carry us to victory next week."

Dutch, caught off guard but not lacking in humor, replied, "Oh, we've got something special planned. Just wait and see."

Dennis, a hint of pink coloring his cheeks, looked up with determination. "Yeah, and Dutch and I talked it over, I've decided. I'm going to dress for the game and be there for every practice."

With evident pride, Dutch added, "You should hear him break down the plays. We could use someone with his football brain on the sidelines."

The boys formed a loose circle around Dennis as he continued to outline his play using the sandy diagrams as a reference.

Missy, Kristen, and Stacy sat huddled on the shoreline, their knees drawn up and arms wrapped around them. The gentle lapping of the water against the shore, the occasional chirp of a bird, and the distant chatter of the boys' discussion created a serene soundscape.

With her innate knack for provocation, Stacy tilted her head and pinned Kristen with a sly look. "You know, Red," she drawled, a hint of mischief in her tone directed at Kristen, "no matter how hard you play the love card, you're not going to anchor Jeremy to this town. College is calling him, and he's going to answer."

Although annoyed, Kristen responded with forced calm: "Jeremy can think for himself, Stacy. It's not for me or anyone to decide where he heads for college."

Stacy inched closer, lowering her voice to a conspiratorial level. "But seriously, with his dad being—you know, Gregg, wouldn't you want to hop on the first train out of here?"

Before the tension grew too intense, Missy intervened with her trademark diplomacy. "Come on, Stacy. We all know Jeremy's relationship with his dad has been rough. But deciding on college? That's a big step, and it's Jeremy's choice."

Stacy rolled her eyes dramatically, "Sure, Missy, but we all see how Kristen's been subtly pushing him to stick around."

Taking a deep breath and diving into treacherous waters, Missy blurted out, "That was before he had that massive blowout with Gregg and stormed out, wasn't it?" She instantly realized that this information wasn't common knowledge.

Stacy's playful facade dropped, replaced by genuine surprise. "Wait, he did what?"

Kristen, clearly blindsided, blinked away frustrated tears. "Why didn't he tell me?"

Reaching out, Missy gently squeezed Kristen's hand, "I'm sorry—I thought you both already knew. He's been dealing with a lot, Kris. He probably needed some space to think."

Stacy's expression softened, her earlier playful jabs replaced with genuine concern. "That explains a lot. I noticed he's been off lately. Walking out on Gregg? That's huge. I just hope he's alright."

Missy nodded in agreement. "Now more than ever, Jeremy could use our support. Can we all be on the same page about this?"

Their conversation was interrupted by a sudden rustling sound coming from the bushes behind them. The girls were on their feet instantly, their faces a mix of alarm and curiosity. The eerie silence that followed only heightened the tension, making the lake's surroundings seem almost otherworldly in the soft morning light.

"Did you hear that?" whispered Kristen, her eyes wide, scanning the dense foliage.

Stacy nodded, her heart racing, "Yeah, what was it? I hope it wasn't a snake; I hate snakes?"

Missy, holding her breath, pointed towards a patch where the bushes appeared to move. "There! Look!"

The noise had not gone unnoticed by the boys. Del and Jeremy, sensing potential danger, rushed towards the girls, followed closely by Dennis and Tomo. They formed a protective semi-circle in front of them, their eyes fixed on the spot Missy had pointed to. The early morning air was thick with suspense.

Del whispered, "Stay behind us, nobody move."

Suddenly, a fluffy yellow flash bounded out from the tall grass, causing everyone to jump back. Before they could react, the creature made a beeline towards Stacy. She barely had time to brace herself before it leaped at her, but instead of an attack, she found herself cradling a small, yellow cat.

Its coat, though slightly unkempt, gleamed under the early sunlight. Vibrant green eyes looked up at Stacy with undeniable affection and trust. As she held it close to her chest, the young feline began to purr, its soft rhythmic vibrations starkly contrasting with the earlier heart-pounding tension.

The gang breathed a sigh of relief, the tension in the air dissolving into a mix of laughter and amazement.

Still cradling the cat, Stacy laughed, "This little guy scared us half to death!" Looks like I've made a new friend."

The rustling had caught everyone's attention except Dutch. When he finally approached the group and saw the small feline in Stacy's arms, his usual tough demeanor crumbled instantly.

"Is that a kitty?" Dutch's usually firm and assertive voice was filled with uncharacteristic warmth. Seeing the cat purring contentedly in Stacy's arms, Dutch's eyes lit up. "Oh my god, he's adorable!"

Kristen and Tomo exchanged amused glances, not used to seeing this side of Dutch. His tough exterior melted away, replaced by a softer, more tender side.

He looked at Stacy with pleading eyes, "Can I hold him? Please? Just for a second?"

Stacy, taken aback by Dutch's unexpected reaction, hesitated briefly before saying, "Sure, just be gentle. And watch out for his claws."

Without waiting for further permission, Dutch gently scooped up the cat and held him close. Surprisingly, the cat immediately seemed to take to Dutch, nuzzling his face and purring even louder.

Dutch cooed with a baby voice that none of them had ever heard before, "Who's a good kitty? Are you a good kitty? Yes, you are!" He scratched the cat under its chin, causing it to lean into his touch, clearly enjoying the affection.

Jeremy and Del exchanged a glance, an unspoken acknowledgment passing between them. Seeing the tough-as-nails Dutch being so openly affectionate was a rare sight. It was a side of him they hadn't seen in years, a reminder of a younger, carefree Dutch who loved animals. "Guess we found your soft spot, Dutch?" Del teased, a smirk on his face.

Dutch, not the least bit embarrassed, shrugged, "What can I say? I have a weakness for cute things, and I love cats. They are the perfect pet. They're smart and snuggly, and they clean themselves. Plus, you never see a cat working with the cops like some dumb-ass dog would."

As laughter rippled through the group, it was clear that the little cat had added a new dimension to their outing, providing a sweet moment of fun amidst the deeper conversations of the night before.

Dutch was adamant, wrapped up in the soft purring and general adoration of the newfound feline friend. "Guys, we're totally keeping him. Just think about it—He can be the cottage's mascot! Our very own Wild-cat!" The realization of the connection between their surprise guest and their school's mascot made Dutch's eyes widen in excitement. "It's like fate brought him here!"

"Look, as much as I love the idea of a Cottage mascot," Stacy said, "he can't stay here."The cottage isn't exactly a cat-friendly environment. He'll need proper care, especially at this young age." She paused, the cat's green eyes looking up at her as she stood next to Dutchie, reaching over and petting his head as he held the tiny bundle of fluff. "My sister works at a vet clinic a few towns over." She offered, "I'll take him to checked out and he can stay with me, but I'll make sure to bring him around. How does that sound?"

Dutch, clearly smitten with the little fur ball, gave an enthusiastic nod, "Sounds great! But I get exclusive visitation rights, okay?"

Stacy chuckled, "Totally fair, but first, he needs a proper name."

Without missing a beat, Tomo suggested, "How about Mr. Belding?" A collective groan from the group followed a stunned silence. Dennis groaned, seriously, Tomo, enough with the 'Saved by the Bell' references."

Tomo grinned mischievously, "Alright, Screech. Since you seem to have a better idea, what's his name?"

Dutch looked over the small cat. "No more suggestions; he's already got a name. Look at him; it's written right across his face. His name is Cheech. End of discussion."

The suggestion was met with approving nods and smiles, and just like that, Cheech, the yellow cat, became the latest addition to their tight-knit group.

They're very own Wildcat.

As the day's events began to wind down, the lake shimmered with the reflections of the setting sun, and the atmosphere was filled with the bittersweet realization of the day's end. Del, breaking the silence, turned to Dutch. "Hey, Dutchie, mind giving me a ride home?" Dutch, his face clouded with emotion, hesitated.

"Sorry, man. I can't." His voice held a hint of defiance, a shield he always wore.

The group exchanged glances, confusion evident in their expressions.

"Why not?" Del questioned; you go right through the valley on your way to The Mills," oblivious to Dutchie's internal struggle.

Dutch took a deep breath, "Look, I am trying to open up and let people in, but the curse—what if it's real? What if this curse is waiting to claim me? And God forbid one of you gets dragged down with me? It's just too risky.

Behind Dutch's tough exterior was a rebel confronting his destiny.

Dutch's voice cracked, "I've started to hope again, to dream of a future. But with this damn curse hanging over my head, I can't let any of you get too close. At least not on the road. I won't let my bad luck, this curse, whatever it is, suck any of you in."

Del shook his head, "Come on, Dutchie! That curse is pure bullshit. Everything that happened— your dad— your mom and Lila was tragic, but you can live in a shadow of darkness waiting for your turn.

He took a deep breath, trying to hold himself together. "You know, after my mom died last year, it was hell." His voice quivered with emotion, "I cried. God, I cried every single day for a month. The guilt I felt after the last time we spoke, where I was such a piece of shit to her, thinking it was just another argument, and then she was gone. I played that moment in my head, over and over, torturing myself." He looked down, wiping a lone tear that had escaped. "But then, I realized that drowning in my guilt and pain wasn't honoring her memory. She wouldn't have wanted that for me. So, I picked myself up and pushed forward, focusing on the good memories, love, and lessons she left behind."

Dutch looked down as Del continued, "I get it, Dutch; I do. I get the pain, the anger, the confusion. But all this stuff you've been through, as hard as it's been, it's just life. Life is messy, unpredictable, and sometimes downright unfair. But it's also filled with good stuff too. You can't let some old ghost story hold you back. You've got so much to live for."

Dutch looked up at Del, his face hardened. "I'm trying to change, man. I'm trying to be better. But this is my rule, alright? If you guys want me on the team if you want me around, then I drive alone—just me and my car. That's how it's got to be."

Jeremy's eyes shifted between his friends, the depth of his thoughts hidden behind contemplative eyes. The evolution he saw in Dutch, the fierce protectiveness and unyielding care he now displayed for the group, was unlike anything Jeremy had seen in any of his lives.

Clearing his throat, Jeremy broke the silence. "Look, we all know everything Dutch has had to deal with. If driving solo gives him peace, we should support that."

Stacy rolled her eyes, her practical nature coming through. "Okay, let's sort out the rides. I've got Del and Tomo. Cool?" she asked, glancing over at Del for a nod.

Kristen, popping a fresh piece of gum in her mouth, said, "That's settled then. Dennis and Missy are with me. And, Mr. Homecoming," she teased, nodding at Jeremy and borrowing Missy's earlier taunt, "you're having dinner at my place tonight. You owe me that much."

Raising his hands in mock surrender, Jeremy laughed, "Okay, deal! But only if your mom serves her signature lasagna."

Del's eyes widened, "Mrs. Ray's lasagna? Oh man, you've got to sneak some out for me, Jer. If you need a place to crash, my doors open. I mean, you've practically become my roommate anyway."

Kristen giggled, winking at Jeremy, "I'll pack an extra-large doggy bag for you, D.C. Just make sure you don't stay up waiting for my 'Bear' here; he owes me some quality time."

Del chuckled, nodded, and fired a playful glare at Tomo. "Hey, Tomo—shotgun!" he yelled, dashing toward Stacy's Bug. Tomo groaned, "Oh, come on, that's not fair!"— laughing as he sprinted after Del.

Stacy gently approached Dutch, who was lovingly holding Cheech. "Hand over the little fur ball. I promise he's in good hands."

Dutch handed over the tiny animal but warned with a playful edge, "Careful with him. I've taught him how to use his claws." He cackled, giving Cheech a final tussle on his head and the cat swiping back playfully.

Kristen swiftly gathered the strewn blankets. "No need to take these.

They're all extras, and I'm sure we'll be back here soon," she said, her voice light. Throwing a playful smirk Jeremy's way, she air-kissed him before hopping into the driver's seat of her car. Meanwhile, Dennis, ever the klutz, scrambled into the backseat, wrestling a bit with the stubborn seatbelt.

Missy let her eyes linger on Jeremy as she got in Kristen's car. The soft intensity in her eyes exposed her feelings. Despite how well she thought she knew Jeremy, recent events peeled back layers, revealing sides of him she never knew existed. She felt an unexpected pull towards him, a curiosity to know more. But shaking her head slightly, she whispered to herself, "Get a grip, Missy,"

Straightening up, she raised her hand in a casual farewell, calling out, "Catch you later," as she slid into the car.

Jeremy and Dutch stood on the cottage's porch in thoughtful silence, encapsulating the emotions of the previous night. The weight of the unspoken words hung heavily between them.

Jeremy turned to Dutch, his expression serious but understanding. "Look man, about the whole driving alone thing," he began, choosing his words carefully, "I get it, Dutch. Everyone has their reasons, and I respect yours."

Dutch leaned against the porch railing, exhaling slowly. "It's just that curse; people whisper about it everywhere I go. Every time something goes wrong in my life, it's as if that fucking curse is taunting me—giving me proof of its existence."

Jeremy nodded, looking out into the distance. "Legends and tales like that have a way of rooting themselves into the soul of a believer. They take on a life of their own, Dutchie," he said, turning to face him squarely, "It's not about how much time you've got or what some old wives' tale says. It's about what you do with the time you have. Making every moment count. Leaving behind something meaningful."

Dutch looked at Jeremy, his eyes reflecting a mix of pain and hope. "I've been thinking a lot about that— about my legacy, about making a difference." He paused, searching for words. "I want this life to matter, however long or short it may be.

Jeremy placed a reassuring hand on Dutch's shoulder. "That's the spirit, man. You've already started making a difference with the team and with us. The past is in the past, but the future? It's what you make it. Curse or no curse."

Dutch managed a weak smile, the weight on his shoulders seeming a bit lighter. "Thanks, man. I needed to hear that."

Jeremy, noticing the shift in Dutch's demeanor, nodded understandingly, a silent gesture of support that spoke volumes between the two friends.

"You better get out of here, man," Dutch continued, the corners of his mouth lifting into a sly grin, "You've got a piping hot lasagna and a piping hot redhead waiting for you." He winked playfully, the sparkle in his eye briefly masking the complexities of his thoughts.

Jeremy laughed, throwing a playful punch towards Dutch's arm. "Classy, I'll see you soon, Dutchie. And, hey," he added, his tone turning serious, "stay safe out there."

Dutch nodded in appreciation of the kind words as he replied, "You too, man."

With a final wave, Dutch climbed into his car, its engine roaring. Jeremy watched him speed away in textbook Dutch fashion, the weight of the day settling over him. As Dutch's car vanished into the distance, Jeremy took a deep breath, contemplating the complexities of life, friendship, and the future.

34

RAYS YOUR HANDS

Jeremy and Kristen stood side by side in the warm glow of the kitchen. The lingering aroma of Mrs. Ray's delicious dinner was still in the air. The hearty meal of lasagna, garlic bread, and a mixed greens salad had been an absolute feast. Mrs. Ray's cooking was always a comforting memory from Jeremy's past.

As they took on the after-dinner chores, with Jeremy washing the dishes and Kristen drying and putting them away, their movements had a meditative rhythm. The soft sounds of splashing water and dishes clinking created a cozy ambiance.

They operated in a comfortable silence, both wrapped up in their thoughts. But that serenity was interrupted when Kristen, her voice softer and more hesitant than usual, ventured, "You know, a little birdie told me about your fight with Gregg."

Jeremy's movements faltered, and he momentarily stopped scrubbing. He responded without turning to her, with a hint of defensiveness in his tone, "Oh? Did they?" he replied, his voice guarded, eyes focused on the soapy pan crusted with baked cheese. Putting down the plate she was drying,

Kristen faced him, her hazel eyes filled with concern. "Why didn't you tell me, Bear? I thought we were open about everything."

He let out a heavy sigh, setting the soapy pan aside. "It's been a crazy few days; it just happened, Kris. I didn't want to bring more drama into your life."

Kristen's fingers lightly touched his forearm, trying to offer some comfort. "You know you don't need to fight every battle alone. The way Gregg treats you sucks. You deserve so much better. I am proud of you for leaving."

Jeremy paused, looking away, wrestling with the emotions inside him. "Thanks, Kris."

Not one to leave things unresolved, Kristen softly pressed, "So, with this new change, does it affect your future plans? Because, you know, I was thinking—"

Jeremy cut her off, his voice slightly strained, "Kris, I need some time. Everything's a mess right now."

She looked at him earnestly, "But now, with this change, couldn't you consider staying close? Maybe UMass or Westfield. I'm sure they'd be happy to have you."

Frustratingly, he responded, "Kris, those options aren't open to me. Westfield doesn't offer athletic scholarships, and I'd be walking onto the team at UMass—I can't afford to pay full tuition, even at in-state costs. Without that scholarship in Vermont, college just isn't possible." His thoughts raced, considering the number of paths he could take, none of which hinged on the cost of education.

College in Vermont was essential to his master plan to reunite with Cassandra. Immersing himself in day-to-day life and keeping a low profile were all part of the build-up to the pivotal moment in his junior year. That's when he'd visit Del at UMass for the weekend. There, at an old dive bar on a night when the stars would perfectly align, he could recreate the night he first met Cassandra—starting their life together again.

Staying in Western Massachusetts, in the five-college system, was a gamble he couldn't afford. The risk of an accidental run-in with Cassandra was too high, and any deviation from their original meeting could mean losing her again. Everything had to be perfectly timed and executed. Meeting Cassandra in that specific spot at that exact moment was critical. Moving to Vermont wasn't just an option; it was a must.

Life twenty-sixth was his shot at getting it right; Cassandra was the endgame. But the early days with Kristen were turning into a high-stakes balancing act. He could feel the frustration mounting, the situation spiraling.

Kristen's eyes shimmered with hope; pressing further, she shared her fantasy. "We can make it work, Bear. Maybe you can start at Holyoke Community and transfer later. You could live here while I finish up at Huxley. My parents wouldn't mind; in fact, I am sure they'd love it."We could even share an apartment in Northampton or something when I'm at Amherst.

Jeremy had been down that road before, going to community college and staying with The Rays, getting the apartment in NoHo, the apartment that Kristen dreamed of. He admitted to himself that, at first, it was great, but it never ended well.

"Look, Kris, just give me some time; it's only been a few days." He looked at her. "I promise everything will work out as it's supposed to."

His eyes met hers, and they were sparkling with a mix of determination and hope. "Alright, Bear," she began, "Promise me you'll at least think about it?"

"I promise, Kris," he whispered, his voice sincere. "I do think about it every day, every moment— it's always on my mind."

He looked deep into her eyes, the weight of lifetimes pressing on him. In his mind, vivid flashes of the past played out— reruns of choices made, the paths taken, and the resulting consequences not just for him but for everyone.

35

LASAGNA BOMB

As Jeremy tiptoed down the stairs leading to Del's basement, the flickering light from the TV cast spooky silhouettes along the wall. The chilling score from *John Carpenter's: Halloween* echoed, getting louder as he crept through the darkness.

Reaching the basement floor, he spotted Del, intently focused on the screen. There, Michael Meyers, with his unwavering malevolence, was stalking Annie Brackett. The room was thick with suspense. Every crunch of Del's popcorn echoed like footsteps in an empty hallway.

Jeremy, always the prankster and sensing the perfect moment, formulated a devilish plan. Moving like a shadow, he snuck closer, remaining unnoticed. As the on-screen terror peaked, with Michael lunging at the unsuspecting babysitter, Jeremy hurled the bag of leftover lasagna he'd brought from the Rays at his friend.

"Incoming!" he shouted as the bag floated in slow motion toward Del's lap.

Del's body responded with fear, triggered by Jeremy's timing as the bag sailed in his direction. He scrambled to make the grab, but for one rare time in his life, the sure hands of Antione Del Coronado did not make the catch.

Hitting him square in the chest, the doggy bag burst on impact, causing it to explode all over its target. Del sat stunned, covered in deep red tomato sauce. The sight, combined with the violent sounds of Michael

Myers claiming his next victim, created an uncanny resemblance to the gory movie scene he was watching.

Del's eyes widened in genuine terror for a heart-stopping moment; the popcorn he'd been munching fell from his lips. He could've sworn he was covered in blood— his blood.

"Ah—you dick!" he exclaimed, staring down at the mess. "This is my favorite Wildcat hoodie!" His frustration was unmistakable. "Is this Mrs. Ray's lasagna? That was supposed to be my post-movie feast! Seriously, dude, not cool, Not cool at all." He groaned as he assessed the damage to his prized sweatshirt. Throwing Jeremy a mock accusatory glare, he quipped, "Hey, remember when we used to be friends?"

Jeremy couldn't contain his laughter, "Sorry, man. The moment was just too perfect. I couldn't help myself.

Getting up and heading towards the washing machine on the other side of the basement hangout, Del grumbled as he peeled off the sauced hoodie. "Let's see if you can be saved," he muttered as he tossed it into the washing machine.

Meanwhile, Jeremy flopped onto the couch, dropping his bag onto the floor with an uneremonious thud. His body language was a mix of relaxation and underlying tension as he stretched out.

Del, cleaning off the last remnants of lasagna from his hands, glanced at Jeremy curiously. "So, how did it go with Kristen tonight?" he asked, leaning against the doorway.

Jeremy sighed, "Typical," he started, his voice trailing off, "She just went on about me leaving for school again."

"I'm not staying in this town," Jeremy said, his gaze drifting away. "I just can't deal with my dad anymore."

"I get it, man— if Gregg was my dad, I'd want to get out of here too," Del offered, his voice filled with empathy.

Del had often dreamt of them both going to UMass, picturing them as roommates, navigating college life together. It was a dream that flickered with the warmth of possibility but dimmed in the harsh light of reality. He knew that for Jeremy, leaving town wasn't just about looking for new experiences; it was a necessary step towards self-preservation. He had seen the clashes; he'd heard the sharp words and the heavy silences that filled the broken Anderson home. It was like watching someone constantly walking on eggshells, never knowing when the next outburst would come.

"I just wish things were different, you know?" Del continued, keeping his eyes on the flickering TV as he spoke, "But you've gotta do what's best for you. And hey, I'll always be here, man. You know that."

Jeremy rifled through his backpack, pulling out Gregg's envelope with a look of frustration.

"Get a load of this," he said as he handed the crumpled note to Del with a bitter laugh, "Classic Gregg. The guy's unbelievable."

As he read the note, Del's mouth dropped. "That dick!" he whispered, the words barely audible yet heavy with emotion and a deep sense of betrayal.

Finally ready to face whatever hidden curse Gregg had left him, Jeremy pulled out the mysterious document he'd been avoiding for the last few days. He inspected it with a mix of curiosity and dread. Settling back on the couch, he felt the weight of the envelope in his hands.

Carefully, Jeremy slid his finger under the sealed flap, tearing it open to reveal the contents. He expected another letter filled with Gregg's usual bitterness and disapproval, but instead, he found a legal document, the pages stapled together in the upper left corner. His eyes quickly scanned the top of the front page, where the words "Deed of Ownership" stood out in bold lettering.

"What is it?" Del leaned in, trying to catch a glimpse.

"It's a deed," Jeremy responded his voice a mixture of confusion and surprise. "To what?" Del's curiosity was piqued.

As Jeremy flipped through the pages, the reality sank in. "The Labrador property. The ruins, the lake, the cottage. All of it." He held the deed up for Del to see, a sense of disbelief washing over him.

Del let out a low whistle. "Man, that's huge. Why would Gregg give you all that?"

Jeremy shrugged, a flurry of emotions playing across his face. "I have no idea." He said as he continued to review the documents. Jeremy's trained eye, honed from lifetimes spent in legal practice, darted across each clause and stipulation of the deed. The legalese was familiar, almost comforting, in its rigidity and structure.

"47.5 acres, lakefront," he murmured under his breath as he traced the property lines on the attached map. It was huge—the entire Labrador property. "This doesn't make any sense," Jeremy whispered, a frown etching deeper lines into his forehead.

In all his lives, the Labrador had been broken up and sold off bit by bit. Some of the land was seized due to Gregg's mismanagement long before the '70s rolled around. The cottage and the 2 acres of land it sat on were supposed to be all that remained in Gregg's hands.

Jeremy knew Gregg's fantasy of restoring the cottage all too well. His father had often talked about turning it into a lucrative rental that might give him a comfortable retirement. But that was just another one of Gregg's pipe dreams.

In every version of Jeremy's life, the cottage would eventually be lost to unpaid taxes, or so he thought. But here it was, in black and white—the taxes were cleared for the next fiscal year, not just for the cottage but for the entire parcel of land.

Confusion spiraled into suspicion. Was this a trick? Was Gregg offloading a financial burden on him? No, the ledger didn't lie; it was all handled.

Jeremy leaned back with the deed resting in his hands. "This doesn't make any sense."

Del watched his friend, a knot forming in his stomach. "Maybe he's trying to make things right? Or, maybe he was, Del paused, " never mind."

"What? Say it, "Jeremy glared.

"It's just, maybe he was drunk and forgot or didn't know what he was doing or something." Del shrugged.

"No, that's not it; my name is listed here as the owner," he said, handing Del the deed. "He knew exactly what he was doing when he signed it over to me. He even said so in his god-awful note, remember. He did this on purpose?"

Del put a reassuring hand on Jeremy's shoulder. "Well, whatever it is, we'll figure it out. You've got the whole property to your name now. That's gotta count for something, right?"

Jeremy managed a small smile, grateful for Del's support. "Yeah. It counts for something." But the question remained: What was Gregg trying to pull? Why now?

The room was quiet except for the low hum of the television, now forgotten in the background. Del's presence was comforting as Jeremy tried to wrap his head around Gregg's unexpected gift. The whole property, with all its potential and history, now legally belonged to him.

"47.5 acres, Del, that's a lot of responsibility," Jeremy said, his voice filled with awe and dread.

Del nodded, "It sure is, but it's also an opportunity, man, a new beginning. You could do anything with it. You could turn it into something amazing."

Jeremy thought about what Del said—a new beginning. Those words stuck with him. The property seemed like a fresh start, a chance to create something different, away from the problems his dad brought into his life.

"And it's lakefront," Del added with a grin, trying to lighten the mood.

"Think of the parties we could have there, the bonfires, the summers by the water."

A ghost of a smile flickered across Jeremy's face. "Yeah, the parties would be legendary."

"But what about your dad?" Del's question hung in the air, the unspoken worries about Gregg's motives and the timing of this deed transfer. Gregg had clearly decided to sign the land over to Jeremy before reset day. Nothing that Jeremy could have done would have caused such a ripple in this life.

Jeremy shrugged, "I don't know, man. Maybe he's had a change of heart, or maybe this is his way of severing ties completely. Either way, I can't let his reasons make my decisions for me. I need to figure out what to do with the property on my own."

Del slapped him on the back. "That's the spirit. And hey, you won't be doing it alone. I'm here for you."

Jeremy smiled, "Thanks, Del, that means a lot."

Del leaned back on the couch, noticing Jeremy's concern. "You need a safe place to stash that deed, right?" he asked, his voice calm and reassuring.

Jeremy nodded, stuffing the papers back in the envelope. "I can't believe I've been carrying this around all weekend. It doesn't feel right, just having it in my backpack."

Del got up from the couch with a decisive energy. "Don't worry, man. I've got just the spot for it. It's totally Gregg-proof—follow me."

They made their way upstairs, down a narrow hallway lined with family photos, and stopped before a stately grandfather clock. Del reached behind it with a practiced hand, pressing a hidden latch, causing the clock face to swing open, revealing a small, concealed compartment.

"This," Del said with pride, "is where I hide my most valuable stuff. The stuff I don't want anyone finding, all my secrets."

Impressed by the hiding place's cleverness, Jeremy handed over the envelope containing the deed. "Secrets, what kind of secrets?" Jeremy asked.

The question brought a smile to Del's face, "I'll never tell," He chuckled, taking the envelope to put it inside the clock.

Jeremy watched as he carefully lifted the door to the hidden compartment, noticing it was empty. "Looks like you've got a lot of secrets in there."

"Haha, what can I say? I'm an open book, dude," Del smirked, "I always wanted something special to hide in here. My mom said I was the only one to know about it— I guess that's my secret."

Del placed the envelope in the compartment and closed the clock face, ensuring it clicked back into place, hiding its contents. "It'll be safe here."

Jeremy felt gratitude towards Del. He was more than just a friend; he was a lifeline in the chaos that seemed to swirl around Jeremy perpetually. "I appreciate it. More than you know."

Del placed his hand on Jeremy's shoulder and sang with a dramatic flair, "That's what friends are for," in his best diva impression, eyes closed and hand on his chest.

"Alright, Whitney, that's enough," Jeremy groaned. "Let's go finish that movie. Michael Meyers is way less horrifying than your singing voice."

As they reached the doorway of the basement stairs, a light knock on the front door captured their attention. "I'll see who that is," Del said. See if any of that lasagna can be saved—I'm starving."

Mrs. Ray's lasagna, once a culinary masterpiece, now lay in ruins on the coffee table in Del's basement. "Well, it's still edible, I guess," Jeremy muttered.

Above him, he heard muffled conversation and footsteps moving across the floor. "That must be Stacy," he thought as he tidied up the dish to make it somewhat presentable.

As the footsteps approached the stairway, he said, "It's a bit sloppy, but it's still good!" Expecting Stacy's typical, vulgar response, he turned around only to find Del descending the stairs with Missy behind him.

Jeremy gave Del a puzzled glance, silently seeking an explanation for Missy's unexpected visit. Del shrugged, diverting his attention to the lasagna. "This seems salvageable; it just needs a few minutes in the microwave. You two chat— I'll be right back."

Jeremy quickly tidied up the sofa. "Want to sit?" he asked. "We were just getting ready to finish watching *Halloween.*

Missy's tone was matter-of-fact, slicing through Jeremy's casual mood. "I'm not here to hang out," she said, rejecting the appeal of the slasher film.

Jeremy's eyebrows arched in surprise. "Oh, then, why are you here? I mean, it's great to see you, but what's up?"

She hesitated before diving into her explanation. "You know my dad's a cop, right?"

Jeremy nodded as her words came out more rapidly, a sense of urgency underlying them. "Is it Dutchie?" he interjected, his mind racing with dread.

"No, it's not Dutch," she replied. "Jeremy, it's your dad. It's Gregg."

"Oh, good Christ! What now?" his voice filled with exasperation and concern.

"I don't know all the details, but my dad has him at the station, and—well, I guess he's pretty drunk." Her eyes held a sympathetic yet uneasy glimmer, bracing for Jeremy's reaction.

His response was laced with a mix of resignation and defiance. "It's not the first time," he scoffed, "He'll sober up eventually. They'll let him out in the morning."

Her expression turned more serious. "Yeah, that's usually how it goes. But my dad said Gregg's been rambling about some pretty strange things, specifically about you. He thinks it might be a good idea for you to see him."

Jeremy's resolve hardened. "No way. I'm not getting sucked into a Gregg vortex tonight. I'm sorry, I'm not going. Please tell your dad I appreciate his concern, but it's better for everyone if Gregg and I keep our distance."

Sensing his hesitation, Missy shifted her strategy. "Can I ask you a question?" Her soft voice invited a deeper connection.

"Sure, go ahead," Jeremy nodded with resignation in his tone.

"Would you say that we are friends?" she asked sincerely.

"Yeah, of course," he responded, nodding again, somewhat puzzled.

"And you trust your friends, don't you?" she pressed.

"Absolutely," he confirmed, his voice firmer this time.

"Then trust me," she said with conviction. "I'll go with you. If it's as bad as you think, we'll leave. I've got my mom's car. I can drive you. Please just go see him."

With Missy's commitment to keep him company, he gave in. "Fine, if you insist. Let me just fill Del in," he said. "I'll meet you in the car."

Her promise to be there for him, to stand by his side, wasn't just a friendly offer; it was a testament to her care and commitment. Their connection was unmistakable, leaving them both questioning the true nature of their feelings.

36

REACHIN'

As Jeremy approached Missy's car, he caught her checking her reflection in the rearview mirror, adjusting her hair, and inspecting her lips for flaws. This small act seemed out of character to him. She had always struck him as indifferent to her appearance, more focused on substance than style. He found this glimpse into another side of her intriguing.

As he opened the car door, the thumping baseline of rap music greeted him, adding another unexpected layer to her. "Really? I never took you for a Hip-Hop fan," he remarked, a hint of surprise coloring his tone.

"Shut up," she replied with a playful tone, her eyes scanning the car's console with determination. After a moment, her fingers triumphantly grasped a cassette of *Digable Planets-Reachin*. With a sense of victory, she inserted the tape into the car's radio. "You've got to hear this; it's my favorite," she said, her voice brimming with excitement.

Her demeanor shifted as the smooth, jazz-infused beats of "Time and Space" filled the car. She began rapping along with the track effortlessly and with confidence. He watched, a combination of amusement and admiration sweeping over him. Her passionate delivery of each line was flawless.

"Time, Space what is that like, just how we livin in the hip-life?" she rapped, her head bobbing in rhythm with the beat and a playful smirk on her lips.

It was both impressive and contagious. Just as he thought she was out of surprises, She sprang this new side of her true self – the reserved and composed girl he knew was now grooving effortlessly to the hip-hop rhythms, and she was absolutely owning it.

He couldn't help but smile, realizing there was so much more to her than he had thought. Her insights into the music offered him a new perspective, not just on the genre, but on Missy herself – a multi-dimensional individual deeply connected to the art she cherished.

Continuing their drive, Missy jumped into her thoughts on the state of the current hip-hop scene, her knowledge spanning a wide array of iconic artists.

"Cube, Pac, Snoop— and of course, Biggie, They're all amazing poets, for sure. But I have a special place for the funkier cuts – I love The Pharcyde, and Tribe is so good," she explained. But this, oh God, this is my absolute favorite. Hold on, I think I have 'Blowout Comb' here somewhere; it's incredible," she said, rummaging through the console for another cassette. "We're really lucky to be living in an era where rap has evolved to what it is today— music and poetry collided." Pinching her finger and thumb together, pressing it to her lips, "chef's kiss, there's so much meaning and depth in their messages."

Her perspective highlighted her knowledge of the genre and her deep admiration for the art form. Her passion for hip-hop was a window into her soul, revealing an infectious depth and complexity. "I might not fully be able to identify with their experiences, but the passion in their storytelling is something I can totally appreciate," she added.

"Wow, you really are an M.C. at heart, aren't you, Miss?" he chuckled.

Something about this moment, her unguarded enthusiasm and the evening's shared vulnerability, made him see her in a new light. Her energy was infectious, and for a brief moment, the weight of their impending visit to see Gregg in jail lifted.

As she turned the radio down, her energy faded into something more thoughtful.

"Can I say something?" she asked, her tone quieter now.

"Of course, and you don't need to ask," Jeremy responded, his face showing he was all ears.

She took a deep breath, her eyes offering a mix of nerves and honesty.

"I didn't expect any of this, especially with you," she started. "For the longest time, I thought I had you all figured out— typical jock, right? Living for sports, homecoming king glory, all that stuff. No offense, but you know, the 'all brawn, no brain' stereotype," she paused abruptly, biting her lip. "I mean, not that you're—" She struggled to find the right words." What I'm trying to say is, since our, uh, 'run-ins,' her fingers awkwardly made air quotes as she held the steering wheel. "Hanging out with you these past few days, I've started seeing things differently, seeing you differently."

Her eyes wandered as if piecing together her new perception of Jeremy. "I was so wrong," she admitted, her voice filled with regret. "You're not just some stereotype. There's so much more to you, and I'm really starting to appreciate that."

It was a messy but heartfelt confession, a stream of consciousness about Jeremy and how their relationship was changing.

"And about the whole homecoming king tease," she added softly, "I'm sorry. It wasn't fair. You're more than those labels. You're actually really kind and thoughtful and surprisingly deep. Finishing her ramble, there was a raw honesty in her look, a mix of relief for sharing her feelings and nervousness about how Jeremy would take this open, unfiltered admission.

He listened intently, his expression softening as she spoke. When she finished, he took a moment before responding.

"I didn't see it either, Miss. I was wrong, too. I thought you were just this goody-goody, overachiever type if I'm being honest. But you're not that person at all." He chuckled lightly.

"You showed up at an after-school sports event, hung out with Dutch Wyatt, of all people, and at an all-night party no less. And now, here you are, revealing some serious M.C. skills. Who knew this Missy Winston was hiding in plain sight this whole time? Not me, that's for sure." He smiled at her, genuine and warm. "I'm really glad you've been hanging out with us."

She smiled back shyly. "Yeah, I guess I've kept a lot of myself hidden. But being around you guys— it's been different, in a good way. I feel like I can be myself, you know?"

"Definitely," Jeremy nodded. "You should show this side more often. We all like it."

Missy's face lit up with a newfound confidence. "I think I will."

As they approached the police station, the mood in the car shifted. The lights cast a somber glow, reminding them why they were there. Jeremy's face clouded over with the weight of confronting his father.

Noticing the change, Missy reverted to her supportive role. "It'll be ok, I promise," she said softly, touching his arm. "I'm right here with you, whatever happens." Her words were a comfort, a reminder that whatever lay ahead, Jeremy wouldn't have to face it alone.

37

JAIL TIME

As JEREMY and Missy entered the police station, their moods shifted. The fluorescent lights cast a harsh glow, amplifying the sense of seriousness that filled the space. As she led the way, her posture became more rigid, a reflection of the formality and gravity of the setting. They approached a desk where a uniformed officer sat, looking up as they walked toward him.

"Hi, Dad," Missy greeted, her voice a blend of respect and familiarity. Her father, a figure of authority in his uniform, looked up, his expression softening slightly at the sight of his daughter.

"This is Jeremy," Missy introduced, gesturing to her friend beside her. "He's here to see his dad."

"Ah, yes, Mr. Anderson," Officer Winston responded, standing up and extending a hand to Jeremy. His tone was professional, yet not without a hint of empathy. "Thank you for coming in."

Jeremy shook the officer's hand firmly, his mind racing with thoughts of what was to come. Despite the formal setting, Officer Winston's demeanor had a hint of warmth, an unspoken acknowledgment of the difficult situation that had brought Jeremy there.

As they were led further into the station, the reality of the situation seemed to weigh heavier on Jeremy. Missy's reassuring presence at his side and her father's understanding approach provided some comfort. Still, Jeremy's apprehension of facing Gregg hung in the air.

The walk down the corridor felt longer than it actually was, as each step echoed in the quiet.

When Jeremy finally saw his father slumped on the bench in the cell, a mix of emotions churned inside him.

Officer Winston roused Gregg with a booming voice, "Anderson, time to get up!" jolting him into a slow, groggy movement.

Gregg's words were elated as he staggered to his feet. "Time to go home!" he exclaimed before stopping abruptly. His eyes fell on his son, and he dropped his head in shame.

"Not yet," Officer Winston interjected firmly. "You two need to talk first."

Jeremy inched closer, but Officer Winston held him back for a moment. "Listen," he said in a lower, more serious tone, "I know this is hard for you, and I don't want to make it any harder, but you need to know he's been talking about some very serious stuff."

Jeremy's heart raced. "What kind of serious stuff?" he asked tentatively.

Officer Winston's voice was grave, "Son, he's been saying things that lead us to believe that he has plans to take his own life. That's why we thought you should speak to him. We're taking this very seriously. He won't be going home tonight; we'll keep an eye on him and make sure he'll be safe before we release him."

Jeremy absorbed the information as it was shared, a heavy silence enveloping him.

Officer Winston continued, "We wouldn't normally do this, but he kept saying something that made me think you should see him."

Jeremy's eyes stayed fixed on his father's disheveled form.

Officer Winston continued, "First off, he was very clear about how proud he is of you. "When we brought him in, he wouldn't stop talking about you, your future, and what a good person you are. Did you recently stand up to him?" he asked Jeremy.

Jeremy, still unmoving, barely managed a nod. "Uh, yeah."

"He loved that you did," Officer Winston said, his voice shifting. "But after a few hours, his typical drunken behavior turned into despair. He kept talking about 'no other way out.' Do you have any idea what that could mean?"

Jeremy shook his head, his frustration surfacing as he addressed Officer Winston. "With all due respect, sir, I'm still struggling to understand why I'm here. This is what my father does. He gets drunk, does stupid things, says things he doesn't mean, passes out and then repeats it all over again. I'm sorry, I can't help him."

Officer Winston's expression was firm. "I think you can, son. Talk to him. He mentioned that you're the only one who would understand."

This revelation gave Jeremy pause. The thought that his father, despite his usual behavior, might genuinely need him and that there might be something deeper in his words was a lot to take in. It suggested a vulnerability in Gregg that Jeremy hadn't considered.

Taking a deep breath, Jeremy mentally prepared himself. Whether or not he felt capable of helping, the gravity of the situation and his father's apparent belief in his understanding compelled him to try.

With a nod to Officer Winston, Jeremy stepped forward to face Gregg, prepared to confront whatever lay ahead.

His voice quivered as he addressed his father. "What was it tonight, Gregg? Vodka? Beer? What'd you have?" he asked, searching for common ground.

Gregg hesitated; his eyes clouded with the weight of his choices. "Ah, you know, all of it," he admitted, his voice filled with defeat.

"Why do you do this, Gregg? You know it won't end well," Jeremy asked, his voice heavy with disappointment.

Gregg's words poured out like a confession. "What's the point? None of this matters. I try, and I try, and it always ends the same way," he rambled, his gaze fixed on the floor. "There's no way around it, no way out. I know you get it. Maybe not now, but you will."

Jeremy's frustration began to surface; his patience was running thin. "What are you talking about? Why did the cops bring me down here? You promised that I was out of your life," he scolded. "We made a deal, and then I find out that you cleaned me out for what? The Labrador? What am I supposed to do with that?

Jeremy's frustration boiled over, his words erupting like lava. "That property won't pay for college; nobody will ever buy it. Everyone thinks it's unsuitable for development, cursed, haunted, and all that stuff. Why do you even still have it? I thought the bank seized it years ago; you've never owned it before," the words slipped past his concrete filter.

"So, you do know?" Gregg asked quietly, affirming his biggest fears.

Jeremy's rage continued, further blasting through his filter, laying bare his truth. His eyes locked onto Gregg's. "Yes, I know," he admitted recklessly, his anger consuming him. "You've never had it at this point in any of my lifetimes."

Gregg's face fell as he blinked away the remnants of his drunkenness, and his demeanor shifted from despair to sobering clarity. He couldn't deny it any longer; his son had inherited the same curse that had plagued their family for generations.

"How many?" Gregg asked softly, his voice filled with genuine concern.

Still reeling from his rage, Jeremy didn't immediately grasp the meaning of his father's question. "How many, what?" he shouted, his confusion and fear intensifying.

Gregg's eyes bore into Jeremy's soul as he clarified, "How many lives, son? How many times have I failed you?

At that moment, Jeremy felt like all the blood had been drained from his body. His eyes welled with tears as he struggled to find the words.

"What? What do you mean?" he stammered, breathing in short, panicked gasps.

Gregg's voice trembled with regret as he whispered, as his eyes filled with tears, "I'm so sorry, son."

Their shared curse hung heavy in the air, and both father and son were left to confront the painful truth of their family's history.

"Forty-Eight, I'm working on number Forty-Eight," Gregg whispered, his voice barely audible. "I guess you're just stuck in one of my bad ones. I promise it's not always like this."

Jeremy glared at his father, a mix of anger and confusion clouding his expression before connecting the dots and breaking down. "Dad, why is this happening to us?"

Gregg's weary eyes met his son's, "I have no idea. I gave up trying to understand it centuries ago. I've tried everything, but none of it matters. Things never change," he admitted with a heavy sigh.

"Twenty-six," Jeremy whispered with his head hung low. "This is my Twenty-sixth life, I've been here less than a week, and it's already going to shit."

"Listen," Gregg said sternly, his tone attempting to be reassuring. "I am sure you haven't done anything that cannot be compensated for."

Jeremy's emotions continued to spiral, moving from defeat to anger in the blink of an eye. "How would you know?" he challenged.

Gregg's response was filled with quiet confidence. "I know, son. I just know," he said, his gaze unwavering. "Look, I'm not going anywhere. They aren't letting me out of here tonight. Let's just talk."

Jeremy took a deep breath as he approached Officer Winston's desk. "Excuse me, sir," he said, his voice calm despite his mixed emotions. I need a favor."

Officer Winston looked up from his paperwork and raised an eyebrow, "What can I do for you, Jeremy?"

Jeremy hesitated for a moment before speaking. "First, could you please send Missy home? She shouldn't have to be here for this mess. Let her know that I appreciate her bringing me in to see my dad. Tell her that I will catch up with her in school tomorrow."

Officer Winston nodded in understanding. "Of course, I'll make sure she gets home safely."

Jeremy gathered his courage for another request. "Could I be let into the cell with my father? I think it'll be safe, and I'm confident he won't be doing anything we need to worry about."

Officer Winston considered the request for a moment before nodding. "I'll see what I can do. Just give me a moment."

Jeremy watched as Officer Winston made the necessary arrangements, hoping that this night, filled with unexpected twists and turns, might lead to some clarity and connection with his father.

———

The two sat in the dimly lit jail cell and talked. For the first time, Gregg and Jeremy, father and son, saw each other as peers with a shared understanding of the joys and pitfalls of their repeated existences.

Jeremy leaned forward and spoke softly, ensuring no one but Gregg could hear him, "This time, it's different; things are changing in ways they never have before."

He told his father about the birthday gifts he'd gotten from Kristen. His brow furrowed as he grappled with the anomalies of this cycle.

"It's always been the same t-shirt and the same pen every single time. But this time, they're different," he explained, a note of disbelief in his voice. "The shirt is similar but long-sleeved and a different color. Instead of the pen, there's this watch."

He extended his arm, showing Gregg the watch on his wrist. "It's not just a different gift; it's more meaningful. Kristen even told me she bought it way before this reset. Nothing I've done in this cycle could have caused this change."

Gregg sharpened with a flicker of recognition. "I've had things like that happen, too," he paused. Events that seemed out of place, different from the script that I thought I knew by heart," he said, shifting uncomfortably on the bench he was sitting on.

"There have been moments, signs I suppose, that I never quite understood," he continued. "Times when a stranger would say something oddly specific from a different life, or when an expected tragedy just didn't happen." He sighed, a long, weary exhale. "I tried to see them as clues, hints of something more beneath the surface of our curse."

For a moment, his eyes lost their focus as if he was peering into a distant past. "But I was never smart or sober enough to figure them out. I drowned in the repetition, in the pain of what we are, never truly looking for the answers that might have been right in front of me."

Jeremy listened as a new understanding dawned within him. His father's admission, the acknowledgment of missed opportunities and overlooked details, added a new weight to his experiences. It wasn't just the differences of this cycle; it was the realization that perhaps, in every cycle, there were always differences, paths not taken, and clues left unexplored. He'd just been too consumed with his plans to notice.

Unfolding his arms and leaning in closer, Jeremy added, "There's more — It's not just about the gifts. It's about people too. You know Missy Winston and Dutch Wyatt?" Jeremy asked, his concern evident.

Gregg nodded, a sad look crossing his face. "It's awful always seeing what happens to those two kids," he replied, his voice heavy with sorrow. "Watching their story end too soon never gets easier."

"I know, I usually try to avoid them, but in this life, I'm drawn to them in a way that I can't explain. It's as if there's some force guiding my path," Jeremy confessed. "I see them in places I shouldn't, in moments I didn't expect. It's like there's an invisible string pulling me toward them."

Gregg listened as his son tried to make sense of his 26th life.

"Dad, there's something stuck in my head that I can't shake," Jeremy continued, "I know I can't stop what happens to Missy and Dutch, and I know I can't save their lives. I've tried before, but I always fail. But this time, it's different. I feel like I'm supposed to do something more, something meaningful, but I don't know how or even why. It's like a puzzle piece that I can't fit into the bigger picture."

Gregg listened, a mix of awe and concern etching his features. "Son, it sounds like you're standing at the edge of something bigger than us, bigger than our curse." His voice was low, almost a whisper. "These connections, this pull towards Missy and Dutch – maybe they're not just random threads. Maybe they're the keys to understanding our cycles or a way out."

Jeremy sat back, leaning against the wall, staring ahead with determination. "I don't get any of it," he said, his voice a blend of frustration and resolve. "I've got plans for this life. I don't want to mess up everything, but I can't shake this feeling off." He looked away, his thoughts racing, caught between his plans and the unknown pull of something greater.

After a brief silence, the topic shifted to Cassandra. "In all my past cycles, reuniting with her was something I could never achieve," Jeremy confessed, the frustration evident in his voice. "But this time, I have a plan built on the one consistent factor in all my lives - Del.

He explained how Del's unchanging role in each life provided a unique opportunity. "Del is the one constant, the one unchangeable piece in the puzzle of my existence. His predictability is the cornerstone of my strategy to finally reunite with Cassandra."

Jeremy's eyes held a flicker of hope as he outlined his strategy. "I know exactly the time and the place to recreate my first meeting with her. It's all about precision, about recreating that initial spark."

He told his father about the original weekend visit to UMass to see Del in life one. He explained how he planned on following that event's timeline, explicitly going into detail. "That weekend, Dad, that's the key. By then, Del will be dating Cassandra's roommate, Leah. It's the perfect setup, and everything will be in place." Jeremy's voice was steady; his plan was not just a dream but a blueprint awaiting execution.

Gregg nodded, impressed by the meticulousness of his son's plan. "That's a well-thought-out approach, Son. Using what you know, the constants like Del and the circumstances of your first meeting, it could really work this time."

"I know it'll work; I know every mistake I have made in past lives. This time will be different; my plan is flawless," Jeremy said with conviction.

"The thing is," He continued," The weekend at UMass won't be for a few years. So, I have some time on my hands."

He shifted slightly, his expression turning thoughtful. "In the meantime, while waiting for that moment with Cassandra, I can focus on helping Missy and Dutch. It feels right to use this time productively, to make a difference where I can without upsetting the natural course of things."

Gregg's question carried a weight of unspoken worry. "But what if none of this works, Jeremy? What if you miss out on Cassandra again? What then?"

Jeremy looked at his father with a solemn understanding. "I know what you're asking, Dad," he replied quietly. "If this fails, then I'll be left considering the last resort."

Their conversation took a serious turn as they discussed voluntary resets, or "forced re-runs," as Gregg grimly called them. This topic wasn't just uncomfortable; it was painful. Forcing a reset wasn't like the usual cycle restarts; it was much worse. The pain from forcing everything to start again was intense, much more than a normal reset.

At that moment, they made a pact. No more forced re-runs or voluntary resets, no matter what. They were going to stick out this cycle, strange changes and all.

Exhausted, his head spinning from the weight of the conversation he'd just had with his father, Jeremy still had one burning question.

"Dad, why did you drain my college fund and leave me with The Labrador?" he asked, his voice a blend of confusion and hurt.

At his son's question, Gregg's expression became pained. "Just like you, I had a plan for this lifetime, son, and as I always do, I failed. A few months ago, something told me that you were in the cycle too, so I signed over The Labrador property, hoping you would figure out how to make it prosper. Usually, in past lives, I'd sit on it out of fear that it would cause too big of a wave if I gave it to you. It was a mistake, and I'm truly sorry if owning it causes a," He paused, "what do you call it again?" he asked.

"Oh, a ripple," Jeremy answered.

"That's right, a ripple," Gregg nodded. "It's funny how we each developed our own vocabulary for these cycles. It's all the same, I guess, waves and ripples, re-runs and resets. So yes, giving you The Labrador was a mistake made after a night of too much booze and self-loathing."

"What about the college fund then?" Jeremy inquired. Gregg sighed. "That was not a mistake; that was another failure. I took the money and booked myself into a rehab on The Cape. I selfishly figured I'd offload the property on you to deal with. You'd figure it out, and I would go and get clean and try to live to my maximum age of 63, something I've been able to do fewer times than I would like to admit."

"So, what happened?" Jeremy asked.

"I was supposed to go today," Gregg admitted. "I chickened out. I couldn't do it, so I bought a bottle, and here we are."

"I see," Jeremy said with a determined look. "Well, you aren't getting off easy. I'm going to see to it that you are checked into that rehab as soon as they let you out of here."

Gregg looked at his son, a sense of pride swelling in his chest. "Thank you, Jeremy," he said, his voice filled with sincerity. "I'm proud of you. And for the rest of this life and all the others to come, I promise to be better for both of us."

As Jeremy was dropped off at home. Exhaustion weighed heavily on him. He needed to get some sleep before school started.

He shuffled into his room and immediately collapsed on his bed. As he closed his eyes, he couldn't help but feel a sense of relief washing over him. For the first time in all of his lives, he knew he wasn't alone in this strange and endless journey.

38

GAMELANS AND REVELATIONS

THE FOLLOWING day came peacefully for Jeremy. For the first time in what felt like ages, he slept deeply. So much so that the blare of his alarm was ignored. Glancing at the clock, he realized there was no way he'd make it to school on time.

His Jeep was still parked at Del's house, and considering the equal distance between the two, he decided to jog to Del's, grab his Jeep, and head to school.

Throwing on the same clothes he'd worn the night before, he raced out the door.

After picking up his Jeep, he swung by Dunkin' Donuts, taking advantage of the perks of youth with a quick breakfast made up of a half dozen donuts and a large chocolate milk. He inhaled his meal, feeling a renewed energy and an early morning sugar rush, as he pulled into the school parking lot just as the second-period bell rang.

He'd salvaged the morning, a small victory in the grand scheme of things. With a renewed focus, he stepped out of the Jeep, ready to face the day and whatever it might bring. As he jogged toward the school entrance, he reminded himself, "Slow and easy." He had no interest in any more clumsy encounters with unsuspecting classmates in the hallways.

His thoughts went to Missy. "I sent her home without saying goodbye," he thought, the guilt weighing on him. Determined to make it right, he made a mental note to find her as soon as possible.

The day unfolded easily as Jeremy settled into the rhythm of high school life. The familiar cycle of classes, lunchtime routines, and hallway chatter made the day pass quickly. But at the end of the day, he'd face a challenge he couldn't ignore: McHale vs. Wyatt, round two.

As the final bell rang, Jeremy caught up with Del. When asked, he swiftly brushed aside his friend's curiosity about the previous night's events with Gregg. Choosing to keep details to a minimum, he mentioned that his father would be checking into rehab and promised to share the rest later—another bedtime story.

Inside the locker room, the atmosphere was tense. Coach McHale stood before the team, his expression grave. "Team, I've weighed our options; dressing Dennis isn't a reasonable solution. If anyone gets hurt during the game, he could be forced onto the field. It's not safe. I'm sorry, there's no way around it, fellas. The season's over," he announced.

With perfect timing, the two Co-Captains and their new recruit entered the locker room before the coach could continue.

Dutch cut in with a bold smirk on his face."Not so fast—Your knight in shining armor is here to save all your sorry asses."

Tomo, who had been dozing in a locker, sat up suddenly. "I told you guys we weren't quitting," he exclaimed, his voice filled with excitement.

The room fell silent as Coach McHale turned to face Dutch. "Wyatt, this isn't a joke," he started, his tone sharp. "You can't just walk in here and—"

"Oh, but I can, Coach," Dutch interrupted, his confidence unshaken. "I'm ready to play, and you know I'm way better than any other option you have."

McHale's expression hardened. "It's not about skills, Wyatt. It's about commitment and discipline. It's about being a team player— things you know nothing about. You think you can just show up, and everything's fixed?"

Dutch looked at the coach squarely, "I'm not saying I can fix everything. But I do give us a fighting chance, don't I?"

The Wildcats watched in silence as the two locked eyes. The outcome of their standoff held the fate of their season in the balance.

"C'mon, Coach, it's the last home game," Dutch pleaded, his trademark smirk on his lips. "Let me help give these guys a chance to play on our field one last time. Who knows, maybe we can even win for a change." This was a straightforward jab at the coach's less-than-impressive record.

The team's reaction to Dutch's comment was divided. Half of them resented his cavalier attitude, clearly frustrated by his lack of discipline and the trouble it often caused. The other half seemed to accept it as simply Dutch, just being Dutch.

Despite the team's mixed feelings, Dutch's athleticism was undeniable. For better or worse, his presence would bring a dynamic they never had.

Aware of this, the coach seemed caught in a moment of decision as he weighed the risks and potential rewards of letting Dutch play.

Finally, with a heavy sigh, McHale nodded reluctantly. "Fine. But this is your only shot, Wyatt. One wrong move, and it's over— not just the game, but the rest of the season, Understood?"

Dutch nodded with a flash of seriousness crossing his face, acknowledging the gravity of the coach's warning.

The rest of the team exchanged looks with a blend of skepticism and hope in their eyes.

This was a final chance to play in front of the home crowd, one more game, and Dutch Wyatt was their wild card. The energy in the room shifted from tension to cautious optimism as they prepared to take the practice field.

Tomo moved towards Dutch, "Here, you can take the locker next to mine," he offered, "I'll help you get your gear." Their interaction was a small but significant sign of the team's willingness to adapt and incorporate Dutch despite the complexities he brought with him. It was a moment of unity in the face of the upcoming challenge.

Before Jeremy and Del could join the others in suiting up for practice, Coach McHale's voice cut through the room. "Captains, in my office. Now!" His tone left no room for argument.

"Yes, sir!" they responded in unison as they followed the coach. As they entered McHale's office, the door closed behind them, shutting off the sounds of the locker room and leaving them in a quiet, more private space.

The seriousness of McHale's demeanor suggested this was more than a routine check-in. Jeremy and Del exchanged a quick, uncertain look as they prepared for whatever the coach had to say.

"Boys, I do not like this one bit. There has to be another way," McHale began, his skepticism clear.

"There isn't, Coach. We've looked into it," Del replied, his tone firm.

"Does he even have the grades to be eligible?" McHale asked, referring to Dutch.

"Sure does," Del said, a hint of pride in his voice. "He's got a 3.0 GPA,". In fact, some of the shop teachers think he's a genius.

"Is that so?" McHale shook his head, partly in disbelief. "Well, do you think he'll stick it out? I'd hate to put the team through a week of practice only to forfeit when he doesn't show up on game day."

"He'll show," Jeremy affirmed confidently. Plus, we still have our original plan in place, just to pad the roster."

At that moment, the locker room door creaked open, and timidly, Dennis peered in. Catching the boys' eyes, he waved from the other side of the glass door.

"No way," McHale objected," shaking his head violently while holding up his hands. I just went over this with the guys. It's too dangerous."

"He won't play, Coach. He'll just suit up. Plus, you should see some of the strategies he's got in his head. Just hear him out," Jeremy urged.

After a brief conversation in which Dennis impressed the coach with his strategies, McHale made his final decision: "Dennis will be with me for game prep and will only suit up if absolutely necessary." Their plan was in motion, and their team's fate was hanging in the balance.

On the practice field, the Wildcat's team dynamic shifted remarkably. They moved with a newfound effectiveness under the guidance of Dennis' innovative plays.

The real game-changer, however, was Dutch at quarterback. His performance was a revelation. His natural talent was undeniable, but what stood out was his attitude. He was receptive to McHale's guidance, executing plays with a focus and discipline previously unseen. This wasn't the same defiant, unpredictable Dutch the team had anticipated. Instead, he emerged as a humble leader, commanding respect and attention in the huddle, something the team never had before.

Dutch seamlessly adjusted to a more collaborative role as Jeremy took the lead in captaining the defense. His ability to shift from a leader to a team player was impressive.

Jeremy, Del, and Dutch revived a communication style and cadence from their Pop Warner days. This allowed them to train the rest of the team in their unique language and cadences, introducing strategies no opponent had ever seen.

The Wildcats drew energy and confidence from one another, creating a synergy that was more than the sum of its parts. The practice session went beyond simply refining their physical skills; it reinforced a sense of unity that had been missing.

By the end of practice, the team had found a new stride. The game against Truman was no longer just another game; it symbolized their renewed spirit and the possibilities ahead when they worked together as a team.

As Coach McHale gathered the team for a final talk. His character, typically defined by a tough exterior and no-nonsense approach, showed a softer side. He commended the team on their hard work and unity, his eyes lingering on Dutch.

"Wyatt," McHale started, his voice striking that perfect balance between 'I'm your coach' and 'I might actually be human.' —"You've thrown me for a loop today. You played like you actually knew what you were doing and kept your attitude in check. That's the secret sauce we need. Welcome to the team. I never thought I'd say this, but I'm glad you are with us," he praised with a respectful nod.

Seizing the golden opportunity to crack a joke, Dutch beamed. "Wow, thanks, Coach! Does this mean we're going steady? Should I clear my Saturday night so we can split a bottle of wine and, ya know, just talk?"

Coach McHale gave Dutch a look, shaking his head, barely concealing a grin he responded with. "Sorry, Wyatt, you're not my type."

But then, Dutch's tone shifted to something surprisingly sincere. "Seriously, guys – today has been a blast. I never thought I'd be back in these pads again, feeling like a part of something. Thanks for letting me be a Wildcat."

McHale, doing his best not to show he was actually moved, quipped back, "Hold the Oscar speech, Wyatt. We still have a game to win." There was an unmistakable glint of respect in the coach's eyes— not just for Dutch's moves on the field but for his efforts to gel with the team.

As McHale wrapped up the practice, the team headed back to the locker room, each player walking away with a bit more pep in their step.

They had created something special between Coach McHale's no-nonsense wisdom and Dutch's unexpected dose of humility and humor. They left the field not just as a bunch of high school athletes but as a team with a real bond, playing for the possibility of finally winning— together.

After practice, the air in the locker room was thick with the familiar mix of sweat, determination, and teenage bravado. Still high on adrenaline, the Wildcats fell into their usual post-practice ritual— joking, rehashing plays, and planning for a weekend still days away.

But Jeremy found himself in a moment of stillness, his mind racing ahead to game day.

Like the previous game against Regional, he knew every move, every call, and every play of the opposing team. But knowledge wasn't power here; it was a haunting reminder of what would come as the game held a painful certainty he couldn't escape.

The game had a deeper purpose for him. It was a critical moment that had become a fixed point in his life.

Destiny would take hold of Jeremy midway through the third quarter. When, in a moment of athletic brilliance, he would leap for an interception, snatching the ball out of the air. With his arm extended before bringing the ball to his chest, he would be crushed from both sides by a pair of Truman defenders, shattering his forearm and leaving him writhing in pain on the turf.

Replaying the event in his mind, he could feel the searing pain, the rush to the ER, and the crushing defeat his team would face without him.

In his past lives, he had attempted to avoid the injury but was unable to evade his fate.

In life 16, he shifted his play, and when the ball was thrown his way, he let it sail past him. There was no collision, no broken arm. However, his relief was short-lived, as destiny had other plans. A series later, while on offense, Jeremy hauled in a pass and immediately received a crippling blow to his knee, ending his football career forever. The severity of the injury caused him to lose his scholarship to Vermont and any future with Cassandra.

Sitting there, with the distant hum of the locker room's buzz, Jeremy sensed the gravity of his situation. The game and the unavoidable injury were reminders of the cycle he couldn't break free from.

He went through all the what-ifs in his head, figuring out the best way to play the game. He decided to lead his team like always, giving Dutch a chance to show everyone the best version of himself and maybe change how they saw him. But to make it all work, Jeremy had to play smart and time everything perfectly.

He thought about the familiar ache of a broken arm, running his fingers over the spot where, in other lifetimes, he had felt the metal hardware under his skin. He knew he could handle the pain of a broken arm. But a more severe injury could destroy his plan for this life.

"Just get through this week, survive the game, and then move on," he told himself. Sure, breaking a bone would hurt like crazy, but he'd been through it before. The pain would only be a temporary visitor that would be gone in no time. He was ready to face it head-on, focusing on getting past this and onto whatever came next.

Del, Dutch, Dennis, and Tomo went to Jeremy's locker with their after-practice plans brewing.

"Hey, we're heading out for burgers. You in?" Del asked.

"I can't," he replied with regret in his voice. I need to get back to Gregg's place—I mean, my house. It's a total mess, plus I've got homework and all."

Del raised an eyebrow. "So, you're not crashing at my place tonight?" he asked. His tone was casual, but there was a hint of concern there. "Don't forget, you owe me a bedtime story. You gotta catch me up on what happened last night with Gregg."

Jeremy gave a small, weary smile. "Yeah, sure, maybe tomorrow. I just need my own bed tonight. After everything that's gone down, I'm beat."

Dutch chimed in with a smirk. "Ah, the pretty boy needs his beauty sleep."

Jeremy shot him a playful glare. "Hey, man, maintaining this level of handsomeness is a full-time job."

The conversation shifted as Jeremy asked the group, "Um, you guys aren't all piling into The Turismo, are you?"

Dutch quickly jumped in, his voice firm. "No way, man, you know my rule. I roll solo. No exceptions."

Del's confirmation brought Jeremy a bit of relief. "Nah, we're just going to walk up the hill. Stacy's meeting us there, and she's gonna drive us all home."

Dennis, chiming in, added something, catching Jeremy off-guard. "Yeah, and I think my sister will be there too."

Jeremy raised an eyebrow, curious as to why Dennis would think to mention that, especially to him.

Dennis continued, "She told me about last night. I think she wants to catch up with you."

Jeremy responded with a soft, understanding smile. "I see," he said gently. "Tell her I'm okay, and I'll catch up with her soon." He then quickly reminded the group and himself of his current romantic situation. "I should probably check in on Kristen anyway," he mentioned, reinforcing that he had a girlfriend.

The conversation shifted back to the more immediate concern of dinner. "Back to The Ray's place, huh?" Del mused. "I wonder what they're cooking up tonight."

Jeremy mentioned casually, "Kristen said something about meatloaf at lunch."

Del cut him off mid-sentence, his voice a mix of envy and hunger. "You bastard! That sounds amazing. Hey, do me a favor and snag me some for lunch tomorrow, will you? And make sure you deliver it peacefully. My wardrobe can't handle another casualty."

Jeremy lingered in the locker room long after his teammates' laughter and chatter faded. As he sat there, lost in thought, the sound of footsteps approached.

Coach McHale, his figure imposing yet reassuring, walked towards him. "Hey, Jeremy," he began, his voice softer than usual. "Are you sticking around for some extra game planning, or are you just trying to avoid the dinner menu at home?"

Jeremy shrugged. "A bit of both, I guess."

Coach McHale sat beside him. "You know, Anderson, I've seen a lot of players come and go," he started, his eyes reflecting memories of countless games and players. "But you've shown a resilience that stands out. Your unwavering commitment to the Wildcats, to never quit, to always fight for your team— it's something that commands respect."

Jeremy sensed the sincerity in McHale's words as a hint of regret crossed the coach's face.

"I haven't spoken much about my time at UMass," he continued. "I know that there are a lot of stories about what happened there. I promise you, none of it is true. They're all just rumors made up by a bunch of kids who know nothing about what it's like to compete."

He paused, looking Jeremy directly in the eyes. "I came back here to coach high school football as a conscious choice. I wanted to get back to the basics. I wanted to help shape young men like you into better players and better people. Nothing could ever compare to how I felt playing in High School, not college, not the pros, and certainly not coaching at UMass. There's something pure about the game at this level.

Jeremy silently listened, absorbing every word.

McHale sighed with a look of sadness on his face. "This season has been tough. Sure, all these losses will build character, but this is your senior year. You, D.C., and the rest of the seniors— you've all played your hearts out. You deserve better than this.

Jeremy looked at his coach in a new light. He saw him as a beaten man who had failed, not a macho blowhard who just didn't get it.

McHale continued, "I just want to get you guys a win before the season ends. But it's more than that. It's about seeing you all grow and come together as a team, regardless of what the scoreboard says."

The coach took a deep breath before dropping a bombshell: "I'm not coming back next fall, Jeremy. This season will be my last one at Huxley. I've got other paths to explore, and I think it's time for someone new to coach the Wildcats. I'm going to tell the team after the game this weekend. For now, this stays between us, got it?"

"Got it." Jeremy replied."

Jeremy was taken aback. With his tough exterior and gruff demeanor, Coach McHale had always been a constant in his high school sports career. He seemed untouchable. He wasn't one to quit like this. Jeremy always thought things would eventually click for him, and he'd start winning games.

"Alright, Andreson, enough of the heavy stuff." The coach said as he stood up, "You better get going. Didn't I hear you say something about a meatloaf to the guys? You don't want to miss that, do you?" Jeremy chuckled, the tension easing. "I guess not."

McHale had shown a side of himself that Jeremy had never seen before — a side that was more human, more real. It was like watching a well-known character from his favorite show reveal a secret past, suddenly making him more relatable and understood.

Exiting the locker room, the drama of the moment and the weight of what lay ahead seemed to blend together. Yet, there was this growing sense of purpose in Jeremy, like the main character in a story realizing his true strength.

The upcoming game was more than just a battle on the field; it was a chance to make a statement to honor a coach who, in his own complicated way, had been their guide and mentor.

Stepping out into the evening, the cool air felt like a scene change, moving from the intensity of the locker room to the calmness of the world outside. Jeremy inhaled deeply, the fresh air clearing his mind. The road ahead was full of challenges, like the climactic chapters of a great adventure, but he felt prepared, ready to take it all on with the passion and integrity that McHale had always preached.

As Jeremy drove home after practice, he mentally sorted through his priorities and the main plot points of his 26th life.

First, there was Cassandra – that part of his plan was still on track, a storyline without any major ripples or waves. The critical objective could still be achieved.

Then there was Dutch and Missy. Jeremy knew that with Dutch leading the Wildcat's offense, the upcoming game would be a defining moment for his friend. It would be a chance to reshape the narrative of Dutchie's legacy.

And Missy was stepping out of her shell and engaging with the group in ways she hadn't in any of Jeremy's past lives. Now a part of the social circle, everyone was creating a richer, more personal connection with her.

With these thoughts came a wave of sadness. Until now, he had accepted the inevitability of losing Missy and Dutch.

In every life leading up to this one, he purposefully kept his distance, avoiding the emotional weight of their inevitable ends. But this time was different—he had allowed himself to truly know them. With this closeness came the piercing realization of the pain he would soon face.

39

YOUR DREAMING

Jeremy's sleep was filled with a series of vivid dreams, each one more intense than the last.

It began with a scene of triumph and the electric thrill of a victory on the football field, the stadium alive with roaring fans and his teammates' wild, unbridled joy.

Soaked in a Gatorade shower, Coach McHale wore a grin that stretched from ear to ear, a look of pure joy and relief marking the grand finale of his coaching career. This victory had eluded Jeremy in so many lifetimes, yet here it was, as real and vivid as if it were happening right now.

But the dream flowed on, changing to darker, more poignant scenes. He found himself in a future where the halls of Huxley High echoed with the absence of Dutch and Missy, two souls who had become as much a part of the school's spirit as they had of Jeremy's 26th life story.

He saw his classmates, filled with sadness and fond memories, coming together in a heartfelt tribute. Laughter mingled with tears as they shared tales of Dutch's escapades off the field and his undeniable charisma on it. Dutch had changed the school's perception of him, leaving behind a legacy that spoke of transformation, courage, and the power of second chances.

The focus of the memorial changed to Missy. Hers was more a gentle, reflective gathering, its impact deeply felt in the tender memories shared. Her legacy was marked by the quiet power of her spirit, a testament to the remarkable things she achieved with her unassuming strength. Her classmates spoke fondly, sharing memories of a girl whose love for life was infectious. They reminisced about her sense of humor, a light that never failed to brighten the darkest days. They recalled her unique ability to connect with anyone she met, leaving a lasting impression on every heart she touched. The tales shared were filled with genuine love and personal connections, painting a picture of a young woman who had truly lived, loved, and mattered.

The air at both memorials was heavy with a sense of peace and deep respect, a fitting tribute to two lives that, though tragically cut short, had woven themselves into the heart of the town.

The stories and memories shared were not just farewells; they were celebrations of lives that, in their brief span, had left profound and lasting impressions on all who knew them.

The dream carried Jeremy into a future brimming with hope and love.

He saw himself growing old with Cassandra. They were on a grand estate, beautifully built upon the grounds of The Labrador, a symbol of new beginnings and enduring legacies. In this future, Cassandra had faced her illness with fierce determination, battling it head-on and emerging triumphant.

In this dream, life stretched long and prosperous. It was a tale of years well lived and loved. He saw himself reaching a peaceful end, a natural conclusion to a journey that had finally broken free from the relentless cycle of rebirth.

Jeremy gently woke up as the early morning light seeped through his curtains. His dreams clung to him like a second skin, warm echoes of it lingering in his heart. He felt a sense of renewal that transcended time as if twenty-five lifetimes' worth of exhaustion had been erased in a single night's sleep.

40

CONFESSIONS OF A VALEDICTORIAN

As JEREMY EMERGED from the locker room, he was startled to find Missy waiting for him, an unusual seriousness etched on her face.

"Hey, Homecoming!" she called out, her voice laced with a hint of sarcasm that didn't quite mask her underlying concern.

Jeremy paused, taken aback. The nickname – a throwback from when Missy saw him as just another high school jock – felt out of place now. It was as if she was hinting at a regression, a step back to a version of him that no longer existed.

"Oh hey, What's up, Missy?" Jeremy asked, his brows knitting in confusion mixed with happiness at the unexpected encounter.

She took a deep breath, her eyes meeting his with frustration and disappointment before laying into him.

"I thought we were friends, Jeremy. But this past week, you've been avoiding me—It's like you're slipping back into this jock persona, all wrapped up in football and nothing else. I thought you were different. I thought you were more than that."

Jeremy felt a wave of guilt. He had been so caught up in his own world, balancing the complexities of his life, that he hadn't realized how his actions might be perceived.

"It's not like that, Missy," he started, but she cut him off.

"And your father," she continued, her voice rising with emotion. "I had to hear from my dad about Gregg going to rehab. Why didn't you tell me? I thought that you trusted me. Now, I don't even know."

He stepped closer, his voice softening. "Missy, I'm really sorry, but I've been dealing with a lot. I guess I didn't realize that I was shutting you out. Gregg going to rehab—I should have told you. There's a lot more to it than him getting sober. I just can't get into it."

Missy's expression softened, the crescendo of her emotions gradually fading away. "I know you don't owe me anything; it's just that," she paused, looking for the safest way to continue, "I just want to be there for you. I just want to really know you, not just the surface stuff. But it's hard when I feel like you're holding back. This past week has been amazing, reconnecting with Kristen and hanging out with everyone. It's all because of you. You brought me into this, and I want to—" she trailed off.

"What, Miss?" Jeremy listened intently.

"I don't know; I guess I just want to spend time with you." She said sheepishly before building courage, "Jesus, I went out with everyone the other night for burgers. I had hoped to hang out with you, but you didn't even show up. Burgers, Jeremy!" She exclaimed with fury, "I am a vegetarian, for Christ's sake!"

"Miss, I didn't," She cut him off again.

"Look, I get it— you're with Kristen. She's my oldest friend, and I know you would never—" she paused, searching for the right words. "I can't believe I am saying this, Jeremy; I just wish it could be different between us."

Jeremy, realizing the admission Missy was struggling to make, looked at her with understanding. "I really don't know what to say, Missy."

At that moment, he knew exactly what to say. He knew he should acknowledge her feelings and admit they were forming for him, too.

The attraction between them was undeniable, but he also knew the ripples such an admission could cause could be irreparable.

He took her hands in his, a sincere look in his eyes; he said, "Missy, I know this has been a crazy week, and I want you to know that I do want you in my life. You've seen sides of me that no one else has. I respect your feelings. I really do."

Jeremy stood there, his heart pulling him in a direction he hadn't planned for. He knew that he needed to navigate the situation with care.

"Missy," Jeremy started, his voice a mixture of sincerity and restraint. "You've become a huge part of my life, perhaps more deeply than I've ever admitted." He paused, each word weighed down by the gravity of unspoken truths. "But I owe you honesty. My life is complicated. I'll admit, I've started to have feelings for you too. But the last thing I want to do is to hurt you."

Her eyes held his as she searched for a deeper connection in his gaze. His hands were gently holding hers, a symbol of his sincerity. At that moment, she felt a surge of courage fueled by her deep feelings for him.

"Jeremy," she said, her voice filled with emotion, "I know life can be complicated. Trust me, I really do. I'm always the one with a plan. You know, set a goal and go for it. But getting to know you wasn't part of any of my plans. And here I am, with all these feelings for you that totally caught me off guard. I get it— you've got a lot going on, and I respect that. And above all, I respect what you have with Kristen. I'm just looking for something honest between us. Can we have that?

Jeremy took a moment, looking at her like he was seeing her for the first time. The evening light gave his eyes an extra depth.

"Missy," Jeremy said, his voice earnest yet uncertain, "hearing all this from you, it's pretty intense. I didn't see it coming either. The way I feel about you," he paused, searching for the right words, his eyes filled with honesty, "it's more than I expected. But right now, considering everything, I think the best way forward for us is to be friends. Really good friends."

She listened, her eyes reflecting understanding and a depth of maturity. "It's a lot for me too. But I respect what you're saying. Being friends, that's something I can do. I trust you, and if friendship is what we need right now, then I'm in."

Jeremy looked relieved, and there was a hint of admiration in his eyes for her acceptance and understanding.

"Thanks, Miss. That means a lot—and being just friends doesn't change how important you are to me.

Missy offered a genuine smile, her heart at ease after sharing her feelings. She was grateful for how respectful Jeremy had been.

Offering a way to move forward, Jeremy looked at her, "Want to come with me to Del's?" he asked with a hopeful note in his voice. "We've got captains' duty tonight, and Kristen will be there. We plan on grabbing some pizza and maybe watching a couple of movies. It should be a good time."

Missy took a deep breath, struggling to keep her emotions in check. She had mixed feelings, but the mutual respect she shared with Jeremy brought her some comfort. "That sounds great," she said, her voice steady despite the undercurrent of deeper emotions. "But, Jeremy, let's make a deal. No matter what happens, we'll always be honest with each other."

His eyes met hers, "I promise," he said, the weight of their agreement settling in his heart. "Honesty, no matter what. It's the only way we'll make it through anything."

41

BROKEN COVERAGE

As the Wildcats conducted their final pre-game walkthroughs in the Huxley High gym, the atmosphere was thick with excitement and focus.

In a quiet corner, Dennis, Dutch, and Coach McHale were deep in discussion, pouring over key offensive strategies with a level of concentration that mirrored the game's importance.

Del and Jeremy took charge of the defensive alignments, confidently orchestrating the team from Jeremy's extensive experience with this game.

"Tomo, you're going to be double-teamed all night," Jeremy instructed with authority. "We're moving you to defensive end. Use a swim move on number 77. Trust me, he'll fall for it every time."

He turned his attention to Del. "D.C., you're going to be shifting between Nickel and Free Safety tonight," he continued, his voice steady and clear. "We need your versatility out there."

His eyes shifted to Dutchie, who was engrossed in practicing Dennis's sideline signals.

"Dutchie will be our spy on the strong side. Their quarterback's got some serious legs. If the pocket collapses, it'll be Dutch's job to contain him and keep him in check." As they ran through the intricacies of the game plan, Jeremy's leadership shined through.

"Any time they shift or adjust, we'll be waiting," he explained, outlining each scenario. "We've got to be one step ahead at all times."

The team listened intently, absorbing every word. There was a sense of unity and readiness, a belief that they were prepared for anything the Truman Beavers threw at them.

As the walkthroughs concluded, the team took a knee, their faces a mix of determination and anticipation. Jeremy looked at them with pride swelling in his chest. This was more than just a game; it was a testament to their hard work and growth as a team.

As the Wildcats knelt before their captains, Del stepped forward with a determined look in his eyes. Clearing his throat, he commanded attention. Every eye in the gym turned to look at him, and in a hush of anticipation, he began to speak.

"Wildcats," Del started, his voice steady and strong, "I want to talk to you about dreams, commitment, and what it means to wear the Huxley blue and gold." He paused for a moment, letting his words sink in.

"For four years, I've played on that field out there. Some of you have been with me the whole time." He looked at Jeremy and gave a gentle nod. "Four long years, filled with loss after loss, week after week. Before every single game, we were dreamers. We dreamed of victory, glory, and celebration, but let's face it, none of our dreams ever came true– our record stands at 0-38. That's my record. That's all our record."

Shooting a glance at McHale's direction, the coach's head dropped in shame. Not my proudest statistic, I'll admit." Del said, swallowing the lump in his throat.

He looked around at his teammates, his gaze unwavering. "But tonight, this game, it's our championship. It's our chance to rewrite the history of this team. To show everyone what we're made of and finally get a win." Del's voice grew more passionate. His words echoed in the silence of the gym. "Think of it like this: we're the underdogs, the ones nobody ever expects to win. Truman has already clinched their playoff spot. For them, a loss tonight doesn't change anything. But for us, for this game tonight? This game is everything."

He leaned in, his expression intense. "They're playing for a perfect season, and who better to spoil that than The Wildcats— the joke of the region, the team that 'couldn't beat anyone.' But tonight, we can change all that."

Del's eyes held with a mix of resolve and fire. "Imagine this – a scrappy, underestimated team taking down an undefeated powerhouse. It's like David vs. Goliath. They might have the size, the record, the reputation. But we have heart. We have determination. And most of all, we have each other." He paused, letting his words resonate with every player there. "Tonight, let's go out there and give it everything we've got. Let's play with the heart of a true Wildcat. Let's make this day one that we'll remember forever – not because it was easy, but because it was the day we stood up and proved ourselves against all odds."

Del stepped back, his speech complete. The team erupted into a roar of support, crowding around their team captain. They were ready. Ready to face their Goliath, to defy expectations, to rewrite their story. And as they left the gym, each player carried with them a sense of purpose, a belief that tonight, anything was possible.

The first half of the game was nothing short of perfection for the Huxley Wildcats. Right from the opening kickoff, they exploded onto the field with an intensity that caught the opposing Truman Tech Beavers off guard. Within minutes, the Wildcats scored two unanswered touchdowns, setting the tone for what was to become an unforgettable game.

Dutch was a force to be reckoned with, playing with a level of passion and skill that seemed superhuman. He moved with fluidity and precision on offense that left the Beavers scrambling. Defensively, he was just as formidable, delivering hit after hit, each one sending a clear message: the Wildcats were here to play.

Standing beside Coach McHale, Dennis proved to be a strategic asset, offering insights and adjustments that kept the Wildcats one step ahead. The Beavers, clad in green and black uniforms, were nothing more than a blur, constantly chasing the uncatchable shadows of the Wildcats' offense.

Jeremy played with an uncanny ability to anticipate plays. It was as if he had choreographed the entire game. Every move and every decision seemed perfectly timed, his presence on the field both commanding and elusive. He easily slipped past defenders on offense, always finding himself in the right place at the right time.

Del, lining up at tailback, was unstoppable. He bulldozed through the Beaver's defense, racking up over 100 yards rushing in the first half alone. His powerful strides and relentless energy added another layer to the Wildcats' multifaceted attack.

As the whistle blew, signaling the end of the first half, the Wildcats found themselves in uncharted territory. They weren't just winning—they were dominating—up by 21 points against the Beavers, a team they had never come close to beating in four seasons. The score wasn't just a lead— it was a shutout, positioning the Wildcats closer to an ever-elusive victory than they had ever been.

The energy in the stands was electric. The Wildcats' fans were making their presence felt, their cheers and chants echoing through the stadium. They taunted the traveling Beaver fans, who sat in stunned silence, unable to comprehend how their team, which had been so dominant all season, was being systematically dismantled.

As the team filed into the locker room for halftime adjustments, Coach McHale gathered everyone together. "Team, I'm proud of each of you. There's nothing better than going into the half with a three-touchdown lead. But let this moment mark the end of your celebration. The score is 0-0 in our minds. We have to play the second half with double the determination we had in the first."

As he continued, the team hung on his every word, "We're making a strategic shift for the rest of the game. Coach Winston will be calling offensive plays in the second half." He motioned toward Dennis and tossed him a reassuring smirk.

Dennis looked at the coach, stunned. "Oh, no way," he responded, his voice trembling. "That's way too much pressure."

"Relax, kid. You'll be fine," Coach McHale reassured him. "You've called every big play in the first half. Let's see what you've got for the second."

From the crowd, Del shouted, "Alright, Big D! It's your time to shine!"

Tomo added, "Hell yeah, Coach Screech, we've got your back!"

As the team rallied around him with exclamations of encouragement,

Dennis' confidence grew. He sighed with a mix of resignation and determination. "Screw it," he said, slipping into his new role. "Alright, offense, we get the ball to start the second half. Let's go over some adjustments."

Jeremy watched Dennis with a mix of pride and concern. This was a new role for Dennis, which could certainly cause some ripples. But Jeremy believed in him. 'He's destined to be a great leader. Why not give him a head start?' he thought.

Then, the dread of what awaited in the third quarter engulfed Jeremy. He wasn't looking forward to the physical pain of a broken arm, but he was resolved to stick to this life's path. This event needed to happen to maintain his trajectory.

Fortunately, he'd be playing defense during the injury and knew how to execute the play when the opportunity arose to limit the severity of the injury. It was a finesse move he'd crafted over countless replays of this very sequence of events.

His mind buzzed with thoughts and strategies. He knew the outcome of every play could tip the scales, but one play, in particular, had to stick to the script. Jeremy had to be ready to take the biggest hit of his life. His heart pounded, not from fear of the injury that awaited him but from the thrill of pulling off a plan only he could envision.

Pulling Del and Dutchie aside, he got straight to the point. "Guys, I've spotted a pattern in the Beavers' offense," he said urgently. "They're finding gaps we don't even know we're leaving open."

Del raised an eyebrow. "We've been shutting them down all game. What are you talking about?"

Jeremy nodded. "You're right, we're shutting them out, but I think they'll figure out our defense in the second half. If they do, we could lose our lead or, even worse, the game. I need you guys to trust me on this." He quickly laid out his plan, making it as clear as possible. "When I shout 'Raptor,' Del, you and Dutch need to spread out, leaving a gap. It'll look like broken coverage, but it's intentional."

Dutch was unconvinced. "Hold on, J—You want us to break coverage on purpose? That doesn't make any sense."

Jeremy's tone was firm and convincing. "I know how it sounds, but hear me out. It's a stunt. They'll cross their tight end over the middle, and I'll be waiting, ready to pick them off. Trust me, it'll work."

Del and Dutchie looked at each other, clearly torn.

"But that'll leave you all alone on defense," Del pointed out. "If they get past you, it's a clear shot to the end zone. We can't cover that distance fast enough."

Jeremy's confidence didn't waver, though his eyes showed he understood the risk. "I've thought about that. Sure, it's risky, but I've got a feeling about this— please, just trust me.— we could seal the game with this one play."

After a moment of tense silence, Del finally nodded. "Okay, we're with you. But don't blow this for us, okay?"

At the beginning of the second half, the Wildcats continued to dominate just as they had in the first. On their second drive, they effortlessly marched down the field, extending their lead to 27-0. But the Beavers weren't ready to give in. Demonstrating superior conditioning, they returned the following kickoff for a touchdown, avoiding a shutout.

Dennis, taking the reins as play-caller, went with a conservative approach. He relied heavily on Del, running play after play to keep the clock ticking, gradually wearing down the Beavers' defense.

The Wildcats' strategy was working flawlessly. Dennis's play-calling was cautious but effective, and the team's execution on the field was nearly impeccable.

———

Jeremy felt a familiar tension knotting in his stomach when the third quarter reached the halfway point. He knew exactly what was coming next. The Wildcats lined up on defense, and Jeremy quickly scanned the Beavers' formation: Power I.

"This is it," he thought. "They've figured us out— It's now or never."

The Beavers' tight end, Joe O'Grady, went into motion. Normally, Jeremy would shadow him, but this time, he had a different plan. He called out sharply to his teammates, "Raptor! Raptor!" Del and Dutchie shifted positions as instructed, leaving an intentional gap in their defense.

From the sidelines, Coach McHale watched in disbelief. "What the hell are they doing? Cover #48!" he screamed, his voice full of frustration. "Jesus Christ, you bozos, he's unmanned!" But his words were lost in the chaos of the play already unfolding.

Jeremy ignored the sideline shouts and focused solely on the Beavers' tight end. As the ball soared towards O'Grady, Jeremy made his move. Timing his leap perfectly, he extended his left arm and intercepted the ball just before reaching its target.

"This is gonna hurt," Jeremy muttered, bracing for impact. Pulling the ball towards his chest, he was suddenly sandwiched between two massive Beaver offensive linemen. The brutal collision stopped him in his tracks and squeezed the air from his lungs. For a moment, everything went silent as he was pancaked between the two giants before they released him, allowing his body to crumple to the turf.

Clutching the ball tightly in an unharmed cradle, Jeremy's mind raced. 'How is this even possible?' he wondered. He had executed the play perfectly; he should be in agonizing pain, but he wasn't.

He had braced himself for the worst, prepared for a painful sacrifice, yet here he was, unharmed, aside from the desperate need for air. Slowly, his breathing began to steady as his teammates were now huddled around him, their faces a mix of concern and disbelief.

"Jer, you alright?" Del asked,

Jeremy nodded, still catching his breath. "Yeah, man— I think so," he managed to say, surprised by his words.

"Sweet Jesus Anderson, you called it!" Dutch Exclaimed.

Just then, Tomo burst through the huddle. Are you good, Jack? He said, yanking Jeremy to his feet.

"Yeah, man—I'm good," he groaned, trying to get his bearings. The referee's whistle blew again, bringing everyone's attention back to the game.

Having sprinted onto the field, McHale reached Jeremy, his expression a mix of relief and confusion. "Son, that was one hell of a play. Are you sure you're alright?" he asked with deep concern.

"Yeah, I'm good, Coach," Jeremy reassured McHale, though he could feel the adrenaline starting to wane, leaving behind a hint of soreness from the collision. "I think I might need to sit out a few plays, though."

McHale nodded, his face etched with both concern and pride. "Take your time, son. That was an incredible interception. We'll manage without you."

As Jeremy made his way to the sideline, his teammates patted him on the back, their faces lit up with admiration and relief. The crowd continued to cheer; their excitement filled the air. Despite his desire to stay in the game, Jeremy knew he had to take a moment to ensure he was okay.

Sitting on the bench, he took deep breaths, each one steadying him more. The team's training staff quickly checked on him, running through their standard assessments. They were as baffled as everyone else that he wasn't injured. "It looks like you just got the wind knocked out of you," the trainer said, a hint of amazement in his voice. But let's keep an eye on you for a bit."

Jeremy watched the game from the sidelines as his team continued their on-the-field dominance.

Dennis did an excellent job keeping the offense moving, and the defense held strong even in Jeremy's absence. It was a testament to the team's will and resilience.

When Jeremy's breath returned and the collision's initial shock faded, he stood up, testing his body for any hidden pains or aches.

Surprisingly, he felt solid and ready to go back in. His body was filled with adrenaline, and he forgot that fate might have other plans for handing him an injury.

"Coach, I think I'm good to go back in," Jeremy said with determination. McHale looked at him, trying to gauge his condition. After a brief nod from the medical staff, he clapped Jeremy on the shoulder. "Alright, get in there and help us close this game out."

Jeremy jogged back onto the field with a renewed sense of purpose. The cheers grew louder as the crowd recognized his return. With his unexpected escape from injury, his focus shifted entirely. Caught up in the energy of the moment, he pushed aside his desire to keep any timeline intact. His only goal now was to secure victory for the Wildcats.

His return to the field gave the team an extra burst of energy. His teammates, drawing strength from his resilience, played with a heightened intensity. The defense, strengthened by Jeremy's presence, became an impenetrable force. Offensively, Dennis executed each play with surgical precision, his confidence amplified by the team's united front.

The crowd's cheers crescendoed into a euphoric roar as the final whistle blew. The Wildcats didn't just win; they dominated, just as Jeremy had dreamt, but the team celebrated their victory with a delightful twist. Instead of the traditional Gatorade shower on the head coach, Dennis was drenched, and his fear of the spotlight was forgotten as he was swept up in the thrill of victory. Tomo and the other linemen hoisted him onto their shoulders, parading him around the field as the embodiment of their triumph.

The once-shy Dennis was now leading a rousing chant: "Cats! Cats! Cats!" as he pumped his fists in the air. His heart swelled with pride at the school's first victory in years.

As the Wildcat fans stormed the field, Jeremy's eyes caught a solitary figure hanging back, watching the celebration from a distance.

Missy stood alone, smiling in his direction, offering a brief wave and a thumbs-up, a silent acknowledgment of his success. Just as he waved back, Del and Dutch tackled him to the ground in a euphoric pig pile. Their screams of joy were so loud and ecstatic that their words were unintelligible, but their message was clear: unbridled happiness and pride in their shared achievement.

Jeremy felt a deep sense of fulfillment, lying on the ground, surrounded by his teammates. This victory wasn't just about the game; it was a celebration of their hard work and the journey they had all taken together.

The Wildcats achieved victory on the football field and created an unforgettable memory of triumph. The joy of exceeding every expectation was unforgettable.

As they stood up, Jeremy, Dutch, and Del were wrapped in the thrill of victory, reenacting the game's key moments with lively gestures and wide, infectious grins.

Del, his face glowing with excitement, turned to Dutch. "Dutchie, if only we had you with us from the start," he exclaimed. "We totally could have won state!"

Dutch, visibly moved, replied, "It's never too late, right? Just being back on the field with you guys was amazing. Honestly, this is the best day of my whole life." Joy shimmered in his eyes, spilling over into tears of happiness.

Amidst their joyful embrace, Coach McHale approached them, his eyes filled with immense pride. "Boys, in all my years, I've never felt prouder of a group of players," he declared.

He looked at Dutch. "Wyatt," he continued, tossing him the game ball. "This is for you, Most Valuable Player.' You've earned it."

The crowd, witnessing this touching scene, spontaneously shifted their "Cats" chant to one honoring Dutchie's remarkable achievement. "Dutch! Dutch! Dutch!" echoed across the stadium, a chorus of admiration and respect.

Dutch stood there, stunned, taking in the acceptance of a crowd that had previously only shown disdain towards him.

Jeremy watched his friend soak in the praise with a full heart. 'Dutch Wyatt's legacy, rewritten,' he thought. He was overjoyed knowing that his friend would always be remembered as a champion regardless of what the future held for him.

The team captains and newly appointed MVP gathered in the locker room to plot their epic victory celebration for the next night. Still riding the high of his MVP honor, Dutch took the lead in planning.

"Do you think we could have it at the Cottage, Jer?" Dutch asked, his voice exploding with excitement.

Jeremy nodded. "I don't see why not. We've still got all our gear up there from last weekend."

The group buzzed with ideas, but Tomo remained unusually quiet. Finally, he said, "Guys, I can't make it. My mom is really pissed at me; I got another write-up from Pritchett for falling asleep in class. I'm grounded for the weekend."

"Sorry, big guy," Del said sympathetically. "We'll make sure to party extra hard for you."

Dutch, already in full planning mode, declared, "I'll take care of the drinks. I'll get a keg. Cold ones for everyone!"

Del chimed in, "I'll handle the guest list. We'll keep it tight, just a few more than usual. It'll be super exclusive, I promise." He added with a wink, "And yes, there will be girls. In fact, I heard Julie Nichols might be in town from Dartmouth. Maybe I can get her to come by. How does that sound, Dutchie?"

Dutch's face turned a shade redder at the mention of Julie. "Oh, man, Julie Nichols? So hot."

The group erupted in laughter at his reaction."

"Alright, Dennis, you're in charge of inviting Missy and Kristen," Jeremy instructed. "Can you handle that?"

"Got it, Jer. You can count on me," Dennis assured him confidently. "

And Del, make sure Stacy knows about it too," Jeremy added. "We can't have a proper celebration without our third amigo."

"Of course," Del agreed. "Stacy's gotta be there. It wouldn't be a party without her."

The planning continued with each member of the group contributing ideas and suggestions. The mood was high-spirited, filled with anticipation for an epic celebration. The victory at the game had set the stage for a memorable night, one where they could unwind and celebrate their victory.

42

KEG PARTY PROBLEMS

As THE SUN began to set, Jeremy worked on building a campfire in front of the cottage. Meanwhile, Del and Stacy were going through a stack of CDs, trying to find the perfect tunes to create an excellent party atmosphere.

Missy and Kristen were a whirlwind of energy. Their laughter mingled with the sounds of their busy work as they transformed the area around the cottage into a vibrant celebration scene. Streamers and balloons bobbed in the gentle evening breeze, adding pops of color against the fading daylight, while colorful Christmas lights, strung up with care, waited for nightfall to reveal their full twinkling glory.

"Anyone heard from Dutch?" Jeremy asked the group, "He was really looking forward to tonight."

"Not since this morning," Stacy responded, settling into a chair with Cheech in her arms. "He mentioned having some errands to run. I know he's excited to see Cheech. I'm sure he'll be here soon," she added as she nuzzled the cat, who was enjoying his newfound celebrity status.

Del, who was giving the boom box a final test, joined in. "He's probably just running late. You know Dutch—always getting sidetracked."

Jeremy, however, felt uneasy. 'Not now—at least let him have tonight,' he silently pleaded to any higher power listening, hoping Dutchie's delay was nothing more than his usual tardiness.

As guests started to trickle in, Jeremy was set at ease as the sound of Dutchie's Turismo broke the evening stillness.

Kristen rolled her eyes at the noise. "I hate that car. It's so trashy."

Quickly defending Dutch, Stacy replied, "Hey, be nice. Dutch is an artist. He's brought that thing back from the dead. You say it's trashy; I say it's Dutchie. And I think it's cool.

Del mocked as he sang mockingly, "Stacy loves Dutchie, Stacy loves Dutchie."

"Shut up, Del; I do not love him. I just admire him. So much pain and such a gentle soul."

Not giving up, Del continued, "Stacy and Dutchie, sitting in a tree K.I.S.S.—"

"Zip it, Antione," she belted, "don't make me kick your ass."

"Alright, I was just teasing, girl, chill." Del soothed.

Having parked beside Jeremy's Jeep, Dutch emerged with a purposeful stride. "Keg is in the back. Get it to the porch," he instructed, heading straight for Stacy.

"Where's my boy? Hand him over!" Dutch demanded as he reached for Cheech. He grinned as he lifted the tiny cat, theatrically singing The Circle of Life from The Lion King. "Nants ingonyama bagithi baba!" he bellowed.

The group erupted into laughter as Dutch continued his playful serenade, holding Cheech aloft like the royal cub he was impersonating. Cheech, for his part, looked utterly clueless yet majestic, his piercing green eyes scanning the surroundings, unaware of his starring role in this impromptu performance.

After the song, Dutch held Cheech close to his chest, snuggling him as he channeled his inner Mufasa. "Someday, Cheech, all this will be yours," he intoned solemnly, gesturing grandly to the world around them. Cheech's expression remained adorably blank, his eyes bright and curious as he gazed at the lively scene. His rumbling purr suggested contentment, or perhaps mild confusion, at being the center of attention.

Jeremy watched Dutch with amusement and fondness before interrupting with a surprising revelation.

"Actually, someday, all of this will be mine," he said with a slight smile. "And by 'someday,' I mean now."

The group's laughter faded into a puzzled silence. All eyes turned to Jeremy, except for Del, who already knew the secret about Gregg's unexpected gift.

"All of it," Jeremy continued, sweeping his hand to encompass the landscape. From the tree line to the lake, the cottage, the ruins—it's all mine." He gazed off into the distance, his tone a mixture of awe and disbelief.

As the group absorbed the gravity of this news, Kristen, confused, asked, "What do you mean it's all yours? How can that be? I thought your family lost this place years ago and that Gregg only owned the cottage."

"That's what I thought too," Jeremy replied, "until the other day. But nope, it turns out it's all mine now."

Dutch, always quick to respond, exclaimed, "Well, shit, man, you're rich! This place must be worth a fortune, even with the ruins and all."

"Not really," Jeremy answered, shaking his head slightly. "Some developers looked at it a while back but were put off by its history."

"History?" Dennis chimed in, intrigued.

Jeremy looked at him with a smug expression. "Ghosts, Dennis, everyone is afraid of the ghosts," he said, holding his gaze for a beat before cracking a smirk. "I guess no one has been serious about it because of the rumors and stories about this place."

As Jeremy locked eyes with Kristen, he sensed a storm brewing. Without a word, she communicated her frustration, mouthing— "What the fuck?" in a way that left no room for misunderstanding.

Jeremy recognized this look all too well; it was the prelude to a major argument, the kind that wasn't easily diffused.

He mouthed back, "I'm sorry," but her fury remained unyielding as she stormed into the cottage.

"What's her problem?" Stacy asked as she watched Kristen storm off.

"Uh, nothing," Jeremy quickly covered, trying to downplay the situation. "I think she's upset that she's just hearing about all this for the first time. I'll talk to her later. I should let her cool off first."

As if on cue, a distraction arrived, much to Jeremy's relief. Cars filled with their classmates began to roll down the dirt path toward the cottage. Heather and the rest of the cheerleaders were the first to arrive. Jeremy seized the opportunity to divert attention from Kristen's departure.

"Thank God!" he exclaimed before addressing Heather. "Kristen's inside, but just a heads-up, she's pretty pissed at me."

"Oh no, what did you do now, Jer-Bear?" Heather teased as she and her squad headed into the cottage.

As some of the kids from the theater group arrived, Stacy sprang up to greet them with her usual enthusiastic charm, introducing them to everyone.

When she got to Dutchie, she joked, "Don't worry; he won't bite." She giggled, gesturing towards Cheech. Dutchie offered a soft smile, slightly uncomfortable with the growing crowd.

Then came a few of Dennis's friends, and finally, a group of their fellow

Wildcat teammates arrived, cars deep, ready to celebrate the previous night's victory.

To everyone's surprise, Tomo emerged from the last car.

"Hey guys!— Mom let me out early for good behavior," he announced, adding to the excitement.

With Tomo's arrival, the party shifted into full gear. The atmosphere was charged with energy, laughter, and music. The mix of people from different circles— cheerleaders, theater kids, and jocks—created a vibrant, eclectic vibe. The night air was filled with the sounds of conversations, the crackling of the campfire, and the rhythmic beats of music.

Despite the lingering concern about Kristen, Jeremy couldn't help but get caught up in the festive spirit. The party was unfolding into a memorable night, celebrating their recent victory and new relationships he'd never allowed himself to have.

As the night deepened, the cottage and its surrounding land – now Jeremy's unexpected legacy – was alive with the joy and excitement of youth.

Dutch, a master at blending into the shadows, was approached by Dennis and a few of his friends. Despite the lively party atmosphere, Dutchie seemed content in his quiet corner.

"Hey guys," Dutch greeted them casually.

"Uh, Dutch, my friends were wondering," Dennis started awkwardly. "Didn't you bring a keg?"

"Yeah, it's in the car. You were supposed to get it up here on the porch," Dutch reminded them.

"Uh, okay. But we don't know how to open it," Dennis said, unsure.

"Dutch chuckled and said, 'Open it? You mean tap it. He laughed and continued, 'No worries. Just bring it up here and grab the tap from the back seat of my car. It looks like something out of one of your chemistry classes.'

"Okay, let's do this, guys," Dennis rallied his friends, following Dutch's directions.

Dutch trailed behind the group to supervise, cradling Cheech in his arms. The underclassmen struggled at first to lift the keg out of the Turismo's hatchback.

"Easy, easy," Dutch cautioned them. "Don't shake it too much, or it'll be all foam." Taking extra care, the boys slowly approached the front porch.

As Dutch followed, Cheech purred softly in his arms.

Just as they reached the top step, one of Dennis's friends, less sturdy than the others, lost his grip. The keg slipped from his hands and crashed onto the porch with a loud bang, startling Cheech. The cat leaped from Dutch's arms and darted off into the woods in a flash.

"CHEECH!" Dutch screamed, his voice laced with panic.

The group froze, taken aback by the turn of events. Dutch, without hesitation, bolted after Cheech into the woods, his concern for the cat over-shadowing everything else.

The party sprang into action, ready to help find the frightened cat.

But, the search for Cheech was brief and half-hearted. Many quickly lost interest, preferring to enjoy the ongoing celebration with its music and laughter.

As Dutch continued to search, his calls for Cheech grew more desperate as he went deeper into the woods. But without any sign of the cat, his determination faded. His heart sank as he stood alone in the dark. He knew that it would be impossible to find Cheech. The weight of his loss felt heavy on his heart, and he couldn't help but feel a sense of hope-lessness.

Feeling defeated, Dutch returned to the party, where there was once excitement and joy but now only heartbreak. He looked around at the laughing and chatting groups and felt disconnected. Seeking comfort, he made his way to Stacy. Her expression turned to concern when she saw the distress in his eyes,

"Hey, Dutch," she said gently, "any luck?"

He shook his head, the worry evident on his face. "No, he's gone. I called and called, but he didn't come back. It's just— he's gotta be so scared."

Stacy reached out, placing a reassuring hand on his shoulder. "Cheech is a smart cat. He'll find his way back. These woods are his home, too."

Sadness was written all over his face. "It's all my fault," he said, his voice filled with regret. "I should've been more careful."

Stacy fixed on him with a stern look. "You stop that right now," she commanded, causing Dutch to snap to attention. "It was an accident, and Cheech will be back. He loves you. He's just afraid of all the people here. He'll come back. I don't want you walking around here all brooding and angry. It's not very attractive."

Dutchie stared at Stacy, slightly dazed. No teacher, school administra-tor, or authority figure had ever put him in his place quite like she had. Her firm yet caring words had a surprising effect on him.

"And don't even think about giving Dennis and his friends a hard time about this. It was an accident." She demanded.

Her expression softened as she pulled Dutch into a comforting hug. "He'll be okay. Let's just give him some time. I'll bet he'll show up once things quiet down."

"I need a beer," he muttered. Is that keg tapped yet?" he shouted over his shoulder toward the porch, where Dennis and his friends were struggling with the keg.

Dennis hesitated before answering, "Uh, bad news, Dutch. When you were looking for Cheech, we tried to tap the keg, and I think we kind of broke it."

Dutch's already simmering frustration began to boil. "Sweet Jesus, Dennis! Are you seriously trying to ruin this party?" he exclaimed, struggling to maintain his composure.

"The tap is on the porch, with the keg," Dennis pointed out, looking equally frustrated.

Dutch shot up and stormed to the porch, where Del was examining the damaged tap. "I don't know, man. Looks like we're screwed," he said, shaking his head.

"No way, not happening. This is our victory party, and I am having a beer," Dutch declared, refusing to let the evening's setbacks dampen their celebration.

"It's all good, man," Del said, trying to console him. "We'll figure something out."

Jeremy joined them as they struggled with the broken tap, his expression one of concern. "Hey guys, have either of you seen Kristen?"

"Nah, man," Del replied, his attention still on the keg. "We're dealing with heavier stuff at the moment."

Jeremy examined the damaged tap closely. "Yeah, this thing is pretty chewed, but don't sweat it. We're all having a good time without the beer. Let's stay cool about this. "I'll catch up with you guys soon. I need to find Kristen."

"Fine, whatever, man," Dutch replied with a hint of frustration. "Go deal with your chick and leave us men to figure this shit out."

After searching high and low, Jeremy finally stumbled upon Kristen in the backyard. They were huddled together in an animated gossip session with Heather and the rest of the cheer squad.

"Hi, ladies," Jeremy greeted them, trying to sound casual.

"Hey, Jer-Bear," Heather replied sweetly, contrasting Kristen's fierce glare.

Feeling shy under his girlfriend's intense gaze, Jeremy asked, "Do you mind if I steal Kristen for a minute?"

The other girls looked between Jeremy and Kristen, sensing the tension, and quietly excused themselves, leaving them alone. Jeremy knew he had some explaining to do and hoped to smooth things with Kristen. Her expression, however, told him it wouldn't be easy.

He let out a heavy sigh, bracing himself for what was to come. "Look, Kristen—"

"No, Jeremy, you look!" Kristen interrupted, her frustration reaching a boiling point. "I'm tired of how distant you've been. You never want to talk about our future. You didn't say a word to me about your huge fight with Gregg or about him going to jail and rehab. And now this..." She waved her arms dramatically, referencing the sprawling estate around them. "All of this land? What the hell is going on, Jeremy?"

Her voice intensified, full of emotion. "You're my boyfriend. These aren't just little details; these are major life events! We're supposed to be in this together, yet you keep me in the dark. I always seem to be the last to know everything. I'm always hearing about your life from other people or I'm finding out in front of everyone. It's not only hurtful, Jeremy, it's humiliating."

Jeremy realized he had neglected Kristen's feelings while focusing on his own path. He always knew their relationship would end, but he failed to approach it with grace in this life.

She continued, her frustration boiling over, "It's not just the big stuff either. It's the everyday things. You're always lost in your own world. When was the last time you asked about my day? Or actually listened to me without zoning out?" Her eyes blazed with raw emotion. "Remember my dance recital last month? You promised to be there, but you didn't show up. You said you forgot, but that was just an excuse. You're always so distracted, Jeremy. And with this whole thing about the land and your family—it's like you're living in a completely different world."

Jeremy felt a sharp stab of guilt, especially about the recital. He couldn't even remember it; it felt like centuries ago. In fact, it was before his life had become so complicated by repeated cycles—before resets when he was simply a clueless teenager.

Kristen inhaled deeply, her chest rising and falling with the weight of her emotions. "I don't know you anymore, Jeremy. You keep everything bottled up until it all just explodes. You're carrying this huge burden and won't let me in. I thought we were a team, but now I'm not so sure." Her words hung in the air, heavy with pain and uncertainty.

Jeremy knew he needed to respond, but the realization that their paths were heading in separate directions was overwhelming. They stood there in silence, each lost in their thoughts, contemplating the future of a relationship that seemed to be unraveling at the seams.

The tense moment between Jeremy and Kristen in the backyard was very different from the escalating situation on the front porch. There, the issue with the broken keg tap had reached a boiling point.

Dutch, still on edge from Cheech's disappearance and now the useless keg, found his frustration mounting as he and Del tried to figure out the situation.

The evening that was supposed to be a celebration was quickly turning into a series of tragedies. "Come on, Del, there has to be something we can do about this tap," Dutchie said, his voice filled with desperation.

Del, examining the damaged tap closely, shook his head. "I don't know, Dutch. This thing is pretty messed up. It looks like it got cross-threaded or something."

Dutchie's patience was wearing thin. "We can't have a victory party without beer, man. This is bullshit!" His voice rose in volume, attracting the attention of nearby partygoers who turned to see what the commotion was about.

Del, trying to maintain a level head, attempted to calm Dutchie down. "Hey, let's not blow this out of proportion. We can still have a good time without the keg.

Dutchie wasn't having it. "No, Del, you don't get it. This party was supposed to be perfect. It's our celebration, our moment, and now it's all going to shit!"

The tension between the two was heavy. In this heated moment, the spirit of the evening was hanging by a thread, with the outcome of this confrontation between Dutchie and Del poised to set the tone for the rest of the night.

In the backyard, Jeremy and Kristen's argument continued. In a moment of desperation, he did something completely out of character. He intertwined a few white lies with genuine feelings, hoping to navigate the turbulent waters of their conversation.

"Kristen, I'm sorry," he began, his voice filled with sincerity. This much was true. He never intended to break her heart.

Continuing, he wove in a lie. "I have no idea what will happen to us."

Then, returning to honesty, "I do love you. I always will. It's just— everything is so heavy right now." He gestured around them, indicating the vast expanse of land as she did earlier. "I'm sorry I didn't share everything about my dad and this place. It's a lot to deal with." He paused, sighing deeply.

In that moment of silence, Kristen saw her opportunity to press further. "But now, can't you at least think about staying?" she pleaded.

Jeremy felt torn. "I get it, Kris. You want me to stay. And until last week, I wanted nothing more than to leave. But now, it's different. I just—I don't know."

It was another truth. The weight of balancing his struggles with the relationships with the people who cared about him most was becoming exhausting, and Jeremy could feel himself nearing a breaking point. His vulnerability was evident in his voice and his eyes.

This conversation was more than just a disagreement; it was a pivotal moment, defining what might come next for them. The fear of what that future might hold— the uncertainty and the potential for more heart-break– slowly crept in, clouding Jeremy's mind with doubt and apprehension.

His heart ached as he listened to Kristen's words. The sincerity in her voice and the genuine concern in her eyes made him yearn to share his entire truth with her. He wished he could break through the constraints of his situation and reveal everything, but he knew that was not just unrealistic but potentially dangerous.

The rule of keeping his true circumstances hidden was concrete and unbreakable. It was a boundary he couldn't risk crossing.

"I know this is all really overwhelming for you," she said softly, moving closer. "I want to be here to help you through it. I just wish you'd let me in more."

Jeremy felt guilty as he looked into her eyes. "Thanks, Kris. I appreciate it," he responded, his voice carrying a note of remorse. I swear that I will tell you everything from now on." The words left his mouth before he could stop them, another lie layered upon the many he felt compelled to maintain. It was a promise he knew he couldn't keep, but in that moment, it was the only thing he could offer to bridge the gap between them.

Despite his best intentions, he was caught in a web of circumstances that forced him to balance his honesty with the necessity of keeping certain truths hidden. This delicate balance was a constant struggle for Jeremy, one that he navigated with a mix of fear, hope, and a deep-seated desire to protect himself and Kristen from the heavier burdens of his reality.

With their tensions temporarily cooling, Jeremy and Kristen made their way to the porch. There, they found Del and Dutchie in a heated debate, each championing a different solution to the keg problem.

Del, visibly agitated, was pushing for a drastic approach. "We should just punch a hole in the keg," he proposed with a tone of desperation. "I saw some tools out back. It can definitely be done."

Dutchie, on the other hand, was adamantly against the idea. "Are you out of your fucking mind, dude? "That will waste half the beer, and we'll get soaked when it explodes," he said with frustration. "The keg looks fine. We just need a new tap. I'll just run to the packie and grab a new one. It won't take long – twenty minutes, tops. I'll pick up some Jägermeister to kick the party into high gear."

Kristen, grimacing at the mention of Jägermeister, interjected, "Jäger, barf. That stuff is so gross. Make it Rumplemintz instead." Her light-hearted comment momentarily cut through the tension, eliciting chuckles from the group and even drawing a brief smile from Dutch. Del, seizing the shift in mood, agreed, "Rumplemintz, huh? That might be better than Jäger for spicing up the party."

Jeremy, sensing the need to de-escalate the situation, intervened. "Let's just calm down, guys," he suggested, hoping to inject some reason into the heated discussion. "No need for drastic actions or a rush into town. We can figure out a simpler solution."

Dutch, however, was not convinced. "That's not gonna cut it, man," he said. The tap is completely stewed. I'll just shoot over to Ryan's on Elm. He always hooks me up, no ID needed," he said with a hint of pride.

Del immediately said, "If you're making a packie run, I'm coming."

Dutch shook his head. "No way, man. You know the rules. I only roll solo. "

"Cut the crap, Dutchie," Del shot back. "Are we fixing this or not?"

Jeremy, seeing the tension rise, offered a compromise. "How about you guys take my Jeep? Del can drive." He hoped this would avoid any potential issues linked to Dutch's 'Wyatt Curse.'

Del was skeptical. "Your Jeep, Jer? The last time I borrowed it, the thing died on me right in the middle of Main Street. It was super embarrassing, man. No thanks. I know you love your Jeep and all, but you're the only one who seems to get it to behave."

Del coming up with an alternative plan suggested. "What if," he paused dramatically, "just hear me out, we take the Turismo, but I drive? We'll be safe, and I'll go slow. Plus, I heard Julie Nichols needs rescuing from a family dinner. We can grab the new tap, some Rumple, pick up Julie, and be back in no time."

Dutchie, after thinking about Del's idea, finally agreed. "Alright, but if you crash my car, I'll kill you."

"Relax, I'm an excellent driver," Del quipped, rocking back and forth as he repeated, "Yeah, an excellent driver," channeling Dustin Hoffman's character from 'Rain Man." Plus, your stupid curse can't catch me. I'm way too fast."

Jeremy's mind raced as he calculated the possibilities. Del's plan seemed to make a strange sort of sense. Based on his experience, Del was invincible. Wrapped in cosmic bubble wrap, he was untouchable by any grim reaper chasing Dutch. The power of his charm would cancel out the danger. He'd keep Dutch safe for the trip to town and back.

Ultimately, Jeremy consented to the plan, though he knew deep down that his friends didn't need his approval.

The trio huddled briefly, Del rallying the group, "Hot 21 breakout on two," he called out, referencing his plan to reunite Dutchie with Julie Nichols. With a "ready, break," He grabbed Dutch's keys and headed for the Turismo, his charm in full swing.

Standing beside Jeremy, Kristen couldn't help but laugh at the turn of events. While veering away from its original celebratory intent, the night had transformed into its own kind of adventure.

As he watched Del take the driver's seat of Dutchie's Turismo, Jeremy felt a mix of worry and reluctant acceptance. 'They'll be fine,' he thought, trying to convince himself. Yet, a nagging sense of carelessness gnawed at him for allowing this to happen.

Dutch's prized possession, the Turismo, was now under Del's control. Jeremy could hear Dutch's voice as he called out instructions.

"Easy, easy, she might not look like it, but she's a gentle lady," Dutch warned; his affection for the car was evident in his tone.

Jeremy watched as the car slowly backed out of its spot. Del was careful, respecting Dutch's rules and the car itself. Dutch's voice guided him, ensuring every movement was just right.

As Jeremy watched the Turismo pull away from the cottage, seeing the car's red taillights disappear into the night left him feeling a strange combination of relief and unease.

43

FIRESIDE CHAT

WHILE WAITING for Dutch and Del to return, Jeremy sat alone on the front steps.

The party had taken over the backyard. Music thumped, and laughter echoed from behind the cottage, where a dance-off and a spur-of-the-moment rap battle were underway. The cheerful sounds of the party seemed a world away from Jeremy's quiet spot by the flickering flames.

Wrapped in his thoughts, Jeremy's gaze was fixed on the fire in the distance until he noticed Missy and Stacy nearby, deep in conversation. Craving some human connection, he joined them.

"You should join the rap battle out back, Miss," he suggested with a playful grin as he sat beside them. "You'd crush it."

Missy glanced up, her eyes sparkling with humor, "Is that Dennis free styling?" she asked, her ears turned to the distinct, amateur rap verses floating through the air.

Jeremy chuckled. "Yeah, it must run in the family," he said, nodding toward Stacy with a nonchalant shrug. The thought of Dennis in a rap battle was comical and oddly fitting for the night's unexpected developments.

As they gathered around the fire, the conversation flowed naturally until Stacy, with a hint of curiosity and concern, broached the topic of Jeremy's argument with Kristen.

"So, what was Bubble Yum's deal, Jer?" she asked, her tone playful yet inquisitive. "Is she in a huff over her hair again?"

Jeremy couldn't help but laugh at Stacy's use of 'Bubble Yum'—he'd always appreciated Stacy's sarcastic pet names for Kristen.

"No, it wasn't about her hair," he groaned, a thoughtful expression crossing his face as he stared into the dancing flames. "We just had some stuff to work through, you know? Things have been intense lately."

As they sat around the fire, the conversation took a turn when Missy, with genuine concern, asked Jeremy about his relationship. "Are you guys good, Jeremy? I swear I'm not probing; I'm just interested."

Before he could respond, Stacy interjected with a hint of irritation. "Ugh, they're just fine. It's annoying, really. They fight, and then they make up or make out, or whatever. It's disgusting." She then turned to Jeremy. "You're so much better than her, Jeremy. She's—well, vapid. She has no real substance. I'm sorry, I just don't like her and never will."

Missy, looking surprised, chimed in. "Why not, Stacy? Why do you hate her so much? I've known Kristen for a long time, and she's not the evil person you think she is."

"That's exactly why," Stacy replied quickly. "What you just did there, Missy. Kristen would never do that. Here I am talking shit about her, and you stood up to question why. Kristen would've just gone along with it."

Missy looked confused. "What do you mean?" she asked.

"It's simple," Stacy explained, looking directly at her. You care, and she doesn't. You took the time to ask about my feelings, but Kristen could never be bothered to do that. It's just gross. Us girls need to stick together. I promise you, if she was sitting here instead of you, she would have joined right in. She would've tossed you right under the bus without thinking twice.

Exasperated, Stacy turned to Jeremy with a stern look. "Seriously, dude," she said, glaring at him as the campfire flames cast dramatic shadows across her face. This chick right here, in case you didn't already know, is your type."

Missy sat quietly. A hint of rose washed her face as she lowered her head. "Thanks, Stace, but we're just friends," she smiled.

The conversation highlighted the contrasting views and dynamics within their group. Stacy's blunt assessment of Kristen contrasted with Missy's defense, painted a vivid picture of their differing perceptions.

Caught in the middle, Jeremy listened thoughtfully, his mind weighing the complex relationships and loyalties that defined their circle.

Missy's blush deepened with a mix of flattery and a hint of longing in her eyes as the conversation unfolded.

Sensing the subtle dynamics at play, Jeremy continued to tread carefully, balancing his words to respect Stacy's strong opinions and Missy's more reserved nature. He acknowledged Missy's commendable qualities but also felt compelled to offer a defense for Kristen.

"Kristen's got her flaws, sure," Jeremy admitted, "but there's more to her than meets the eye. She's complicated, and yeah, a bit immature, but her heart's in the right place."

Stacy, usually quick to judge, seemed to mull over Jeremy's words. Her look softened with a sign of deep respect and understanding. She may not have been Kristen's biggest fan, but she respected Jeremy's decision to navigate his path in the relationship.

Missy, on the other hand, was quietly thoughtful. Though she had feelings for Jeremy, she wasn't driven by jealousy. Her more profound wish was for a different outcome, but she knew the importance of gracefully handling the situation. Balancing her newly rekindled friendship with Kristen and her feelings for Jeremy was delicate.

As they continued their conversation by the fire, their attention was diverted by a light blue Buick Skyhawk slowly approaching. As the car parked, a lone figure emerged from the shadows, adding a new dynamic to the evening.

Julie Nichols stepped into the light, catching the group's attention. "Hey, is my sister here? Sarah Nichols?" she asked, looking around. "She told me there was a party here. I would have been here sooner, but my folks had me locked down for dinner. I swear, I come home from college for one weekend, and it's like I can't have any fun at all."

Missy, ever the helpful one, offered to assist. "I'll help you find her. They're all out back," she said as she got up to help Julie find her sister.

The mood shifted as Stacy, perhaps feeling the weight of her earlier comments, turned to Jeremy with a more somber expression.

"I'm sorry, dude," she began. "I can't say I didn't mean what I said about Kristen. It's just that I know she's not great for you. It's just hard to see you with someone who doesn't seem to value you the way you should be."

Jeremy nodded, understanding where Stacy was coming from. "I know, Stace. And I appreciate your honesty. I'm just trying to figure things out, you know? It's complicated."

Stacy's tone hinted at frustration as she addressed Jeremy's situation. "Complicated? Really?" she scoffed. "You're eighteen, for Christ's sake. Just break up with her. It's our senior year; you've just helped win a huge game, and now there's this totally gorgeous, extremely smart, blonde babe who's definitely into you. And you're still hung up on Kristen?"

She shook her head in disbelief. "I mean, come on, dude. You're choosing someone like Kristen over a girl with actual substance like Missy. You're not seeing things clearly. She's the real deal. I'm not into girls, but I can even see that she's something special. She could make anyone reconsider their preferences, you know?"

Jeremy listened, taking in Stacy's perspective. Her blunt words, though harsh, were laced with genuine concern for him. He knew Stacy always spoke her mind, regardless of how her opinions might be received, and he respected that.

The fire crackled between them, casting warm light over their faces. Despite having lived countless lives, Jeremy found Stacy's words refreshing. It was as if she wielded a special power, making the invisible visible.

Her straightforwardness made him question his feelings, forcing him to reflect on his obsession with Cassandra. Had he been so focused on his quest that he missed the chance for something real with Missy?

As soon as the thought entered his head, he pushed it away. With her tragic fate set in stone, pursuing Missy felt like chasing a mirage. Jeremy had achieved his goal for Missy—her acceptance into the group and her true self was finally being recognized. With a sense of closure, he could let her memory shine for who she truly was.

44

COSMIC STOMP

DEL CAREFULLY PARKED Dutchie's Turismo behind Ryan's Liquors, the storefront's neon lights illuminating the car's exterior.

"Stay here," Dutch said sharply. "I'm still pissed that you lied about Julie waiting for us."

"Look, Dutch, I swear," Del began, trying to explain himself. "Her sister told me she'd be home. I thought she was interested— I promise." "Dutch shrugged dismissively, clearly disappointed."

"She's probably a waste of time anyway." He was still grappling with the loss of Cheech earlier in the evening and the mishap with the keg tap, and now this failed setup with Julie only added to his frustrations. Del, sensing Dutch's mood, attempted to lighten the atmosphere.

"Hey, man, there are plenty of girls back at the cottage. Let's just get a new tap and head back. I wasn't trying to—"

Dutch cut him off, "Save it. I'll be right back." He stepped out of the car and headed into the store, his mind a whirlwind of thoughts.

Alone in the Turismo, Del reflected on the situation. He didn't mean to mislead Dutch but understood his friend's frustration.

Meanwhile, Dutch, walking through the aisles of Ryan's Liquors, felt a wave of blame wash over him. He had wanted the party to be perfect, a celebration to remember, but it felt like everything was spiraling out of control. He hated himself for his reactions earlier – the outburst over Cheech, the frustration with the keg – realizing that his desire for a flawless evening might have been unrealistic.

Looking for the Rumplemintz, he considered adding hard liquor to a party that hadn't started well. "This stuff is gross, and we don't need a bunch of puking cheerleaders," he mumbled to himself, pausing in the aisle of various bottles to take a moment to breathe. He knew he needed to let go of the night's mishaps and focus on salvaging what was left of the party.

As Dutch returned to the car with the new keg tap in hand, he got back into the Turismo and turned to Del with a more subdued expression. "Hey, man, I'm sorry for being a dick earlier," Dutch began. "Sometimes it's hard to keep everything bottled up, you know?"

Del nodded, understanding the weight of his friend's struggles. "I get it, man. It has to be tough. I will always be here to listen, but have you ever thought about talking to someone, like a professional or a school counselor or something? Maybe they could help you deal with everything. It's a lot for anyone to handle."

Sitting back in his seat, Dutch absorbed his friend's suggestion. "You know what? Maybe talking to someone isn't such a bad idea." His voice carried a new tone of determination. "I'll give it a shot. It's worth a try, right?"

Del's response was immediate and supportive. "It's definitely worth trying, man. Life's too short, you know? You never know what might happen if you try. It could be really great for you."

Dutch nodded with a newfound sense of purpose. "I promise, Del, I'll try. That's all I can do, right?"

Del nodded back, his approval clear. "That's all I'm asking, Dutch. Just give it a chance. You might be surprised at how much it helps."

Del, seeking to lift Dutch's spirits further, continued, "You're a hero, man. Leading the Wildcats to victory like you did last night that's no small accomplishment. You've turned things around so quickly. You're stronger than you think."

Del grinned, "Remember how people used to react when you showed up? 'Fucking Dutchie,' they'd say with a groan. But now? Now it's 'Fucking Dutchie' with respect, maybe even a bit of envy. People see you differently now, like a celebrity or something. And man, I'm proud of you!"

Dutch let out a small laugh, a mix of appreciation and disbelief. "A hero, huh? I don't know about all that. But thanks, buddy. You're a good friend, not just to me but to everyone."

The two prepared to head back to the cottage with the energy shifted to a positive outlook for the future.

"Let's make this a night to remember," Del grinned. "I bet we can make it back in less than 15 minutes."

Dutch scoffed playfully, "C'mon, man, you're not giving my car enough credit. Just hit it, and I bet we're back in ten."

As they raced against the clock, Dutch calmly coached Del on navigating the Turismo. "Easy, lay off the gas a bit. Trust her; she'll get us there," he said coolly, his eyes fixed on the road ahead.

Turning off the paved street, the car's tires crunched on the dirt road that led through the dense woods toward the cottage. "Easy, man," Dutch warned as they approached a bend. "There's a tricky turn up ahead. She'll slip if you give her too much gas."

The car's engine roared in response to Del's cautious acceleration.

"Okay, around this turn, it's pretty much a straight shot. You can open her up," Dutch instructed the anticipation building in his voice. A few more minutes, and we'll be tossing down cold ones."

Del, feeling a rush of confidence, prepared to push the car to its limits. But as the road straightened out, he struggled to see through the darkness that enveloped them. Flipping on the Turismo's high beams, Del squinted against the sudden flood of light.

In a heart-stopping moment, the bright beams illuminated a small figure cowering in the middle of the dirt road.

Both boys gasped in surprise. "CHEECH!!!" Dutch yelled, recognition and horror mixing in his voice.

Reacting instinctively, Del jerked the steering wheel, desperately trying to avoid hitting the terrified cat. The Turismo, caught off guard by the sudden maneuver, veered violently. Del fought for control, but it was too late. The car skidded across the dirt road, its tires losing their grip.

With a sickening crunch, they careened into a ditch. The force of the impact was just the beginning, as the car, unable to stop, began to roll over. Metal twisted and glass shattered as the Turismo tumbled, each roll a terrifying symphony of destruction.

Dutch and Del were thrown about helplessly, leaving the world outside a blur of motion and chaos. The car finally came to a rest, its battered frame a twisted wreck in the ditch, the echoes of its demise hanging heavy in the air.

45

THE AFTERMATH

THE LIVELY ATMOSPHERE surrounding the cottage was suddenly interrupted by a horrific sound in the distance. The tearing of metal and a thunderous crash rolled through the woods.

Jeremy's instant reaction was one of alarm. His heart pounded against his chest, a foreboding sense of dread engulfing him. Meanwhile, Stacy, propelled by instinct and concern, didn't waste a second. She sprinted into the darkness, her figure quickly swallowed by the night as she raced towards the crash.

Simultaneously, alarmed and confused, Kristen and Missy burst through the front door. Their faces were mirrors of anxiety. "What was that?" they exclaimed together, their eyes searching Jeremy's for an answer.

Jeremy's mind was a whirlwind of fear and realization. 'It's happened,' he thought in panic. The worst-case scenario he had dreaded was unfolding—the Wyatt Curse had struck, and Dutch was gone.

His thoughts immediately turned to Missy, realizing the dire implications. 'Screw ripples, and waves, screw all of it; she wasn't joining Dutch; his emotions flaring, he turned and looked at her, "Missy, stay here. Do not leave, I mean it," "He demanded with such intensity that allowed no room for argument." Turning to Kristen, he added, "Kristen, keep her here, no matter what. She cannot leave." His words were frantic, and his expression was one of deep concern.

Jeremy's abrupt command took Kristen and Missy aback. The severity in his voice was uncharacteristic and alarming, yet they could not deny the earnestness behind it.

Without another word, Jeremy dashed to his Jeep and drove off.

When he arrived at the crash site, his heart was in his throat, expecting the worst. But the scene before him was something he hadn't anticipated. There was Stacy, sobbing uncontrollably, in the arms of Dutch, who stood silently, his arms hanging limply at his sides. The Turismo was a mangled mess nearby, steam hissing from its busted radiator, barely recognizable from the twisted metal.

Pulling up close, Jeremy quickly hopped out of his Jeep, trying to compose himself amidst the chaos.

"You good, Dutch?" he asked, his voice laced with shock.

"Yeah, I'm good, but the car is toast," Dutch replied, "It was Cheech. He was in the middle of the road. Del swerved to avoid him and lost control."

"Oh shit, Del!" Jeremy exclaimed, his concern shifting as he rushed to the driver's side. "Yo, Del, you alright?"

"I can't get out, Jer— The door is jammed," came Del's strained voice from inside the wrecked car.

Jeremy motioned for Dutch to help. Together, they managed to pull Del out through the opening where the driver's side window had been. He struggled to his feet, visibly disoriented.

"You sure you're okay, man?" Dutch asked, his voice laced with concern.

Del glanced back at the Turismo's wreckage, his expression one of guilt. "Man, Dutch, I'm so sorry," he murmured, his eyes wandering off.

"Antoine," Stacy said sharply, snapping her fingers in front of his face. "Are you okay?"

"Ah, my head is killing me," Del muttered, his words slurred.

"That's it. Get him in the Jeep," Jeremy ordered firmly. "We're taking you to the hospital."

"Wait, no, I'm fine. Let's just go back to the party," Del protested weakly." Dutch needs to get his make-out session in with Julie Nichols—" His voice trailed off, clearly indicating he wasn't in his right mind.

"No, Del. You need to get checked out," Jeremy insisted. Everyone, get in the Jeep. There will be other parties."

As they pulled up to the cottage, a hush fell over the crowd gathered outside, sensing the gravity of the situation. Jeremy quickly got out and addressed everyone, his voice firm yet filled with concern.

"Give him some space, everyone. We are taking him to the hospital." Missy, waiting anxiously with the others, immediately stepped forward,

"Yeah, he's not okay. We need to go, and I'm coming with you. My mom's on duty tonight. She'll bring Dr. Clarke to see him right away."

Jeremy nodded in agreement, then turned to address the partygoers. "Alright, everyone, the party is over!" he announced authoritatively. "Please start packing up and head out."

Kristen approached Jeremy, her expression soft and understanding. "We got it covered, Bear," she said. "Go take care of Del. I'll make sure everything is good here."

Jeremy nodded thankfully at Kristen before turning back to the Jeep. Without hesitation, Missy hopped into the passenger seat. Del, who was slumped in the back seat, clearly in pain and disoriented, struggled to address the group. "Sorry, everyone, I didn't mean to ruin the party."

With Del appearing to get worse, Jeremy quickly got behind the wheel, his mind focused on getting him to the hospital as quickly and safely as possible.

Jeremy drove with a sense of urgency, his thoughts a mix of concern for his friend and relief that they were on their way to getting him the help he needed.

In the tense silence of the Jeep, Jeremy's muttered ramblings filled the space with an air of confusion and concern. "This doesn't make any sense. It's supposed to be Dutch, not Del," he murmured, shaking his head as if trying to dispel his thoughts.

Missy gently placed her hand over his on the Jeep's stick shift, trying to ground him in the present. "Jeremy, I'm here," she said softly. "Whatever it is, you can talk to me."

"You wouldn't understand," he said, his voice full of frustration and fear. "Del was supposed to be untouchable." His statement, more to himself than Missy, hinted at an inner conflict detached from their reality.

Missy's concern deepened as she listened to him. She could sense the gravity of his internal struggle. She understood that it was about more than just the accident.

"Breathe, Jeremy," she said gently, her hand still resting over his. "We'll get Del looked at. He'll be okay."

However, Jeremy was caught in his thoughts, pulling him further away. "And you—you're still here. Why—" he trailed off, his voice laced with confusion.

Taken aback by his question, Missy responded sincerely, "What do you mean, why am I still here? I'm here because I'm your friend and care about you." Realizing that Jeremy was struggling with more than just the accident, Missy decided to focus on getting them to the hospital. "Let's just get there," she said, her tone steady.

Feeling grateful, Jeremy looked down at her hand resting on his. Turning his hand over, he firmly grasped Missy's, their fingers entwined in a mutual understanding of support and concern.

As they approached the hospital, the bright lights of the emergency admissions entrance cut through the night's darkness. Missy, recognizing the need for immediate action, sprung out of the Jeep as soon as it came to a stop.

"Stay here," she instructed Jeremy, her tone reflecting the seriousness of the situation. "I'll run in and get my mom. We need to get some help out here with a gurney for Del. We probably shouldn't move him anymore."

"Alright," Jeremy agreed, watching Missy as she dashed towards the entrance. He stayed in the Jeep, his attention shifting back to Del, who was clearly in pain and disoriented.

Jeremy's heart raced; his eyes fixed on Del's motionless form in the back seat."Del, you've got to be okay, man. You have to be," Jeremy pleaded, his voice trembling with emotion.

The urgency of the situation broke down the concrete walls he had carefully built around his secret—the secret of his repeated life cycles and the roles his friends, especially Del, played in each of them.

"Del, you don't know this, but you've always been destined for greatness," Jeremy began, his words spilling out as he laid out his top scenarios for Del's futures past.

"In my twelfth life, you made it to the NFL. You were the starting tailback for The Dallas Cowboys; you were a legend, a Hall of Famer.

In life twenty-two," he continued, "you were a senator. You wrote laws that change the world. You've always grown into a good man in every life I've lived."

Del, despite his weakened state, managed a faint response. "Jer," he whispered, his voice barely audible, causing Jeremy to immediately perk up, and lean closer. "Yeah, Del? What is it?"

"I hate The Cowboys," Del murmured, a hint of his usual humor flickering through the pain. The corners of his mouth briefly turned upward.

A small, relieved smile crossed Jeremy's face. "I know you do, buddy," he replied as a momentary lightness touched his heart despite the gravity of the situation.

Before he could process the exchange further, Jeremy sensed someone behind him. Turning around, he saw Missy standing there. "Sorry, I didn't want to interrupt," she said softly. "They're coming out now. Dr. Clarke is going to see Del right away."

Jeremy was about to ask how much she had overheard when a team of orderlies arrived. They carefully loaded Del onto a gurney and swiftly wheeled him into the hospital for immediate medical attention.

As Del was taken away, Jeremy's mind continued spiraling. He was relieved that his friend was getting care while he battled with anxiety over what Missy might have heard of his revelations. The weight of his secret, the curse of his repeated lives, and the potential consequences of his unintentional disclosures hung heavily on him.

As he watched Del being whisked into the hospital, Jeremy felt the total weight of his situation. His secret, so long guarded, might now be exposed. But in that instance, his friend's well-being was the most important thing. The implications of his confession would have to wait. For now, Del's safety and recovery were all that mattered.

Missy and Jeremy waited in the hospital lobby as their friends arrived to support Del. Kristen and her cheerleader friends were the first to come.

"How is he?" Kristen asked, her voice laced with worry.

"I'm sorry, we still don't have any information on that," Jeremy replied with a somber tone.

Kristen pulled him in for a warm embrace and whispered into his ear. "Don't worry, Del is tough, and he'll pull through this. Let's stay positive."

Dutch, Stacy, and Dennis arrived next, each carrying their mix of concern and anxiety. Stacy, in particular, was visibly shaken, her usual composure replaced with raw emotion. They found a bench outside the waiting room, sitting together in silence, each lost in their thoughts and prayers, seeking comfort in their own ways.

The hospital waiting room gradually filled with familiar faces. It was as if the entire Huxley High student body and administration had shown up to pray for Del's recovery. The sense of community was strong, a testament to the young man's impact on those around him.

The last to arrive was Del's father, his face showing signs of worry and fatigue. Jeremy immediately stood up to meet him, a knot of apprehension in his stomach.

"Uh, Mr. D, I'm sorry," Jeremy stammered. I'm not entirely sure what happened." He began recounting the events leading to the accident.

Del's father gently interrupted him. His demeanor exuded a wisdom that seemed to transcend the ordinary. His words were carefully chosen and deeply resonant.

"Son, it doesn't matter how this happened or why," he began, his voice steady with a profound depth. "What matters is that we are here together, united in our concern for Antoine. Life is a complex series of events and decisions. Some of these are within our control, and many are not. Moments like these remind us of our shared humanity, vulnerabilities, and how much we need for each other." He paused as his eyes met Jeremy's. "Every one of our choices leads us to where we are. I believe these choices are not entirely ours to make. There's a greater force at play, a form of divine intervention that guides our paths."

His words seemed to echo Jeremy's thoughts and experiences.

"We can try to understand the reasons behind our actions and the motivations that drive us. But the truth is, some things are beyond our comprehension. We are part of a larger design, a grander plan we cannot understand." His eyes, filled with otherworldly compassion, stayed on Jeremy.

"The decisions we make," he continued, "are the footprints we leave behind. Some footprints are deeper and more defined – the details of our larger decisions. Others are faint, almost invisible, and seemingly insignificant choices we might overlook. But at the end of the day, they all line the path we've traveled."

In Mr. Del Coronado's spiritual offering, there was an acknowledgment of the predetermined nature of life's journey, a sentiment that resonated deeply with Jeremy's own experiences of living multiple lives. It was as though he understood the very essence of Jeremy's existence, the repetitive cycles, and the burden that came with such knowledge. His words offered a sense of peace and understanding.

The waiting area was tense as everyone anxiously awaited news on Del's condition. The sound of approaching footsteps broke the silence. Dr. Clarke's presence immediately drew the attention of Del's friends and family. Del's father stood up as the doctor approached, displaying a stoic calmness despite the worry in his eyes.

As Dr. Clarke prepared to deliver his update, Del's father gestured toward Jeremy. "Please, whatever news you have, share it with us both. He's Del's brother."

Jeremy felt a mix of gratitude and apprehension as he stepped closer.

Dr. Clarke took a deep breath before speaking, his voice gentle yet filled with the weight of his message. "I'm afraid I have some difficult news," he began, "Del sustained a significant impact to his head in the accident. Despite our best efforts, the injury was too severe. I'm very sorry, he's gone."

The words landed like a physical blow, sending a shock wave through Jeremy's body. He felt as if the ground had been pulled from under him; his heart sank with a paralyzing grief.

Del's father closed his eyes as he processed the devastating news. When he opened them again, his face had a deep sadness and a quiet strength. He touched Jeremy's shoulder, a silent message of shared grief and support.

As the room observed their reaction, no announcement was needed. The two men's expressions painted a picture that needed no explanation.

Jeremy was sent reeling. The room and the people around him felt distant as if he were observing everything through a thick, soundproof glass. The reality that Del, his best friend, was no longer with them was a cruel twist of fate, something his mind struggled to accept.

'He was supposed to be bulletproof,' Jeremy thought, the phrase echoing in his mind. In every one of Jeremy's repeated lifetimes, Del had been a consistent presence who had attained greatness. His absence now created an unfathomable void, disrupting the fabric of what Jeremy had always known and experienced.

Del had always been the invincible, unbreakable spirit in Jeremy's life. He was more than a friend; he symbolized resilience and success, a person who had always triumphed and excelled. The thought of Del being so suddenly and tragically taken away was not just shocking; it contradicted the very patterns Jeremy had come to expect.

The waiting room, filled with the quiet sounds of mourning, felt like an alien landscape to him now. His tears blurred the faces of friends and classmates, their expressions of grief mirroring his own. But for Jeremy, the pain was compounded by the confusion and disbelief that such a foundational part of his existence could be irrevocably altered. At this moment, the surreal sense of detachment was his mind's way of shielding him from a reality too painful to embrace.

Jeremy's thoughts raced through the many cycles of his life, each marked with its own highs and lows, victories and struggles. It was as if every moment, every experience, stitched together to form the fabric of his existence, and the common thread in this fabric was Del.

Now sucked into a world of confusion and grief, Jeremy was grappling with an unfamiliar sense of solitude. He faced reality for the first time without Del's presence, and the thought was shattering.

This realization brought a profound new depth to Jeremy's emotions. He hadn't just lost Del; he had lost a cornerstone of hope, potential, and purpose in this life. Without Del, the chain of events that would shape this existence unraveled – there would be no Cassandra, no reason to continue the journey of life twenty-six.

At that moment, Jeremy understood what he had to do. Despite the agony it entailed and the promise he had made with his father, he recognized that he had to let go of this life. He had to embrace the unknown and willingly step into the abyss of a voluntary reset. It was the only path that offered hope and a way to reunite with Del in a different life with a fresh start.

46

THE FAREWELL

FIVE DAYS AFTER THE ACCIDENT, under a somber sky, friends and family gathered to say goodbye to Antoine Del Coronado. The air was heavy with a shared grief, and the atmosphere at the cemetery was one of respectful mourning. The service was a testament to Del's impact on those around him, a final tribute to a life that had ended too soon.

Jeremy had deliberately held off on resetting himself until after the services. Part of him clung to the hope that enduring this pain might somehow alleviate the agony of what was to come or at least lend him a new perspective. It was a desperate grasp at finding meaning or relief during an excruciating experience.

Del's casket lay at the center of the gathering, beautifully adorned with blue and gold flowers – the proud colors of Huxley High's Wildcats. It was a fitting tribute, representing the spirit and strength that Del had embodied in life. The colors, so vibrant against the somber tones of the cemetery, spoke of Del's vitality and the legacy he left behind. As the service proceeded, Jeremy stood silently among the mourners, his mind filled with memories spanning multiple lifetimes. Each eulogy, each shared memory of Del, was a reminder of the profound void his passing had left. The Wildcats had lost not just a teammate but a friend, a leader, and a source of inspiration.

In the background, the subtle sounds of nature – the rustling of leaves, the distant call of birds – seemed to underscore the finality of the occasion. The reality that Del was truly gone was inescapable, and with it came a deep sense of loss, not just for Jeremy but for everyone who had known and loved him.

Pulling up to the cottage, Jeremy's eyes swept over the property one last time. In his mind, he envisioned an alternate ending to the party – one where laughter and cheers for the Wildcats' win filled the air. "Well, it was a nice try," he thought, his heart filled with regret.

His plan was simple yet final in its execution. He would hike up to the rock – a place that had become significant in his youth, before cycles– and leap. The details of the act were blurred in his mind, a vague intention overshadowed by the weight of his decision.

His steps were slow and deliberate as he climbed the hill. Reaching the top, he sat down and looked across the sprawling property. The Labrador's ruins, bathed in sunlight, seemed almost surreal. They were a reminder of the passage of time and the layers of history that the land had witnessed. The calm and serene lake was very different from the turmoil in Jeremy's heart.

As he settled on the rock, he allowed himself a moment of reflection. He thought about the events of this twenty-sixth life. He thought about how it would be one of his shortest lives, filled with chaos and unexpected turns. While each life he lived brought unique challenges, joys, and sorrows, this one had been particularly chaotic. Losing Del and the unexpected turns with Dutch and Missy weighed heavily on him.

Sitting on the rock, taking in the view, Jeremy felt a sense of closure. This life was coming to an end. With a deep breath, he prepared himself for what was to come. The leap from the rock was more than just a physical act; it was a release from the current cycle, a step into the unknown of the next life where he'd carry the memories and lessons of this past life just as he'd done 25 times before.

As he stepped closer to the rock's edge, preparing himself to take the leap that would force his reset, an unexpected call from below abruptly pulled him back to reality.

"Jeremy? The voice rang out. "Are you up there?" The sudden interruption caused him to step back, his heart racing.

"Yeah, who's there?" he yelled, trying to identify the person disrupting his solemn moment.

The sound of footsteps crunching on the gravel and grass grew louder as they made their way up the hill towards him. "Hang on, I'm coming up," the voice called out again, filled with concern.

"Missy?" Jeremy asked, recognizing her voice. A mix of emotions flooded him. Deep down, he felt relief, but on the surface, he was frustrated by the intrusion on his planned final moment.

"Hang on," she called up to him, her steps quickening with urgency. A moment later, she appeared from the path, her expression a mix of worry and relief upon finding him.

"What are you doing up here?" she asked, her eyes scanning his posture, his position at the edge, and the pain on his face.

Jeremy, caught off guard by her presence, struggled to find the right words. Her unexpected arrival had thrown a wrench into the plan he had resigned himself to. He stood there, facing her, the moment's significance hanging heavily between them.

"I thought you might come up here," Missy said, her voice gentle. "I saw your Jeep and figured you went for a hike. I just wanted to see you." She paused, "We haven't really spoken since— "she trailed off.

"Yeah, I know," Jeremy interrupted, his voice heavy with grief. "Listen, you should just go home. I'm working through this in my own way. I don't want company." His stance was one of someone deeply mourning, seeking to process their pain alone.

Missy, however, was undeterred. "You don't have to be alone," she said softly, her eyes conveying a deep understanding.

"Miss, look, I can't explain it," he began, his voice filled with frustration. "I'm dealing with this the only way I know how. You wouldn't understand."

Looking directly into Jeremy's eyes, she offered a challenge wrapped in kindness. "Try me," she said, her expression reassuring. "Seriously, I'll listen to anything you need to say. Just give me a chance."

Missy's sincere offer to be a friend, in his moment of despair, he felt a shift within his spirit. Perhaps letting out his thoughts and sharing the weight he had been carrying could offer relief, even if temporary.

With a defeated exhale, he uttered, "Fuck it, why not."

He sat down on the rock, and she joined him, ready to listen to what he had to say, without judgment, to whatever poured from his troubled heart. He felt an unexpected sense of freedom as he broke his long-held concrete rule of silence.

"Remember a few weeks ago, when we were all up here for the first time? Sitting by the fire, talking about reincarnation?" his voice, unsteady at first, gained strength as he spoke.

"Yeah, of course I remember," she replied, her voice filled with encouragement and openness.

"What if I told you, for me, it's real, very, very real?" his words came out in a rush, almost as though he feared being interrupted or disbelieved.

As he explained his cyclical existence, he avoided specific details from his past lives and focused on the overarching timelines and patterns. Surprisingly, she didn't challenge or judge his revelations. She just listened, her expression one of genuine interest and understanding.

Putting some of the pieces together, she interjected, "Wait, so two weeks ago, the day you nearly ran me over and knocked me down on the stairs—That was your first day in this life?"

"Yeah, it was," he confirmed with apprehension.

Her understanding deepened. The strange coincidence of their first encounter and the intensity of their interactions made sense now. She thought, "So you know everything that's going to happen before it does because you've lived through it before?"

He dropped his head. "I thought I did, Miss, until now." He spoke of ripples and how adjustments could cause effects. She listened intently as she tried to piece it all together.

He shared his plan for life at Twenty-Six. He told her about his best life, his first one. The one with Cassandra. He told her that Del was always a constant in every life, the reason he'd met Cassandra, and that he'd never lost him before this life. It was this revelation that connected the dots for Missy.

"Oh my god, it makes so much sense now," she said, remembering Jeremy's conversation with Del in the Jeep before he was brought into the hospital.

She admitted what she had heard before Del was wheeled into the hospital, "That bit about playing for The Cowboys, that really happened," She paused, "I mean, for you, it did, in one of your lives, it really happened?" she asked, a note of amazement in her voice.

"It sure did," Jeremy replied. "It was one of my better lives."

"And he's always outlived you, every time?" she asked, impressively rolling with the complex details of Jeremy's existence.

"Yeah," he confirmed.

"I see," she paused, making more connections. "And because he's gone, you won't meet your wife?"

He nodded.

"Oh my god, Jeremy, this has to be so awful for you." Her face fell, and a chill seemed to wash over her as she looked over the edge of the rock she was sitting on, seeing the jagged landscape below.

"Wait, so you aren't planning on—" she asked as she mimicked the motion of jumping off a rock with her hand. "That's why you're here?"

He looked at her, silent, the gravity of his intent hanging between them.

"Jeremy, don't," she pleaded, her voice filled with urgency. "Please."

Overwhelmed by the weight of his emotions and the gravity of the situation, Jeremy broke down beside Missy. His tears were a testament to the deep pain and confusion he felt.

"I can't, I don't know any other way," he sobbed, his voice choked with grief. "Without Del, there's nobody, no Cassandra, no future."

Her voice was firm yet filled with compassion, and she responded, "You can, Jeremy. I know you can. Please think of the pain and how selfish it would be. We all just buried Del, and now you want us to go through losing you, too? You may think it won't matter because you'll be off in your next life, but you'll leave us all in this one without you."

His sobs continued, but as he listened to her, a realization dawned on him. He had never considered that forcing a reset would devastate everyone he'd leave behind. The thought that his decision to leave this life would cause more pain and loss for his friends was something he had failed to see.

In his desperation to escape the pain of losing Del, Jeremy hadn't fully grasped the selfishness of his plans. Missy's words reminded him that his life was intertwined with others and that his presence and choices affected more than his existence.

As he sat there, weeping and wrestling with these new insights, he began to understand the broader impact of his decision. The idea of causing more grief and sorrow to his friends was something he couldn't bear.

Missy's presence and her willingness to confront him with this harsh reality forced Jeremy to look beyond his suffering and to consider the feelings and lives of those around him.

At that moment, he faced a crossroads. One that required him to weigh his pain against the pain he might cause others. Her words resonated with a clarity and understanding that he hadn't expected but desperately needed.

As she looked at him, her eyes seemed to be staring directly into his soul. "I want you to listen to me, Jeremy, "she said, her voice stern yet genuine. "I want you to know, first and foremost, I believe you. I may not completely understand it, but I believe you." She put her arm around him and pulled him close." You need to realize what a tremendous gift you have. You've been given lifetimes worth of experiences with your best friend, and you'll probably have more. I think in this life, the universe is challenging you. The powers greater than us are pushing you into an uncomfortable place where you don't know the future."

Her words filled him with a sense of purpose he hadn't realized was missing. He had been trying to manipulate the outcome since the start of this life. He had never considered that there might be greater forces at work. Powers that didn't approve of his attempts to control and shape his path.

"You even said that from day one of this reset, you had a plan," she continued, her voice gentle yet filled with conviction. "You said that you were trying to use your experience to manipulate this life's outcome for your benefit. I can't imagine any higher power being a big fan of that."

Her words were filled with wisdom that resonated deeply with him. She spoke with a gentle assertiveness, her ideas forming a pathway to a different approach to life—one he had never considered.

"Let's think about the what-ifs," she continued, her voice steady and encouraging. "What if you decided just to live this life with an open mind? Accept the time you have, and don't exploit your experience to chase fame and fortune. Instead, try to find what makes you happy. Find your place in the world and be a good person. After all, that's all any of us can really do."

Her suggestion was simple yet profound. It proposed a life lived without the shadows of past experiences or the drive to manipulate the future. It was about finding joy in the everyday and happiness in the little things.

Absorbing her words, Jeremy felt a shift in his heart. For the first time in a long time, he looked forward to the days ahead, not with a plan or a mission, but with an openness to experience life as it came, one day at a time.

"I'll make a promise to you right here," Missy said, her eyes locking with his. "I'll guard everything you've shared with me for the rest of my life. No one will ever know. If you ever need someone to talk to about it, or if things get out of control, find me, and I'll listen, I promise."

As he looked at her, his eyes reflected gratitude and relief. "Thanks, Miss," he said, gaining his composure. "I can't tell you how much that means to me. Knowing I have someone who understands and I can trust changes everything."

He paused for a moment, taking in the view one last time. "We should probably head back down," he suggested, standing up and offering her a hand to help her up. She nodded in agreement, accepting his hand with a gentle smile.

As they began their hike down the hill, there was a comforting silence between them. It was the kind of silence that comes with mutual understanding and shared experiences.

***

As they approached the cottage, they saw Kristen's Z24 and Stacy's Bug parked alongside Jeremy's Jeep, telling them their friends were waiting for them. Jeremy let out a sigh, showing his apprehension.

"They need you, Jeremy," Missy said softly, sensing his hesitation. "And you need them too. It'll be okay, I promise. I'm right here with you."

He nodded, taking a deep breath as they reached the porch. Kristen was sitting on the stairs with Dennis and Stacy, and Dutch was on the old couch. They greeted them with soft, sorrowful smiles that spoke volumes.

"Hey, guys," Jeremy said, his voice filled with gratitude and sadness. "I'm glad you're all here."

Together, connected by tragedy, they would share their sadness and memories and find comfort in each other.

***

Gathered on the cottage's front porch, they began their private memorial for Del. Each taking turns, sharing stories and memories. He had touched each of their lives in profound ways. The stories evoked both laughter and tears, creating a collage of memories that celebrated his life and the joy he had brought to them.

A heavy silence settled over them as the final words of remembrance were spoken. Emotionally spent, they each retreated into their thoughts, wrapped in a blanket of quiet contemplation.

Suddenly, a subtle rustling from the edge of the woods broke the silence, drawing everyone's attention. At first, it was faint, but as the rustling grew steadily, all eyes turned towards the source. Out of the shadows of the trees, Cheech emerged. His movements were filled with purpose, cutting through the somber atmosphere like a ray of light. With an agile leap, he jumped into Dutch's lap.

"Oh man, Cheech," Dutch exclaimed, his voice cracking with emotion as he hugged the cat. "I can't believe you came back. I'm never letting you go." He sobbed.

As Cheech nestled comfortably into Dutch's lap, the group couldn't help but feel an overwhelming emotional connection. It was as if Del had guided Cheech back to them, a gesture of love and care characteristic of their lost friend. This was more than mere coincidence; it felt like a tender, deliberate message from Del, reassuring them that he was still with them. At that moment, they all knew that while he wasn't physically there, his spirit was.

As the evening sky transitioned from the warm hues of sunset to the deeper blues of twilight, the group gathered closer, united by the day's emotions and Del's memories. In the quiet that surrounded them, a shared resolve began to take shape—a commitment to honor his memory in how they lived their lives.

"We should make a promise," Stacy suggested, her voice steady despite the tears in her eyes. "To live as Del did, with kindness, laughter, and loyalty."

Dennis, his eyes lifted towards the star-filled sky, chimed in with a thoughtful tone. "And let's not forget to face each day with the same positivity Del always had." His voice carried a mix of nostalgia and inspiration, resonating with the heartfelt commitment shared by the group.

Dutch leaned forward, his strong arms wrapped protectively around Cheech, who purred contentedly in his embrace. The night of the accident weighed heavily on his mind, and as he spoke, his voice carried both vulnerability and determination.

"The night of the accident," he began, his gaze distant for a moment before focusing on his friends, "when we were out at Ryan's, Del said he thought I should see someone, talk about everything that happened to me, my family, all of it." He paused, his fingers gently stroking Cheech's soft coat as if seeking comfort. "I think I'm gonna do it," he continued, his tone resolute. "The truth is, I've been carrying this shit around for way too long." He let out a heavy sigh, his eyes reflecting the weight of his past. "But I'm done with all the bullshit, no more anger. I'm done hating myself."

His voice grew stronger as he spoke with a fire of determination burning inside him. "I'm going to try to be a better guy, not just for me, but for all of you. I'm going to treat each of you with the respect you deserve. We're in this shit together, and I'm going to let any of you down."

His words hung in the air, a promise of redemption and growth, spoken in the colorful language that only Dutch could muster. As he held Cheech close, it was clear he was ready to face his demons and become the person he knew he could be.

Absorbing the moment's energy, Missy offered her perspective, her voice filled with a newfound understanding. "Del had a way of rolling with the punches," she reflected. "We should try to be more like that. I know I spend way too much time worrying about my big plans.

She paused, her gaze drifting over to Kristen. "Until these last few weeks, I was so focused on my future that I never let anyone get to know me. It cost me years with my best friend," she said, giving Kristen a soft, regretful smile. "I would never have gotten to know any of you, Del included, if I hadn't let you all in." Her eyes brightened as she continued, "Del always just flew by the seat of his pants. Everything seemed so effortless for him."

Jeremy, feeling a surge of agreement, jumped in. "That's the Del magic in a nutshell right there. He never sweated the small stuff, didn't try too hard, and never beat himself up when things didn't go his way. He kept positive, and positivity was attracted to him."

"I think having a plan is good," Missy added, her eyes flickering with determination as she glanced over at Jeremy. Her voice was filled with conviction as she continued, "But if we can't be flexible, we could miss out on what's happening around us. Life is like a rollercoaster, you know? Sometimes, you just have to hold on tight and enjoy the ride."

Jeremy nodded, his eyes meeting Missy's in silent agreement. He understood her message loud and clear,

Their shared stories and memories painted a clear picture of Del's way of being—his effortless charm, unwavering positivity, and remarkable ability to make connections with anyone.

Together, they committed to keeping Del's spirit alive throughout their lives. Embracing his easygoing and positive outlook was their tribute, a way to keep his spirit alive and honor their friend's legacy.

Kristen, who had been quietly reflective, spoke up with determination. "I've been thinking," she began, her gaze drifting over the group before settling on Jeremy. "I need to make a change too. I need to stop being— well, a bitch; I don't want to judge people anymore," She shot a glance at Dutch, "and I am going to let things happen the way they're supposed to."

She paused, a hint of vulnerability in her eyes. "I just want to work hard to make those I love happy," she continued, her words sincere. "I want to be more understanding, more patient." She paused, "Del always had a way of bringing out the best in people, and I spend way too much time putting people down. It's not right. I'd rather be someone who helps others, just like Del did. I'm done making people feel bad about themselves." She dropped her head, feeling ashamed. "It's not who I am—it's ugly."

Her statement was met with the group's nods and soft smiles, each understanding the depth of her commitment. It was a significant moment for Kristen, an acknowledgment of her desire to grow and embrace the positive aspects of life inspired by Del's memory.

Jeremy, moved by her words, reached out and gave her hand a reassuring squeeze, a gesture of support and acceptance. He looked at each of his friends, feeling a sense of solidarity and purpose. "Del may not be with us physically, but it sounds like he left us with something priceless— his approach to life.

He paused, a soft chuckle escaping his lips as he reminisced. "Del lived easily like the world was a playground and every moment an opportunity to find joy. He didn't just walk through life; he danced with a rhythm all his own. It was infectious, you know? His spirit was like a guiding light in the dark, showing us all how not to take life too seriously." He sighed a gentle, wistful note in his voice. "I'm sure gonna miss him."

The words he had just spoken about Del, about living easy, resonated deeply, stirring something that had long been dormant. He decided to "roll with it," embracing the unpredictable tides of his twenty-sixth life with open arms and a full heart. He would give up chasing his meticulously drawn plans, nor would he attempt to manipulate the flow of life to fit into a rigid plan of his own design.

Instead, Jeremy envisioned a path inspired by Del's philosophy on life. He saw himself waking up every day with a sense of curiosity rather than a checklist of goals or a list of dos and don'ts. He imagined making decisions based on what felt right in the moment rather than a well-organized strategy. This new approach felt like a breath of fresh air.

Jeremy realized how, for lifetimes, he had been so focused on his plans and ambitions that he missed the simple joys around him—the laughter of friends, the beauty of adventure, the thrill of an unplanned journey. He thought about Del's effortless way of finding happiness in the little things and his ability to turn the ordinary into something extraordinary.

Living like Del meant more than just a carefree attitude; it was about being present, fully and completely. It was about listening to the rhythm of life and making it your own. It meant being able to ride the waves of change and trusting that there was always a melody to be heard and a dance to be danced.

As Jeremy sat with his friends around him, bathed in the fading light of the day, he made a silent promise to himself. He would live the rest of this twenty-sixth life with a spirit of openness and adventure. He would let life unfold in its mysterious ways, finding joy in the unexpected. He would honor Del's memory by living each day with an open heart, his soul free to enjoy the journey.

47

THE NOOK

THREE YEARS after graduating from Huxley High, Jeremy returned home carrying a mix of nostalgia and anxiety. Now a junior at Vermont State, his life had evolved, yet the past still hung on to him.

Gregg's late journey to sobriety couldn't undo the years of damage he'd done to his liver, and he was now confined to a hospital bed. Sitting beside his father, Jeremy clung to the hope that Gregg might find a gentler path in another life.

After a visit with his father, Jeremy was swiftly pulled back into the life he had left behind.

Stacy had been begging him to come home for a visit since he'd left for college. Finally succeeding, she brought him to a local dive bar in Amherst, where Dutchie had gotten a job as a bouncer. It was the same bar where Jeremy had met Cassandra so many lifetimes ago, The Nook.

Over a few beers, Jeremy and Stacy jumped into a sea of memories and life updates. The last few years had been challenging; Dutch had put off finding counseling, but eventually, after an emotional breakdown the previous summer, he decided it was time to honor his promise to Del and get some help. Stacy had been his anchor throughout.

In their conversation, Jeremy's thoughts often drifted to Del. That night by the fire when Del had playfully pointed out Stacy's feelings for Dutch— a prediction that now had become a reality. The couple shared a small apartment in South Hadley near Mt. Holyoke College, where Stacy was a Junior. They were a perfect match.

Catching Jeremy up to speed, Stacy laughed, recounting their land-lord's initial no-pet policy, which quickly changed upon meeting Dutch and his imposing yet endearing persona. Cheech, now a cherished part of their lives, was a testament to their growing bond.

As Stacy excitedly shared details about her upcoming theater produc-tion and classes, Jeremy listened intently as his vision occasionally drifted to Dutch. He reflected on the strange twist of fate that spared his friend's life, a life that was traded for Del's. It wasn't resentment that filled Jeremy's heart, but relief. Relief that the black cloud that once hung over Dutch had vanished.

As the two finished their pitcher, Jeremy was ready to call it a night. The long drive from Vermont and the visit with his father had drained him.

Listen, Stace, I should probably get going," he interjected gently, rubbing his eyes. "This has been great, but it's been a long day."

Stacy, undeterred, shot back with mock indignation. "Oh hell no!—You're not pulling that shit with me. It's barely ten o'clock – the night is still young!" Her plea was playful yet insistent.

Unable to resist her persuasive charm, Jeremy conceded with a small smile, "Alright, one more. But I gotta drive, so make mine a Sprite."

"Fine, you're so responsible," she teased, waving over the bartender.

As Stacy engaged in a lighthearted conversation with the bartender, Jeremy's attention was involuntarily pulled back to the door, and his heart skipped a beat at the sight unfolding.

Kristen was handing her ID to Dutch with her usual impeccable style. She snapped her gum, just as she always did, and her hair gracefully fell around her face. Jeremy found himself completely captivated, unable to take his eyes off her. It had been years since he last saw her.

Their relationship had been a defining part of his final year at Huxley. Unlike previous lifetimes, they had stayed together through it all. After they lost Del, they needed each other, but ultimately, a few weeks after Jeremy graduated, they decided to end their relationship. There was no dramatic breakup, no heated argument—just a mutual understanding that their time together was over. Kristen had let him go, releasing them both into their futures with a graceful acceptance.

Her sudden appearance at the pub, with her characteristic flair, stirred a mix of emotions in Jeremy. He watched as she snatched her ID from Dutch, her expression revealing a hint of irritation – clearly, Dutch still enjoyed pressing her buttons.

"Fucking Dutchie," Jeremy thought with a soft smile, observing the brief exchange.

As Kristen's gaze swept the room, her eyes found Jeremy's. She instantly transformed, adopting a flamboyant wave and striding towards him with her signature sashay. "Hey stranger!"— she exclaimed with a bright smile, her voice a familiar melody to Jeremy's ears. She leaned in, kissing his cheek softly, a gesture of warm familiarity.

"Hey Stacy!" she greeted with the same sweetness.

"Hey Red," Stacy responded with playful sarcasm.

Kristen's presence seemed to light up the space around them. "I'm so glad you guys are here," she said enthusiastically. "This place can have a lame crowd sometimes. Too many townies."

Jeremy found himself caught in Kristen's sudden whirlwind of energy. Her vivid and lively presence contrasted with his mellow, reflective mood. He observed her, noting the subtle changes time had brought her, yet so much of her remained the same.

Kristen's infectious energy filled the air as she bubbled with excitement. "This is going to be a fun little reunion. I'm so excited," she beamed.

The scene abruptly shifted before Jeremy could probe further about the reunion she mentioned. A tall young man appeared behind Kristen, spinning her around with an ease that spoke of familiarity. In an instant, they were locked in a passionate embrace, their lips meeting in a moment that seemed perfectly choreographed. Kristen's squeal of delight was unmistakable.

Jeremy turned to Stacy, who was amused and slightly disgusted by the display. But Jeremy's attention was quickly drawn back as the couple separated.

Jeremy's expression registered pure shock as he recognized who it was. "Dennis!" he blurted out, unable to mask his surprise.

Stacy, meanwhile, raised her hands to cover her face, stifling her laughter and awaiting Jeremy's reaction. She glanced through her fingers at Dutch, who was also awaiting Jeremy's response to the sudden twist. When their eyes met, Dutch just shook his head and shrugged at Jeremy, silently acknowledging his bewilderment.

However, Jeremy's focus quickly returned to Dennis as the couple parted, revealing him fully.

"Holy shit, man!" Jeremy boomed," You must've grown a foot!" He couldn't help but marvel at Dennis's striking physical transformation, who now stood with an imposing and confident presence. Dennis, visibly sheepish and a touch uneasy, offered a tentative smile. "Oh hey, Jeremy."

The awkwardness of facing Jeremy, the ex of his current girlfriend, was evident in his demeanor despite his efforts to appear nonchalant.

Stacy cut through the awkwardness. "Oh yeah, they're a thing now." Her tone was dry, laced with her typical blunt humor.

Jeremy, still processing the unexpected coupling, nodded slowly. It was an odd match, yet somehow, it made perfect sense. Kristen, picking up on his surprise, chimed in, "Oh, you didn't know? I thought your buddy here," she gestured toward Stacy with a teasing smile, "would've filled you in by now."

"No, the topic of your love life didn't come up," Stacy retorted playfully. Her mock disdain for Kristen called back to an earlier, more complicated time in their relationship.

Jeremy, eager to squash any tension, turned to Dennis with a sincere expression.

"Well, I think it's pretty great, you two, together; seriously, it's awesome," he offered, extending his hand to Dennis in a gesture of goodwill. "As long as you both are happy, that's all I care about. Plus, you guys look perfect together."

Kristen beamed, wrapping her arms around Dennis's waist. "Yeah, we are happy, and we do look good together," she affirmed with a contented smile, her typical vanity showing through with a hint of sarcasm. "He just gets me." She added before kissing him sweetly.

As Jeremy looked around, his eyes inevitably drifted back to Dutch at the door, checking in on his old friend. The evening unfolded with one surprise after another.

At that moment, Jeremy recognized the beauty in life's unpredictability. Each individual's path was uniquely their own, weaving through a collection of evolving experiences.

As Jeremy watched his friend check IDs at the front door, he observed Dutch's demeanor shift when he was handed what appeared to be fake IDs by a pair of underage kids, eager to blend in with the older crowd. Dutch's temper flared up, his frustration evident as he informed the young men that he'd be keeping their IDs.

As Stacy watched, she couldn't help but chuckle. "He really loves this job. It gives him the freedom to haze young kids," she commented, amused. "It's perfect for him."

The group watched as Dutch confronted the underage patrons with a stern, "Listen, you turds, your IDs are mine now. Beat it before you make me do something I'll regret." His words seemed to fall on deaf ears as the young men stepped closer, pleading for the return of their fake IDs and promising to leave if they got them back.

As Jeremy watched the heated interaction, the evening took yet another unexpected turn when Missy stepped through the door. Slipping past the underage kids and offering a quick hug to Dutch, she scanned the room. When her eyes finally landed on the group, she waved in her typical, understated, and sweet manner, slightly frowning at the scene unfolding with Dutch and the rebellious young men.

With Missy's entrance, the atmosphere in The Nook changed as if charged by her presence. She moved with cinematic grace, like a slow-motion scene, her elegance and poise transforming the space around her.

Jeremy was rendered speechless. His characteristic eloquence seemed to have deserted him, reverting him to an awkward version of himself reminiscent of how Dennis once was.

As Missy approached with her radiant smile, she greeted everyone warmly. Her natural charm and grace were evident. Jeremy captivated yet unable to articulate his thoughts, watched as she effortlessly mingled, exchanging greetings and hugs. She had always been attractive to Jeremy, but now her allure had a new depth and maturity.

He felt himself becoming more awkward as he observed the scene. As she chatted with Stacy and Kristen, her laughter was light and engaging, and she occasionally glanced his way. Her eyes twinkled with amusement and curiosity as if sensing his internal struggle.

When Missy finally turned to greet Jeremy, she did so with genuine warmth. "Hey, homecoming," she said sweetly, with no hint of mockery. Her smile was sincere as she embraced him tightly, pulling back only to look into his eyes, making him feel like they were the only two people in the room. "How are you?" she asked.

"Good, Miss, really good," Jeremy replied, his voice slightly strained.

Missy took a seat beside him. "I thought you were at B.C.," Jeremy asked, recalling her previous plans. "Wasn't that the plan?"

"That *was* the plan, yes, and it was great for a while, but plans change," she replied, her voice echoing a sentiment from the night of Del's memorial. "Classes were good, grades too. I even made some terrific friends— can you believe it? But it didn't feel right. Something drew me back, so I transferred to Amherst with Kristen. We're roommates now, and it's amazing."

"That's really great, Miss," Jeremy nodded, impressed.

"It can be lonely sometimes, though," she added. "Kristen spends almost every weekend with Dennis at his fraternity house."

"Dennis is in a frat?" Jeremy interrupted, surprised.

"Oh, yes. Big D is quite the party animal now. He's studying sports management at UMass, and Coach McHale helped him get a spot as the football team's equipment manager. He's on the sidelines every game. He really is living his best life."

As Missy spoke, Jeremy couldn't help but draw parallels. "I guess he's filled with a bit of that Del Coronado magic, huh?" he said with a smile.

Missy's thoughtful agreement with Jeremy's observation about Dennis added depth to their conversation. "It's as if a part of Del's soul lives on in my brother," she mused, pausing to reflect. "Honestly, I think there's a little piece of him in all of us.

"Kristen is studying nursing, of all things! Can you believe it? And Stacy," her expression brightened, "has transformed into a fearless performer. I saw her one-woman show last spring. She wrote, acted, directed, and designed the whole thing— It was incredible!"

Jeremy's voice carried a note of regret. "I heard about that," he said. "She wanted me to see it, but I couldn't bring myself to come back."

Missy, intrigued, probed gently, "Why not?"

He hesitated, shrugging. "I don't know. I guess I was scared," he confessed, dropping his voice. "Scared of what coming back would mean." Jeremy was careful with his words, knowing Missy understood his cyclical existence but not the full extent of her and Dutch's intertwined fates. Yet, he felt a sense of peace, believing they were now safe.

"I guess I just needed some time," he added, glancing away.

Missy looked at him with empathy. "Well, time is something you'll always have," she reassured him softly.

They talked long into the night, well past the pub's closing time. Dennis and Kristen had left earlier for an after-hours party at his frat house. And as Dutch finished locking up, Stacy ushered Jeremy and Missy outside. The final four lingered briefly for goodbyes. Missy was the first to leave, her silhouette gradually disappearing into the night.

Stacy turned to Jeremy, her tone serious. "You know what, Jeremy Anderson, my oldest and dearest friend? You, sir, are a fucking idiot." Her words caught him off guard. "If you don't chase after her immediately, I swear to Christ, I will kick your ass right here, right now," she threatened.

Dutch joined in with a serious tone, supporting her threat, "And I'll help her."

"This is your moment, Jeremy. Get the girl! Go! Now! Run!" Stacy urged, pushing him forward.

Spurred by Stacy's words, Jeremy's heart raced. His mind focused on a single thought – he had to catch Missy and tell her he needed her. In this twenty-sixth life, the quiet, happy existence Missy had suggested was impossible without her. He sprinted, rounding the corner, and when he did, that's when the lights went out.

Jeremy was unaware that Missy had turned back, intending to return to him and they collided, causing them to tumble to the ground. Jeremy instinctively held her in his arms.

"Oh my god! Missy! Are you alright?" Jeremy gasped.

Missy, slightly dazed but with a hint of humor, joked, "Jesus, Jeremy, we've got to stop running into each other like this." Her comment, a classic cliché for the moment, brought a brief, nervous laugh from Jeremy amidst the unexpected chaos of their reunion.

He held onto her tight as a sea of emotions swirled within his heart. He opened his mouth to speak, but the words caught in his throat.

"Missy, I—" he stuttered, his heart pounding in his chest.

Before he could finish, she gently interrupted, her voice soft. "I know," she said, looking directly into his eyes. "Me too."

He looked at her, the urgency of his sprint replaced by the moment's intensity. All the unspoken words and the events of their complicated past seemed to hang in the air. They remained on the ground for a few seconds, the world around them fading. It was just Jeremy and Missy and the connection that had somehow endured through the twists and turns of their lives.

Eventually, they helped each other to their feet, still holding onto one another, refusing to let go. As they stood there, the night's earlier events— their shared history, everything that had happened between them– all seemed to pale compared to this unexpected moment of honesty and vulnerability.

As they held each other close, their bond solidified, transforming into something unbreakable and enduring. It was as if the universe had carved their connection in stone. The cosmic forces that first drew them together in the early moments of life twenty-six seemed to be at work once more, weaving their destinies together in synchronicity. This time, neither Jeremy nor Missy wanted to resist the pull.

As they embraced, they found a sense of completeness. Their bodies aligned effortlessly, mirroring each other in form and presence. Simultaneously, their souls seemed to unlock new depths within each other, filling a void they never knew existed. In each other's arms, they discovered a wholeness, their hearts aligned, their souls one. It felt both exhilarating and right.

Life's uncertainties and challenges lay ahead, but in that moment, under the soft glow of the streetlights, all that mattered was their connection. Jeremy and Missy, united by an unbreakable bond, would step into the future together, ready to embrace whatever surprises it would bring. Their journey, marked by fate, was only beginning, and they were prepared to face it together.

48

LIFE TWENTY-SIX

May 5th, 2037:

Jeremy had lived his life filled with freedom and peace. He had allowed events to unfold naturally and never tried to force or manipulate the timeline. Yet, in a twist of fate, he found himself called back to The Hollywood Roosevelt Hotel.

Throughout his adulthood, Jeremy's career flourished. He had become a multifaceted land developer known for rejuvenating historical properties. Because of this, he caught the attention of the hotel's management company. As always, at least for Jeremy, the landmark had faded from its golden age splendor, and the owners believed that Jeremy was the key to restoring the hotel to its former glory. Accepting the project felt like more than a professional decision; he was being pulled back to where he was supposed to be.

Missy, his partner in this life's journey, understood the significance of this trip. Their life together had been an open book, built on a promise of honesty made on a solemn day in 1996.

However, the realization that May 5th, 2037, would arrive during this trip weighed heavily on both of them. Fully aware of the implications of this date, Missy was heartbroken at the thought of not being by her husband's side during his final moments.

In his ever-caring and thoughtful manner, Jeremy reassured her that everything would be alright. He made all the necessary arrangements to ensure she would be cared for after he was gone, and he made a heartfelt promise to look out for her in life Twenty-Seven. This was a vow that transcended time and space, a testament to the depth and resilience of their bond.

As Jeremy arrived at The Roosevelt, he felt as though he had come full circle. The hotel, steeped in his personal history and memories, symbolized a journey spanning multiple lives. Preparing to step into the unknown of his next life, Jeremy carried with him the love, experiences, and lessons of life twenty-six – particularly those shared with Missy, the woman who had changed everything for him.

Checking in at the hotel's front desk, the subtle yet significant changes since his last reset didn't escape his notice. The touchscreen kiosks he remembered were now replaced by a more modern, streamlined system of QR-coded check-ins meant to be easily accessible with a smartphone.

"Oh, this is the first thing to go," he mused silently, mentally jotting it down for his presentation scheduled the next day– a presentation he knew he would never get to deliver.

Fully aware of his existence's cyclical nature, Jeremy understood that setting a meeting for May 6th at noon was an exercise in futility. Once settled in his room, he meticulously compiled his notes and recommendations for the hotel's revival. He set up a delayed send on his email, planning to share his vision with the meeting attendees the morning after his expected departure to the next life. It was his way of leaving a legacy gift, a contribution to the lives and the world he would leave behind.

Jeremy found himself thinking beyond the scope of his own existence for the first time. He thought about the future of this timeline in his absence. The idea that his work and his impact could live on beyond his physical presence filled his heart. It was a new perspective for him that extended his sense of purpose and connection to the world.

This change in perspective marked a notable shift. It involved acknowledging the temporary nature of his physical self while realizing the lasting impact of his actions and ideas. As he prepared for his next life, Jeremy took comfort in knowing that his contributions to The Roosevelt and the world would make a difference.

As he sat in his room, his thoughts drifted to Del, his best friend, and brother in spirit. Unlike previous cycles, where the approach of a reset filled him with unease and a sense of loss, this time was different. Reflecting on his life, he felt a surge of celebration and joy. His heart was full, not just with the memories of what had been, but with the anticipation of reuniting with Del. It was a comforting thought, bringing a peaceful smile to his face.

324

He picked up his phone and knew his next call would be difficult. Dialing Missy's number, he braced himself for the emotional conversation ahead. When she answered, his voice was calm but full of emotion. He took the time to reassure her, to express how deeply he loved her and how important she was in helping him find peace in life twenty-six.

"Your life is a gift," he told her, his words tender and genuine—"Fill it with joy, just as you have filled mine." As the words left his mouth, he thought back to his first life with Cassandra and her request before she passed—a request he failed to honor.

He spoke of their souls meeting again, a statement that, for him, was not just a comforting thought but a fact grounded in the reality of his existence. It was a promise he could keep, a certainty that transcended the physical limitations of their current life.

The conversation, though difficult, was filled with a sense of peace and understanding. As they said their final goodbyes, there was an unspoken acknowledgment of the depth of their connection. It was a bond that would endure beyond time and space.

Hanging up the phone, he felt a sense of closure. He would face this reset with acceptance and a heart full of gratitude for the life he had lived this time around.

As he looked out of his hotel room window, taking in the view of the city one last time, he was ready for whatever came next, secure in the knowledge that the bonds of love and friendship are eternal.

With the reset drawing closer, Jeremy thought about Missy's teenage advice about breaking away from rigid plans and paths. Her words echoed in his mind, inspiring a shift in his usual approach to waiting for this life to end.

"Why do I do this the way I always do? Sitting here, getting drunk, and waiting?" he thought. "This life had been different from all others; it only made sense that the end should be different, too.

With that thought, he decided to change the script of his usual routine. He threw on a blazer and went down to the hotel bar with a sense of purpose in his step. Settling into a seat, he decided to forego his regular pre-reset scotch, and instead, he ordered a Sprite and asked for a menu.

The woman beside him, busy rummaging through her purse, glanced over and said with a hint of sarcasm, "Sprite, huh? Sounds like you're in for a wild night," she chuckled. "I've got so much crap in here; I can never find anything," she continued as she finally found her phone buried in the clutter of her bag.

Jeremy turned to offer a polite, casual smile, but the moment their eyes met, something extraordinary happened. It was as if the universe itself had orchestrated this encounter. In her eyes, he found something familiar, something magnetic.

-It was Cassandra.

Jeremy's surprise was evident as he caught her gaze. Her quick realization that there might be a reason for his choice of non-alcoholic drink was typical of the Cassandra he remembered – intuitive, perceptive, and quick to adapt.

"Oh, I'm so sorry, that was very rude of me," she apologized with genuine concern.

"No, it's fine," Jeremy replied, trying to regain his composure; his heart raced with excitement and disbelief at this encounter. "You just remind me of someone I used to know."

"Really?" she asked, a playful glint in her eye. "She must be beautiful."

Jeremy couldn't help but chuckle, feeling almost starstruck by her presence. "Yeah, she sure is," he thought but didn't say.

Cassandra, ever gracious, gestured to the bartender. "Let me get your drink. I feel bad for making fun. Red wine for me, please, and I've got his soda."

"Thanks, but you don't have to do that," Jeremy replied, still reeling from the situation. "I know," she said with a smile, "it just seems like you could use a day-maker. Sprites on me! I'm Cassandra, by the way," she said, extending her hand.

Jeremy took her hand, resisting the urge to reveal he knew exactly who she was. "Uh, Jeremy— Jeremy Anderson," he introduced himself.

Recognition flickered in Cassandra's eyes. "Wait, I know you from somewhere, don't I? She looked at him, trying to place his face.

Stuttering and still in shock, Jeremy stuttered, "I, uh—I don't think so."

"Wait, I know; you're the guy with that place out east. In The Berkshires?" She exclaimed.

Jeremy played it cool. "Not the Berkshires, but yeah, that's me."

"The Labrador!" she exclaimed, her memory finally clicking all the pieces into place. "I read the article in Travel Magazine about it. You rebuilt that place. Oh, it's fantastic! We stayed there last Columbus Day weekend. We're planning to go back this summer for a full week. It's amazing! You did a great job bringing that place back to life."

"Thanks, you're very kind," Jeremy replied graciously. "It's been my life's work. I'm very proud of it."

"Well, you should be. We love it," Cassandra exclaimed with genuine admiration. "You've got the whole package going on there."

Jeremy asked, curious about her current life, "So, what brings you here? You said that you are from Amherst, right?"

"I didn't, but you're right. What are you, psychic?" she responded with a slight nod and a giggle.

"Oh, sorry, I thought you said something about Amherst," Jeremy sank, crucifying himself internally.

"It's fine, lucky guess," she said, not giving the comment a second thought. "I'm in town to speak at an event tomorrow night, and I'm a bit of a wreck about it."

Intrigued, Jeremy asked politely, "What kind of event?"

She gestured to a small pink ribbon pinned on the lapel of her blazer. "I'm a survivor," she revealed. Jeremy felt a rush of emotions flood through him. "She beat it!" his internal voice screamed as a sense of pride and relief washed over him.

Cassandra opened up about her story, speaking with a candidness that seemed to suggest a deeper connection between them. She talked about her husband, a doctor, who insisted on regular health checkups for their family. It was during one of these routine checks that her cancer was discovered earlier than it ever had been in any of Jeremy's lives. With the early detection and her husband's profession allowing her access to the best possible care, she beat it.

She spoke of the trials and tribulations, some eerily similar to the challenges she had faced with Jeremy by her side, yet this time, in this life, her story had a different, more triumphant ending.

Cassandra continued, "I'm a writer, and I've written quite a bit about my experience. I've been invited to share my journey. It's an honor, but honestly, I'm terrified."

Jeremy, moved by her openness and resilience, offered words of encouragement. "I'm sure you'll do great. If you can beat cancer, public speaking shouldn't be a problem for you," he said with a supportive smile.

As they sat at the bar together, Jeremy and Cassandra's conversation took them through the landscapes of their lives. Cassandra shared photos of her two children, their joyful moments captured during vacations and holidays. Jeremy found himself genuinely engrossed in these snapshots of her life.

When the topic shifted to his own life, Jeremy spoke fondly of Missy.

Upon learning that they never had children, Cassandra responded with gentle empathy, suggesting, "Maybe in another life."

"Yeah, maybe," Jeremy replied with a note of wistfulness in his voice.

Their exchange was filled with laughter and a sense of connection that bridged the gap between two seemingly new acquaintances. For Cassandra, this was a fresh interaction; for Jeremy, it was a nostalgic reunion and a novel experience at the same time.

Time flew by as they chatted, and before Jeremy realized it, his watch read 8:15 PM. He had let the evening get away from him, surpassing the usual time he had set for himself on these crucial nights.

Jeremy's face flashed with panic, but he quickly regained his composure. "This has been great, Cassandra. A real pleasure," he said sincerely, standing up from the table. "I should head back to my room. I need to finish preparing for an important meeting tomorrow."

He briefly explained his presence at The Roosevelt – consulting on revitalizing the historic hotel, much like his successful project with The Labrador.

Cassandra expressed her admiration. "They're lucky to have you here. It will be amazing if you can do anything close to what you did with The Labrador to this place."

"Thank you," Jeremy said, touched by her words. "Oh, one more thing, when you plan your next visit to The Labrador, call and ask for Dennis; he's my business manager. Tell him you're an old friend. He'll make sure you and your family are treated like royalty."

After exchanging respectful goodbyes, Jeremy rushed back to his room, his heart racing. Sitting on the bed, he watched the clock and mentally prepared himself.

"Okay, five more minutes. This will be fine. This will all be fine," he reassured himself. Reflecting on the life he had just lived, Jeremy felt a sense of contentment. He had learned valuable lessons, lived with love and joy, and left a positive impact.

As the clock edged closer to 8:35 PM, he found himself praying for the first time in a long time. He prayed for release from the cycle, for peace, for no more resets. He wished for an end to the continuous loop of lives, hoping that this time, he could find eternal rest and leave behind the endless journey of rebirths and rediscoveries.

As the digital numbers on the clock silently shifted to 8:45 PM, he braced himself for the inevitable, a ritual ingrained in his being after so many resets. His muscles tensed involuntarily, a physical manifestation of his mental preparation for the pain and disorientation that came with a reset.

He closed his eyes, his breaths becoming shallow and rapid. Every nerve in his body seemed to be on high alert, anticipating the familiar jolt. He waited for the pain that had become a dreaded companion at the end of each life cycle. His hands clenched into fists, a subconscious effort to ground himself in the reality of the moment.

His mind raced with memories and sensations from previous resets. He remembered the sharp, electrical surge that would course through his body. The anticipation of that pain, the discomfort that signaled the end of one life and the start of another, hung heavily in the air.

His entire body was wound tight, like a coil ready to spring. He could almost feel the tickle of electricity on his skin, the air around him charged with the impending shift. Every second that passed felt like an eternity, each tick of the clock amplifying the tension that gripped him.

As the moment reached its peak, when Jeremy was fully prepared to endure the familiar agony, to embrace the end of this life and the start of something new—

Nothing happened.

Jeremy remained still after the initial wave of surprise and confusion, his body frozen in anticipation. The first five minutes passed silently, each second ticking with agonizing slowness. He half-expected, half-hoped for the familiar sensations to begin at any moment, but the room remained still, the only sound being the quiet hum of the air conditioning and his steady breathing.

Ten minutes crept by, and Jeremy's sense of disbelief deepened. His mind raced with possibilities, questions, and a growing realization that perhaps this time was different. He sat motionless, his eyes fixed on the clock, watching the minutes pass without incident.

A half-hour later, the reality of the situation began to sink in. There was no pain. No disorienting leap into a new existence. The reset, the event that had punctuated every one of his lives, simply did not happen.

Jeremy's anticipation gradually gave way to a profound sense of stillness. He relaxed back into his chair, letting out a breath he hadn't realized he'd been holding.

He wanted desperately to call home, to tell Missy that he was still alive, to start the rest of their lives together, but he was afraid that would be premature. He was scared that the reset was still to come, but with a slight difference, much like many events in the early days of his life.

At that moment, he thought about the Nirvana t-shirt Kristen had given him on his 18th birthday—the same design, yet a different color. Jeremy wondered if this was what was happening now. Maybe the reset was running late for no other reason than it felt like it.

He sat and waited, his body still, his breathing calm and even, his mind anything but at peace.

If the reset wasn't coming, what did this mean for him? For his future? The familiar framework he had always relied on was gone, and in its place were limitless possibilities.

As he sat there, waiting, lost in contemplation, the exhaustion of the emotional rollercoaster began to take its toll. His eyelids grew heavy, and the adrenaline that had fueled him through the evening was now giving way to exhaustion.

Slowly, sleep crept up on him. His thoughts became less coherent, fading into the background as the gentle pull of slumber took over. In the quiet, dimly lit room, Jeremy drifted off, his body and mind surrendering to the rest they so deeply needed.

The serene stillness of the morning in Jeremy's hotel room was abruptly shattered by the phone vibrating furiously in his pocket. Roused from a sleep that felt like it had spanned decades, his eyes opened slowly, struggling to adjust to the light of the new day. Wrestling the device from his pocket, he put it to his ear, answering it with a gruff, groggy voice, "Hello?"

"Jeremy Anderson!" The voice on the other end scolding him was unmistakably Stacy's. "Where have you been? I swear to God, I was just about to fly to Los Angeles myself and personally hunt you down and kick your ass."

Hearing Stacy's voice, although aggressive, was comforting to Jeremy. "Oh hey, Stace," he replied, his voice still heavy with sleep.

"We've all been trying to call you since last night. Missy is a wreck; she's been locked in her room, sobbing all night. She won't tell anyone what's wrong," Stacy continued, her worry evident.

Jeremy scrambled for an explanation while trying to piece together the reality of waking up to a day he had never lived before. "I must've forgotten to plug my phone in before bed. I'm sorry. Everything is okay, I promise," he said as his mind raced. "Tell Missy we spoke. I'll call her right away."

The concern in Stacy's voice was unmistakable as it came through the phone, "What's going on, Jeremy? I've never seen her like this. What can I do? Tell me."

"Everything is fine, Stace, I swear." Jeremy insisted, his voice steady and reassuring. "I'll call her right now."

Stacy's voice, somewhat muffled but still discernible, reached out to someone nearby, "He's said he's calling you now."

A shaky voice in the distance called out, "Wait, is it really him?

The background noise swelled with the sound of a door bursting open and hurried footsteps.

Through the muffled chaos, he heard Missy's voice rise in a crescendo of desperation as she ran towards the source of the call before snatching it from Stacy with a flurry of movement. The line was filled with muffled sounds as the phone changed hands in the brief struggle.

"Fine, just take my phone," Stacy's half-exasperated, half-amused voice receded into the background, leaving a playful threat hanging in the air, "Tell him he's going to get it from me when he gets back in town."

As Stacy's voice grew quiet, Missy emerged on the other end, clearer now, carrying a mixture of skepticism and fragile hope.

"Hello?" she sniffled, her voice filled with hope. "Jeremy?? Is it really you?"

"Yeah, Miss, it's me, I'm here, I'm okay," Jeremy responded, his voice brimming with a complex blend of emotions.

After a moment of silence on the line, Jeremy heard her voice in a quiet, barely audible whisper. "I knew it— I knew you'd be here," she sobbed softly.

Jeremy recounted the extraordinary events of his evening –starting with the unexpected meeting with Cassandra.

"There I was, Miss, sitting across from her, trying to make sense of everything. Honestly, I felt star-struck. There was this person who I had spent centuries trying to reconnect with. She was right there— right in front of me."

On the other end of the line, Missy clutched the phone tighter. Her heart raced, and her thoughts spiraled as she hung onto his every word.

Jeremy's tone softened, carrying a warmth that bridged the physical distance between them. "But here's the thing," he whispered, profound emotion in his voice, "at that moment, with Cassandra right in front of me, I only thought about you."

There was another brief silence as Missy processed his words, the weight of his confession causing her heart to skip. "Jeremy," she finally whispered back, her voice trembling with the magnitude of her feelings, "this is incredible."

He went deeper into the night's unfolding, his voice full of excitement as he spoke of the frantic dash back to his room and how he braced himself for a reset that never came.

"As I waited, my mind was exploding in a million different directions," he confessed. "I just sat in my room and thought about it, waiting to be thrown back to the beginning, back to Huxley, seeing Del again, starting all over again. Just as I always have, I prepared for my next life. I packed my memories, cataloged my lessons, and made sure that I had everything I needed to remember for the next life."

He paused, and though they were miles apart, Missy could picture the vulnerability in his eyes. "I've chased so many things: happiness, fame, wealth, Cassandra, and when the reset never came, I realized something, something I never knew. I realized what I needed."

Missy held her breath, sensing the depth of his following words.

His voice cracked, heavy with emotion. "This entire time, Miss, I never knew I needed you."

Missy's voice shook with emotion. "Jeremy, hearing those words from you, it's like a dream I never dared to believe in. I've always wished for a forever with you. Knowing we have that chance now is all I could ever want."

For Jeremy, Cassandra would always be the unforgettable melody of a song cut short, her love a deep, resonant echo of what might have been. She would forever be a cherished presence in Jeremy's heart—a constant reminder of the depths to which someone can love and lose. Cassandra might have been the right choice for another version of Jeremy, but in this life, in this reality, it was Missy who completed him.

Now, every day was a gift, and every moment was something to live for. The once infinite resource of time was now transformed into a wealth of love and appreciation for each new day. Every surprise life threw at him, good or bad, was a chance to celebrate—each one a step in the adventure of a life that was truly his own at last.